# TAMING THE TEASE

*Book 2 of Stronghold Doms*

## GOLDEN ANGEL

Cover art by Wicked Smart Designs
Edited by MJ Edits

❧❦❧

**Thank you so much for picking up my book!**

Would you like to receive a free story from me as well? Join the Angel Legion and sign up for my newsletter!

# ACKNOWLEDGMENTS

Thank you to every single person who has ever written to me with supportive words or encouragement deserves an acknowledgement. Being a self-published writer isn't easy, and making the step was both scary and thrilling. I would have never done it without the support of my fans. However, there are some particular special thanks which need to be said.

A huge thank you to Katherine, who has been a huge help to me since the beginning of my journey into the world of self-publishing. I'm not sure I could have done it without you, and I know for sure I wouldn't have done it as well without you. You help keep me on track, motivated, and always thinking about the next step.

Another huge thank you to Nick, who provided me with a very detailed and constructive male point of view while I was writing this novel. This book would definitely be shaped slightly differently without you, and I can't thank you enough for helping me to keep it well-rounded and appealing to both sexes. Plus, all the other little things you pointed out that helped make this a better story than it would have otherwise been.

And as always, thank you to my wonderful husband for his love and support of my dirty mind.

۔

❧   I   ❧

At exactly 11:01 pm, Maria made her escape. The engagement party had started at 8 pm, which meant she'd suffered through three hours of ecstatic young ladies squealing, men making ball and chain jokes, and the inevitable flood of well-intentioned but ultimately insufferable remarks directed at her from friends and family members alike. Three hours was enough, even if the party was for her sister.

Making her way past the bright green lettered banner reading Congratulations Lara and Victor, Maria fervently sent up a prayer of thanks that it was summer instead of winter, so she didn't have a coat to give her away. Even with the AC running full blast, the restaurant's private dining room was stifling due to the large crowd of people who were all drinking, eating, and expelling excessive amounts of hot air.

That's if anyone even noticed she was leaving. Pretty much all of the attention was on Lara and Victor, which was as it should be, and Maria wasn't jealous. Envious yes...

Lucky Lara. The youngest of the Arias sisters and the third one to get engaged. Maria didn't begrudge her sisters any happiness, but as the oldest sister and the only one with no husband and no husband in her near future, the situation wasn't exactly comfortable. With all of her sisters doing the whole marriage thing while Maria wasn't even in a relationship, there were too many people at the party who thought she needed comforting or encouragement, or—worst of all—advice on how to get a man. Most of them were related to her and had the best of intentions, so she couldn't even be rude to get them to leave her alone.

Maria made a face. She didn't need advice on how to get a man, she just needed to find the right man for her. And if she was single at her youngest sister's engagement party, well that didn't mean anything except she hadn't found the right man yet. Anyone who thought differently could suck it.

The hot night air hit her like a blast, the humidity making it feel even worse than it was. Gotta love Maryland weather. At least July usually wasn't quite as bad as August, but it made her curly hair even more unruly than ever. Which was why she had it pulled up in a pretty bun, but she knew the little bits of fluff and frizz would already be lifting. Hairspray? Ha, her hair laughed at hairspray.

"Running away so soon?"

Ugh, great. Just what she needed, another run in with Victor's best friend Jeremy. Pasting a smile on her face, she ignored the cloud of smoke around him and gave him a little wave, hoping she could flee. Victor was a doll, but his best friend was a complete scrub. She didn't care that the slang term was over a decade old, it was the best way to describe him.

And she didn't want no scrub.

"Hi Jeremy, bye Jeremy."

"Hey, come on Maria, I feel like we got off on the wrong foot..." Jeremy jogged after her, giving her what he obviously thought was a charming smile. He was a decently attractive guy, although not nearly as attractive as he thought he was. "If I'd known you were Lara's sister, I would have never said what I did."

Maria walked faster, although in her heels it wasn't like she could truly outrun him. "So you don't mind telling complete strangers that you'd totally hit on them if they weighed less, but since I'm Lara's sister it's not okay? That's just charming."

"I think you're hot, just bigger than I like 'em. Doesn't mean we can't get along. Let me make it up to you, I'll take you out to dinner tomorrow."

Oh hell no. The stupid overconfident smile on his face hadn't even budged. Like he actually thought she would let him take her to dinner.

"Go away, Jeremy. I have no interest in you and I don't know why I bothered to try and be friendly and introduce myself in the first place. Oh wait... yes I do. Because I was trying to give you the benefit of the doubt after Lara told me what a dog you were. Then it turned out she was right."

Since she had reached her car, she had the satisfaction of seeing Jeremy wince and look surprisingly sheepish. "I know... I know... but, you didn't tell her, right? And you won't? I know she doesn't like me... but Victor and I have been best friends since we were five. I'm trying to do better around her."

"You know what might help? If you didn't completely suck as a person," Maria snapped, fed up with his selfishness and shallowness. "Don't try to do better 'around her,' try to do better period. If you're having problems with your friendship with Victor, maybe it's because he's finally seeing you for the self-involved jerk you actually are. Change that and maybe both he and Lara will think better of you."

For a long moment Jeremy just stared at her and Maria pulled her car door open, figuring they were done. Unfortunately, it had just taken that long for his tiny brain to process what she'd said and come up with a response.

"You know, you wouldn't have such a stick up your ass if you could find someone to fuck you... and if you looked like your sisters, that wouldn't be such a problem."

Gripping the steering wheel so tightly her knuckles turned white, Maria turned on the car and revved the engine. At least she had the satisfaction of watching Jeremy turn tail and run, realizing she was sitting in a vehicle that could definitely be used as a weapon. Unfortunately, such a drastic act would only have more negative consequences for her... She'd probably have to apologize to him later, her sister would be upset, and she might end up in jail. Plus, everyone probably would ascribe her single status as somehow being behind her motivation to run the scrawny bastard over.

The thing was, Maria did look like her three younger sisters. At least, their faces looked alike. Jeremy was referring to the fact that when it came to body type her sisters all took after their mother whereas Maria had the same body type as her dad's sister. Aunt Rhonda was a beautiful, curvy, voluptuous woman who had also been the only one in the family not to hassle Maria tonight about her lack of romantic success. She adored Aunt Rhonda.

It's not like she was out of shape. She loved her curves now. Although, when she was growing up she'd felt like a clumsy, overlarge duckling in a family of graceful, slim swans. Not that any of them made her feel like she was anything less because she was a bit bigger than them, no that was left to the douchebags of the world like Jeremy. If Maria was a meaner person, she would tell on him to Lara.

Her baby sister would have him sliced, diced, and served up with some cumin sprinkled on top.

Hell, if it wasn't for him being Victor's best friend and best man in the wedding, Maria might have done the same thing. But she wanted to escape more than she wanted a scene in the parking lot, and she didn't want to cause any waves during Lara's wedding and especially not within the wedding party. That was the last thing she needed.

Ugh. She needed some serious stress relief. Even with the AC going full blast the humidity of the air still making her dress stick to her skin, making her long for the cool embrace of water all around her, drowning out the noise of the world.

The pool was her little bit of escapism. A place to just be.

SHE WAS OUT THERE AGAIN.

Rick did his best not to look. Even if he did have a perfect view of the pool from his window, that didn't give him the right to stand there and watch the swimmers. Especially ones who turned him on, since it made him feel like a creeper.

This particular swimmer was out there often, during both the day and the night. People weren't really supposed to be there at night when there wasn't a lifeguard on duty, but it seemed like she was the exception to the rule somehow. That or she just didn't care about the rules. He did check on her every so often, to make sure she was okay out there on her own, but just standing and watching somehow seemed an invasion of her privacy.

Even if she was in the apartment complex's public pool.

Besides, he should be sleeping instead of watching her. Rick tried to keep his schedule close to school hours even during the summer, so it wouldn't be too much of a shock to his system when fall came. Normally, he would be teaching summer school, so it was easy to have a routine close to normal working hours. His recent move prevented him from teaching this summer, so he needed to find other ways to make money over the break before starting at the new school this fall. Other ways which translated into other schedules, which meant a bit more trouble sleeping, which meant he was watching her instead of getting some much-needed rest.

So far this summer he'd mostly been doing odd jobs for his friends at their companies, earning extra money from them.

Adam owned his own head hunters and temp agency, placing workers in full time or temporary positions at other companies, and that was where Rick was spending most of his time. After that he was helping out Patrick Murphy, the owner of the kink club where he and his friends usually spent their weekend evenings. Patrick owned Stronghold and he hated doing paperwork. Plus, there was always a need for someone behind the bar or working security. Rick had become the on-call man at Stronghold for the summer, which wasn't a bad thing. It had given him an opportunity to meet more of the submissives than he had before, which was good.

Now that he was living closer to Stronghold, he was hoping to meet a submissive he could have a real relationship outside the club with. Since last summer, four of his friends had found a special woman to be with—granted, two of them were in a relationship with one very special woman, but that counted—and he wanted a relationship too.

Glancing out the window, he looked down at the woman in the pool, floating on her back. She was all curves, tucked into a barely-there bikini. He liked curvy women who were confident. Which was probably why he had such trouble keeping his eyes off of her whenever she was down there.

It was definitely time to go to bed, despite his urge to stay up and watch over the pool woman. Not his responsibility. But moving away from the window was almost physically painful, and as soon as he'd brushed his teeth and gotten ready for bed, he found himself right back in the same spot watching his midnight mystery woman.

PLOWING THROUGH THE WATER WAS ALMOST LIKE MEDITATING FOR Rick. One of his favorite things about his early morning swims was the fact that there was no one at the pool. Although today he was a little bit more tired than usual, having stayed up long past the time he should have been in bed. When the woman in the pool had finally gotten out, wrapped her luscious curves in a towel, and headed back to the building—his building, he knew she lived one floor down although he didn't know which apartment—he'd finally managed to get his ass into bed.

Which was why he deserved the extra burn and strain this morning. He shouldn't have stayed up to watch over someone who didn't want or need it, or even know he was doing it.

Creeper.

Spraying water as he exhaled and dunked his head back in, Rick had to remind himself to kick his legs. It was too easy to just pull himself through the water with his arms, but he needed the leg work out, too. Anything to drain himself of the excess energy he seemed to be carrying around.

Maybe he should reconsider Patrick's offer to put him into the Introduction Scene rotation. Although he went to the club every weekend now that he'd moved to the area, he still hadn't found a submissive he really clicked with. He played of course, and had even had some mutually satisfying scenes, but either the woman wasn't interested in extending their interactions beyond the club or something just didn't gel completely.

Doing Intro Scenes would mean interacting with more subs. After all, it had been a month of going to the club on a regular basis and he was just as likely to sit at the bar chatting with his friends as he was to scene. So maybe he just needed to find a way to put himself out there more.

Heck, half the reason he'd moved up here was so he could be closer to Stronghold. The other half of the reason had been that he hadn't been thrilled with the way things had been going at the school he'd been teaching at. The principal had had the tendency to play favorites, with both the teachers and the students, and unfortunately seemed particularly favorable to those who cause drama. It was not a situation Rick was willing to put up with. He'd already been somewhat dissatisfied with the school, even though he loved his students, and he'd become so frustrated with his love life that moving away from it all just made sense.

Here, he was closer to his friends, he was starting at a new school, and hopefully he'd be able to find a relationship which actually could go somewhere. When he'd been living almost two hours away from Stronghold, most of the submissives he was meeting also lived two hours away from him—or more. Which was a hard sell for when it came to dating. Of course, now that he was living here, somehow it hadn't been any easier to find a woman he actually wanted to have a relationship with.

Reaching the end of the lane, Rick grabbed onto the wall and pulled himself against it with his arms, spreading them along the upper edge which was starting to heat up in the sun. The pool was starting to get a little busier now; he wasn't the only one here anymore although he was the only one swimming laps.

As he glanced over towards the entrance, his muscles tightened, and he recognized the dark-haired woman he often watched from his window. They actually hadn't been at the pool at the same time before. She tended to go in the evening—or late at night—and Rick usually swam in the morning. She was wearing a bright purple bikini with pink polka dots and a matching dark purple sarong tied at her curvy hips, which peeked open to show a generous amount of leg when she walked. This was closest he'd ever been to her and at this range he could see how very nicely she filled out her bikini top, the large globes of her breasts jiggling as she walked.

Most women her size wouldn't have the confidence to carry off a bikini, but she looked completely comfortable in her own skin. Deservedly so—she was fucking gorgeous. Her dark hair was piled up on top of her head, a mass of curls precariously perched and appearing far too heavy for her long neck. The college guys near the entrance were checking her out, also uncaring that she was more voluptuous than current beauty standards. She was hot, confident, and luscious.

Rick didn't usually describe women as luscious, but that was the best word for her. In his head, it was always the description that came to mind whenever he saw her. As always, seeing her stirred a physical reaction, despite the cold water of the pool. He liked women of all shapes and sizes, but he did have a particular soft spot for ladies with more curves. Maybe because he'd always been a bit of a cuddler. Mostly, though, he was drawn to confidence. He liked sassy women and always had. Something about the way she moved hinted she was just his type.

Maybe he should just go over and introduce himself. Flirt. Ask for her number.

Yeah, and then when she turned out to be completely vanilla and possibly freaked out by his needs, then living here wouldn't be awkward at all. Rick liked his new apartment. His motto had always been don't piss where you eat—in other words, don't get involved with your neighbors. It just never ended well, and the only solution was to move away.

Not an option.

Time to go. He could go visit Liam at his dojo and join into one of the classes or help with paperwork or something. Or hit up Adam's office and visit with him and Justin. Or any other million things that didn't involve sitting here and checking out his hot neighbor who was now flirting with the college guys.

"HAVEN'T SEEN YOU HERE BEFORE," THE DARK-HAIRED COLLEGE hottie said to Maria, grinning at her as she laid out her towel.

After Asshole's remarks last night, it was nice to have some male attention that was unequivocally positive, even if the two guys were definitely too young for her.

"I'm usually not here this early in the morning," she said with a smile, not an overly friendly one but not entirely dismissive either. Still, she didn't really want to get wrapped up in a conversation with them, she just wanted to lie down and bake in the sun for a little bit. Terrible for her skin, but she'd put sunscreen on and she wanted the warmth.

Swimming in the pool last night when it was empty had been calming, soothing. Today she needed warmth and background noise and guys checking her out. Validation at its finest.

Getting out her sunscreen, she slathered it over her arms and then her chest and stomach while the two guys watched. Hiding a smile, Maria pretended she didn't notice them practically salivating while she smoothed the white cream over her breasts. The bathing suit she'd worn today was meant to draw attention. Her sisters liked to call her a tease. Maria preferred to think of it as appreciation awareness. Guys needed to know that plus size girls were hotties too.

These two definitely seemed to appreciate her efforts. Too young for her, but maybe they'd take the lesson back to school with them.

"Would you mind helping me with my back?" she asked, just a little bit coquettishly. Guys putting on sunscreen tended to turn the process into almost a massage—and she could definitely use one.

Okay, maybe she was a bit of a tease, but she wasn't harming anyone.

The two hotties jumped up, the one with reddish hair grabbing the bottle of sunscreen before his friend could. "No problem, just turn around," he said, grinning eagerly.

Maria smiled sweetly before turning, pretending she hadn't noticed the male posturing. The best way to get continued male attention was to ignore it. Made them think their competitiveness had gone unnoticed and work harder to get the attention they wanted.

Dios mio!

There was a Greek god getting out of the pool.

She barely noticed the strong hand rubbing sunscreen into her shoulders as she stared across the blue expanse at the man getting out on the other side of the pool. Tall, blond hair darkened by the water, and the kind of body women drooled over in front of their own boyfriends and husbands. Hell, just looking at him Maria had the urge to fan herself.

When he turned to walk over to the chair his towel was draped over, red bathing suit clinging to the long, lean muscles of his legs, she could see his profile was just as attractive as his back. How had she not seen him before?

Then again, this really was way earlier than she was normally at the pool. Her dreams had been rather troubled, which was what had gotten her up this morning. Although if he was here in the mornings, even if it was only a couple of times a week, she might have to change that.

Not that a guy like him would ever talk to her. Maria might love her curves, but she was very aware that most guys who were into lots of exercise and having hard bodies liked skinny, muscular little girls who matched their physical perfection. She had the muscles, but it was under soft flesh and even if she starved herself, her bone structure was too big to ever be truly skinny. So why bother trying to force herself into a mold she'd never fit?

But she could certainly appreciate the eye candy, even knowing the appreciation would likely not be mutual.

She watched, fascinated, as he dried himself off, running the towel over his short hair and then down his body. Squeezing her thighs together, she grinned. Hello new fantasy fodder! Sure, she got tired of using her vibrator to get the big O sometimes, but having new imagery always helped to spice that up a bit.

The man looked over, directly at her it seemed, and Maria froze. College hottie behind her was saying something as he moved on to covering her lower back with sunscreen, but she didn't register a single word he said. How could she when there was a man who looked like that actually looking at her?

And then he looked away, tossing his towel over his shoulder and heading toward the exit, and Maria remembered to breathe again. Talk about potent!

She turned away, reminding herself that it's not like he would ever return her interest. In fact, he was going through the exit without a second glance back. There was no way he'd felt the same thing looking at her as she'd felt looking at him. Pasting a smile on her face, she turned back to thank the guy who had helped her with the sunscreen.

Still, she couldn't help but glance after the Greek god. After all, he had a very nice ass... and it was headed straight into her building. Holy crap! He must be the new guy upstairs. Mrs. Pierce next door had mentioned he was a "good looking young man"—Holy Understatement, Batman!

He'd been living there for what, close to a month? Maybe she should do the neighborly thing and bring him some brownies later. Not that she thought he'd be interested in her, but if he wasn't a total jerk then it might be fun to flirt... and if nothing else, she wouldn't mind getting a closer look than the view afforded from across the pool.

🐚  2  🐚

**M**aria spent a frustrating morning at work dealing with suppliers and an irate Executive Chef at the restaurant she worked at. Murphy's Meals was a wonderful, family owned restaurant that was considered a community staple, but since it wasn't a chain, sometimes the suppliers could get a little sketchy about their shipments. One of the annoyances of being a small business.

She loved her job most days, not in the least because she loved the owners, James and Jeanne Murphy. She'd worked here as a hostess in high school, eventually becoming a server. Right after college she'd done some job hopping and she'd come in to have a comforting meal, a bit depressed and frustrated because she just couldn't figure out what she wanted to do for her career, and Jeanne had sat with her and listened. And at the end of it, Jeanne had offered her a job as daytime manager until she could figure out what she wanted to do.

That had been three years ago. She'd taken over the position with enthusiasm, and although she occasionally had to cover evenings it wasn't common enough to be a nuisance, and she made enough money to cover her expenses. It turned out she loved her job and it had become her career rather than a placeholder position. Plus, she got to interact with people all day, and at a place like Murphy's, she didn't have to pander to asshole customers when they came in. They were more likely to be banned than catered to.

When she finally got off work around 8 pm—she'd stayed to help through the dinner rush—she checked her phone to find she had seven missed calls and four new voicemails. Groaning, she scrolled through the missed calls. All three of her sisters had called her, and her mother had called her four times. She wondered whether the voice-mails were all from her mother or if everyone had left one.

Plugging in her hands-free device, she started her car while she listened to them. One from each of them. Well at least they weren't all from her mom. Maria didn't think she could take that much haranguing right now. All four messages said basically the same thing, just delivered in different words and different tones of voice: We missed you last night, looked around and you were gone... where did you go and are you okay?

Ick.

Every single one of them, worrying over Maria's single state and thinking she must be taking it hard that her youngest sister was getting married. It would be a hell of a lot easier to take if everyone would stop acting like she must be upset over it. There was nothing more guaranteed to make her upset.

"Sorry, but I'm not calling any of you back," she muttered under her breath.

It was times like this that she cursed having three sisters. She'd never really had a best friend outside of them, she hadn't needed one. Of course, she'd had female friends, but it was her sisters she'd always been closest to. After college she'd lost contact with the friends she'd made there, and she'd never really made any new close friends. It was her sisters whom she hung out the most with, whom she vented to, shared secrets with...

And she could really use someone to vent about her sisters to right now. They had good intentions, but her entire family was driving her up the wall.

"Screw it."

Sitting alone in her apartment with her phone turned off, eating Ben & Jerry's, might not make her family feel any less troubled about her, but it sure as hell made her feel better. What was wrong with having a night like this anyway? Maria liked sitting and watching rom-coms by herself, eating whatever the fuck she wanted. Okay, it'd be more fun with her sisters here, but the point was she didn't need a man.

Although it might be nice to get laid.

Mmmm... she wondered what the Greek god from this morning was doing. Just knowing he was in the same building made her feel all tingly and hot. Unfortunately, the moment she started considering ditching the ice cream and grabbing her vibrator, someone knocked on her door. For just a quick second, a porno-esque fantasy ran through her head—maybe her thoughts had drawn him. Maybe he was at her door, hunkalicious and needing something from his eager neighbor.

When she peeked through the keyhole, her fantasies took a swift retreat. Recognizing the gray curls of Mrs. Pierce, she shoved down her disappointment (which was silly anyway since obviously the Greek god wouldn't be knocking) and opened the door.

"Good evening Maria, I'm sorry to bother you," the older woman said, peering up at her with an apologetic smile. In her early eighties, Mrs. Pierce insisted on living in her own apartment with her own things. Although her granddaughter stopped by on a regular basis, she often relied on her neighbors for help with little things.

"No problem, Mrs. Pierce, what can I do for you?" she asked.

"I'm making cookies and I thought I had enough brown sugar, but I'm half a cup short. Do you think you might have some?"

"Of course, I'll be right over with it."

"Thank you dear."

Well so much for a night of dreaming about the Greek god. Maria knew from past experiences with Mrs. Pierce that she was now in for an evening of giving up detailed descriptions of everything going on in her and her sisters' lives, hearing about every last detail of Mrs. Pierce's granddaughter's life, and eating some seriously delicious cookies. All in all, right now, it sounded kind of relaxing. Plus, she knew Mrs. Pierce would be delighted to hear all about Lara's engagement party, and the older woman wouldn't be one of the people clucking over Maria's single status. Mrs. Pierce firmly believed in holding out until the right man, no matter how long it took.

It was an attitude Maria fully appreciated.

⚜

LEATHER, SWEAT, AND SEX. THAT'S WHAT THE DUNGEON OF Stronghold smelled like. The sounds were even more erotically disturbing. Screams. The crack of leather against flesh. Moans. Whimpers. Begging.

It wasn't even making him a little bit hard.

Okay, that was a lie, he was a little hard, but being at half-mast wasn't where he should be, not when he'd just finished a scene of his own. The blissed out little subbie he was unhooking from the spanking bench had been wonderful, but Rick just hadn't felt anything with her. Feeling desire, even if he wasn't interested in the woman in question beyond a scene, hadn't been a problem before, but apparently it was now.

Fortunately, sex was one of Anna's hard limits within the club. She was a newer sub and still getting used to public scening. She wasn't comfortable with the idea of sex in public yet, although she'd consented to manual and oral stimulation, and the use of toys.

Rick loved watching a woman orgasm just as much as he loved watching a woman writhing with need when she was denied climax, but tonight neither had done much for him. He'd been into making sure Anna got what she needed—the lack of spark or real connection between them wasn't her fault—but he was glad her own boundaries barred any real sexual contact between them.

"Thank you, Sir," she said, glowing up at him as he wrapped her in a blanket. With her red cheeks, slightly reddened eyes, and happy smile, she was the very image of a well-satisfied submissive. It made him feel slightly better.

Twenty minutes later, Anna was well enough to return to the locker room on her own two feet, and Rick found himself back at the bar with his friends. For once Andrew wasn't behind the bar, he was off scening with Ellie—a very sweet submissive and masochist who had absolutely no interest in a Dom beyond the scene, and therefore was a good match for him—but Adam, Angel, and Patrick were all sitting at one of the tables, chatting. Rick strode over to join them.

"I doubt she'll be around again anytime soon," Angel was saying to Patrick as Rick walked up. The pretty brunette was obviously emphasizing her Asian heritage this evening, the design on her corset had a mandarin neckline with a deep keyhole showing off her cleavage. She was wearing a collar made out of matching fabric, and her hair was up and held in place with chopsticks, keeping it off her neck. Adam's fingers were running back and forth along the back of her collar, and Rick recognized the territorial look in his friend's eye.

The aggressive, blond haired, blue eyed Dom wasn't used to waiting for what he wanted, but Angel was no pushover, and so she wouldn't be wearing his collar anytime soon. Just recently she'd announced that she didn't care how much of her stuff was in his house, she wasn't officially moving in until they'd been together for a year.

Suffice to say, Adam had been more possessive than ever after that. Of course, he didn't think she was going to leave him just because she didn't want to move in, it was just his natural reaction to her declaration of independence.

"Who are we talking about?" Rick asked as he sat down at the table, giving Adam and Patrick a nod and Angel a smile. Naturally tactile, she leaned over to give him a hug. Rick pulled her in tight, smirking at her Dom over her shoulder.

"You're supposed to ask permission before letting another Dom touch you," Adam growled, tugging on Angel's hips to pull her back. Rick let his hands linger down her arms as she pulled away. Adam glared at Rick through narrowed eyes. Superficially, the two of them looked rather alike, although Adam had facial hair and tended to be compared to a Viking. In both looks and demeanor. Whereas Rick was usually seen as more clean cut and easy-going.

Rick grinned and winked at Angel, eliciting another growl from Adam.

"Oh stop it, it's just Rick. Sir."

Ever since Adam had realized Angel didn't exactly run on his leash, he'd been remarkably easy to tease. It wasn't something any of their group of friends got to do very often, and for the single ones—like Rick and Andrew—it was fast becoming their favorite game. Patrick didn't play, but then again Angel didn't encourage him either. She definitely encouraged Rick and Andrew.

Eventually Adam was going to stop putting up with it.

"Do we need another lesson on manners, sub?" the blond Dom asked, biting her earlobe. Angel's eyes half-lidded as she shivered. He had her pulled up against his body, nestled between his legs, rather than allowing her to sit on her own stool. Rick watched enviously. Not that he disliked being a voyeur, but his enjoyment of watching them was also tinged with his jealousy.

"If it pleases you, Sir," she replied, a sultriness to her voice.

"If you'd behaved, it would have pleased me sooner. Now you'll have to wait. Brat. Now answer Rick's question."

Angel pouted as both Rick and Patrick laughed. Every so often she would try to top from the bottom and it was always amusing to watching Adam catch her at it. He always kept her guessing as to how she'd be punished for it.

"What was the question again?" she asked.

"Who's not coming back here anytime soon?" he repeated, waving at one of the subs serving drinks. He'd been here often enough for them to know he just wanted a glass of anything on tap.

Making a face, Angel sighed. "Leigh. Ever since she got back together with dickhead, she's been doing whatever he wants to do. I don't think she's even told him about this place, there's no way he'd be okay with her coming here."

"That's too bad." Their group had rather liked Angel's best friend. She was sweet with a sunny disposition, despite the fact she'd met them all after a recent breakup with her long-term boyfriend—a.k.a. dickhead. Rick thought she might even be a bit submissive. She was definitely attractive enough to appeal to him. A little small on top, but he'd definitely appreciated her well-rounded hips and ass.

The generously endowed tease he'd seen at the pool flashed through his head, cutting right across his mental image of Leigh. Yeah, those were some delightful proportions. Anna's had been close to those... but there was just that little something missing. A spark he'd felt from just looking at pool-girl. That spark had definitely been absent when he'd met Leigh too.

"Yeah, I really wish she'd just give up on him, but something always sends her back."

"We feel the same about Jared," Patrick said, looking at her sympathetically. Well, as close to sympathy as his expression ever came. The scar running down the side of his face, leftover from a playful sword fight in high school with his best friend, tended to twist his expressions a bit. "Haven't talked to him in days."

Angel made a face, wrinkling her nose in a manner that was as adorable as it was disdainful. "Yeah, I didn't think there was anyone worse than Michael, but Marissa definitely takes the prize. I understand Leigh's relationship better than I understand theirs."

"We've been wondering for years if he'll ever manage to get away from her, but every time she draws him back in," Rick said, turning to accept the beer the submissive had brought him. The pretty blonde imp gave him an inviting smile, but he just kept his own smile neutral and nodded his thanks before turning away.

"Don't feel like playing again tonight?" Patrick asked, once the server was out of earshot. Rick just shook his head. Maybe if he saw someone he actually felt a stirring of interest in, but he wasn't going to force another disappointing scene tonight.

"I wish I had more female friends," Angel muttered. The guys all looked at her, their expressions ranging from amusement to disbelief. It was well known that Angel preferred guy friends to girls, although she'd become fast friends with Jessica, Hilary, Lexie, and Olivia. They and Leigh were the exceptions to her rule; something Adam struggled with but tolerated for her sake. "What? I do! I'm sure if I had them, they'd be awesome, and then I could hook Rick up."

"What about me?" Patrick asked, pretending to be affronted. Angel shot him a look that was probably supposed to be significant, but which glanced right off of him. Whatever message she had been trying to convey, either Patrick didn't get it or wasn't interested in hearing it. Interesting.

Rick had been so caught up in his own search for a submissive, he hadn't even thought about Patrick. Then again, the club owner hadn't exactly said anything about wanting a permanent sub. Hell, if Rick remembered correctly, he hadn't even played in the club in months. Perhaps he had the same problem Rick did?

"Anyway," Angel said, turning her attention back to Rick. "I just feel a little bad. All my friends are guys... I'm useless."

"Far from," Adam said, squeezing her hip. "Although I wouldn't mind if you had more girl friends as well."

"Where's Master Michael been?" Rick asked, deliberately throwing out the name just to grate on Adam. The two men got along pretty well, despite Michael being a very old, very good, almost intimate friend, of Angel's. A dominant and a sadist, the two of them definitely had some chemistry when the group had first met him, but that had seemed to fade as she and Adam had become more involved. Still, while Adam tolerated Angel's male friendships, and had even become friends with her roommates, any mention of Michael seemed to up his level of possessiveness.

"Settling into the area," Angel said with a wave of her hand. "Adam's been keeping him employed during the daylight hours, but he's been trying to find some theater gigs in the evenings."

"I'm sure he'll be back at the club when he has the time," Adam said blandly. Not fooling anyone.

Good submissive that she was, Angel turned slightly sideways to lean into him, as if sensing Rick's teasing was getting to be a little too much and Adam needed a show of her love and devotion to him. Which also made Rick feel a bit bad. Teasing Adam was fun, but he didn't mean to take out his own frustrations on his friend. Definitely time to stop. Although, now he doubted Adam would care much, as Angel curved into his body, her face nuzzling into his neck.

Damn. What Rick wouldn't give for a submissive who read his own moods that well. He could actually see Adam relaxing as Angel rubbed up on him.

"So," he said, turning to Patrick to give the two a bit of privacy. "How—"

Shouting at the entrance cut off his sentence. Will was standing guard at the door, blocking whoever was trying to get in. Rick's eyes widened as he recognized the very irate, very frustrated, very feminine voice.

"Dammit, Will! Get out of my way! I'm allowed in there now!" Lexie's shriek was easily heard over the music, and all conversation had stopped the moment someone had started yelling. Everyone wanted to know why there was a commotion in Stronghold, where there was very rarely such a thing. In fact, Lexie had been at the center of the last commotion, at the Valentine's Day party when things had gone a bit south with her now-ex, Trevor.

Out of the corner of his eye, Rick saw Patrick wince.

"You didn't..." None of the guys had been particularly comfortable when Patrick started letting Lexie on the main floor of Stronghold. They all tended to view her as their little sister, especially since Jake, her big brother and Patrick's best friend, was overseas fighting in Afghanistan. That made them all feel especially bound to look after her.

However, all of them knew it would be a really, really bad idea to try and renew the restriction.

"You didn't!" Even though Angel's words were the same as Rick's, they were said in a completely different way. He'd been almost as awed as wary; she was obviously outraged on Lexie's behalf. "Patrick —MMmmmfff!"

Adam's hand had found its way over her mouth and he was whispering in her ear. Probably telling her to stay out of it. Patrick just shot a glare at all three of them and then got up, unfolding his large frame from the barstool he'd been sitting on, with all the reluctance of the mountain about to make its trek to Mohammed.

"Some of the Doms were starting to ask me if she was available for scening," he said flatly. Rick shuddered. Not with their Lexie, dammit. Obviously, the Stronghold Doms were starting to get ideas just because she was in the main room. None of her self-appointed big brothers were going to stand for that.

"Mmmff, mmm mmMMMMMMMMMFFF!"

Although if Angel's reaction was representative of the submissives' reaction, which Rick had a sinking feeling it probably was because all of the subbies loved Lexie, then this was going to cause a lot more problems than Patrick had anticipated. Seeing Angel was actually trying to kick Adam's ankle in her struggle to get free and speak her mind, Rick decided it might be marginally safer to follow Patrick as he headed to face off with Lexie. Plus, he wanted to know what was going to happen. He was only human after all.

As they approached the entrance, they could see a couple of people in the lobby, watching with amusement. Will looked completely relieved to see Patrick coming. Tiny little Lexie might be the size of a pixie, but she was a vicious one. Like the ones in Harry Potter, but with even more bite. Rick didn't have any doubt that she might have tried to start forcing her way in physically if she hadn't seen Patrick coming to sort out the situation, and Will would have then had to worry about hurting her. It was a lose-lose scenario for the Dom and he knew it.

Seeing Patrick headed towards her calmed Lexie down a bit—she had stopped bouncing and shouting and was just waiting for him to reach her.

"Lexie," he said, in his deep voice, nodding at her. Rick positioned himself along the wall so he could see both of their faces. He couldn't help but grin as Will sidled out of their way, back into the lobby. Which meant Lexie was marginally standing inside the club, but that couldn't be helped.

"Don't you dare stand there acting like nothing's wrong! You said I could come onto the main floor from now on!" Lexie jabbed her finger into Patrick's chest, her head tilted back to glare up at him. Tonight she was wearing another one of her fishnet shirts with a bright blue bra underneath, one matching her eyes exactly, and a short black skirt. Rick was just relieved to see she was wearing a bra, for a while she'd been donning electrical tape and pasties and they'd all worried she was about to move to being completely uncovered beneath her see-through tops. The return to a bra was surprising, but also reassuring.

The slight quiver in her voice was not.

Patrick heard it too, tensing and hesitating from whatever he'd been about to say. Shit. The big man looked over at Rick, as if searching for some kind of support against the thread of hurt in

Lexie's voice. Rick shrugged but stood his ground; he was going to be silent support.

"We're not going to have another party for a while, Lex, you don't really need to be on the main floor."

"It's not about need you big lump, it's about finally getting to spend time with my friends in their usual hangout!" The unhappy ragged quality to Lexie's voice was definitely increasing, indicating she was moving closer to tears. Rick shifted uncomfortably backwards but Patrick shot him a glance that said don't you dare.

"It's not a good place for you, Pixie."

Yeah, the big man was definitely losing control if he was calling her by her childhood nickname, the one which only Patrick and Jake were allowed to use.

"My friends are all in there. So it's a good place for Angel and Hilary and Jessica, but not for me?"

"They're submissives."

Lexie's chin came up stubbornly as she crossed her arms under her chest and stared up at Patrick. Suddenly her stance was a lot more challenging than upset. "I could be too. I want to be, if it's the right man."

The undercurrents of this conversation were starting to make Rick feel extremely uncomfortable. They'd all noticed the tension which had sprung up between Lexie and Patrick over the past year, but no one really talked about it. Neither Lexie nor Patrick had seemed to push the status quo... until now.

Shit.

Now he wished he'd stayed at the table with Angel and Adam, even though they (like everyone else) were watching the scene at the front door. He doubted they could hear what was being said. The little looks Patrick kept shooting at him begged Rick not to leave him alone with Lexie.

Normally Rick would be entertained by seeing Patrick on the retreat for once, but not about this. Fuck. It was one thing for Lexie to have a crush or for Patrick to see her as all grown up—that was pretty hard to miss considering the outfits she chose to wear to Stronghold— or even be attracted to her... another for either of them to actually do anything about it. Did Lexie really understand the kind of relationship Patrick wanted? That he demanded?

"You can come in. But only if I'm here or one of the other guys is here to sit with you," Patrick said, apparently deciding to completely ignore her challenge. Rick let out a breath he hadn't known he was holding.

"Fine. Oh look, you're here." Lexie looked over, directly at Rick. "Hey look, Rick's here too. Hi Rick. And over there are Angel and Adam. That's three Sentinels to sit with me. I guess I get to come in."

Obviously royally pissed, Lexie pushed her way past Patrick and headed for the table where Adam and Angel were. Rubbing his head, Patrick stepped over to where Rick was standing, as grinning patrons began to trickle in through the doorway.

"She's going to be the death of me," Patrick muttered. "Not to mention my reputation."

Rick snorted. "No one's going to blame you for giving way to her. Although if she wants anyone to think she's submissive, she's going about it the wrong way."

Something in Patrick's expression tightened as he looked across the room to where she was now seated, her back to him. "She's not coming in here if one of us isn't here to keep an eye on her. Or I'll fire her ass and then she won't be able to come here at all."

Deciding it wasn't prudent to inform Patrick it would be better to tell Lexie that than Rick, he just nodded. Not that the big man was even looking at him, he was already pushing off the wall and heading to join the conversation happening at the table. Where he and Lexie would probably act like the confrontation had not just happened. Eventually something was going to have to give between the two of them.

Feeling too tired to go back and pretend like the very air around them wasn't filled with tension, Rick just slipped out the front door and headed out. As far as he was concerned, his night was over. Lexie could make do with two Sentinels.

$\mathcal{H}$   3   $\mathcal{H}$

S troke, stroke, stroke, and breathe; stroke, stroke, stroke, and breathe... Rick preferred to breathe on every third stroke when he was swimming freestyle. It was how he'd been taught, and he found that twisting his head from side to side rather than always coming up on the same side meant his neck got a more symmetrical workout. He didn't know why it mattered to him, but it did.

Sometimes he felt like he was getting old and set in his ways.

Gliding the last couple of meters into the wall, he came up for air and stretched out his shoulders. This morning he'd done a longer workout than usual. He'd needed to burn off excess energy again.

Sexually frustrated much?

He nearly groaned when he saw the lusciously curved brunette, apparently venturing out in the morning for the second day in a row, this time tucked into a bright red bikini with tiny ruffles edging the top and bottom. Ruffles were dumb, in his opinion, but on her they didn't detract from her attractiveness. The screaming red color suited her dark hair and tanned skin perfectly.

The rest of the pool area was nearly empty. There was a young mother with her toddler on the opposite side and an older man Rick recognized as a fellow lap-swimmer, and the tempting brunette. Who was putting her stuff down on a lounge chair only two away from where he'd left his towel.

There were plenty of other lounge chairs further away, but he saw the way she was looking at him out of the corner of her eye. She'd deliberately chosen a location near his things.

Interest stirred, along with his cock.

Stop it.

No getting involved with the neighbors. Obviously, a reminder that bore repeating. Besides, he might be reading too much into things. Maybe she hadn't been looking at him at all. Or maybe she'd only been looking at him and wondering if it was his towel sitting so close to her chosen spot.

Ugh. He was starting to sound like a teenage girl inside his head. Great.

Ducking back into the pool, he kept swimming. But the entire time he was also picturing the brunette and that wasn't good either. He swam faster.

Ten laps later he glided back into the wall and came up breathing heavily. One quick look over in the brunette's direction nearly had him groaning again. She was laid out on her stomach and she'd undone the top of her bikini, leaving the expanse of her back completely bared to the sun. Why that was so sexy, he wasn't sure, but somehow a woman with her bikini top undone was always an erotic tease. Maybe it was just the vain hope that she might forget to redo it before sitting up.

Yeah.

Time to go home again. He was done with his workout and while he'd originally been planning to spend some time drying out in the sun as the day heated up, he knew he wouldn't be able to relax and enjoy it with her only two chairs away. Pulling himself out of the pool, he did his best not to look at her as he padded over to his chair and picked up his towel. Rubbing it roughly over his face, he took the moment to regain his balance, unsure of why her mere presence unsettled him so badly.

Slipping on his sandals, he slung his towel around his neck and headed toward the exit.

"Hey, do you have a second?"

The sound of her sultry, sleepy voice, tinged with just the faintest hint of an accent, had Rick doing a quick about turn. Yep. Sunbathing beauty was looking up at him with a smile, her head and shoulders raised just enough to make his cock twitch in hopes he was going to get to see something scandalous. Teenage fantasy type stuff, but a man never grew too old for it.

"Sure," he said, taking a step toward her. He knew he was looming over her a bit, but the position helped him regain some of his equilibrium. Damn she looked good from this angle. The bikini bottoms were clinging to the well-rounded cheeks of her ass, which was soft and cushy looking—the kind of ass a man wanted to grab onto or spank the hell out of. Rick wanted to do both. The fact that her bikini was red only made visualizing it easier. "What can I do for you?"

Her eyes brightened, and her smile deepened, revealing a dimple on her left cheek. Rick had never thought he had a weakness for such things, but on her...

Reaching into her bag, she pulled out a white tube. "Can you get my back? I can just feel the heat coming down and I don't want to turn over yet."

"Sure." The word was out of his mouth for a second time, his body eagerly taking over for his brain. Not that his brain would have been able to come up with a good excuse to get out of her simple request. But at least his brain knew it was a bad idea. He could have hesitated instead of jumping on the excuse to touch her.

"Thanks."

That sleepy, sultry smile was doing all sorts of havoc, but he had a lot of practice at keeping his face expressionless. Still, he didn't want her to think he was unfriendly, so he gave her a small smile back as he squirted the white cream onto his hand.

Yeah, don't think too hard about that.

Her deep brown eyes went down to a half-lidded state as she watched him sit down on the chair next to hers and reach over to her back. Soft. Warm. Pliable. Rick tried to concentrate on smoothing the sunscreen in evenly rather than on how silky and inviting her skin was.

"Mmmmmm..."

Giving her a quick glance, he saw her eyes had closed and she had a little smile on her face, looking very much like the cat who got the cream. Satisfied. Sexy.

"My name's Maria."

"Rick."

❧

MARIA PEEKED AT THE GREEK GOD. GOOD GRIEF HE WAS GLORIOUS up close. Chiseled jaw with just a hint of stubble, which hadn't been visible from further away because he was so fair-haired, stunning blue eyes, and a truly friendly smile. And the way he was looking at her back as he rubbed the sunscreen across it said maybe he wasn't like a lot of the other super fit guys she'd met, maybe he didn't judge women based on their size just because he was so... fit.

"I think I'm one of your upstairs neighbors," she said, to make conversation. "You moved into 304 right? I live right next to Mrs. Pierce."

He laughed, and it was probably the nicest sound she'd ever heard. Rich, sincere, and deeply sexy. Yum. "Mrs. Pierce with the grand-daughter named Catherine who is halfway through college and spends her weekends volunteering at her local animal shelter? I believe I might be familiar with her."

"Yep, that's her," Maria replied, giggling. She had a small pang of disappointment as she felt his fingers sweep across her back in a movement that indicated a 'finishing touch.' "She's really sweet as long as you don't mind hearing some of the same stories over and over. Most of them are pretty interesting though."

"Thanks for the warning," he said with a smile, getting to his feet. "It was nice to meet you Maria, I'm sure I'll see you around."

"Bye," she called after him as he turned and walked away.

The retreating view was nearly as appealing as the front. Especially with his bathing suit clinging to his legs and butt.

Not that she should be looking. He was obviously a nice enough guy and not a jerk, but he hadn't tried to stay and talk to her or anything. But he hadn't shut her down either. Maybe he had stuff to do today. Maria wondered what he would do if she tried to actually flirt with him.

She liked the idea of flirting with someone who was as hot and seemingly nice as him. Her mind started spinning a little fantasy where they became friends and she could take him to Lara's wedding, just to thumb her nose at Jerkface Jeremy. That made her giggle again; picturing the look on Jeremy's stupid face. Heck, perhaps they could become more than friends... she doubted a guy that good looking was anything but a player, but hey, she could live with that as long as he was good in bed.

And going by the careful way he'd massaged her back as he'd been rubbing the sunscreen in, the gentle but firm press of his fingers, she was willing to bet he was good. Most guys didn't have that kind of attention to detail if they were bad in bed.

"Mmmmmm...." she said again, thinking about the possibilities.

The sun soaked into her back until she couldn't bear it anymore and she turned over, reapplying sunscreen to her front. That got the attention of the two college guys she'd been talking to yesterday. They were across the pool in about the same place they'd been before, setting down their stuff. Both of them waved at her and she waved back, winking and jiggling a little bit.

A little shiver went up the back of her spine as goosebumps popped out all over her skin. She had the strangest feeling someone was just behind her, watching... but when she looked, no one was there.

Weird.

SHE WAS IN THE OFFICE WHEN HUMBERTO, ONE OF THE SERVERS, came back to let her know she had family in the house. Lara and Victor to be exact. She still hadn't actually called any of her family back, although she'd texted all of them just saying she'd been tired and had gone home but hadn't wanted to interrupt the celebration. She should probably just be grateful they hadn't descended on the restaurant en masse. Besides, this was Lara's favorite restaurant, so it was very possible they were here just for that and not to ask her about her sudden disappearance from the party.

Hopefully Jeremy hadn't said anything to Victor about their little confrontation. Not that Maria had done anything wrong, but who knew how the little douche canoe would have spun things. How someone as awesome as Victor could have such a butt monkey for a friend...

"Hey guys!" she said, pasting a smile on her face as she walked up to their table. Lara looked as effortlessly gorgeous as ever in a light blue t-shirt and shorts, and Victor was her perfect match in his khakis and green polo shirt. They'd been seated at one of the corner booths and were snuggling in the corner of it. If she wasn't so happy for Lara the sight might have been a little gag-worthy. "Is everyone taking care of you so far? No one's spit in your food?"

"Mariiiiiia!" Lara said laughing, dragging out Maria's name the way she'd done her entire life. "You're so bad, as if anyone here would ever do that."

"That's because you don't know how many of our servers are in love with your fiancé," Maria teased back, winking at Victor who grinned his appreciation. "And now that he is your fiancé, they might not be above taking a little bit of revenge."

Her younger sister rolled her eyes. "It's a good thing Ryan's our server then."

"You know Ryan is one of the servers in love with your fiancé, right?"

"Yeah, but I asked him to help me plan the wedding. He'll protect me," Lara said smugly.

Maria had to laugh. It was true, Ryan loved weddings. In fact, he wanted to be a wedding planner, but he needed to build up a portfolio to help him attract customers. If Lara wanted his help then she'd get a wedding planner for cheap and be able to help him out by providing pictures and a reference. A win-win for everybody.

"Is that the only reason you came in today?" she asked in mock anger. "Stealing my employees away from me?"

"That and for the crepes."

"You and your crepes," Victor said laughing, squeezing Lara tightly against him. She gave him an absolutely adoring look and Maria felt a little twinge of jealousy. Only because she couldn't remember a time any man had looked that way at her or she at him. Kinda sucked. Fortunately, Victor broke eye contact with his fiancé before Maria had time to become uncomfortable or feel like a complete outsider, looking back up at her with an inviting smile. "We were hoping you might be able to sit down and hang out with us for a bit, too."

Man she liked Victor. He was absolutely sincere in his invitation, not at all awkward or reluctant to spend some time hanging out with his fiancée's sister, even though they were on a date. So she sat down with them and they chatted, and talked a bit with Ryan and she got to hear some of the ideas Victor and Lara were batting around about the wedding. As a bridesmaid she knew she was going to hear a lot of wedding talk over the next year, but she was okay with that.

She talked with them until about halfway through their meal, when she went back to work, letting them have the rest of their date to themselves. Their visit did make her feel better, especially since—unlike the rest of her family—they didn't make any remarks about her single state or seem to feel the need to tiptoe or be "considerate" of the fact that she was single. They just talked, shared their joy, and had a good time. Which was exactly how she wanted it.

THE REST OF THE WEEK, MARIA DIDN'T MAKE IT OUT TO THE POOL while the Greek god was there. Which was disappointing. She ended up having to work later than usual a couple nights and was just too exhausted the next morning to get up early enough. Not that it kept her from the pool but being there just wasn't nearly as exciting without the possibility of running into him.

And it kept her thinking about how he lived just a floor below her.

Maybe it would be worth it to reach out to him. Just see what happened.

At the worst, she could try to make a new friend, right?

Every so often, she actually had a full Saturday off. This was one of those weeks and she decided to make some granola. A guy with a body like his who worked out every morning probably wouldn't want a plate of brownies, but she could make some pretty killer homemade granola. It was healthy, easy, and gave her an excuse to more formally welcome him to the neighborhood.

Yeah, most people weren't this kind of neighborly anymore, but that was okay. He had no way of knowing she didn't normally do this. She had mentioned Mrs. Pierce when they'd talked, so he knew she was friendly with at least one of her other neighbors. The others she all knew by name, which wasn't too hard since there were only three floors of apartments, with four apartments on each floor except the ground which only had three plus the laundry room. It was part of why she liked living in a garden apartment; even if you didn't know your neighbors, you at least knew who they were after a couple of months.

The smell of toasted oats, almonds, and coconut filled her apartment as she got ready. When she took the tray out of the oven, everything looked nicely browned and crispy. Yum. Just give it time to cool and then she'd add something a bit sweet, maybe raisins or even chocolate chips. Or maybe just a bit of honey.

She'd picked out her favorite pair of jean shorts— - not daisy dukes because she didn't like her ass cheeks hanging out, but they fitted her curves nicely and came to just about three inches under her butt, which meant she was still showing off a fair amount of leg but she didn't feel like she was showing too much—and a bright blue tank top. Thick straps with a deep V-neck edged with lace, it had an empire waistline so the fabric under her bust it fluttered a little more freely, covering the parts of her stomach she wasn't a huge fan of. Strange how she could feel totally confident walking out in a bikini, but she didn't like it when her clothing was stuck to her rolls.

Maria shrugged. Just one of the many contradictions of being a woman she supposed.

Since her hair was relatively well-behaved today, curling without too much frizz, she decided to let it fly free. Chances were she'd put it up later, but sometimes she liked the feeling of the big mass bouncing around her shoulders and upper back. It just felt fun. Plus, she'd been told by a lot of men that they loved seeing her hair like this. Although, most of them wanted to touch it and run their fingers through it which just made her want to smack them. Naturally curly hair did awful things when people ran their fingers through it.

Mixing the granola up with some raisins, deciding against the chocolate chips, Maria hoped he would be home. It was the middle of the day on a Saturday though, so her chances should be pretty good. Unfortunately, she wasn't on the side of the building where she'd have a view of the pool, but if he followed his usual pattern it was too late in the day for him to be there anyway. Humming to herself, she wrapped up the granola in the red-colored plastic wrap she had left over from Christmas.

When she rapped on his door, she shifted back and forth on her feet, feeling a bit nervous and hoping he really was as nice as he'd seemed at the pool.

"Coming," she heard him call.

Well, at least that answered the question about whether or not he was home. She shifted her weight again, finding a comfortable position and pasting a smile on her face before she could talk herself into abandoning the granola at his door and running. It was just nerves. Totally normal.

The door opened, and she nearly dropped her jaw. He was wearing a black tank top that was practically suctioned against his gorgeous body and a pair of workout shorts and he looked absolutely, effortlessly delicious. The dark color of his tank top just made his golden boy looks even brighter and his blue eyes glow even bluer. Everything about him screamed confident male, from the shaggy mess of his hair to the way he was leaning against the door frame. It wasn't until a slow smile crept across those expressive lips that she realized she was staring.

"Um... hi again. I brought you some homemade granola. You know, to welcome you to the neighborhood. Officially. I was gonna make cookies, but I wasn't sure if... um yeah." Mentally screaming at herself to shut up, Maria thrust the granola at him. His eyebrows went up in surprise, but he accepted the offering, the warmth of his hand brushing against hers and making her skin tingle as he took the packet of granola from her.

She was just about to flee until she realized his eyes had dropped to her chest and he was making a slow perusal of her own outfit. Warmth flooded through her and she suddenly felt a million times more comfortable. When his eyes came back up to hers, unashamed of his blatant examination, she was able to smile at him completely naturally.

"Thanks," he said. "It looks delicious. And for the record, snicker-doodles are my favorite."

"Favorite?"

"Kind of cookie." His smile was almost blinding. Maria did her best not to swoon. "But I've never had homemade granola before, so that's something to look forward to."

"It's really easy to make."

"I'll have to get you to teach me sometime." He glanced over his shoulder, she couldn't see at what. "I'd invite you in for a drink or something, but I was actually just about to head out to hang with some friends."

"Maybe some other time," she said, letting some of her natural flir-tatiousness slip into her manner, since he seemed like he might be receptive. It felt like there was a little spark, a little connection between them. Sure he might be a player, but he was hot and she was single and not looking for anything serious. "I'm the daytime manager at Murphy's Meals, if you ever wanna come in and visit. I can get you a drink for free."

Rick gave her a long measuring look and she actually got the impression of his eyes shuttering a bit, shutting her out. The change was subtle but abrupt and she blinked. The connection between them had shut down just like that, which told her she hadn't been imagining it. Something that didn't exist couldn't disappear, and she definitely felt the loss.

"Sorry, I probably won't be able to do that."

She huffed, bringing herself back fully upright, thoroughly annoyed at the abrupt rejection. Especially because she had a feeling she knew why he'd suddenly gone cold. She shouldn't have been surprised a guy who looked like him would be willing to have a drink with a girl who looked like her in private, but not out where someone might see them.

"Shocker," she said with an eye roll, falling back on her normal defense of sarcasm. So much for being neighborly, but whatever.

Guys like him really pissed her off. Jerks who didn't hide their asshole tendencies were at least honest. Although she knew she wouldn't be quite so defensive if she hadn't been hurt by the sudden shut down. She really hadn't expected it.

As she was about to turn and flounce away, his free hand snapped out and grabbed her arm. Not hard enough to hurt, but it was not a gentle hold either. Maria jumped. Damn he moved fast.

"What do you mean by that?" he demanded.

She raised an eyebrow and rolled her eyes at him, shoving down the hurt where he wouldn't be able to see even an inkling of it. Seriously? He wanted to question her when he'd been the rude one? Well fine, she'd never been one to hold back on blunt honesty. Maria had no problem laying it out for him.

"I'm just saying I should have expected someone as in shape as you wouldn't want to be seen out in public with me. You're nice enough when there's no one around to see or judge you, but not when someone might be watching. Guys like you are so predictable."

"That's not what I meant."

"Sure it wasn't." Derision laced her voice. First Jeremy, now him. Although at least Jeremy was obviously an ass. And she wasn't attracted to Jeremy, didn't care what he thought. Rejection from Rick had gotten under her skin in a way no other guy had in a long time. "Look, I don't really care if you're a jerk, I'm used to it. I just don't know why you bothered pretending not to be one. If you're going to be an asshole at least be an honest one."

The little growling noise he made under his breath didn't frighten her, although he was going to get it in the nards if he didn't let go of her and soon. It was amazing how many guys didn't want to think they were 'that way' and got pissy when it was pointed out to them. Maria considered it her duty to shove their prejudices in their faces. Some of them even came out the better for it. Besides, she wanted to get under his skin the way he'd gotten under hers.

Which is why she was shocked when he flipped her around and pressed her up against the wall. What the—? For some reason, even though she was trapped between the wall and what looked like a very angry man, and probably should have been screaming for her life, she didn't feel threatened. Just turned on, like he'd flicked a switch in her body. Blinking, she stared up into a pair of furious blue eyes. His body was long and hot and very... very... hard.

Everywhere.

Her breath caught.

"Sweetheart," he said, breathing out the words in a low, intimate tone; one that was both somehow patronizing and sexy. Something she wouldn't have thought possible before this moment. "I'm not going to meet you out in public for a drink, because you have no idea what a guy like me wants at the end of the night. Because I don't just want a good night kiss at the end of the night. I don't want to just come in for "coffee" and tamely get into bed, touch your body, and lick you from head to toe... I want..."

He broke off, his voice ragged, and his pupils dilated. Maria was panting, both a bit frightened and completely exhilarated by his response. What did he want? Something sexual, for sure.

He obviously wasn't a sexual predator, but he must have some kind of—what did people call it?—a kink that went outside the norm. What was it?

When he stepped away, her body felt the loss of it immediately. She remained braced against the wall, staring up at him, feeling slightly abandoned as his eyes shuttered again. The hot, hungry look in his eyes was gone as quickly as it had appeared.

"I'm sorry, Maria." He hesitated as if he wanted to say something else but didn't know how to phrase it. "I didn't... I don't..." He sighed and looked away. "Thank you for the granola."

"Rick?" She found herself in the strange position of wanting to reassure him. Especially since she had a feeling she'd come to a snap judgment herself. But what did she say. He looked at her, with those very blue eyes, obviously uncomfortable and a little ashamed. "It's okay. I... I mean, it's really okay. I'm sorry I made an assumption."

He thawed a little bit, but not back to the person she'd first encountered when he'd opened the door. "Thanks. I guess I'll see you around."

And then he was back in his apartment with the door firmly shut before she could respond. Although she was bristling again over his abrupt dismissal. Dammit.

He was hot and attracted to her. Maria was more intrigued than she had been when she'd first knocked on his door. What had he been holding back?

She'd gone a while without sex and she would be willing to work around some preferences.

Muttering to herself, Maria went back upstairs. Maybe she should leave him alone. But she didn't really want to. Especially now that she knew he was attracted to her. So he hadn't wanted to talk about whatever it was he wanted to do to her in the hallway, she could understand that.

She was so going to make sure she ran into him again. When he had the time for a drink.

GROANING, RICK BANGED HIS HEAD AGAINST THE WALL AND THEN glared at himself in the mirror. It wasn't really suave to hide out in his bathroom while he waited for Maria to vacate the hallway, but then again, he'd left suave behind about ten minutes ago, hadn't he?

"Get it together, Winter."

He was going to be late to the dojo, which Liam was probably going to kick his ass for. Although at this point, he could use the work out... pressing himself up against all of Maria's soft curves had been a huge mistake, but he'd just reacted. Without thinking.

Not his normal M.O.

When she'd implied he didn't like her because of her body though, he'd kind of just snapped. Ha. All those soft, luscious curves packed into her tank top and shorts combo, plus her inviting eyes and sweet, babbling shyness when she'd handed him the granola had completely disarmed his defenses. Every intention he'd had of keeping things neighborly had gone completely out the window and he'd gotten a little too friendly.

Then he'd tried to back off and she'd taken it in completely the wrong way. Which made him want to go around punching whatever guys had ever given her that impression about her body. Although she hadn't been insecure or hurt. No, she'd been marvelously, wonderfully, justifiably angry.

So damn sexy with those sparking dark eyes.

No wonder he'd nearly blurted out his desire to put her over his knee, spank her ass and then tie her up and work her over until she was begging to cum... and then continue to torture her some more. Yeah. Definitely not the kind of thing he needed to announce in his hallway. Or to her, period. Although for just a moment, when he'd pushed up against her and she'd looked up at him with those big dark eyes, all hot and bothered, he'd though for just a moment...

Maybe.

Maybe there was a submissive buried beneath all her tease and sass. But then again, maybe that was just his wishful thinking.

Feeling like an idiot, he went back to his front door and peeked out the peephole. As far as he could see, she wasn't there. He was both relieved and disappointed. Which meant, as far as he could tell, that he was also an idiot. Grabbing his gym bag, he opened the door and couldn't help glancing around the empty landing. Just in case.

Nobody was around. No noise from upstairs.

Time to get his ass to the dojo where his friends could give him all the smacks he needed to get his head back on straight.

## 4

As Rick had predicted, Liam was merciless when he showed up late. He gave Rick enough time to stretch and then threw him immediately into the forms with the others, being twice as picky about Rick's movement and placement as anyone else's. Rick didn't mind; it meant he had to concentrate, to fight any distractions in his thoughts.

Like a certain curvy brunette with soft skin and invitation in her eyes.

"Focus," Liam snapped out, right next to his ear, and Rick jerked his attention back to the matter at hand.

Caught.

Out of the corner of his eye, he saw Chris smirking at him, obviously amused both at his distraction and how he'd been called out on it. Normally that was Chris' position. He usually got bored during the non-weapons forms after a while. Gritting his teeth, Rick bent his knees slightly and slid into the next form, concentrating on his balance and trying to ignore Chris' superior looks.

There was a larger group of them than normal at the dojo—even Jared had managed to make it in for the evening. The only people they were missing were Andrew and, of course, Olivia, who rarely came since she preferred Krav Maga. Having a larger group was nice because once the class portion was over, Rick had a large choice of sparring partners.

"Jared?"

More than one person turned to stare at his choice. Normally Jared only sparred with Patrick or Liam; he was big, and he had a tendency to hit hard when he was sparring. On top of that, he was devilishly quick for a man his size; often, bigger meant slower, but that wasn't the case with Jared.

"Looking to get your ass kicked?" Jared asked, a smile slowly spreading across his face.

"Maybe a little bit," Rick admitted. "But I think I'll still give you a run for your money." His form wasn't always perfect, because he didn't come in often enough, but he was fast. Fast enough to dodge a lot of what Jared would throw at him, but he almost thought he'd welcome the pain when Jared did connect.

Someone needed to smack his head on straight after his performance this morning with Maria, that was for sure.

"Your funeral," the big man said cheerfully. Quickly tilting his neck so his ear was almost touching his shoulder and then snapping it back, the loud crack as Jared stretched out his muscles was ominous. Strangely, it just made Rick feel even calmer. Maybe he really did want to get his ass kicked. A kind of atonement for even thinking about trying to start something with his neighbor.

"I'll referee," said Liam. He glanced over at the other four. "Who's refereeing and who's sparring?"

"I'm gonna ref," said Patrick. "Justin and Adam are going first."

"I'll spar loser," said Chris with a grin. He pushed his sweat-matted dark hair out of his eyes.

"You can spar me next," Liam said, amusement showing in his hazel eyes as chuckles went around the room at Chris' muttered curse. Theirs would be a particularly uneven match. Even more so than Rick and Jared, and no one thought Liam would go easy just because Chris was probably the worst about coming to the dojo on a regular basis.

Facing off against Jared, Rick had just a split second to wonder if he'd made a mistake. There was a lot of tension in Jared's big frame, and they all knew he'd been having issues with Marissa again. Maybe he should have let Patrick take on Jared and let someone else less wound up have a go at him.

Then again, maybe it was better that they'd be taking out their aggression on each other.

Jared moved silently, without the shouts which usually accompanied a move, and Rick quickly dodged out of the way. He sent his own leg kicking out behind him, hoping for a lucky strike, but Jared was too canny for that. Instead, Rick found his foot caught and he was flipped straight onto his back, nearly knocking the breath out of him. His lungs burned a bit as a muscle in his back twinged. He'd be sore there tomorrow.

"Point. Get it together, Winter," Liam said, sounding amused. "Whatever bug you've got up your ass, you'd better let it go and get your nose to the ground."

"Or what, you'll smother me in your girlfriend's weird old sayings?" Rick asked as he pushed himself back up. Jared and Chris—who was obviously more interested in watching him and Jared than watching Adam and Justin—both laughed. Hilary was known for constantly using out of date phrases, thanks to her dad who was a university professor and had a bit of an obsession with the English language. The habit had started to rub off on Liam, something they all enjoyed giving him a hard time over.

"Or I can tell Hilary you called her weird."

"Hiding behind your girlfriend is cheating, but Hilary can check out the bug in my ass anytime," Rick taunted, laughing as Liam growled a mock threat, gesturing for Rick and Jared to get on with their match again.

He and Jared bowed to each other again and then began circling, more cautiously this time. Out of the corner of his eye he could see the other sparring match, but he forced himself to focus. That was the whole point of this exercise, wasn't it? Trying to make himself concentrate.

It got a bit easier after Jared accidentally knocked him on the chin with his elbow. That fucking hurt, but the pain made Rick buckle down and finally get his act together. He and Jared exchanged a flurry of kicks, turns and hits, which ended with Jared rubbing his stomach where Rick had kicked him and Rick feeling like he'd gotten hit by a freight train. Tomorrow he was going to be bruised in multiple places and, unlike Jared whose dark skin rarely showed a mark, Rick's would be green and yellow, maybe even a bit black and blue.

By the end of the bout, Jared had thoroughly kicked his ass and they were both breathing a little easier, their inner tension gone. That was the beauty of sparring, for them. A way to work out major aggressions in a safe environment. Slumped next to each other against the wall, they watched as Liam and Patrick tormented Chris in what was supposed to be a free-for-all between the three of them but was looking more and more like two-on-one. Justin's supposed refereeing was leaving a bit to be desired, as Chris pointed out whenever he had the breath.

"So... women troubles?" Rick asked Jared.

"I'm pretty sure that's the definition of Marissa," Jared rumbled, rubbing his hand over his bald head in a motion that looked like frustration, exhaustion, and resignation all rolled into a ball of despair. Sadly, not an unusual look when it came to Jared and Marissa. "You?"

"Had a bit of a run-in with my new neighbor this morning. She... made it clear she's interested in me."

"You aren't?"

"No, I am."

"Submissive?"

"No idea."

Jared chewed over that for a minute while Patrick wrestled Chris into a headlock while Liam started drumming on Chris' bent over back. They cheered Liam and Patrick on, with only Adam rooting for Chris to break the hold—which he eventually did by catching Patrick with his elbow perilously close to the gonads. He was still laughing as he rolled away from them, yelling "Red! Red!"

"Too bad we're not in the club!" Liam shouted as he pounced. He and Chris began rolling around on the floor while Patrick laughed and started pushing their rolling bodies with his foot. Rick was a little surprised to see how chipper Patrick was being. He'd expected him to be nearly as wound up as him and Jared.

Then again, if Lexie was behaving and not entering the club unless she had adequate chaperonage, Patrick didn't really have a whole lot to complain about at the moment. Especially if she wasn't pushing for more than that like she had in the past. Patrick was always more relaxed when Lexie wasn't pushing boundaries and she was acting more like the good little vanilla girl all of them wished she actually was.

Although, Rick had noticed more of them were becoming resigned to the realization that she probably wasn't vanilla and one day she would probably be in the club, and not just on the main floor. Even though no one talked about it, Rick thought they had all probably observed the same thing as him. Patrick was fighting a serious attraction to his best friend's little sister and she wasn't making it easy for him.

"If she's not submissive, probably better to stay away," Jared said, dragging Rick away from his thoughts and surprising him with both the advice and the bitterness in Jared's voice. "There's nothing worse than being in a relationship built on a false premise."

The group of them, other than Jared, had long held the opinion that Marissa wasn't really submissive, but this was the first time he knew of that Jared had indicated he might share the opinion.

"Is there anything I can do, man?" Rick asked quietly, not wanting to draw their friends' attention. They were still laughing and playing in the middle of the floor, oblivious to the serious conversation happening along the wall. Jared didn't often open up much about whatever was going on between him and Marissa, and if he was doing so now then Rick didn't want to break his trust.

Jared stared up towards the ceiling for a long moment. "No. It's my own fault. Nothing you can do."

Hesitating for a moment, because he didn't really want to hand out unwanted advice, Rick decided to just go for it. "You don't have to stay with her, you know."

"I tried to break up with her a couple weeks ago," Jared said quietly, still staring up at the ceiling. Rick wasn't even sure the other man was really aware of Rick's presence. It was like he was a pot that had been overfilled and set to boil, and now the water was sliding over the sides, but it wasn't by choice. "She locked herself in the bathroom and told me she was swallowing all the pills in the medicine cabinet. I had to break the door down."

Rick sucked in a breath. "Fuck."

"Yeah."

"Had she?"

"She was holding the bottle."

"Do you think she'd really have done it?"

"I don't know."

But he wouldn't take the chance. That was something Rick knew instinctively. None of them would. Their entire group of friends was demanding, stubborn, and occasionally cruel in the bedroom, but they would never allow someone in their care to come to any kind of harm.

Part of Rick wanted to point out that, of course Marissa knew she hadn't been in any real danger. She was still manipulating Jared, knowing he would get to her in plenty of time. Even if she had swallowed the pills there would have been plenty of time to get her stomach pumped. But he also knew that while Jared might know she was playing him intellectually, it was another thing to live it and he was too much of a caretaker to let his damaged girlfriend go if she so desperately wanted to stay with him. Rick was starting to wonder if she was actually that manipulative, or if she really might be more than a little damaged.

"Isn't she seeing a therapist?"

"Yeah."

"Fuck."

"Yeah."

"I'm sorry, man."

Jared just shrugged, but Rick saw his eyes flit over to where Adam and Justin were standing on the sideline. They were cheering on Liam, who was now using what looked like some kind of pro-wrestling move on Chris. Tossing him to the ground where Chris made his body shake like he was having some kind of seizure—just like the pro-wrestlers in the 80s did. Patrick pretended to be throwing down the People's elbow onto Chris' chest, a move made famous by the Rock back when they'd all actually watched that stuff.

Suddenly he understood why Jared had opened up specifically to him, why he'd felt comfortable enough to do so.

Adam, Liam, Justin, and Chris were all in happy relationships. Even Patrick and Lexie had some kind of weird thing going on between them that, while it wasn't a relationship, might be one day if Patrick ever let it. If Andrew had been there, maybe Jared would have talked to him, but he wasn't, and Rick was.

For the first time, in a long time, Rick was glad he was single. Because that meant Jared hadn't had to hold everything inside while looking around at all his happy friends.

He looked at Jared, whose expression had settled into morose. Elbowing the big guy in the side, Rick started to push himself up out of his sitting position.

"Come on, let's jump these assholes and make this a Battle Royale."

It took a moment, but then a smile spread across Jared's face. "Fuck yeah man."

Rick reached out his hand and yanked Jared to his feet. They both let out war cries as they dove into the fray, Rick going for Liam while Jared aimed for Patrick, knocking them off Chris. It took Adam and Justin less than two seconds to figure out what was going on, and then Rick grunted as one—possibly both—of them landed on his back.

"Austin 3:16 says—you're going down!" Chris yelled as he bounced up to his feet, pumping his fist in the air.

Chaos reigned.

"Maybe he has a foot fetish. In which case, you should definitely stop by to say hi to him after this."

Maria giggled as her sister Jackie wiggled her toes at her lasciviously. The pedicurist clucked a scolding sound at her and Jackie contritely put her foot back on the rest, even though it wasn't the one the pedicurist had been attending to. Jackie was generally considered the prettiest of the Arias sisters, with her long black hair and striking green eyes. She had the same thick hair as Maria, but without the frizz and curl, and her naturally tanned skin only made her wide eyes all the more stunning.

Growing up, all of the sisters had been envious of Jackie, especially once they'd realized their boyfriends were easily distracted by her. Not that it was her fault, but it had happened. It would have been easy to hate Jackie if she wasn't so damned nice on top of everything else. Maria sometimes wondered if Jackie felt almost apologetic for her looks. She knew her sister had often felt guilty whenever someone's boyfriend would become fascinated with her. Especially since she definitely never encouraged them.

Jackie had been happily married for the past two years to a wonderful man named Daniel, who was well aware his wife had attributes that went far beyond her physical beauty and appreciated every bit of her. He wasn't bad looking, but a lot of people tended to be surprised when they saw him because he didn't have Jackie's movie star good looks either.

Maria thought her sister was wonderfully lucky to have found him.

"Is that why you have a standing appointment for a pedicure every two weeks?" she teased back. "Because of Daniel's foot fetish?" To her surprise, Jackie blushed. Maria gaped. "What?! No way!"

"Shhhhh," said Jackie, her cheeks turning even darker pink as she waved her hand at Maria gesturing her to speak more softly. The pedicurists would still be able to hear, of course, but it always seemed like there was some kind of code of silence between clients and pedicurists. Maria was sure they heard the weirdest things. "I wouldn't call it a fetish exactly but, yes... he does love it when I get a new pedicure. And he likes to kiss and suck on my toes sometimes, but that's as far as it goes."

"I had no idea." Maria tried to keep from giggling, knowing this was a serious subject to her sister, but it was just so hard not to picture it in a comical way. "Do Ava and Lara know?"

"No, and I wouldn't be telling you this if you hadn't brought it up, so don't tell them."

"I won't if you won't," Maria said, referencing the fact that Jackie had somehow managed to coax her into talking about Rick. She'd managed to avoid her good-looking neighbor for several days now. It wasn't too hard as long as she stayed away from the pool in the early mornings.

She hadn't been avoiding him because she didn't want to see him again. She'd been avoiding a chance run-in, while she thought about how best to approach him next. And she'd been wondering what it was, exactly, he wanted to do to her that he didn't want her to know about.

"I've already promised not to," Jackie reminded her, making a face.

Secrets were sacred among the sisters, mostly because it was so hard to keep one for any length of time. Maria had needed someone to spill to, Jackie had been the next sister to see her, she'd noticed how distracted Maria had been and well... one thing led to another and Maria had found herself spilling about the entire incident.

"I could live with a foot fetish," Maria announced, nodding her head thoughtfully. Laughing, Jackie shushed her again. Maria grinned, amused at how easily embarrassed Jackie was by the revelation. "No seriously, I mean, that doesn't sound so bad. A man who wants to worship my feet? That's close enough to 'at my feet,' right?"

"I can recommend it," Jackie said with a little smirk, wiggling her glossy dark red toenails on the foot the pedicurist wasn't working on. Her face became a little bit more serious. "What if it's not though? What if he's into something like swinging or having sex in front of people?"

Maria contemplated the idea, watching as her own pedicurist put the finishing touches on her bright pink nails. Swinging didn't sound like fun, she wasn't a sharing person. She also didn't really know how she felt about exhibitionism. There was something exciting about that, but it was also sharing in a different way. People would be watching an intimate moment. Still. She didn't like the idea of giving up on a hot guy just because he might be into something different than she'd ever done before. "I mean... you should never say no until you've tried something, right?"

"Oh no... you wouldn't..." Jackie moaned. "Mom would kill you."

"Mom would never know." She gave Jackie a look, raising her eyebrow, although she couldn't quite shake the guilty feeling either. Jackie was right, their mother would so not approve of Maria thinking about doing something kinky. But what mom didn't know couldn't hurt her. She seriously doubted Jackie had ever discussed her husband's foot fetish with their mother. "He's really hot. And nice and seriously sexy. It's a good combination. Plus, I'm not exactly thinking serious relationship or marriage... I just need something uncomplicated and fun for a bit."

"I don't know why you're not thinking marriage," her sister muttered, giving her a dire look.

She shrugged. "Because thinking marriage has never gotten me anywhere."

"Oh Maria..." Jackie's voice trailed off, suddenly sympathetic and a bit worried.

"Oh no you don't," Maria pointed her finger right at Jackie's face. "I am perfectly happy like this. I haven't given up on love and marriage and babies and all that jazz, but it's not like I've met anyone recently who I'd want to get serious with. And I have met someone who's hot and seems nice, and if I learn a little something from it then that's not a bad thing, right?"

The look Jackie gave her was unconvinced but resigned. "I guess."

"Good." The pedicurists put the finishing touches on both of them, smiling and shooing them over to the table where they could let the polish dry under UV lights. Wiggling her toes, Maria grinned. "Now let's go let our feet bake and talk about where we're going to go for lunch."

They ended up going to a hole in the wall restaurant a couple of storefronts down, since they felt lazy and didn't want to drive anywhere. The food was surprisingly good. Maria was enjoying her day off and spending some time with her sister. Especially since Jackie seemed to have gotten the message about not bothering her about her romances. Maria still bet there was a pretty good chance Jackie was going to contact her within the next week about some friend of Daniel's Maria just "had" to meet. But she could live with that.

In the meantime, she was so not going to let Rick get away just because he was a little shy about whatever it was he liked to do in the bedroom. Right now, Maria was feeling up for a little exploration. She just had to figure out how to approach him again, without scaring him off. Maybe even just showing him that he hadn't managed to scare her off would do the trick.

SINCE HE WASN'T EXPECTING ANYONE, WHEN HE HEARD HIS doorbell ring, Rick checked the peephole. Immediately, he recognized Maria, nibbling her lower lip as she waited outside his door. He nearly groaned.

It had been almost a week since he'd last seen her and made a complete fool out of himself. A period of time during which he'd been heavily distracted by working a job for Adam, trying to figure out what to do about Jared and Marissa and whether or not he could tell someone else without breaking Jared's trust, and mentally prepping himself for the next time he ran into Maria. Of course, he'd thought their next meeting would be a chance run-in, he hadn't actually expected her to come to him.

Why had she?

And why did he find that so appealing? As a dominant male, he usually wanted to be the hunter and didn't like being chased but seeing her outside his door made his entire body come alive in anticipation.

Taking a deep breath, Rick opened the door, trying to keep his expression open without showing his pleasure at seeing her. This was exponentially harder when her face brightened the moment she saw him. He couldn't help but wonder why she was so pleased to see him after the way he'd treated her... had she liked being pushed up against the wall? Had she been excited when he'd trapped her? Considering she'd shown up at his door again, without an invitation, she wasn't exactly acting like a submissive but maybe...

Cut it out.

"Maria, good morning," he said, determined to keep things neighborly and civil between them without anything more. "What can I do for you?"

Almost as if she was ignoring his demeanor, she smiled brightly at him. Her curls were pulled back into a fat, bouncy pony tail of curls and she was wearing a knee-length fluttering blue skirt and a white tank top with matching blue edging showing off a generous amount of cleavage. There was no doubt she knew what looked good on her and used it to her advantage. Rick would be quite happy to fall into her cleavage and snuggle in like a bear hibernating in winter.

"I was hoping maybe you'd have time to invite me in for that drink," she said cheerfully, giving him a look bordering on flirtatious but wasn't quite. Almost as if she was inviting him to flirt with her but wasn't trying to push the envelope.

Rick was surprised at how much he wanted to do so, to get to know a little bit more about her and what made her tick. To test the waters, so to speak. Hell, they didn't even really know each other. Ineffable attraction, that's what it was.

Animal attraction maybe.

"I don't think that would be a good idea," he said, determined to stick to his guns. Having her come into his personal space was a terrible idea. Every little step he took toward getting to know her better, toward bringing her into his life, would probably just make him want to take more. She was a dark-haired temptress, offering inducements without knowing what the consequences might be for herself.

"Come on, it'll be fun."

Maria just slipped past him, before he could react, too surprised by her brashness to stop her. Dammit, he was tired if he couldn't even keep one woman from getting through his doorway. Possibly stress induced fatigue from everything he'd had going round his head since the last time he saw her.

"Maria," he growled, turning and holding the door open wider to indicate that she should get her gorgeous ass back outside, but she cut him off with another encouraging smile.

"Come on Rick, I promise I won't bite. Unless that's what you like..." She fluttered her eyelashes at him flirtatiously, but the look she gave him was more inquisitive than anything else. He had to stifle the urge to laugh, forcing himself to keep his expression serious and unwelcoming. "I have to admit, you made me very curious."

Ignoring the open door, Maria stepped closer to him, tilting her head back to look at him with those beautifully dark eyes. Her voice was becoming breathy, filled with intrigue. Great, apparently, he'd woken up a curious little kitty who wanted to come out and play. "Exactly what is it you want to do to me? I'm willing to be... very open-minded."

Rick narrowed his eyes at her, wishing his body wasn't so very keen to take her up on her offer. While he might not be overly dominant outside of the bedroom, unlike some of his friends, he definitely should not have found her blatant come on so damned appealing. What was it about her? Or maybe it was just the way she was challenging him, as if begging for a punishment. He'd always had a soft spot for submissives who were teases.

But she wasn't a bratty submissive and he needed to remember that.

"I think it's best if you go," he said. "I'm not looking for open-minded, I'm looking for someone who wants the same things I do."

"And how do you know I don't?" she asked, pressing those gorgeous soft curves up against him. Rick nearly groaned as his body reacted immediately and her eyes got wide. She knew damned well he had a hard on now, not that she needed any encouragement. "It's not like I'm asking you to be my boyfriend, I'm willing to experiment... and we can have a good time."

Now that pissed Rick off. He didn't even need to pretend to glower now. As if she realized she might have misread him, she took a tiny step back. Not far, but just enough, as a slightly puzzled expression went across her face.

"And what makes you think I'm just looking for a good time?" Rick demanded, torn between the desire to shove her out the door or drag her back to his bedroom and show her just exactly what she was asking for.

"I mean... you're a guy... aren't guys always up for a good time? And... I mean, look at you. Guys who look like you do... they're... usually players," she said, but her voice was hesitant. As if she was remembering the last time she'd made an assumption about him and how wrong she'd been then. Maybe even remembering the way he'd pressed her against the wall to prove he absolutely did find her attractive and he had no problem with her curves.

Rick truly wanted to hunt down every male she'd had an interaction with throughout her life and beat the daylights out of them. What made this gorgeous, confident woman have all the stereotypes about men that she did?

Unfortunately, he had a feeling her life experiences probably backed up all those stereotypes.

At one time in his life, he might have too. A sexy curvy girl showing up on his doorstep and offering a good time would have seemed like Christmas. But that wasn't what he wanted now, and it grated on him that he'd apparently already been assessed and judged by her.

"Well I'm not," he said, stepping forward and slightly to the side, forcing her to change her position so her back was to the open doorway. He knew he was crowding her, trying to herd her toward the door, but she didn't back up as much as he thought she would. His voice was low, fierce, because he didn't want the neighbors to hear what he was saying if they were home, but he wanted her to know he was one hundred percent sincere with everything he said. "I'm not the kind of guy who's going to fuck a woman he doesn't want to be seen in public with. I'm not the kind of guy who's just looking for a good time. I'm not interested in being someone's experiment. And I'm not interested in flirtatious little teases who are just looking for a cheap thrill."

With every sentence he took another step toward her, forcing her to back out into the hallway as her big eyes widened even further. She was finally out of his apartment, out of his space, and part of him was incredibly disappointed by that. He needed to give her a damned good reason to stay away from him.

Deepening his voice, deliberately making it rougher and more forceful, Rick stared directly into her eyes, packing his pent-up frustration and heat into his gaze.

"If you knock on my door again, Maria, I will put you over my knee and spank your ass until it's a hot cherry red. And I'll enjoy every second of it."

With that he slammed the door practically in her face.

His chest felt tight as he turned away from the door. Damn, but he'd hated doing that. Hated intimidating her, hated threatening her, hated how his cock had been rock hard the entire time he'd been doing it. At least he'd given her just enough information to indicate what exactly it was he liked to do in the bedroom, which should scare her off. Especially with the manner he'd delivered it in. He hadn't imagined the shock and spark of fear in her eyes before he'd closed the door.

That kind of response, as long as it was tempered with excitement, was like manna to a Dom. He hated the part of him which had enjoyed that, because he knew it wasn't going to be followed up with a hot scene that would temper her fright with pleasure.

What he hated most of all, was the disappointment sweeping through him when he realized she would probably never darken his doorstep again.

## 🙐 5 🙒

**H**oly crap... holy crap holy crap holy crap holycrapholy-crapholyCRAP!

Maria's knees actually felt weak as she slammed her own apartment door and then pressed her back against it. Her heart was pounding. Not like he was chasing her or anything—he'd made it pretty clear he wouldn't be doing that—but Maria had so not been prepared for that kind of confrontation.

He wants to spank me?

If it hadn't been for the way his eyes had sparked and flared with interest as he said it, she might have thought he was just trying to scare her away with something outrageous. But there was no mistaking the fact that even just saying the words definitely got him hot and bothered. The question was, did it get her hot and bothered too?

She didn't know. It was one thing to contemplate getting it on with a hot guy who might want to lick her feet or maybe wear her panties, but Rick had made two things very clear: he wasn't just looking for a good time and he wanted something which had never been on her menu. Like... seriously... spanking? People actually did that?

Okay, she wasn't a complete idiot, she knew people did that, but somehow his golden boy, Greek god good looks didn't lend itself to the way she would have pictured a spanker.

How did she picture a spanker? Well, she'd seen that movie, Secretary, so maybe a little bit like James Spader. Or maybe some Goth kind of guy who dressed in leather and chains. A super conservative throwback to the 1950s guy who wore pressed suits and considered himself the Head of the Household. None of those descriptions came anywhere close to Rick though.

Man, she was really good at stereotyping and she hadn't even realized it. Not a pleasant realization. She always hated when people stereotyped her, and she'd now done it to Rick multiple times. Even knowing she'd already wronged him once.

And he had given her a lot to think about.

Dammit.

She really needed more female friends. More than ever she needed to talk through some of this stuff with someone, but her choices were rather limited. She could either fess up to Ava (ha!) or Lara about what was going on or she could go back to Jackie, but she didn't know how any of her sisters would react to the idea she was interested in a guy who wanted to spank her. Or that she was tempted to let him. Sure, they'd all talked sex before, but not like this.

As the oldest, she also felt like she was supposed to be the mature, responsible one, never mind that they had all gotten married before her. There was something inside of her saying she had to set a good example. Somehow, getting spanked just didn't seem like it would send that message. She was supposed to be strong and independent and all that good feminist stuff.

So why did she feel more excited than outraged?

WHEN BROOKE, ONE OF HER SERVERS, CAME LOOKING FOR HER THE next day at work with a call of distress from Janet, the hostess, she was glad to get out of the office and away from the paperwork, even though it meant dealing with a pain in the ass woman who insisted on a window seat despite the fact she didn't have a reservation.

"Yes, I understand the table at the window doesn't have anyone sitting at it right now," Maria said calmly, wanting nothing more than to smack the snobby looking woman across the face. "However, we have a reservation which should be arriving any minute who specifically requested a table by the window. As all the other tables by the windows currently have people seated at them, and none of them will be getting up any time soon, and you do not have a reservation, I'm sorry but I can't seat you at the window. It wouldn't be fair to the person who made the reservation for that table. We're happy to seat you at any other table in the restaurant."

The snobby woman was with a friend, who was grimacing and looking apologetically over her shoulder at Maria. Maria sent the other woman a quick little smile as the snobby one rolled her eyes and made a disgusted noise. Even if this woman was a bitch, it was obvious her friend wasn't, and Maria felt a little bad for her. It must be embarrassing to be out with someone who so obviously felt entitled and was basically making a scene that made both of them look bad.

There was no way in hell Maria was going to put out someone who had the courtesy to make a reservation with a specific request, in order to cater to some bitch who thought the world should just bow down to her.

"This restaurant is just awful," the woman fumed, furiously tapping her perfectly done French manicure on the top of the hostess stand. Click, click, click, click. "Every time I come here, the staff is slow or rude or both, you management people never do anything to help, and the food isn't even great!"

Stifling the fury she felt at such a derisive summation of what Maria considered her restaurant, well aware of the wide-eyes of Janet who was watching the entire thing, not to mention the serving staff in ear shot, Maria gave the woman her brightest smile.

"Well then," she chirped, in her most friendly and upbeat manner. "May I ask, what brings you back?"

The woman gaped like a fish as her friend burst out laughing. Maria could hear the choked gasps and laughter of the staff. Out of the corner of her eye she could see several of the servers making a beeline for the kitchen where they'd be able to laugh themselves silly. And probably share what she'd said. Next to her, Janet was having a sudden coughing fit. Stoically, she held her bright smile, blinking and waiting for the woman's response.

"Well I never!" she finally huffed and turned on her heel to go outside.

"Sorry... new money... thank you," her friend choked out before following.

"Have a nice day!" Maria called out after them.

Next to her, Janet finally started cracking up. She was a sweet girl, senior in high school, but sometimes the more demanding guests could roll right over her. Which is why she'd sent Brooke for Maria, because she'd known the right thing to do, she just hadn't known how to handle the woman.

"Oh my God... Maria, you are so bad!"

"I was perfectly polite."

"And still, so bad!" Janet shook her head, still giggling as she wiped the tears from her eyes. "I don't know how you kept a straight face."

"Lots of practice," Maria said with a grin. That and she'd been pissed enough that even her retort hadn't made her want to laugh.

"What did the other woman mean by 'new money'?"

Maria sighed, making a face. It was a problem they were probably going to have more often, although hopefully most of the people like that woman just wouldn't come by, because Murphy's was so not going to cater to them when they were being unreasonable. "You know the new housing development down North Hill Road? About five minutes away? A lot of people moving in there are people who are just starting to become rich. Old money, like the people we get from Mansfred Park, tend to be polite, classy, and not rub it in your face. They're used to having money and influence. New money means they feel like they have to step all over you to prove how much better they are than you."

"So, no class." Janet made a face. "I hope we don't get a lot of people like her in here... I wonder why the other woman was with her. She seemed nice enough."

"Maybe they were friends before," Maria said, shrugging. "Or maybe they're forced into being friends because of business or something. Who knows. Anyway, don't let people like that push you into doing things which will mess up the way the floor is running. Murphy's has plenty of business, we don't need to antagonize people who play by the rules by indulging people like her."

"Okay. Thanks Maria."

"That's what I'm here for," she said, smiling.

She was going to have to tell Ava about the little interlude later. Ava loved hearing work stories, especially about the craziness difficult customers could bring into the restaurant. It was definitely amusing, after it was over, although while it was happening Maria could usually feel her patience wearing thin.

Deciding she should go check on the kitchen, she wove her way through the dining room, stopping at a table here and there, saying hi to the regulars who were there. One table wanted her to sit and have a drink with them, but she refused. Sometimes James or Jeanne would do that with the regulars, but they were owners, not managers. It made a difference in privileges.

When she stepped into the kitchen, Ryan hooted and started to applaud. The other servers in there immediately followed suit, as did the chefs. Obviously, restaurant gossip had already made quick work of spreading the word on how she'd dealt with the bitchy woman. One of the reasons people loved working at Murphy's was because they knew the management wouldn't force them to cater to people who were rudely unreasonable.

"Thank you, thank you," she said, taking a laughing bow before giving them a mock-stern look. "Now back to work!"

They all chuckled, not that they needed to be told they were in the middle of a rush. But they appreciated the joke.

By the end of the shift, Maria was exhausted. She finally got home around eight o'clock, starving and feeling a bit burnt out. Lunch had gone smoothly enough, but the dinner shift had seemed cursed. Not only had there been a major pile-up on one of the major roads nearby, causing half the servers and bussers to be late, but they'd had some trouble with the hood over the wood burning oven in the kitchen and it had started pouring out smoke...

Fortunately, it happened before they had any guests in the restaurant, but the entire kitchen had filled with smoke and she and the evening manager, Blake, had talked with the Executive Chef and realized they couldn't open for dinner that evening. She'd called James and Jeanne to let them know. Then she and Blake had called every single person on their reservation list, the staff who hadn't made it in yet, and then had to call around and find a repair person who could come in early tomorrow morning. It had been a major pain in the butt all around.

The good news was that tomorrow morning was not her shift.

The better news was that she had leftover casserole in the fridge and wouldn't need to make dinner.

Settling herself on the couch with her meal and a very generous glass of wine, Maria let her mind drift to the Rick and spanking issue, which she'd managed to forget about for most of the day. Shocking, considering that last night she'd barely been able to sleep while her mind had turned over the possibilities.

She still didn't think she liked the idea of being spanked. On the other hand, for some reason, part of her did like the idea of a man who took charge in the bedroom. When was the last time she'd been with a guy who really knew exactly what he wanted and went for it?

When Rick had been looming and intimidating, she'd been creaming her panties in a way she'd never done before with any other guy. Well, maybe for Chris Hemsworth. But definitely no man in her real life had ever made her feel so weak-kneed or flushed and squirmy, and Rick had done it twice now.

Maybe she could put up with spanking. Especially since he said he wasn't just a good-time guy, and she believed him. If he was seriously looking for a relationship, and he was attracted to her then she'd be crazy to pass up at least getting to know him better. After all, when was the last time she'd met a guy she was this attracted to? That's if he still wanted to get to know her after yesterday.

She was sure he thought she was a flirt. A tease. A good-time girl just like she'd assumed he was. That's how she'd acted around him.

So maybe she needed to do something a little different.

RICK FIGURED HIS MORNING WORKOUT WAS JUST ABOUT OVER, HE was debating between doing another two laps or just finishing his work-out now when he saw the pair of legs hanging down in front of the wall he was approaching. Steering himself slightly to the side so he could grip the wall, he came up for air, pulling off his goggles at the same time so he could actually see. Maria smiled blindingly bright at him as he blinked at her. She was back in the red bikini, water droplets on her stomach and thighs from his splashing as he'd approached, and her hair was piled in her usual heavy bun on top of her head again.

Being so close to her made his fingers itch to reach out and touch her. His shoulder was within an inch of her calf, so close he could swear he could feel the heat of her skin. Her very nearness set him on edge, wondering what she wanted from him now. Wondering why his threat to spank her hadn't kept her far, far away from him.

"Hi. I hope I'm not interrupting. You're usually done with your workout about this time," she said cheerfully. As if their confrontation at his front door hadn't happened two days ago.

"I was just finishing up," he said, carefully keeping his voice non-committal. He wasn't sure what she was up to now. After all, he'd only warned her to stay away from his apartment, not from him entirely. That might have been a mistake, although he hadn't thought she'd pop back up again. Definitely not so quickly. He cursed the pleasure that rose up in him at her presence, the hope that she might be interested in what he was offering.

"Don't you get bored? Swimming laps? I can't stand it. It's even worse than running because you can't listen to music or watch television while you're doing it."

"I think that's why I like it," he said, leaning back against the rope keeping the lap lane separate from the rest of the pool. If it was later in the day he'd feel the need to get out of the lane so someone else could use it, but right now there wasn't anyone at the pool who would want to. Just some kids, a couple of teenage girls who were eyeballing the college frat boys that had shown up, and a few parents who obviously just wanted to laze about in the sun. "It's almost like meditating. Since I teach high school, I like the quiet."

"What do you teach?"

"English. I'll be starting at Franklin High School this fall."

"Bet you're going to cause a stir among the girls," she said, kicking her legs a bit, not quite enough to break the water, as she grinned at him in a conspiratorial way, inviting him to share the joke.

Rick studied her, more than a bit confused. Everything about her body language said she was relaxed and being friendly, but her last remark was definitely flirtatious. For a minute he'd thought perhaps she'd decided to just be friendly and ignore the attraction between them, maybe as a way to prove to herself that he hadn't scared her. Now he wasn't sure what she was doing.

"Do you go running often?" he asked.

The little amused look she gave him said she hadn't missed his evasion away from being flirty. Even that made his cock stir. Good thing he was still in the pool. Because right now all he could think about was ways to wipe the little amused smile from her face.

"Not really, why?"

"You shouldn't listen to music while you do it. My friend Angel teaches a women's self-defense class and that's one of the things she stresses, always being aware of your situation and that means being able to hear what's around you."

"Or someone might jump out and put you over their knee?" she asked, teasingly, but he could see the curiosity in her eyes.

Telling his dick not to get too excited, Rick looked back at her, considering his response. He couldn't help it, the way she was looking at him, the fact that she continued searching him out. It had to mean something, didn't it? "Is that something you'd actually be interested in?"

To his surprise, she looked away, not meeting his gaze for the first time. Not meeting the challenge. It was almost... submissive.

Wait for her to actually answer before you jump all over her, Romeo.

"I don't know," she said, softly, turning back to look at him. But as soon as her gaze met his, her eyes lowered again, and he had to stifle the urge to pull her down into the pool with him so he could get a little bit closer. See what other reactions he might be able to surprise from her. She peeked at him from underneath her eyelashes. "I thought maybe we could just start with flirting."

Rick wanted to make a comment about how two days ago she'd wanted to start with sex, but he stamped down on the urge. Not only would it be rude, but it would be entirely counterproductive. He'd been very clear about what he wanted, and if she was still truly interested in getting to know him, and she hadn't been completely scared off by the threat of a spanking, then he shouldn't push her away immediately.

While he would have preferred to meet someone at Stronghold, someone who was already familiar with the lifestyle, he also realized so far that hadn't exactly been working. Neither had his resolve to stay away from his gorgeous neighbor. At the very least, maybe as they got to know each other, the initial attraction would fade. As long as she wasn't throwing herself at him, just looking for a hot night, then he could keep his own impulses under control.

He glanced over at the clock on the lifeguard's station wall.

"Unfortunately, I have to go," he said, letting his reluctance show. "I've got some stuff to do today."

"Okay." This time her bright smile didn't completely hide her disappointment or the little flash of hurt.

Damn. He didn't mean for it to be a rejection.

"I really do have some stuff to do," he said, apologetically. "I'll be back here tomorrow." He gave her his own best flirtatious smile. "If you want to come by and chat... or flirt."

Her smile changed, subtly, becoming more natural. "Okay. I'll see you then."

"Good."

Since he didn't dare touch her, Rick pushed himself over to the other side of the lane and pulled himself up the ladder. Just being so close to all her gorgeous bare skin and those lush curves had his dick half hard. If he actually touched her, he was pretty sure he'd be sporting wood for everyone to see. Maria was already moving her legs out of the swimming lane and into the regular part of the pool.

He watched as she slipped down into the water, sighing with pleasure as the cool liquid enveloped her skin. Thank God for a clammy cold bathing suit or that might have done him in.

Looking up at him with those gorgeous dark brown eyes, she smiled. The red suit was clinging to her curves and he could clearly see the outline of her nipples from getting into the cold water. "Have a good day."

He cleared his throat. "You too. I'll see you tomorrow."

"Looking forward to it."

The sultry way she said it made the simple words incredibly flirtatious. Rick just nodded his head and turned to go get his towel. Otherwise he was never going to be able to make himself leave the pool.

Unfortunately, he'd promised Justin some help in the office today. Adam hadn't found someone to hire as Justin's assistant yet, because there wasn't quite enough work for a full-time position, and so Rick had said he'd come in and do what he could to help.

But he could let them know he'd be a little bit late tomorrow.

After a quick shower and change into office clothes, Rick couldn't help glancing out the window at the pool. Maria was still down there, he was sure it was her, in the pool splashing and horsing around with what looked like those two college frat-boys. Gritting his teeth, Rick made himself turn away and get his ass out the door, telling himself he wasn't jealous.

He wasn't.

"EARTH TO RICK... HELLO RICK..."

Blinking, Rick gave himself a little shake and focused on Justin's amused dark eyes. "Yeah? Sorry, what did you say?"

"Are you feeling okay, man?" Adam asked. "That's the third time in the past half hour you've completely zoned out."

They were all in Justin's office eating lunch together, which was what usually happened whenever Rick came in to work. Adam had the neatest desk, but it still had a lot of paperwork on it, and Rick's desk tended towards the messy side since he wasn't in every day. Although, to be honest, his workspace always seemed to be organized chaos. He managed to be neat at home, but it just doesn't translate over to work for some reason.

"I'm fine."

"Are you thinking about a woman?" Justin asked.

"Why is that the first thing your mind goes to?" Which wasn't really an answer. Rick knew he was being a bit evasive, but he just didn't really know what to say to his friends.

There wasn't exactly anything concrete between him and Maria, he was spinning fantasies. About all he could tell them was that he was hung up on a woman and he couldn't stop thinking about all the dirty things he'd like to do with her, and on top of that, he kept thinking about how he could adjust things in his life to make a relationship with someone like her work.

That he was thinking about things like making her dinner when she was home from work late, which he'd noticed she did, thinking about how to reduce her stress and get her to relax... the things a boyfriend would do for his woman. Or a Dom would do for his sub.

Yeah, he was so not spilling his guts over lunchtime.

"Because Jessica told me Olivia told her you're having girl problems."

"What the fuck," Rick said, not exactly angry, but more than a bit confused at how that had happened. "How did Olivia know?"

Stupid question. Even as he asked it, the answer popped into his head. Damn Jared anyway. He'd probably thrown Rick under the bus to get Olivia off his case about Marissa. Not that Rick entirely blamed him. Olivia was like a rabid dog about Marissa. And this was another good reason why he didn't want to just blab about himself to his friends; the gossip grapevine was out of control.

Justin just shrugged, obviously not particularly interested in where the news came from as he was in confirming it. "So is it a woman?"

"A neighbor," Rick said shortly. "There is no problem. We're just friends." As soon as the words were out of his mouth, he knew it wasn't true. They weren't really friends. Hell, up until this morning, he'd been trying to chase her away from him, and he still wasn't sure he should change his tactic.

Normally he would have probably been a little more willing to share with his friends, which is probably why they had noticed he wasn't really keeping up with the conversation. While he tended to keep things close to his chest, he'd always been pretty open about his desire to find a girlfriend and submissive. But he found himself reluctant to talk about Maria. Not just because he wasn't sure where things were going with her, but also because he didn't really want to share her yet.

The only reason he'd done so with Jared was because he'd been so frustrated and pissed off with himself. Now he was starting to think maybe he and Maria could be more than friends, but he didn't want to talk about it. Talking about it, before anything had actually happened, felt almost like jinxing it. Superstitious nonsense, but Rick still couldn't quite shake the feeling.

Besides, if things didn't work out between him and Maria, he didn't need the teasing.

With the raise of one eyebrow, Adam said everything he needed to without even opening his mouth. Justin just smirked. Bastards.

"So how are things going with Angel?" Rick asked, changing topics to something he knew Adam would find uncomfortable. "Is she moving in yet?"

Predictably, Adam scowled. Which meant he was still working on getting his girlfriend to do what he wanted. Adam tended to be dominant outside the bedroom as well as in, although he wouldn't admit that. He just liked to think of himself as a bit of a control-freak. Angel was definitely submissive, but not so much in her day-to-day life. So far, she was still insisting she wouldn't be moving in till she and Adam had been together for at least a year. "Most of her stuff is at my place."

"But she's still paying rent for her room at her house, right?" Rick asked, teasing. Nothing like bringing up Angel's living arrangements to get Adam's nose out of other people's business. It made him all sorts of cranky. Especially because her current room was at a house with three guys.

Rick had met all of her housemates and they were all nice guys. Angel treated them all like brothers, but it had definitely been hard for Adam to get his own possessive tendencies under control when it came to Angel's friends. Most of which were male. All things considered, Rick thought Adam actually dealt with it pretty well. He got along with Angel's friends, the fact that she lived with a bunch of guys wasn't why he wanted her to move out–he just wanted her to live with him, and for the most part he didn't get super caveman on her.

The big blond grumbled something about semantics under his breath while Rick and Justin grinned at each other.

"Speaking of living arrangements, did you know Liam bought a ring?" Justin asked.

"What? Already?" Rick tried to remember when Liam and Hilary had met... it was getting close to a year. Wow. He felt an immediate rush of excitement and happiness for them, and at the same time, the usual wistful envy he got whenever he thought about his friends' relationships. That was the emotion which had helped spur his move north; seeing how happy his friends were in their relationships.

Liam and Hilary's relationship was especially encouraging for him right now, because Hilary had been a complete newbie to the scene when she and Liam had first met. Actually, if he remembered correctly, Liam had actually tried to scare her off at first. But, as Jessica's best friend, he hadn't been able to entirely avoid her, and she'd kept showing up at the club. When she'd shown up for an Introduction Scene, Patrick had paired them together purposefully. So they'd had a happy ending.

Unfortunately, Maria didn't know any of his friends, so it wasn't like she was just going to show up at Stronghold out of the blue. That would be way too serendipitous. Hilary had had Jessica to support her and urge her out of her shell. If Maria was going to come to Stronghold, the person getting her there would be Rick. Now that was an idea.

"I don't think he's going to ask her right away, but he has the ring."

Adam grinned, obviously nothing but happy for their friends. Of course, he wouldn't be feeling envious right now. He had a girlfriend and could look toward doing something similar in the future. They all knew Angel was going to move in with him eventually, the only question was whether or not Adam would be able to get her in on his timetable or if she'd stick to hers. "Think he'll do it at the club?"

"No."

"Why not?"

"Cuz he's romantic."

"What's not romantic about that?"

"And you wonder why Angel won't move in with you," Justin taunted. Adam scowled again.

"I can be romantic."

"Maybe you should ask Olivia for some advice," Rick said, laughing at the big blond's affronted look. Adam was glaring at Justin who looked remarkably like Chris as he snickered. Those two had definitely rubbed off on each other now that they were in a relationship with the same woman. Justin had relaxed, and Chris had become more dominant. It was kind of interesting to watch. "She's gotten pretty close to all the women."

"Yeah, isn't she supposed to be our friend?" Justin asked. "Now she's on Lexie's side about getting into the club."

Even though they were finished eating, none of them seemed inclined to get up and leave. Rick was especially enjoying the camaraderie. Hanging out during the day and just talking wasn't something he'd gotten to do when he'd lived in Virginia. Before his move he'd always been the last grape on the vine, getting his gossip when he finally came to the club or if he happened to talk with one of them on the phone.

"I might have to burn my eyeballs," Adam said dryly. "I was already having nightmares about those nipple shirts she was wearing. There was less tape every week. Thank God she stopped that."

"Isn't anyone else curious about why she stopped it?" Rick looked at both of his friends who seemed a little surprised at his question. "Seriously, she's been pushing the limits the entire time she's been working at the club, why suddenly stop doing something she knew was getting to us?"

They all looked at each other in silence, mulling over the question.

"Maybe she realized it was really upsetting us?"

Adam gave Justin a look of complete disbelief. "Yeah, she seemed real concerned about it."

"Maybe Patrick said something to her," Rick suggested, just to see his friends' reactions to having Patrick and Lexie mentioned at the same time. Justin coughed and looked up in the air while Adam shifted uncomfortably in his seat and stared at his desk. Yeah. "You know he's going to let her in there sometime. Probably with him."

"Better him than someone else," Adam said, although he didn't sound entirely convinced. Like Patrick, he definitely would have preferred it if Lexie was entirely vanilla and had no interest in being at the club. Although, he also hadn't been hovering over Lexie as much since he'd started coming to the club with Angel. His girlfriend definitely took the majority of his attention.

Justin shook his head. "I guess... I mean... it's just weird. I don't like thinking of her like that."

"I don't think Patrick does either." Adam sighed, rubbing his hand over his goatee, the way he often did when Angel was badgering him about something. A sign of frustration and resignation. "I doubt she would have listened if he'd told her to cover up, anyway."

"Who can understand women anyway," Rick said, thinking about Maria's inexplicable behavior.

For all her self-assuredness, she seemed to have had some very set ideas about how he would react to her. Not to mention her brazen flirting at his door in contrast to how she'd acted with him this morning, which had been mostly friendly with just a little bit of flirting. Both of which had appealed to him. Really, it was just her that was appealing, in any form.

He still couldn't decide if she'd toned back her approach because of his reaction, or if she was just naturally flirtatious and trying to be friendly. Trying to figure out what was going on in her head was completely impossible. After he'd basically threatened her with a spanking, he thought he wouldn't see her again. Just a few days later she was ambushing him at the pool and showing off all those gorgeous curves.

Better than at his door where he had to fight off his urge to drag her back to his bedroom. Run his tongue along her curves and see what she tasted like. Bury his hands in all her wild hair. See if her body was as soft and welcoming as it looked.

"I think we've lost him again," Justin whispered, making Rick blink and focus back on his two friends.

They were grinning at him expectantly. Like teenage girls awaiting a particularly juicy bit of gossip.

"So... about your neighbor..." Adam drawled.

"Oh look at the time, better get back to work," Rick said, pushing his chair back as he stood and grabbed the remains of his lunch to throw away. He definitely wasn't going to talk about Maria to his friends. Just mentioning her to Jared had already had unforeseen consequences.

And there wasn't any point in mentioning her, because there wasn't anything going on.

# 6

"So if you had a time machine, and could go back to anytime, where would you go and what would you do?"

Rick gave Maria a look. "Seriously?"

It was the fourth day in a row she'd shown up early enough to see him at the pool once he'd finished his work out. The first two days they had just chatted while she dangled her legs in the water next to him. Yesterday there had been someone else wanting to use the lap lane and so they'd both ended up in the main part of the pool, floating around and talking. She'd learned he had a married older brother who lived in Pennsylvania. Rick spent the holidays with them when they weren't visiting their parents, who had retired to Florida.

This was the first summer in a long time he hadn't spent teaching summer school, and he told her about the odd jobs he was doing for some of his friends. From what he said, she definitely got the impression his group of friends were very close and spent a fair amount of time together. Something she envied, considering her recent revelations about her lack of close friends outside of her family.

She was trying to get to know him better. And flirt a little. So far, the more she got to know him, the less frightening being spanked by him sounded. Although it still didn't sound like something that would be good.

Splashing him a bit, she cocked her head inquisitively. "Seriously. Where would you go and what would you do? This answer will give me great insight into the workings of your mind. I swear."

Rick rolled his gorgeous blue eyes and leaned back into the water, letting it roll over his shoulders. Damn. She never got tired of looking at him and seeing the way the water shifted over his muscles. Little droplets ran down the lines of his body and made her want to press her tongue against his skin to lick them up.

They didn't touch each other, ever, while they talked. They just kind of circled around each other in the water, half-treading it. It was almost a metaphor for the way they were dancing around their attraction to each other.

"You know, my immediate thought is to say I would go back and see one of Shakespeare's plays at the original Globe, during the time he was writing, but the other day I was listening to a comedian who said he'd go back and stop George Lucas from making the first three Star Wars movies. I think I'd have to do that."

"Really? You were listening to a comedian who was talking about this exact topic?" Maria couldn't help but laugh. Rick had definitely not struck her as a sci-fi kind of guy. Good thing she hadn't actually said anything like that out loud. He didn't need to know she'd still been trying to fit him into some kind of box. She really needed to cut it out.

"Patton Oswalt," Rick said, grinning at her. "He's not the only one. Dane Cook did a segment on time travel too."

"Okay, so why stop the new Star Wars movies?"

This time the look Rick gave her was frankly disbelieving, with a little bit of shock thrown in for good measure. "Are you kidding me? You actually liked them? I might have to..." His voice trailed off, which was too bad because it had gone kind of growly and hot.

"What?" Maria looked at him curiously. Had he been about to say "spank her?" Because of some movies? Or was she just being hopeful? And how stupid was it that she would be hopeful he might?! Maybe just because, as flirtatious as he'd been, he definitely hadn't hinted at wanting to do anything with her past talking at the pool in the mornings.

Knowing he was still interested in doing naughty things to her would be nice. At least, that's what she told herself, ignoring the tingling excitement and hope she'd felt when she had thought he was going to threaten to put her over his knee.

Rick just shook his head. "Nothing. Never mind." His voice had gone back to normal, although laced with near-horror and disbelief. "But you actually liked them?"

Maria just splashed at him, shaking her head as she laughed. Boys. They got so serious about the weirdest things.

"I've never seen them."

"Oh, well that explains it."

"I never saw the originals either." She knew the statement would get him.

Clutching at his heart, Rick went down. Laughing, Maria bounced forward to grab for him as his other hand waved dramatically above the water, like he was trying to signal for help. Latching onto his wrist she pulled him back up. It didn't even occur to her that this was the first time they'd touched since... well, since she'd been in his apartment. And now they were both slick and wet, and practically naked since bathing suits really didn't cover much of anything.

His hard body skimmed along hers as he came back up, not even an inch away from her. The suddenness of his nearness made her gasp a bit and she felt her nipples immediately hardening. Shaking the water from his hair and face, Rick snapped his arm around so he was holding her wrist instead of the other way around. His strong grip was like a shackle around her arm and she couldn't even explain why she felt suddenly breathless.

The slow smile spreading across his face made her want to melt and she was starting to lean into him, sure he was going to kiss her, when he gently pushed her away. At the same time, his smile changed into something less fraught with tension. Maria scowled. He was distancing himself again. Acting like she was too dumb to decide for herself whether or not she was interested in him.

Well, maybe dumb wasn't the right word. But he did act like she was a little kid who didn't know any better and was about to play with fire. It bugged the crap out of her because, with him, she had started to think she wouldn't mind getting a little bit singed.

"How can you never have seen the original Star Wars?"

Back to being nothing but friendly. Maria inwardly sighed. "I grew up with all sisters remember? I might have seen them when I was little and just not remember, but I don't think so. It just wasn't our thing. We liked some guy stuff, like superheroes and stuff but none of us were ever into Star Wars or Star Trek."

"Such a deprived childhood."

Laughing, she splashed him again. "I didn't know you were such a nerd."

"Star Wars isn't just for nerds," Rick said looking affronted. "Although even if it was, they're still great movies. You should watch them sometime."

"Maybe if I had someone to watch them with," Maria said, giving him a flirtatious little smile. Angling for a little bit of attention from him that would push the boundary line he'd drawn between them.

He just gave her the stupid neutral smile she was starting to hate so much, as he glanced up at the clock. "Yeah, they're more fun to watch with company. Anyway. I have to go."

"Alright, bye," Maria drawled, as if she couldn't care less, still feeling a bit miffed. She made sure to "accidentally" splash him again as she turned away. It wasn't that her feelings were hurt, exactly, because she was pretty sure he was definitely attracted to her. The way he acted with her wasn't quite like rejection, it was just like he was trying to warn her off or something.

So why bother talking to me in the first place?

"I'll see you tomorrow?" he asked, actually sounding like he wanted to. And that was what got her hooked back in all over again. Hope. Always the little bit of hope keeping the door between them open.

"Yeah," she replied, flashing a little smile over her shoulder. She would be here.

Sneaking peeks at him as he got out of the pool, she almost wanted to fan herself. Seriously, the man was smoking hot. He already had taken over a pretty much permanent place in her sex fantasies. Every time she had a hot one, it was with a guy who looked exactly like Rick. Except he wouldn't push her away or put up walls to keep her out.

It wasn't just that he was sexy, and she was attracted to him, she liked finding out the little things about him that broke her assumptions. Like his taste in comedians and love for Star Wars. She felt comfortable with him, like she could talk to him about anything. Rick had to be one of the most nonjudgmental people she'd ever met. He didn't care if she talked about being a little envious of her sisters, or how she'd once cried when she went jeans shopping for two hours and couldn't find a single pair that actually fit, or how she once broke into a pool after hours to go skinny dipping. Not something she could do at this pool unfortunately. And no matter what they talked about, he just accepted her for who she was.

If only he would take that one step further and accept the attraction between them.

Lying on her back, Maria floated, determined not to look at him because she didn't want him to catch her peeking. It was embarrassing enough to keep practically throwing herself at him. He did respond though—he did—before he'd back off. So it wasn't like she was making a complete fool out of herself, although she was starting to feel foolish.

He'd already warned her he wanted to spank her. If she was still flirting with him, didn't that send the message she was willing? At least, she was willing to try. Sure it was a little weird, but she could deal with that. As long as he didn't want to actually beat her or anything.

It was damn frustrating.

Maybe she needed to be more direct again.

FEELING A BIT LIKE HE HAD A TARGET ON HIS BACK, RICK GOT OUT of the pool. He enjoyed spending his mornings with Maria, he truly did, but it was getting harder and harder to control himself around her. Today, when she'd touched him, he'd nearly forgotten he'd decided to be hands-off with her.

They were attracted to each other, but that didn't mean she had any real idea of the things he wanted to do to her... even though she'd stopped acting like all he wanted was a fuck buddy or a one-night stand, she still didn't seem to take him very seriously. He liked her. A lot. Taking things farther would make it too hard for him not to get emotionally involved—heck he already was, and they weren't doing anything more than talking on a daily basis.

It was better to just keep things on a friendly basis until he was really sure she wanted something more.

Looking back over his shoulder, he nearly groaned out loud. It was only the nearby presence of a couple of older women, old enough to be grandmothers, that kept him from doing something so obvious. Maria was floating on her back again, her breasts looking like soft purple mounds, water droplets decorating her stomach, her eyes closed as if she was in bliss. It made him want to get right back in there with her.

Fortunately, he was helping out Liam at the dojo today so he was forced to leave the pool area. Otherwise, he didn't know how much longer his self-restraint would have held out.

If only she was submissive and wanted a relationship.

The words rang in his head like a taunt. If only, if only, if only...

ANOTHER FRIDAY NIGHT AT THE CLUB AND BEING HERE WAS MORE frustrating than ever. After spending close to two weeks talking to Maria almost every morning, he didn't feel the slightest glimmer of interest in any of the very attractive, very willing submissives who gave him inviting little looks. When he'd come in, Lexie had smirked at him and told him word had gotten out that he was looking for something more serious than just club play.

Just what he needed on a night when he couldn't gather up any kind of interest in the women here at all.

"You look like shit."

Great. More of just what he needed.

"Well thank you darling, and you look stunning, as usual," he said, baring his teeth at Olivia in a poor imitation of a smile. He'd chatted with Andrew for a bit before settling down at one of the bar tables.

Once Andrew had gotten too busy to talk, Rick had been keeping an eye on the submissives who were settling down in the lounge area, waiting for a Dom to ask them to play. Looking at a distance was more appealing at the moment. More than one of the subs was trying to catch his eye, but since he was sitting far away, he could pretend not to notice.

"As if I care what you think," Olivia said, but she was smiling as she said it. She did look good, her breasts tucked into bright red vinyl, her favorite color, and the rest of her covered in black leather. The red should have looked terrible with her hair, but somehow it never did. Going by the tight fit of her clothing, he assumed she probably wasn't there to do any serious play either. Not unless there were some hidden invisible flaps or something to allow easier access to her body. Maybe she was just in the mood to beat on some naughty subs. "Seriously though, you look like shit."

"I'm feeling better and better by the minute with you here to cheer me up." Sad, but true. Olivia's ribbing had actually put a small smile on his face he couldn't quite push back. "Just like shit in general or in a specific manner?"

"Well, before I sat down you had the vacant look of a stoner, combined with the circles under your eyes, the wrinkles on your fore-head from scowling, and you don't look remotely interested in playing with any of the subs who are trying so hard to get your attention. Which, considering all your talk about moving here so you can have an actual relationship with someone, is highly illogical. Oh, and you haven't touched your drink in the past two minutes."

"What are you, Sherlock Holmes?"

Olivia just smiled smugly, but her blue-gray eyes were concerned. "I hear you're having woman troubles. Want to talk to an actual woman instead of those useless wankers we call friends?"

"Okay, now I know you've been watching BBC again, you only call us wankers when you're on a British kick."

"See? I'm not the only one with powers of deduction. So what's up?"

Sighing, Rick leaned back slightly.

It was doubtful he'd be able to shake Olivia unless someone more interesting came in, which was unlikely at this point. Adam and Angel were upstairs in one of the private rooms. Downstairs in the Dungeon, Justin, Chris, and Jessica were scening; he'd watched the two Doms tie their girlfriend to a spanking bench before he'd wandered back upstairs. Watching the triad was always hot, but he hadn't been able to shake the melancholy envy wrapped around him, stronger than ever, while they'd been starting their scene.

Liam and Hilary weren't coming in, so at least he didn't have to watch them, too. He wondered if Liam might propose this weekend. So far, they were all waiting for the announcement, but Liam was keeping them all on tenterhooks, waiting for him to actually get down on one knee. Jared was off for the night and Lexie was at the front desk which meant Patrick was probably barricaded in his office. Unless something really crazy happened at the bar with Andrew, he had Olivia's undivided attention.

"How much did Jared tell you?"

"Pretty much everything you told him, I think," Olivia said, her smile turning a little grim. "He really didn't want to talk about Truckstop. I can't blame him... if I ever get my hands on that little thundercunt..."

"You and me both," Rick said, deciding it was best to distract Olivia from her line of thought. If she got pissed enough, and Jared and Marissa did happen to come to the club tonight, who knew what would happen. "So you know I have a neighbor and she's not submissive. That's not exactly what I would call a real problem."

"So then why are you sitting here instead of finding someone to play with?"

Why indeed. Because compared to his level of connection with Maria every other woman here just didn't seem as interesting. Because, even though they'd done nothing more than talk at the pool, for some stupid reason it felt like a betrayal of her. Because he was an idiot.

"What's her name?"

"Maria." It wasn't that he said her name, it was the way he said it. He could hear it echoing in his ears, wistful and possessive at the same time. Dammit. Olivia smiled at him. "Nothing's going on. I've just... chatted with her a bit."

"How often is a bit?"

He took a sip of his beer, which had gotten warm while he'd been sitting there not drinking. Still, warm beer was better than no beer, especially if he was going to talk about Maria. "Every morning," he admitted in a low voice. "She shows up at the pool when I'm finishing my work out and we talk."

"Uh huh."

"It's nothing like what you're thinking," he said. "We're not flirting. I mean, not really. She's sweet and got a great sense of humor... she's easy to talk to. Kind of sassy. Smart too, she manages a restaurant. But you know, neighborly. She brought me homemade granola."

"Uh huh."

"I just talk to her about day-to-day stuff. We're getting to know each other, in a neighborly way. We just talk about normal things, like, she's got three younger sisters and two of them are already married and the youngest, Lara, just got engaged. That doesn't bother her though, just how her family and their friends treat her, like she should be bothered by it. But she's not. She's got incredible... strength of character. Which sounds boring, but it's true."

"Uh huh."

It was Olivia's third 'uh huh,' when normally she was quite vocal, that made Rick realize he'd started babbling. About Maria. And his voice had gotten warmer and more excited as he'd done so. He glared at the smirking redhead across the table from him.

"But she's not submissive, so don't even think about it."

She just rolled her eyes. "How do you know she's not submissive?"

Half an hour later he'd pretty much spilled his guts out, going over every detail of his initial interactions with Maria while Olivia listened thoughtfully. He'd even gotten a second beer to replace the warmed one. Olivia could probably have gotten work as an interrogator if she'd ever wanted to. It felt kind of good to finally unload everything to her.

"So you think she's not submissive because of how she came onto you initially?" Olivia asked.

"Don't ask that like I'm an idiot... she just doesn't seem submissive."

"Not all submissives are obvious. Remember Angel?" Olivia

smirked at him. When he'd first met Angel, it had been at a different club, one closer to Rick which he'd wanted to check out in hopes his friends could meet him at a kink club halfway between them every so often.

Unfortunately, Chained had been a letdown, but they had met Angel there. She'd been posing as a Domme, trying to get comfortable with the scene and clubs on her own, and he, Chris, and Andrew had all been taken in. Only Adam, who was generally considered one of the best at reading body language, had figured out that something was off, and even he'd second guessed himself over and over again until she'd shown up at Stronghold for her Introduction Scene as a submissive.

"Bad example, she knew she was submissive and she was faking it. I haven't seen any indication from Maria that she even knows what being submissive is."

"She still came to talk to you after you threatened to spank her," Olivia pointed out. A male sub walked by on his way to the Lounge, giving her a longing look, but she didn't even notice. Too involved poking her nose into his business. Olivia did like to be a problem-solver; he sometimes suspected she liked it as much as she liked dominating submissives. "That means something."

"Yeah, she has no sense of self-preservation."

"Or... she's not opposed to the idea." Smirking at him Olivia hopped up from her barstool. "The only person stopping you from getting what you want, as far as I can see, is you."

Patting his shoulder, Olivia turned and walked away, heading straight for the Lounge and the sub that had just walked by. The well-muscled man perked up the moment he saw her coming. Apparently, she had seen him after all.

Damn it was annoying when she did that.

Finishing off his beer, Rick returned to the bar for another, and chatted with the Doms, Dommes, and couples who ended up there throughout the night. Nothing serious. Nothing heavy. None of them asked him why he wasn't playing down in the Dungeon although he could see in their eyes that they were wondering.

Andrew definitely was curious, but, unlike Olivia, he wasn't the type to pry information out of someone. Which was good, because Rick wouldn't have had a good answer for him if he'd asked.

✧

I'M SUCH A STALKER.

She hadn't meant to be, but she'd gotten home late from the restaurant and had recognized Rick getting out of his car. Friday night... she couldn't help but wonder what he'd been up to. And instead of getting out of her car, she'd sat in the darkness and watched him. She wondered where he'd been that he was wearing what looked like leather pants—leather pants in the summer? As far as she knew he didn't have a motorcycle. The only motorcycle in the parking lot belonged to some dude in the next building over.

So why the leather pants?

Not exactly date clothes. Thankfully, because she had the sinking feeling Rick on a date with someone else would crush her hopeful little heart.

Where had he been?

Or was he wearing them because he was expecting late night company? Even though it was after midnight, she'd waited in her car for half an hour, waiting to see if someone else showed up. Butterflies of nervousness had assaulted her the entire time. If someone had, she probably would have followed them into the building to see if they'd go to his apartment.

She probably would have been out there for another half hour if she hadn't seen the lights in his apartment go out.

Because I'm a crazy stalker.

Crawling into bed a lot later than she'd intended, Maria decided she needed to do something bold. Something to show him that she wasn't disturbed by the idea of being spanked by him—although she wasn't entirely sure of the truth of that. Spanking could be hot, though, right? It didn't always have to be painful. Not that she knew anyone who had actually been spanked since they were a kid, so she was going off of the few romances she'd read which had a bit of light spanking in them.

She liked him. She really liked him. Not just a "hey I want to hang out and be friends" kind of interest, although she'd settle for that if he truly didn't want more with her, but she got the feeling his attraction to her was just as strong as hers to him. For some reason he was fighting it. So it was up to her to do something to push him past that.

Once she'd decided on a course of action, the pent up energy keeping her awake faded away. Rolling onto her side, she hugged one of her extra pillows, smiling to herself.

Surprisingly, she got a pretty good night's sleep. That morning, for the first time in days, she didn't go to the pool to see if he was working out. Nope. She spent the morning shaving, buffing and polishing and then going through her wardrobe. Every inch of her was all soft from her lotion, every inch of her except a thin landing strip of her pubes had been shaved off, and every inch of her was buzzing with excitement.

When was the last time she'd done something this crazy?

Had she ever done something this crazy?

Amazing how crazy could be so exciting. Her heart was pounding like it might just beat its way out of her chest and she didn't need to put her fingers to her wrist to feel her pulse, she could actually see it. With her nipples narrowed to hard little points, brushing against stiff fabric as it moved while she walked, she made her way down to Rick's apartment.

It had taken her three tries just to get out her own door because she'd turned around and second guessed herself, until she'd finally told herself to nut up. Hell, even if this blew up in her face, she still wanted to do it. A dramatic, crazy, and wild impulse. Because where had being safe gotten her? Single and lusting after a guy who kept pushing her away.

Hey, if he was going to suggest something as wild as spanking, then maybe she needed to show him a little wild to convince him to take a chance with her.

Taking a moment to steady her nerves, she forced herself to breathe deeply, glancing around even though she knew no one was in the stairwell. She felt incredibly paranoid, not too surprisingly. Rapping her knuckles on his door, she just prayed he was home, because if he wasn't, she didn't think she'd be able to get up the courage to try this on him again.

When she heard footsteps nearing the door, all of her muscles tensed, as she stamped down the urge to bolt.

Oh my God, oh my God, oh my God...

The door opened, and Rick was standing there. Gorgeous as always in a simple gray t-shirt and jean shorts. The moment he saw her, he started to smile, and then a little crease in the center of his forehead appeared as he took in what she was wearing. Maria smiled. She hoped it looked confident, even though she felt like it probably looked more sickly than anything.

And then she opened her trench coat.

Before she could take another breath, she was yanked inside his apartment and pressed up against the wall next to his door, which was quickly slammed shut. He tugged the trench coat back over her breasts, his forehead against hers and his lips only an inch away from a kiss. Maria knew her eyes were wider than they'd ever been in her life.

Excitement, fear, anxiety, and hope roiled around inside of her. Yeah, he'd liked that. This close to him she could see the wild look in his eyes, the dilated pupils, feel his chest as he breathed in deeply. The press of his hips against hers as something very big and very hard dug into her stomach.

"What," he growled, "the fuck are you doing?" It wasn't the nice, friendly tone he usually had when he talked to her. Nope. His voice was low, dangerous, and it did funny things to the inside of her stomach. Yeah, she was creaming herself already. This was definitely the side of Rick she'd hoped to invoke with this little stunt.

A tremulous little smile crossed her face and her voice wobbled when she answered him. "Looking for a spanking?"

Rick groaned and closed his eyes, his body pressing even harder against hers as his hips rocked, and she felt the hard ridge of his erection jutting into her stomach, rubbing against it. Sucking in a startled breath, she wriggled a little as his hands slid from her trench coat down to her sides, resting on her hips. Holding her in place against the wall.

The movement made her nipples rub against the stiff fabric of the coat even more, which made her squirm again.

"Hold still," he gritted out between his teeth. Maria froze. His tone was that of a man at the end of his rope, and she really didn't know which way he was going to jump. Holding her hips in place, he pulled back and she felt a wave of disappointment wash over her. Dammit. But the look in his eyes made her belly flutter. The trench coat was still covering most of her, his hands helping to secure it to the front of her body, but he was looking at the little bit of skin still revealed like he wanted to lick every inch of it. "It's not just about spanking, Maria."

"Then what's it about?" She wanted to know. Because damn... this was hot. And she wanted sex. With him. Dates too, if he wanted, but mostly she was tired of pretending this attraction between them didn't exist. Dating would be great, because she liked him, and she would love to date him, but at the end of the day she'd be satisfied with just sex if that's all she could get.

Being held against the wall, trapped, feeling like he could overwhelm her at any second was just damn sexy. She loved the growling, crackling note in his voice, the way his thumbs were caressing her hips, and the power he seemed to have over her. It was exciting. Even the idea of getting spanked right now sounded pretty exciting. All hot and bothered like this, going over his knee and having her ass up in the air so he could touch her however he wanted, sounded pretty great.

His eyes hooded as he stepped back, studying her and she got the strange sense he was hesitating because he felt vulnerable. Even though he didn't at all look it. Maria was sure she looked pretty vulnerable as she pulled the edges of the trench coat back together, covering herself more completely. Was that a flash of disappointment she saw in his eyes as she re-dressed herself?

"Come over tonight at eight o'clock. Wear something sexy and black." His voice was deeper than usual. There was no mistaking his words for anything but a demand.

"Is this a date?" She didn't even mind his presumptuous orders, coming from him it was really hot. Any other guy she'd been with in the past would have gotten the cold shoulder for trying something like that, but somehow Rick made it exciting. It felt natural from him. Not like he was trying to force himself on her, but like he had an agenda and he expected her to follow through with it. Or not. But if they were going to do this, it was going to be on his terms. It made her insides flutter and her pussy clench.

"No. If you still want to go out after tonight, then I'd like to take you on one," he said. Now she bristled, because the tone of his voice made it seem as though he didn't think she could handle whatever it was he was planning.

"Fine. I'll see you at eight." Chin held high, she flounced out, tightening the belt of the trench coat around her, deliberately not looking at him. Fortunately, there were no neighbors in the hallway to see her rather ignominious exit. The door closed behind her before she could say goodbye, but in the grand scheme of things that didn't matter.

They were going out tonight.

Which meant she needed to get her ass back upstairs and search for something to wear. At least he'd made it somewhat easier, but she knew she was going to agonize over it anyway.

## 🕉 7 🕉

**D**ressed in a short black skirt that hugged her thighs and a black lacy tank top with a lining over her breasts and stomach, showing a large portion of her cleavage through the lace where there was no lining, Maria was feeling pretty good. She'd let her hair stay down, her long curls rioting down her back and framing her tanned skin with all the black. Bright red lipstick was the only splash of color she allowed herself. Even her shoes were unrelieved black strappy heels.

It wasn't the kind of outfit she'd normally wear on a date, more like something she'd wear to go out dancing with her sisters—back before they all got married and still wanted to go dancing—but it made her feel good. And Rick had said tonight wasn't a date. Besides, she wanted to keep him drooling over her.

All afternoon she'd been reliving the press of his body against hers, the way he'd trapped her against the wall, the intensity in his blue eyes when he'd been inches away from kissing her. It drove her nuts that he hadn't.

Her heart hammered in her chest as she studied herself. Sexy. Confident. And dressed exactly the way he'd told her to. That last still made her feel a little uncertain—she knew exactly what her sisters would say if they knew some guy had dictated her clothing choices for her—but she was too excited to really care. Besides, since he hadn't told her where they were going, it only made sense that he help her know how to dress, right? That's what she told herself anyway.

"I can do this," she whispered to herself, smoothing her hands over her outfit. It definitely hugged her curves more than it used to, which made her wonder if it was too much... "No, stop it. You've done this already."

Time to go before she chickened out.

Her heels clacked on the stairs as she made her way down, feeling rather breathless. Before she reached Rick's door, it opened, which made her wonder if he'd been listening for her. Blue eyes stroked over her figure, examining her from head to toe. Taking the opportunity to do the same, Maria sighed inwardly at how good he looked. Also wearing all black, he had on the leather pants she'd seen him in before and a black t-shirt that hugged his body, showing off his muscles and golden tan. The blue of his eyes shone brightly, even in the negligible light of the hallway. He gave her a short nod of approval when he was done looking her over.

"Good enough for you?" she asked, feeling both irritated and nervous at his close scrutiny.

A little smile curved his lips, not mocking exactly, but definitely amused. "You look perfect. Good enough to eat in fact."

Warmth spread through her as a blush rose in her cheeks. Not something that happened to her on a regular basis. Suddenly she felt a little off balance, a little less confident even though he'd just complimented her. And a little more excited.

"Thanks... um, you were wearing those last night," she said, gesturing towards the pants, feeling the need to get the attention off of herself.

Rick raised his eyebrow. "Was I?"

Realizing she'd just given herself away, Maria blushed again. Dammit. "I was in the parking lot when you came home, and I saw you. Are we going to the same place you were at last night?" she asked, hoping to change the subject.

"Yes." Reaching out his hand, he smiled again when she automatically put hers in his. His palm was warm but not sweaty, and when he curled his fingers around hers she felt a little jolt of electricity right down her spine. "Come on, let's go."

The ride was surprisingly relaxing. Although Rick wouldn't tell her where they were going, the conversation flowed easily enough. After all, they'd been talking just about every morning for the past week. She told him about the latest drama going on at work with a new female server and the two guys trying to get her attention, apparently not realizing she was obviously crushing on one of the line cooks. Mostly he just listened and asked questions as they drove downtown, making Maria even more antsy.

It had been a while since she'd been downtown, and she still didn't have a clue where he was taking her. When she tried to tease it out of him, he just shook his head and refused to answer.

"It's better to show you," was all he would say.

Annoying.

When they pulled up to what looked like a warehouse, with a parking lot full of cars, she was intensely curious. As far as she knew, there wasn't much around this area, and while the cars made it obvious there was something here, she wasn't sure what it could be. At least there were plenty of cars. She was already questioning her sanity a bit for letting him take her somewhere without telling her their destination. It's not like she really knew him, not very well.

Considering they were in what seemed more like an industrial district, his mysterious behavior and their all black attire, she was almost a little bit worried he was going to reveal he was a vampire or something. Obviously she'd been reading too many urban fantasy books lately. But hey, their current surroundings would be the perfect location for him to lure her to if he was.

"Where are we?" she asked, looking around the lot. There was another couple getting out of a car and walking towards the door, which made her feel a little better. The man was wearing similar clothing to Rick and the woman was wearing a short, shiny red skirt even shorter and tighter than Maria's, paired with a black bustier that pushed her breasts up as if offering them on a platter. She was clinging to the man's arm as she tottered on insanely high heels which made Maria worry about the woman's ankles.

"Stronghold," Rick said. When she turned to look at him, his face was impassive, and she realized he'd been watching her watch the other couple. There was a tension in his voice she hadn't heard before, although his tone was smooth and controlled. She suddenly got the impression he was showing her something he wanted her to like and was nervous she wouldn't. "It's a club I go to sometimes."

"For dancing?" Somehow that just didn't fit with him, or with the couple who had just gone through the plain looking door. It definitely didn't fit with the anxiety she sensed in him.

"No. Although there is a dance floor. Come on." Turning away, Rick opened his door and got out. Definitely nervous. He usually wasn't so abrupt when he talked to her. Although she could see he was on his way to her side of the car, she opened the door and got out without waiting for him. Sometimes chivalry was nice, but she always felt stupid just sitting in a car and waiting for a guy to open it, as if she couldn't handle it herself. Holding a door open for her to walk through made sense, sitting and waiting in a car didn't.

He just gave her a little smile and pushed his hands into his pockets, turning to walk briskly towards the door the other couple had gone through.

Step into my web, she thought. But she followed anyway.

The tension in his shoulders seemed to grow as they approached the building. Which only fed her curiosity. Seriously, what was behind the door?

A lobby, it turned out. And not a particularly flashy one. She could hear music coming from the far door, which was guarded by a giant. An attractive giant with creamy dark skin and melting chocolate eyes, but still a giant. While Rick made her feel kind of dainty, he didn't actually make her feel petite or small. Especially when she was in heels. The giant did. He was tall and broad and nicely muscled, wearing nothing but leather pants to show off his muscled chest and shoulders, a line of dark hair going down from his belly button into his pants.

A hand wrapped around her arm, pulling her gaze away from the giant's crotch. Oops. Not her fault, the happy trail had led her there.

"Try not to check out my friends," Rick said, a little wryly.

"I wasn't checking him out," Maria said. "Not in that way." She glanced over at the giant who winked at her, and she knew he'd heard. "Not that you're not very attractive."

The deep rumble of laughter made her grin as Rick pulled her over to the desk where a very perky and alert little black-haired pixie was practically bouncing in her seat. The leather dress she was wearing had cut outs all over the bodice and gave the impression of exposing more than it covered. It looked fantastic against her pale skin, emphasizing her slight figure and the curves she did have.

"Hi Rick," she chirped, big blue eyes peering at Maria from thick black lashes. "You brought a guest. The subs are going to be devastated."

Subs?

Before she could ask, Rick was introducing her to the pixie. "Lexie, this is Maria. Maria, this is Lexie."

Now that was a name she recognized, although she hadn't expected to meet the young woman this evening. Maria grinned. "The one who's growing up too fast?"

Lexie rolled her eyes, which really were a stunning shade of bright, crystal blue, contrasting sharply with all her dark black hair. Literally black, just as dark (or maybe even a shade darker) than Maria's. But where Maria's was long, curly and unruly, Lexie's was short, sleek and straight.

"Is that what he said?" she asked. "Growing up too fast? You'd think I was still a child the way they treat me, none of them wants to acknowledge I'm actually grown up." She shot Rick a look, but he was acting like he hadn't heard her say a thing. Maria giggled.

There was definitely a sibling-type vibe going on between these two, and if she read between the lines of what Rick had told her, Lexie definitely had a plethora of "big brothers." Poor thing. From Rick's description, Maria had been expecting someone much younger and more immature, but it was obvious that, although Lexie was young, she was definitely a woman and not a girl, and she seemed pretty put together for her age.

"Well it's nice to finally meet you," Maria said, reaching her hand across the desk Lexie was sitting at. "Rick talks about you a lot."

"Oh?" Lexie asked in real surprise as she automatically clasped Maria's hand back. She hesitated on what to say next. "That's... surprising. Rick's actually not usually a talker."

"Really?" Maria asked, now surprised herself. She also realized Lexie's hesitation must have been because Lexie hadn't heard anything about Maria. But the young woman obviously wanted to reassure Maria with an explanation of why that might be so; which was all the more interesting because Rick did an awful lot of talking for her.

"In our group of friends, I usually don't need to talk," Rick said. "Everyone else is doing plenty of talking without me." There was a hint of exasperation in his voice, and Maria couldn't help but giggle. He'd mentioned before that his friends could be like gossiping girls. Apparently either he hadn't mentioned her to his friends, or none of them had mentioned her to Lexie, but she wasn't going to get hurt feelings over that. He'd brought her out with him tonight, and that's what counted.

"Especially now that Olivia and I aren't the only girls," Lexie said gleefully. She gave Maria a huge smile and squeezed her hand before releasing it and looking back at Rick. It seemed like she wasn't just friendly, but she was genuinely pleased to see Maria with Rick. Which Maria found fascinating. "Are you two going to play tonight? Does she need to fill out forms?"

Play? Forms?

"No, I'm just showing her around the club," Rick said, the tension returning to his frame as he shifted closer to her. Almost like he was worried she would try to run. Maria decided to keep her mouth shut and her ears open, hoping Lexie might give her some more hints about what the night might hold for her.

Unfortunately, Rick just told Lexie he'd see her later and took Maria's arm, steering her towards the door with the giant guard. Maria waved a goodbye to Lexie who waved cheerfully back at her and then had to turn her attention to a ringing phone. When she had turned back around, the giant had shifted so he was partly blocking the door-way, watching her and Rick approach with an arrested expression on his face. His dark eyes seemed to be studying her, not judging, but just taking note of every detail about her while judgment was pending.

"Rick."

"Jared." Rick paused and then she felt, more than heard, him sigh when Jared didn't move out of the way. "This is Maria. Maria, this is my friend Jared."

"Hello," Maria said, tilting her head back to look up at him. Holy crap he was big. The way he was looming over her, making her feel like she was being weighed on scales that she didn't know the purpose of, made her feel uncomfortable. Which, in turn, made her feel snarky. "You're a little bit scary, did you know that?"

A small smile twitched the edge of his mouth. "I try."

Rick snorted. "He's actually a big teddy bear, don't let the height fool you."

"I was thinking more along the line of all the bulging muscles, but whatever," Maria muttered under her breath, purposefully loud enough both men could hear her. Jared laughed although Rick looked a little less pleased.

"So how do you two know each other?"

"We're neighbors," Maria said, a little surprised when a flash of recognition went through Jared's eyes; she felt Rick tense beside her. After Lexie, she had been prepared to meet a bunch of people she'd heard about but hadn't heard about her. Apparently, Rick had said something to Jared, at least. From their reactions she couldn't tell if that was a bad or good thing.

"It's nice to meet you," Jared said, giving her a small smile as he moved back to the side of the door and out of their way. "I hope you enjoy yourself tonight." There was some kind of ulterior meaning laden in his voice that she didn't understand. It was like everyone else was speaking a language she'd learned, but wasn't fluent in, and she was missing some kind of important subtext.

Talk about frustrating.

But nothing they actually said gave her any reason to ask questions, and if she was imagining it then she'd look like an idiot for saying something about it.

"We'll see you later," Rick said, putting his hand on the small of her back and propelling her through the door. Maria gave Jared a little smile as they went through.

The music was loud, but not so overpowering that people couldn't talk, she noticed. There was a bar and a dance floor, although almost no one was on it at the moment. The couples there were involved in erotic bump and grinds, their bodies almost plastered together. That seemed a little unusual for a club, since they weren't surrounded by singles or groups of women dancing together, but not entirely out of place. The bar was right in front of them, and there was a lot of leather and latex gathered around the tables and on the stools.

Rick was still pushing her forward, watching her face, although she wasn't entirely sure what he was waiting for. Then she saw one of the pictures behind the bar and gasped.

It was a black and white, gorgeously done, of a woman bent over some kind of bench. The picture was taken from the side, but it was obvious she was naked except for the thick black cuffs at her wrists and ankles, restraining her. A blindfold was over her eyes, her breasts were hanging down on either side of the bench, and there was a man standing behind her. Nothing of his body could be seen from about mid-chest up, but he was obviously wearing a suit and he was holding a riding crop which he was trailing along the white expanse of her ass.

There was something intensely erotic and also rather frightening about the picture. Maria felt her cheeks flushing and paling in reaction. The press of Rick's fingers against the small of her back let her know he was still there, but he didn't try to move her away from the picture. She looked over at the next picture behind the bar, which had a man on his knees, some kind of metal cage around his erection, while a woman stood with her legs far apart, one hand on his hair, dragging him face first into the V of her legs. Even though his hands were cuffed behind his back, the cage around his bait and tackle looked both scary and painful, and he obviously had no control over the situation, the expression on his face was blissful.

And none of it was anything she'd ever seen in any kind of bar or club.

"What is this place?" Her voice was barely a whisper, the question more rhetorical than anything else, but Rick answered anyway.

"A BDSM club."

"BDSM?"

He sighed, but it didn't sound like he was mad she didn't know or impatient or anything. More like he was reluctant to explain. "Bondage, Domination, Sadism, Masochism. Although most of the letters have multiple meanings, that's probably the most popular denotation."

No wonder he'd been reluctant to explain. He obviously expected her to start running. Which was absolutely what she should do.

Run, run, run, as fast as you can...

But then she'd never been a very good gingerbread man, she was more like Hansel and Gretel, eagerly entering the witch's house. Sweet seduction... but was Stronghold a trap or something else entirely? She'd heard about stuff like this, but she'd never known anyone who actually did it. Or, at least, they hadn't admitted it to her. No wonder Rick had been so reticent, it wasn't exactly something people encouraged conversation about.

She looked around the room. "Is there more?"

The main floor didn't look like much more than a regular club, although she now noticed there were people actually kneeling on the floor over in a little space lined with chairs and small couches. There were some people sitting in the chairs as well, talking to those who were kneeling. The BDSM thing did explain why there were only couples on the dance floor and why they were pressed so closely together. They were there to have sex and be spanked and... well, who knew what else. A lot of the men and women at the bar were dressed like Rick. There were servers, with trays, who were wearing a lot less and were weaving through the people kneeling on the carpeted area, serving them drinks.

Like, wearing a lot less. Maria actually felt kind of overdressed. Most of the women were wearing nothing but underwear, and if they were covering their top with a corset they had on nothing but a thong on the bottom. Some had a skirt on, but their breasts were either entirely exposed or barely covered with what looked like tape. One woman who was kneeling and talking to a man in leather pants and a leather vest was wearing nothing but a see-through g-string and jewelry on her nipples. Yikes.

It was scary, but also almost natural looking. No one was acting as if there was anything weird going on, no one was staring or leering— some of them were checking each other out, but it was in a hot sexual way. Not a creepy, smarmy way. The people on the dance floor were the same; half-naked, and yet the sexual energy between dance partners seemed natural and beautiful. So much so that it had taken Maria a couple of glances to realize the people in the different areas weren't exactly dressed.

"There's private rooms upstairs and downstairs... and there's a Dungeon downstairs."

"A Dungeon?" Maria could hear the uncertainty wavering in her voice. Half-naked people were one thing, torture was another. "Like... with a rack and chains and stuff?"

Rick laughed. "No rack. Some spanking benches, a few Saint Andrew's crosses, and some tables. There are chains, but mostly ropes and leather cuffs." He paused. For all his apparent calm, he was definitely still tense. "So, what do you think? Do you want to stay here or check out the other floors?"

Come into my parlor...

"I have to pee," Maria said honestly, rather than answering his question. It was true, but mostly she desperately needed some space to gather her thoughts and acclimate herself to this new norm. He'd just whacked her with a metaphorical brick and now he was asking if she wanted more? She just needed a breather for a moment. "Is there a bathroom anywhere?"

"Yeah, this way." To her surprise, instead of just pointing the way, Rick led her over to the doors on the opposite side of the room. She noticed more than one person watching their progress with interest, including some seriously intimidating looking men and women, and she was suddenly glad he'd decided to lead her there instead of just letting her cross the room on her own. More than one woman kneeling on the floor gave her a dirty look. Maria assumed because she was with Rick.

Interesting.

"Here you go. I'll be over there," he pointed back toward the bar, "but I'll keep an eye out for you. Take as much time as you need. No one will bother you in there."

"Thanks," she said, a bit shaken by the implication someone might 'bother' her elsewhere if he wasn't there to watch over her.

The bathroom was actually a locker room. There were several other women in it, chatting and comparing outfits in one of the three rows of lockers. Maria tried not to gawk when she saw one of them had hoops in her nipples and her labia and was brazenly flaunting all of her jewelry in front of the others. One of the women, a tall redhead, smiled encouragingly at her as she passed, as if sensing Maria was feeling out of her depth.

Giving the woman a weak smile back, Maria hurried to where she saw some stalls and some much-needed privacy.

Locking herself into the tiny cubicle, she sat down rather heavily on the toilet, her knees feeling kind of shaky and weak. What was she doing here? Was she really this desperate? No, of course she wasn't. That was a stupid thought. It wasn't desperation which brought her here, that was just her fear speaking. She'd been curious. And attracted to Rick.

This was just a lot more than she'd bargained for. No wonder she was unsettled. The jerk hadn't even given her the slightest bit of a heads up! Then again, would she have believed him? Or even realized how serious he was? She'd kind of brushed off the idea of being spanked as a kinky thing to be indulged in once in a while. Obviously she'd had no idea how kinky he really was.

Would he want to tie her up? That was bondage. So what about the other stuff? Domination, Sadism, Masochism... Okay, domination sounded like it might be kind of fun. And she had to admit, she went all weak in the knees when he was pressing her up against walls and going all alpha male. That was hot. But she didn't know anything about any of this, how much more would be expected of her?

Nebulous images of various fetishes she'd heard about ran through her head... and seriously, sado-masochism? Maria was pretty sure she didn't like to hurt people or the idea of being hurt by someone. If other people wanted to party like that, well it wasn't any of her business, but she didn't need to try it to know it wasn't her cup of tea. Just the idea made her shudder, and not in a good way.

Still, how was she going to discover what Rick liked, what Rick wanted to do with her, what she and Rick might be able to become, if she didn't learn a little bit more?

All she had to do was step out of this bathroom and tell him to take her to one of the other floors, or to take her home. Decisions, decisions.

## 8

O nce Maria had gone into the bathroom, Rick turned around and started the long walk toward the table at the bar where he could see his friends waiting. Maybe it was a good thing she obviously needed a moment to collect herself, before he intro-duced her to all of his friends.

Because literally all of them except Olivia had shown up tonight and apparently none of them were playing right now. He doubted any of them would leave to play until they met the woman he'd just brought to the club. At least he'd already gotten Maria past Jared and Lexie.

Nosy bastards.

He really wished they weren't here tonight, he was having enough trouble keeping his cool around Maria. The image of her at his door, in nothing but an open trench coat, was practically burned into his brain. The dark coat had framed her gorgeous curves perfectly, her tanned skin had glowed against her lighter skin the exact shape of her bikinis, letting him know exactly what small expanses he hadn't seen before. Those heavy, curving breasts with brown-tipped nipples that had been puckered and eagerly pointing at him. The small landing strip of closely cropped hair that didn't at all cover her pussy.

It was an image that had haunted him, even though he'd only seen her exposed body for a few moments before he'd been able to cover her up. A few more moments and he would have dragged her back to his bedroom, fuck the consequences. It had taken all his control not to anyway. And now he was going to have his control tested in front of all his nosy friends.

Although it wasn't just the guys, Jessica and Hilary were both craning their necks toward the girls' locker room and he was pretty sure if Adam hadn't had a firm grip on Angel, the friendly brunette would already be heading after Maria. She looked about ready to pop right out of his lap given the opportunity. Well, this is what he got for making his desire for a relationship so plain and then bringing a complete unknown into the club. If he'd just spent the night playing with another sub, it would have never garnered this level of interest.

"Hi Rick."

"Hi Rick."

"Hi Rick."

It was like being greeted by a chirpy Greek chorus, but he couldn't help the smile spreading across his face as the three women beamed up at him. Angel was practically bouncing against Adam, which was probably at least part of the reason for the man's long-suffering expression. He was a pretty self-contained person, but he'd admitted to Rick that he enjoyed Angel's exuberance even when it tried his own sense of dignity.

"Hey," he said, gesturing to Vickie, one of the submissives serving drinks to the tables scattered around the bar. Since Andrew was apparently off for the evening and hanging at the table, she was the one who knew his usual order best.

Settling into his seat, making sure he had a clear view of the door to the women's room, he remained deliberately quiet while everyone exchanged looks with each other. Too bad he didn't have anyone to lay bets with on who would speak up first. Angel opened her mouth only to close it again when Adam's arm tightened around her. He couldn't see the look she shot at her boyfriend over her shoulder, but he did see the quelling glare Adam gave her. And the pout on her lips when she turned back around.

Hiding his smile and pretending he hadn't noticed, he accepted his beer from Vickie and took a sip. Out of the corner of his eye he saw Jessica straighten up and then subside again, no need for either of her Doms to settle her down. She would argue with herself in her head about whether or not to be nosy.

"Alright Rick," Chris said, leaning forward on the table with his elbows. "I give. Who's the chick?"

Damn. He would have lost money on that one, he'd been sure it was Patrick who would ask first, considering he owned the club. "Her name's Maria. Be nice. This is her first time in a club. She's a complete newbie."

That got some raised eyebrows.

"So why bring her?" Patrick asked, a frown settling on his face. As a rule, Patrick didn't approve of newbies coming into Stronghold without going through some kind of screening by him.

It wasn't a requirement, as long as the newbie had a sponsor for the evening, but not too many people went around it. The only reason Rick did was because he knew they weren't going to be playing, he was just going to be showing Maria around. Waiting to see her reaction.

"I like her."

"And?" That was from Justin, who knew Rick too well to think he would bring a newbie to Stronghold just because he liked her. Especially after he and Adam had already tried to pump Rick for information about her.

He took another swallow of beer to fortify himself. "It didn't scare her off when I told her I wanted to spank her."

There was a wealth of information admitted in one sentence. The fact that he'd tried to resist, how she'd been chasing him, that he wasn't completely in charge of their relationship so far, and that she might be open to what he wanted. He could tell Justin and Adam were definitely amused at his expense, probably already plotting questions for the next time he ate lunch with them.

"That's a bit of a risk," Andrew said quietly. His somber expression wasn't at all usual for him, but considering what they were talking about, Rick couldn't blame him. Andrew's last relationship had crashed and burned as Andrew had discovered his needs and his girl-friend's inability to handle them.

"I figure she'll either run scared or be curious," Rick said, a bit grimly. Part of him wasn't sure whether he was hoping to scare her off. But why? He'd been looking for someone to become involved with, but he'd wanted someone already in the scene. He'd been resisting her for so long. So why had he set her up like this? His dick had taken over when he'd seen her naked, and now they were here, and he was talking to his friends, he was already second guessing himself.

Unfortunately, it was too late. He'd been glancing at the door to the women's room every couple of seconds, waiting for her to appear; so he happened to be looking straight at the door when she finally did, looking calmer, and determined, with her chin raised. Something in his chest tightened even as the blood surged to his cock. This wasn't just sexual attraction. She got to him on an emotional level as well. Which shouldn't be too surprising, considering how much time they'd been spending together.

He was so screwed.

She stood out, in her sexy but—compared to most of the people in the room—modest outfit. All her glorious hair framing her face and shoulders. She obviously wasn't a Domme, but her strong stance made her appear to be a challenge. More than one dominant in the lounge area was already looking her over, mostly the ones who enjoyed a bratty submissive who needed to be taken in hand.

Immediately Rick got to his feet and walked to meet her, feeling incredibly possessive as he noticed the dominants looking at her. He wanted to claim her in front of them. She came straight at him, not looking to the left or right, her entire focus completely on him. It was strangely intimate and incredibly sexy.

Stopping in front of her, so close they were almost touching but not quite, Rick brushed the back of his hand over her cheek. Subtly, so subtly he wasn't even sure she was aware she was doing it, she pressed her cheek into his hand as it passed. He wondered if she realized what that kind of connection revealed to the people who were watching, that they would all understand she was with him for tonight. They would all think she was his submissive. Even if it wasn't quite true, he couldn't help but feel quietly triumphant.

"Okay then?" he asked softly, suddenly worried she was going to ask to leave. His emotions clashed. For some reason part of him wanted her to not be able to handle this, but another part of him was nervous with hope.

"Yeah... I think so," she said, giving him a tremulous smile at odds with the defiant tilt of her chin. "Who are the people you were talking with? Your friends?"

"Yeah," he said, dropping his hand to slide it down her arm. Immediately he felt a tremor go through her body as her lips parted in reaction to his touch, eyes widening a bit. The kind of response which made his senses come alert, wanting to explore it. He wrestled the impulse down. "Come on, I'll introduce you."

For just a moment she looked like she might try to escape back into the locker room, but as his fingers threaded through hers, she straightened her shoulders and nodded her head. "Okay."

Why he felt the need to hold her hand, he didn't know. It wasn't a customary way of leading a submissive through a club. Maybe he was sensing some need of hers, some kind of craving for normalcy in this strange world he'd led her into. Poor thing must feel a bit like Alice, fallen down the rabbit hole. As he led her back to the table, he could feel her fingers tightening around his, the only indication of nerves he could see.

Of course, Patrick and Adam might see more. They tended to be particularly observant Doms, the best out of the group at reading body language. All of them were good at it, but Patrick and Adam sometimes picked up on things that the rest of them didn't.

All of them were smiling, except Andrew, but even he didn't look unwelcoming. Just like he was examining her, taking in every nuance of her movements. Rick didn't take offense to it, he knew Andrew, like Jared, was just worried because of his own experiences. He didn't want Rick to get hurt. But neither of them would be unwelcoming to Maria, and she had obviously passed Jared's appraisal before he'd let them in the door.

Besides, like Lexie, the girls were more than making up for any unsmiling faces. Angel actually was bouncing now, and so was Jessica. Hilary was slightly more reserved, but the pretty blonde's face was lit up like it was Christmas. They were all so obviously thrilled to meet anyone Rick brought to the club and he could only thank his lucky stars they were there. Not that he didn't love his male friends, but as a group they were pretty intimidating. The girls provided the softer edges which were needed for a newbie like Maria.

He introduced Maria around, keeping a firm hold on her hand, mostly because she was clinging to it. None of her anxiety showed on her face or in the way she was answering Angel and Jessica's questions, but he felt her need for support through her fingers. So he didn't let go, even when more than one of his friends raised their eyebrows at the fact.

Not like any of them had room to talk. Liam rarely let Hilary out of arm's reach and preferred her tucked directly beneath his arm, either Justin or Chris were almost always touching Jessica in one way or another, and Adam's lap had practically become Angel's permanent seat. Then again, it wasn't like Maria was his girlfriend.

"I've been there, I love that place!" Angel exclaimed as Rick tuned back into the conversation. "We'll have to come in and visit sometime."

"Absolutely," Maria was saying, her fingers slowly relaxing in Rick's grip. He doubted anyone could be unaffected by the open friendliness coming at her from all sides. "I mostly work during the day but I'm usually there for happy hour too."

Crap, he should have been paying more attention. His focus was all over the place, comparing his friends' relationships to him and Maria, thinking about showing Maria around the club, trying to act nonchalant about introducing her to his friends, all of it adding up to being distracted from the actual conversation going on around him. The girls were already making plans and he didn't even know if Maria was going to want to see his face after she got a good look at the rest of the club.

"Hey," he said, gently interrupting as he gave her fingers a squeeze. "Let's head upstairs so you can look around."

She looked up at him and for a moment he thought she was going to refuse, stay within the safety of the other women, but then she seemed to gather herself in and nod her head. While he was glad the girls were all eager to welcome Maria, it probably would have been better if he'd taken her around the club first. See if she even wanted to be welcomed to the group.

THE UPSTAIRS OF STRONGHOLD WAS AN EYE OPENER. RICK SEEMED much more focused on her now. When he'd first introduced her to his friends he'd seemed pretty distracted. She'd always thought she and her sisters had using significant looks between each other down to an art, but he and his friends had been having an entire conversation without saying a word. Fortunately, the women had all been a lot more open. Maria had immediately liked all three of them, maybe because they'd been so obviously ready to like her too.

And whoo-boy… his friends! Probably the hottest congregation of male friends she'd ever seen gathered in one place. Most of them wearing at least one article of leather clothing, which really didn't hurt when it came to the dangerous, bad-boy appeal. But it hadn't been so much their looks, although all of them were attractive, as the sheer amount of power that seemed to radiate from all of them. Maria hadn't felt so out of depth in her entire life. If it hadn't been for their much sweeter, much more approachable girlfriends, she probably would have been too intimidated to speak a word.

She was a bit curious about Jessica. Rick had mentioned her in the past, Maria had gotten the impression she was Justin's girlfriend from what he'd said. But, even though Justin had been sitting next to her, Chris had been stroking Jessica's hair in a manner more intimate than friendly. And Justin hadn't seemed to have a problem with it, which seemed a little strange.

Was that normal in a place like this?

Maria was all for live and let live, and Jessica hadn't seemed to have a problem with it, but Maria hoped it wasn't something that was just expected. Because she wasn't sure she'd want to be with a guy who wanted to share her… and she definitely didn't want to share. Right now she felt pretty out of her depth and she really didn't know what

Rick expected of her, which was pretty scary. Kind of exciting too, because her stupid body was really enjoying the way he was taking charge of her.

Stronghold's second floor was somewhat reassuring when it came to the sharing thing. Not all of the rooms had the shades open for people to look in, but quite a few of them did, and they were showing couples. Although being able to see them was still a bit unnerving.

"They know we're watching?" she whispered, her eyes glued to the sight of a couple in what looked like a high school locker room. The woman was wearing a cheerleading uniform and was laid out on the bench, her legs draped over the man's shoulders, skirt flipped up, and moaning as his head moved up and down between her thighs. Watching through the window seemed both kind of creepy and kind of hot in a forbidden way.

Rick's body seemed to lean closer to her, making all the hairs on her arm stand straight up as his lips practically pressed against her ear. "They wouldn't have left the window open if they didn't want people to watch. You know what exhibitionism and voyeurism are?"

"So they're getting off on knowing people might be peeking in?"

"Yes. They're not the only ones who are getting off on it. You like watching." His finger ran down the center of her back and Maria shivered, stepping away as she blushed deeply.

"How do you know that?" Her voice came out as a little squeak, fortunately no one else in the hallway seemed to be paying attention. It was true, but it definitely wasn't something she would have admitted. Even in the dim light of the hall she could see Rick's eyes glowing a bright blue as he stepped closer again, a little smile on his face. For some reason the slight curve of his lips made her shiver again as her head tilted back.

Fuck... he was crowding her into a wall again. He really liked to do that. And it was shameful how much she liked it when he did. If she'd been sitting, she would have been squirming in her wet panties. As it was, she pressed her thighs together hard, trying to dampen her reaction.

"Because," he said, his smile growing as he put his hands up on either side of her, trapping her with his body, but not touching her at all. Every inch of her skin seemed to ache for him to lean in and press against her. What was wrong with her? "Your breathing picked up, your cheeks turned a little bit pink, you licked your lower lip, and your nipples are hard as little diamonds." He watched her face, which was turning even redder and she could feel it even though she couldn't stop it. "Plus, now your pupils are dilating."

His breathing was getting a little ragged too. Maria felt like her throat had seized up. All she could do was stare back into his brilliant blue eyes, unable to move, waiting for whatever was going to happen next. Which had never happened to her with a guy before, and it was seriously the most exciting thing she'd ever experienced. It felt like her body was thrumming, completely on edge, and if he wanted to do something kinky to her in the hallway she knew she wouldn't stop him. People could totally watch if they wanted.

Watching her expression for just a moment longer, Rick eased back, and Maria found she could breathe again. "Come on, let's look into some other rooms."

Maria glared at his back as he turned away. She was all hot and bothered and he wasn't even going to kiss her? What did a girl have to do to get some attention around here? Then again... she really did want to see what else the club had to offer. And she was secretly relieved, because now that her brain was working again, she was back to feeling unsure if she would really be okay with people watching them. Something about having Rick right there, taking over, made her just want to roll over and do whatever he wanted. Scary shit, even if it was exciting.

There was a movie theater where people could watch the exhibitionists in another room next door, but there wasn't currently anyone on camera. Rick shrugged and said it happened every so often. Most of the other rooms in use had drapes in place, keeping out the voyeurs, but there was one that looked like an office they could peek into. A gorgeous blonde in flaming red latex had a man in a suit, with his pants around his ankles, bent over the desk and was spanking him with a large wooden paddle. His hairy butt was already a bright red and his loud yells were just audible through the window.

Maria gasped. "Oh my God... what are they doing?"

"Don't worry, that's Lloyd and he loves it," Rick said, watching impassively. Obviously, unlike the other scene at the end of the hall, this one didn't interest him as much. "If he didn't, he would say his safe word. Most people have their own personal safe word, but the club safe word is 'Red.' Say the safe word and everything stops. See him?" He pointed at a man in a vest coming up the stairs and looking into the windows, slowly walking down the hallway toward them. There was a bright red badge pinned to his vest in the shape of a keyhole. "He's a Dungeon Monitor, they come around on a regular basis listening for safe words which aren't being honored, although Patrick works hard to keep out the assholes who would do that. If someone ignores a safe word, their membership is immediately revoked. Period."

"Okay." She blew out a long breath, still slightly horrified by what looked like abuse. This had better not be what Rick meant by spanking her. The man in the office was jerking forward with every loud THWAP of the vicious paddle, she could hear the sob in his voice as he yelled out. The amount of trust involved in something like that was almost astounding, it suddenly occurred to her.

Not only would the person taking the punishment have to trust that their safe word would be honored, that the blows would stop when it was said, but the person giving the punishment would have to trust the word would be said when it was needed. That there wouldn't be any vacillating or putting up a front, while resentment simmered beneath. Especially in the case of when a man was on the receiving end. The woman was incredibly intimidating, Maria didn't doubt Lloyd would be a match for her if he wanted to. But she trusted him to take the paddling, to tell her when it was too much, and not to try and retaliate. And in turn, he trusted her with his ass.

The Domme stopped swinging the paddle, letting it drop to her side and putting her free hand on Lloyd's bottom and rubbing it roughly over his abused skin. And his moan was nearly as loud as his yells had been. Maria gasped as he turned slightly to respond to something the woman said and his rigidly hard cock, leaking fluid from the tip, came into view for a few moments. Beside her Rick chuckled. "I told you he likes it. He's in here almost every week. The Dommes love him because he's both eager to please and wants to be punished every time he comes here."

"What's he being punished for?" Maria asked a little faintly.

Rick just shrugged, tugging on her hand to pull her away from the window as Lloyd got back into place and the blonde lifted the paddle again. She didn't try to resist. She didn't really want to watch any more of that. "For a lot of the submissives and dominants who aren't in a relationship, the 'punishments' are usually more of a fantasy scenario than anything else. Like role-playing."

"And for couples?"

"A lot of the real punishments are handled in private, but sometimes a dominant will handle a minor transgression with a less severe punishment scene at the club. That's what we call funishment, because it's more about pleasure than anything else. Sometimes, if someone breaks the rules here, they'll be punished publicly."

"Remind me not to break any of the rules," Maria muttered, shivering a little as Rick led her back down the stairs.

He just laughed. "Don't worry, I won't let you."

The confident arrogance in his voice should have made her laugh, but she just found it reassuring. There was something very protective about his stance next to her, that made her feel safe. As they walked, he put his hand in the center of her lower back, sending a shiver up her spine. All night he'd been touching her in one way or another. Nothing overtly sexual or flirtatious, but just as if it was something unthinking and natural. It made her feel a lot more secure, walking around a sex club filled with people who liked to paddle each other's asses.

"So are you taking me to the Dungeon now?" she asked, teasing, as they made it back to the main floor and turned the corner to go down another set of stairs. Out of the corner of her eye she saw his group of friends, who were watching them go. Jessica raised her hand and waved, and Maria smiled at her before the pressure of Rick's hand had her heading down the next set of stairs. She was slightly in front of him, but the connection of his touch made her feel like she wasn't alone.

And then they walked into hell.

FUCK.

He should have asked Patrick what was going on in the Dungeon tonight. Or gone down to check it out for himself before taking Maria down.

The second he saw Christina, trussed up to a frame, with her Dom, Paul, standing in front of her, he knew he was fucked. Christina and Paul didn't come into Stronghold often, but when they did everyone stopped to watch. They enjoyed some of the more extreme aspects of BDSM play. Paul was a sadist and Christina was a masochist, and even more than that, Christina tended to be noisy and she liked to beg—beg and be ignored.

The scene was obviously just beginning. Christina was trussed up to a large frame in the center of the room, more than half of the occupants of the Dungeon were watching rather than engaging in their own scenes, as Paul stalked around her, scowling. Although her expression was fearful, Rick could also see the anticipation and excitement in the lines of her body and the hardness of her nipples.

"Please Master!" she called out, in a high shrill voice as he walked around behind her. "I'm sorry! Don't hurt me!"

The only response was the sound of a cane slicing through the air and then Christina's body jerked as it landed on her rounded ass, and she screamed, high and shrill.

"Master, I'm sorry!" Another scream. "Please, stop!"

Although they were standing at the bottom of the steps, and had a fairly obstructed view of the proceedings, it was obvious enough even to a complete newbie like Maria what was going on. He felt her gasp, tense, and turn to flee up the stairs.

"Maria, wait!"

Even in heels she could move fast, and he cursed himself for not being quicker to turn her around on the stairs once he'd realized what was going on in the Dungeon. Once he realized what a scene like this must look like to someone like Maria.

Chasing her up the stairs, he cursed under his breath, hesitating to reach out and grab her once he was close enough—not sure how she would react. And then she was slipping through the people on the dance floor, headed for the far wall were the locker rooms were. He followed, close enough to touch her, but ambivalent about whether or not to actually do so.

She plowed right through the door of the ladies' room, leaving him standing on the other side, basically wringing his hands like the idiot he was.

"Dammit..." he muttered, shifting back and forth on his feet. The locker rooms were considered sanctuaries for each gender. Following her in there wouldn't just get him into trouble with Patrick, but with all the Dommes and probably all the other submissives too. But the urge to get to her, to comfort her, to explain to her was overwhelming. Panic was welling up inside of him, along with his self-flagellation for idiocy.

Then, suddenly, he was surrounded by women, who had come at him from behind. A hand gently patted his shoulder, as Angel, Jessica, and Hilary all looked up at him, big eyes and creased brows.

"Don't worry, we got this," Angel said as she pushed past him. "Go sit down."

Bossy little thing. She was lucky Adam hadn't heard her talking like that. Using that kind of tone in Stronghold would get her ass beat. Immediately Rick tensed, reminded of the scene downstairs and why he was standing outside the ladies' room, helpless.

"What happened?" Hilary asked, pausing with her hand on the door, keeping it from closing all the way after Angel had gone through it.

"Christina and Paul are starting a scene." His tone was flat. Gruff. Even to his own ears it sounded odd.

At least no further explanation was necessary. Hilary had seen one of their scenes before and it had distressed her even as it had fascinated her. He felt Jessica's fingers tighten on his shoulder—in sympathy? encouragement?—and then she and Hilary were both through the door. He had only a moment to glimpse the inside of the room, enough to see Maria wasn't anywhere within the line of vision from the door, and then it closed again.

Shutting him out.

Clenching his fists, he debated whether or not to follow them. It chafed that Maria had gone somewhere he couldn't follow. He almost wished she had gone out to the car and demanded to be taken home. At least then he would know what was going on.

"Rick, step away from the door."

He groaned. "Olivia," he said, reluctantly, as he turned around. Just what he needed.

Unlike the girls, who had been encouraging and supportive, Olivia obviously suspected he had something to do with Maria fleeing from him. Then again, she could just be reading his guilt. Or he could just be projecting because of his guilt.

The fierce redhead raised one haughty eyebrow at him, obviously displeased he still appeared to be thinking about encroaching on feminine territory. Suppressing an aggravated growl, Rick stepped away from the door.

"Come on, Patrick wants to talk to you," she said, turning and walking back toward their table.

Under other circumstances, he doubted Olivia would have ever deigned to play messenger for Patrick. He was willing to bet she didn't trust the other guys to keep him out of the ladies' room. Really, all it would take was one successful breach and the sanctity of the unspoken rule probably would have been broken forever. Rick doubted he was the first Dom who ever wanted to follow his sub into the locker rooms. The Dommes would, as a group, be pretty pissed about it though. For some reason, none of them ever seemed to have the same need. Olivia would say that's because none of them ever fucked up with their subs the way the Doms did.

He could feel the curious stares of the other Stronghold patrons as he made his way through the room, following Olivia. Rick was not normally the kind of Dom to be found at the center of a scene like that. He rarely did anything to draw attention to himself or what was going on in his personal life. Which was partly why the attention focused on him when the subs had realized he was looking for something more permanent had bothered him so much.

Rick slid into the seat between Olivia and Chris, who gave him a sympathetic whack on the back, and across from Patrick. It was the only seat left open and it had obviously been purposefully positioned so he wouldn't be distracted by watching the door to the locker room. In order to see it, he would have to turn his head.

"What happened?" Patrick demanded, almost as soon as Rick had settled into his seat. The big black man looked more concerned than anything, but he was obviously upset about seeing a woman Rick had brought to Stronghold running through the club in distress. Nothing like owning a BDSM club to bring out the control freak in a Dom.

"Paul and Christina were just starting their scene. I didn't realize they were down there... I don't think she..." Rick sighed. "Maria wasn't prepared." Guilt welled up in him again. He hadn't done a very good job of preparing her.

"You didn't tell her what to expect?" Patrick asked, raising one eyebrow. On his left, Rick could feel Olivia bristling. He groaned inwardly; he really didn't need Olivia deciding to mother hen Maria. His stubborn little tease was hard enough to handle on her own.

"I thought it would be better to show her," he said, although even as he said the words he could feel a flash of uncertainty flicker through him. Why hadn't he sat her down to talk things through? Maybe not beforehand, but once they'd arrived... he could have tried to explain. Tried to prepare her for some of the things she might see. Sure, she'd handled watching Lloyd pretty well but that should have just been a good opening. He couldn't have known more extreme players like Christina and Paul were down in the Dungeon, but they definitely weren't the only ones who did scenes which didn't appeal to Rick personally and would be difficult for a newbie to understand.

"Does she understand Christina enjoyed what was happening?" Patrick pressed.

"I'd just finished explaining safe words to her upstairs," Rick said, struggling against the urge to turn his head and look at the door to the ladies' room. He would know the second Maria came back into the room by his friends' reactions. "She took watching Lloyd well enough."

"You... are you... ARGH!" Olivia made a noise halfway between a scream and a growl as she threw her hands up in the air. "What is wrong with you? I thought Adam had taken the prize for idiocy in the club, but it looks like we have a new contender."

"Hey," Adam scowled at her.

"You were an idiot and you know it. Although at least you also knew Angel had some idea what she was getting herself into, so she didn't get completely blindsided." Even though Rick was keeping his head down, he could feel Olivia's glare. He didn't even try to argue. Testament to how guilty he was feeling. "So you dragged the poor thing here, and she looked absolutely terrified when I saw her in the locker room earlier, then dragged her all over the club without giving her any preparation or a clear explanation about what was going on, and then took her down to the Dungeon and you're shocked she went running?"

"Of course I'm not shocked," Rick snapped back. "It's nothing I didn't expect in the first place." Lifting up his gaze, he glared, only to meet Olivia's flat, gray eyes without even the slightest sparkle of silver in them. Behind him, he could hear Liam and Andrew murmuring something to each other, but he couldn't tell what. Adam just shook his head and shot Patrick a look, but Patrick was too busy groaning and looking up at the ceiling to notice. Fortunately, he couldn't see Chris or Justin's reactions. Like he didn't know he'd screwed up. "I should have never brought her here in the first place."

"That's what you think you did wrong?" Olivia gave him the most pitying, derisive look he'd ever gotten from her. "I was wrong, you're not an idiot. You're well on your way to being hopeless."

"What?" Honestly confused now, Rick turned his head to look around at his friends, seeing if any of them understood any better than he did. They all looked back rather blankly and then turned, almost as a group, to Olivia for explanation. At least he wasn't alone.

"Men." She rolled her eyes, crossing her arms under her breasts in a contemptuous motion. "Let's see. Going by what I've seen so far tonight, and the overview Chris gave me, I'll try to break this down for you. She likes you. Enough that she came here, met all your friends, didn't run out the door when she realized what kind of club it was, stoked up her courage on her own in the bathroom after all of that sank in, went on a tour with you, saw Lloyd getting his ass beat, and still didn't run until she was presented with what probably looked like something brutal, unloving and non-consenting... am I right?"

Rick winced and nodded.

"Then she still didn't run for the outside world. She ran for the bathroom. Not only is she still counting on you to take her home after this, but she didn't even leave the club. Beyond all of that, I seriously doubt you would have brought her here if you didn't have some suspicion that she's at least a little bit submissive. So. Given all of that, and your obvious attraction to her as well as your stated desire for a real relationship, please explain to me why you have done everything in your power to fuck it up before it even started."

His jaw was hanging open as Olivia's words blasted through him, along with her fierce glare and the shocked but comprehending expressions of all of his friends, and he couldn't think of a single thing to say.

"I... I—"

Olivia's slate gaze softened slightly. "I'm going to hazard a guess you're freaking out a bit, because you finally found someone you connect with, on more than one level." Uncrossing her arms, she leaned forward and placed one hand on his forearm, which was resting on the table, muscles tensed along with his jaw as anxiety swirled around his stomach. "You're a bit of a romantic. That's not a bad thing but I'd bet money you're already thinking all sorts of long-term thoughts and are worrying she's going to reject you. So you're testing her to see if you should even be thinking that way. But that's not fair to her or you. You two just met. Stop thinking in the long-term. It's too much pressure, and it's too soon to start testing her to see if she might be the future-Mrs.-Winter. Now you think about that, and I'm going to go check on your girl."

Giving him an almost motherly kiss on the side of his head, Olivia hopped off her bar stool and sauntered towards the locker room.

Still utterly at a loss for words, Rick looked back up at his friends.

Adam sighed, giving him a look of deepest sympathy. "Sucks when she's right, doesn't it?"

"Here," Andrew said, pushing his beer across the table. "You need this more than I do right now, I'll get another."

Chris just slapped him on the back again, shaking his head.

"So is anyone else wondering what the hell Lexie is up to?" asked

Justin, taking the attention from Rick, which he was immediately grateful for. Patrick scowled.

Rick slowly relaxed as his friends followed Justin's lead and picked up a conversation around him, sensing he needed some space to think. If he wanted to talk about what Olivia had just said to him, about her dissection of his motives and behavior, then they'd be willing to listen. But they also respected he probably really didn't want to talk about it.

He was too busy castigating himself for needing everything spelled out to him by Olivia, rather than realizing it on his own. Maybe he really was an idiot. Or maybe Olivia just understood women better than any of them ever could, which was probably a more realistic explanation.

Adam caught his eye and gave him a rueful grimace. Seeing the look, Justin raised his beer just a tiny bit, as if in acknowledgement and Rick knew they were all thinking the same thing: one day, it would be really nice to be the one to explain things to Olivia.

# 9

Maria was moving so fast for the stall she'd occupied before that she barely even noticed the startled looks she got from the few women who were in the locker room as she went past them. Fortunately, all the stalls were empty. She barged right into the one she'd been in before and locked the door behind her, sitting down on the seat and wrapped her arms around herself as she tried to get her panic under control.

Something inside of her jibbered, screaming at her to get out and away from Rick. Like, seriously, what the hell? The woman had been begging to be let go, pleading to escape her punishment, and not a single person had made a move to help her. They'd all just stood there watching—including Rick. The scene with Lloyd upstairs had been one thing, it had made her uncomfortable, but how was she supposed to be okay with what was going on in the Dungeon? She'd justified the man's spanking by the fact that he'd obviously enjoyed it, but he hadn't been asking for mercy. He hadn't been tied up and unable to escape.

Her breathing was getting faster as her fear and panic coiled around inside of her, confusing thoughts and terrifying images swirling around her head and only escalating her anxieties. Even though she hadn't seen the marks the long, awful stick had left on the woman downstairs, her imagination was supplying her with all sorts of possibilities. Bruises. Welts. Cuts. Maybe even blood. What the fuck?!

"Maria?"

It was a woman calling her name. Not Rick. Thank heavens. Maria couldn't face him yet. Why had he chased after her instead of helping that woman? She'd been begging her Master to stop. And apparently no one cared.

"Maria? We know you're in here, where'd you go?"

Although she couldn't completely distinguish who went with which voice, she knew immediately who had followed her in. Footsteps moved closer into the bathroom area, probably pointed in the right direction by the women in the locker room.

A tentative knock on the door and she recognized the pink heels as being Hilary's. She couldn't see Angel or Jessica's feet, but she knew they were there.

"Maria? Can you come out? We just want to talk to you... we know you saw... look, can you come out and we can explain?"

"Explain?!" Even to her own ears her voice sounded a bit screechy. "How can you explain..." Her voice trailed off. She couldn't even bring herself to say the words.

"Maria, I know this is going to sound a little weird, but I promise you, Christina liked what was happening. She wanted it."

That just sounded like a rapist's defense. Weird was an understatement. But then again, her brain reminded her, Lloyd had liked what was happening to him too, hadn't he? At first Maria hadn't understood that either.

"It freaked me out too, the first time I saw them." That was Hilary again. "Liam and I do role play, but not like Christina and Paul do it."

"Role play?" Maria lifted her head. Yeah, it hadn't looked anything like any role play she'd ever heard of—what happened to something nice and simple like French maid outfits? But her panic was slowly subsiding under the other women's calm. They'd all seemed like reasonable women before. Not the kind of people who would stand by while someone was being beaten and raped. Then again, she hadn't thought Rick would be either.

There was silence on the other side of the door for a long moment.

A silence fraught with tension, as if there was an unheard conversation happening.

"Maria?" She was pretty sure Jessica was the one talking now. "How much did Rick tell you about Stronghold?"

"Nothing before we got here," she replied, feeling a small surge of anger over the fact that he'd been so close-mouthed. Then again, he'd probably been afraid she wouldn't want to come. He might have been right. Three small gasps outside the door made her feel a bit more justified in her anger.

"He told you nothing?"

"That... that..."

"Nincompoop!"

Maria couldn't help it, she burst out laughing. The epithet was just so unexpected and yet so completely true it surprised some humor out of her. She could hear the others giggling too.

"Seriously? Nincompoop?" she heard Angel say. "Come on Hil, you can do better than that."

"I kind of like nincompoop," Maria said, ruefully, getting up off the toilet seat and unlocking the door. That little bout of humor had washed away the last of her fear, along with the obvious support she was getting from the three other women. It didn't sound like they were going to try to push Rick on her or chastise her for her reaction.

Three smiles greeted her as the door opened, showcasing various degrees of sympathy, encouragement and relief.

"Come on," Hilary said, reaching out and taking Maria's hand, her voice full of sympathy. "Let's go sit down and talk."

"Yeah, we'll do what Rick should have done and actually tell you about the club, and then you can ask us any questions you want," Angel said, turning and heading back toward the locker room area and the benches there. Her curls bounced as she shook her head angrily. "What the hell was he thinking? Stupid idiot."

"Shhh," Jessica hissed at her, looking around the locker room quickly. Fortunately, it had been deserted, as if the previous occupants knew Maria would need both support and privacy. That or the other two just hadn't wanted to get mixed up in whatever was going on. "Look around before you say things like that. You know the

Dommes will tell on you to Adam if they hear you disrespecting a Dom."

Maria tensed, and Hilary squeezed her hand encouragingly, as if reassuring her Angel wouldn't be in any real trouble.

"They'd also agree with me."

"That won't save you from getting spanked," Jessica scolded as she sat down on one of the benches.

Turning back around, Angel caught the look on Maria's face and her almond shaped eyes went wide. Even with the explanations Rick had given and the casual way Jessica and Angel were talking about it, Maria couldn't help the reaction she had after what she'd seen downstairs. "Oops, sorry. I didn't think about how all of that would sound... trust me, I don't mind getting spanked. Well. Most of the time. Shit..." She looked at Jessica and Hilary. "How do we explain this?"

"Let's start with this," Jessica said, as Hilary and Maria sat down on the opposite bench, facing them. "Maria, how much do you know about BDSM and kink?"

"Um... well Rick explained what BDSM stands for once we got here. And upstairs he explained Lloyd had a safe word and he could have stopped the spanking if he wanted to. But... the woman downstairs... she was begging that guy to stop." Hearing the tremor in her voice, Maria felt her anxiety welling up again. Especially since neither Jessica nor Angel looked shocked, they just kind of shrugged at each other as it if it was completely normal for a woman to beg for mercy and not have it granted.

"Christina and Paul are a bad place to start," Hilary said. "They're kind of extreme. But trust me, Christina has a safe word and 'no' or 'please don't' aren't it. Red is the club safe word, which everyone will recognize, but she probably has her own personal one too."

"A safe word is a word which is easily recognizable as not belonging in the scene," Angel said, taking over the explanation. "Mine is 'uncle,' like in 'say uncle.' Saying 'no' doesn't get me shit, but if I say my safe word, Adam will stop whatever he's doing immediately. Although the only time I've ever had to use it is when he accidentally made one of my wrist restraints too tight and my hand started to tingle." She rolled her eyes and exchanged a grin with Jessica. "He practically panicked when I said it, thinking he was being too rough with me, and then you should have seen the way he acted over my wrist. All I wanted was for him to loosen the cuff, not stop the scene entirely. Now I know better and I say 'yellow' if I have something I need to tell him like that, so he doesn't freak out."

Their easygoing demeanor was just as reassuring as what they were telling her. In the privacy of the locker room, with no one else around, it wasn't like they could be pressured by their men or their friendship with Rick. This felt like girl talk, the kind she would have with her sisters—if her sisters ever talked about stuff like this.

"Safe words can mean different things to different couples," said Jessica, leaning forward earnestly. Which gave Maria an incredible view of her breasts. Not that Maria normally noticed things like other women's boobs, but in the corsets Jessica and Angel were wearing it was hard not to notice when either of them leaned forward. She couldn't help but wonder what Rick's reaction would be if she wore something like that. "For all of us, it stops the scene, but for some people a safe word is just like 'pause.' Like when Angel says yellow. I know in some of the Master-slave relationships it can actually end the relationship entirely, so it's really rare for it to happen, but the choice is always in the submissives' hands. From what I've seen of Christina and Paul, I'm not sure what he could possibly do to get her to safe word. She's kind of an extreme masochist, and she likes rougher role play."

"Yeah, tell me about it," Hilary said, and Maria turned her head to look at the pretty blonde. She was wrinkling her nose, but her soft brown eyes were filled with amusement. "First time I saw them together, he had her hog-tied and she was screaming 'rape' while everyone watched. I was lucky. We came in at the end of their scene, so she orgasmed about thirty seconds later, otherwise I might have been traumatized, even with Liam reassuring me she was fine."

"What is her safe word?" Angel asked the other two, sounding curious. "Does anyone know?" Hilary and Jessica shook their heads. "I might have to ask her sometime."

"So... she likes pretending she's being raped?" Maria asked, still a little confused.

Angel gave her a lopsided smile. "Yeah. I don't get it either, but Stronghold's very much 'to each their own.' All the dominants and submissives have their own personal kinks, and a lot of them are looking for a partner whose kinks match theirs. We can tell you with absolute certainty Rick's kinks don't involve anything extreme. There's not a lot of secrets here, and especially in our group of friends."

"What do you mean, his kinks?" Maria asked, a little worried about what Angel might consider extreme. Not because Angel seemed untrustworthy, but because Maria didn't have a barometer for this kind of thing.

"Well, all the guys are kind of into different things, although they also have a lot of similarities," Angel said. "Adam's got a major thing for spanking and bondage—"

"Also, he's a complete ass man," Jessica interjected with a giggle. "And I don't just mean to look at." Out of the corner of her eye, Maria could see Hilary make a face, her own head was trying to catch up with exactly what Jessica meant.

"You guys are going to scare the newbie," Hilary said, her tone slightly scolding although she also sounded amused. She turned to Maria. "Liam's not at all into anal sex, fortunately, because no matter how much these two talk it up I'm not really interested. We do a little bit of anal play with toys and stuff sometimes, but that's about as far as I want to go and thankfully that's all he wants too."

"What if he wanted more?" Maria asked, almost surprising herself by asking a question now.

Listening to this conversation was fascinating, still girl talk, but worlds away from anything she'd ever talked about with her sisters. And it really was helping her that all three of them were so open, although she still wasn't sure if this was the kind of thing for her. She felt like she was soaking up the knowledge, storing it all away for further contemplation.

Hilary made a face. "I guess if he really wanted it, I'd try it, but if I didn't like it, that would be that. We don't have the kind of relationship which includes me doing things I don't like, although some people are turned on by that. Like Christina."

"I like it when Justin and Chris push me," Jessica said, blushing a little bit. "But they never do anything I can't handle, although there are certain things we don't do very often."

"So... you're with both of them?" Maria asked, hoping her voice didn't sound judgmental. She truly wasn't trying to judge, it was just she'd never heard of such a thing, although it did explain the dynamics she'd seen earlier.

"Oh good grief, he really didn't tell you anything," Hilary muttered.

"Yes, I'm with both of them," Jessica said, her voice even. Obviously she was used to people not being entirely sure what to make of such a revelation. She'd blushed over talking about them pushing her boundaries but not about the fact that she was in a relationship with two men. "Last summer I went to this um... kink school basically, like a summer camp but for adults who want to learn about sex and different kinds of kink, and they were both instructors there." She rolled her eyes. "Little did I know. We all worked at the same company back then, and they knew I was going to be there. I was so pissed off when I got home and realized they'd known who I was all along... but we really connected at school and they both wanted to date me, and they were sure they wouldn't break up their friendship over trying to date me, but I just couldn't choose between them. Didn't help that they taught the ménage a trois class together at the school, so I knew how good it could be with both of them. It's not always easy, but we're making it work."

"Wow..." Maria blinked, trying to assimilate all the information just handed to her. The others waited patiently, although she got the feeling that mostly they were waiting for her reaction to Jessica's unusual relationship. Hey, she didn't think it was what she would want for herself, although now that she thought about it some aspects seemed like they could be pretty fascinating, but she didn't know what her mother and sisters would say. They'd probably have a meltdown of nuclear proportions. "I think I could use a school like that, after today. Would've helped a lot anyway."

Relaxing at Maria's acceptance of everything she'd just been told, Jessica grinned at her in a conspiratorial way. "It was pretty fantastic... although it was also kind of weird. At first, I felt a little slutty, because I was having sex with someone different in almost every class, but it was a lot of fun too. I don't think I could be where I am today if I hadn't gone, it really opened up my mind."

"Tell me about it... and then she comes home and she's all bondage this, bondage that..."

"Like you hadn't already been reading all the dirty books on my e-reader," Jessica said laughing, shaking her finger at Hilary. Her hazel eyes sparkled at the memory.

"So then I get dragged to Stronghold," Hilary said, ignoring Jessica. "Met Liam... he was a total jerk at first and then the next thing I know I'm asking for an Introductory Scene, probably half because he told me to stay away from the club. Of course, Patrick made sure Liam was assigned to me to do the scene, and we did some role play... and then I was hooked. Both on the lifestyle and on him. We just clicked with what we like,. He's more into ordering me around and making me hold still while he teases me until I'm ready to beg him to let me cum than anything else, although we both really do have a good time with the role play." The dopey grin on her face was so cute, and yet so at odds with her words. It was incredibly charming. "It's fun."

The look the three women exchanged then was the kind Maria sometimes had with her sisters. Not a conversation, just a cama-raderie, a sharing of something special. They were all completely different in looks and—apparently—interests, but they all had the same self-satisfied, content expressions of women who were happy.

Expressions she recognized from her sisters' faces. So apparently it didn't matter whether a relationship was more conventional or a little bit kinky, it could still affect a woman the same way. That was nice to know... that was, if she was going to stick around Rick.

She was still mad she was discovering all of this now from his friends, rather than from him. Not to mention that, even with their explanations and evident happiness, she didn't know if this kind of thing was for her.

"What are Rick's... um... kinks?" she asked, a little hesitantly. "He said he wanted to spank me..."

"Oh good, so he's communicating a little bit, at least." The new voice made Maria jump, along with the other three. She couldn't see Hilary's face, but both Angel and Jessica beamed at the woman who was coming towards them, having somehow slipped silently into the room without any of them noticing. The stunning redhead was the same woman Maria had seen in the locker room the first time she was there, the one who had smiled at her encouragingly. The same smile was on her face as she straddled the bench next to Jessica.

The tight leather pants she was wearing didn't look like they should be that flexible, but she didn't even wince as she settled down. Her top was leather too, showing off an expanse of pale midriff as well as a generous amount of cleavage. Somehow the combination was both sexy and intimidating.

The woman held out her hand, and Maria automatically took it without thinking.

"I'm Olivia."

"Oh!" The connection lit up in Maria's brain and she smiled as Olivia released her hand. Although Rick had never described his friends physically, the aura of authority and confidence around Olivia was just what she had always pictured. "Rick's told me about you."

"Well that's good, considering what he hasn't told you," Olivia said, rolling her eyes. Wide and gray, they were like calm, reassuring pools. Somehow, even though no one had said anything, Maria got the feeling they were all deferring to Olivia in some way. Rick had said she was a ballbuster. That confident gaze regarded her thoughtfully, reminding her a bit of the way Jared had looked her over when she'd first come in, but in a decidedly more friendly manner. "So you want to know about Rick's kinks?"

"Yeah... I know it's not like any of you have had sex with him, so you won't know personally, but anything..." Maria's voice trailed off as every head turned towards Jessica. Who had turned a beet red.

Her mouth hanging open, Maria tried to stamp down the jealousy suddenly flooding her stomach. Jessica had had sex with Rick? Dammit, she liked Jessica. She didn't want to feel like suddenly clawing the other woman's big brown eyes with their extravagantly long lashes out. Something hard settled in the pit of her stomach, it roiled and churned, making her feel nauseous.

"Well... um, you know that school I mentioned?" Jessica asked, her hazel eyes big in her face, silently pleading with Maria not to be upset with her. "I met Rick there too, he was an instructor. It wasn't..." She sighed and looked at the others as if appealing for help. "It was just part of class. I never thought I'd see him again, and even when I did... there's nothing between us. It's always been Justin and Chris for me. Rick and I have never been anything but friends."

"I see," Maria said carefully, pushing down the bile in the back of her throat. She was not going to be that girl. There was no reason to think Jessica was lying to her. Not to mention, she was in a monogamous relationship. Well, as monogamous as someone could get with two men. But they'd both seemed possessive of her, like they weren't willing to share her with anyone else. Jessica had been nothing but friendly to her, and surely she wouldn't be like that if she had anything but friendly feelings for Rick.

"You're going to run into more people who have had sex with Rick if you date him," Olivia said bluntly. Maria got the impression Olivia didn't often sugarcoat her words. "Although not as many as these three do. Rick just moved up here recently and he didn't come as much before that. People here scene together, and that sometimes includes sex. Some submissives can get attached to dominants they've scened with, and vice versa, but the boundaries are pretty clearly spelled out."

"Which is why I don't make friends with the other subs," Angel said under her breath, avoiding Olivia's amused gaze. She winked at Maria, returning her voice to speaking volume. "Most of them are nice enough though, no one's out to steal anyone's man. They want their own. Doesn't make them like me, but they respect the relationship."

"Except Marissa." Jessica made a face as if the name left a bad taste in her mouth. That was another name Maria recognized, and not in a good way. Interesting how Rick's opinion of Marissa was definitely backed up by the females in the group.

"Let's not talk about Truckstop," Olivia said, waving her hand as if to ward off bad spirits. Her expression was completely blank, as if she was holding back her distaste by sheer effort of will. "The point is, the club is kind of incestuous in a way. If you come here often, and you aren't in a relationship, you're going to scene with the other singles. That's just something you'll have to get used to and accept, if you decide you want to be with Rick."

Well at least Olivia didn't just assume Maria was going to want to be with him. Sure he was drool-worthy, fun, funny, sensitive, sexy as all get out, and she had a lot of fun being around him, but she was more than a bit pissed about how he'd handled tonight. It also didn't help her uncertainty that she would be able to deal with everything being thrown at her. Yeah, she'd had so-called meaningless sex before. It could be a lot of fun, but it wasn't like she spent time around the guys after they were done with each other. Or introduced her boyfriends to them.

Then again, since Jessica was dating his friends, it's not like Rick would have much of a choice about hanging out with her. And Jessica was really nice. And in a committed relationship. So did it matter?

"So," she said, taking a deep breath. She was already in the pool, might as well hit the deep end while she was here. Who knew if she'd have the opportunity to ask the questions again? Pushing down her jealousy, she forced a calm expression onto her face when she looked at Jessica. "What are Rick's kinks?"

"Oh, I haven't actually experienced them firsthand," Jessica said, looking somewhat alarmed. "He just taught the Basic Intercourse class at the Venus School."

"There's a Basic Intercourse class? Man... maybe I should just go to the school," Maria said, laughing and feeling some knots in her shoulders loosen. Strangely, knowing Jessica hadn't had kinky sex with Rick, indulging in all the things he wanted, somehow made her feel a little better. Even though she didn't know much about BDSM, it seemed like fulfilling each other's fantasies would be more intimate than just regular sex.

"I wanted to go too, but Adam said no," Angel said with a little sigh, although it wasn't really regretful. Kind of smug actually.

"Spanked your ass for even thinking about it, didn't he?"

Angel's smile was like the Cheshire cat's after licking a bowl of cream. "I'm just going to say it was a good night."

"We're getting off-track ladies," Olivia said, although her smile was indulgent. It suddenly struck Maria that Olivia's position in the group was incredibly familiar; that of the big sister. A protective leadership role, but the kind of leader who knew when to step aside and let someone make their own mistakes. A guiding hand, but not a prohibitive one. Those gray eyes found their way back to Maria's, still contemplative, but kind. As if she already considered Maria to be one of her own. Was this how Maria's little sisters felt? It was distinctly odd to be in the receiving position. "Rick likes and a bit of impact play —spanking and flogging—but his biggest fetish is orgasm play."

"Orgasm play?"

Angel made a face and Jessica shuddered. Hilary just shrugged slightly, although her own expression wasn't entirely serene. Apparently orgasm play wasn't necessarily the fun thing it sounded like.

"Usually denial of, sometimes forced orgasms. Although he's not extreme with it, like some people can be." The little smile hovering on Olivia's lips seemed to indicate it was something she enjoyed as well; she had a slightly faraway look in her eyes, as if she was picturing something else. Or someone else. "It's more about control than anything else. The knowledge that they are willing to withhold their own pleasure in an attempt to please you. Having that kind of control over another person. Keeping your partner just on the brink of pleasure, keeping them from actually crossing the edge... and then when they do, it's... beautiful."

Pressing her thighs together, Maria sternly told herself it probably wasn't as pleasant as Olivia made it sound. Jessica was looking at Olivia like she was crazy.

"It's also hell when you're the one not allowed to cum." Jessica snorted. "Trust me, I've thought about safe wording more than once when Justin and Chris are making me hold back."

"But you haven't, have you? And it's been worth it, hasn't it?" Olivia asked in a superior tone. That's when Maria realized, Olivia wasn't a submissive like Angel, Jessica, or Hilary. She was dominant. Like Rick was. Maybe that's why the others deferred to her so easily.

Looking at her, she definitely seemed to have the same confidence and aura his male friends did. Kind of nice seeing it in another woman. The others were confident, but this was a different kind of power.

"Yeah, once they finally let me cum, it's awesome," Jessica said, although her tone was a bit derisive, like she still wouldn't choose the experience on her own. Maria could understand that. But it really did sound kind of hot... being tied up while Rick played with her until she was begging him to let her cum. Her thighs pressed together again as something wild and needy surged in her pussy.

A lot of the things she'd seen and heard about tonight didn't appeal to her, but that image did.

Still... that didn't make up for she was hearing about what Rick wanted in bed from other women. One of whom had actually slept with him. If someone had told her that was going to happen tonight, she would have never come. Now that she was here it kind of made sense, but it was still something which would have normally been a major warning signal to stay away.

Her head was so confused. So was her body, apparently, because she was still kind of hot and bothered by the half-formed images flitting through her mind of Rick looming over her with his hands between her legs while her own hands were tied above her head and she moaned and begged him to—

Okay, yeah. Enough of that.

"Think you're ready to go back out into the club?" Olivia asked. Maria looked up and realized the other woman was watching her quite closely. She blushed, wondering if Olivia could see any of her thoughts on her face. Man she hoped not. Talk about embarrassing. Like the other woman didn't know enough about what was going on in Maria's life already, whereas Maria didn't really know anything about her.

"Yeah... I think..." She paused, trying to gather herself. "I think I'm ready to go home, actually," she said slowly.

"Oh..." Hilary looked disappointed, and a bit worried. "I hope we haven't scared you away."

"Oh no, it's nothing any of you have done," Maria said, a bit of steel finding its way into her voice. Yeah, she was still ticked at Rick for his little trick tonight. Talk about a surprise date. "I just need to... think. Process. Figure out how I feel about well... all of this." She waved her hand.

"Understandable," Olivia said, standing up. Angel looked like she wanted to say something, but when Olivia gave her a look she subsided. Yeah, Olivia was definitely dominant. "Stop by the front desk on your way out and let Lexie know I said it was okay to give you my phone number."

"Me too," Angel said.

"Us too," Hilary said, waving at Jessica, who nodded her head in agreement. "Even if you don't get together with Rick, you can still hang out with us, right?"

Maria smiled gratefully. Nice to know the connection she felt with them wasn't one-sided, although she didn't doubt they'd try to play matchmaker given the chance. "Yeah, I'd really like that."

Olivia basically herded them out into the main club area as they each grinned and either hugged Maria or squeezed her hand, and Maria noticed more than one woman made a beeline for the locker room door after giving Olivia a dirty look. Apparently she had the redhead to thank for their continued privacy while they were in there, which made her feel both guilty and relieved.

Across the room, at the table they'd been sitting at before, she could see Rick's back and his friends as they all took notice of their girlfriends coming towards them. Heads came up, watching with expressions both admiring and protective. After all, they weren't the only ones watching. And Maria had to admit, she could see why.

They were a diverse group, with Olivia in all leather, Jessica in her tight corset and short skirt, Angel's latex dress and Hilary's more demure but still sexy pink top and shorts. And Maria, in the black clothes she'd wearing to a regular night out, definitely not in line with the outfits everyone else in the room had on. It made her feel a little out of place, not to be dressed for sex like the others were, but at the same time she was glad. Now that she was paying attention, she could see more than one man checking her out—and not being at all shy about it. Which would have been awesome if they all didn't scare the crap out of her. Not because they were scary in and of themselves, but because who knew what they'd want to do with her?

Seeing his friends' reactions, Rick knew the women had finally come out of the locker room. Taking a deep breath, he turned around, preparing for the worst. Instead he saw Maria, walking in the center of the woman, looking around with a calm expression. As though she was soaking everything in, maybe even seeing it with new eyes.

He bristled as he noticed how many of the other Doms were eyeing the small group with appreciation, but he couldn't blame them. The girls looked hot. If he hadn't been so nervous about how Maria was doing, what she might want now, he'd probably have even enjoyed the way it looked like they were following Olivia like they were her ducklings.

Olivia had been completely right. He'd been putting way too much pressure on the situation, and on Maria. Which hadn't been fair at all. There were things he could have said to prepare her. Hell, once they'd gotten in the club and he'd started explaining BDSM to her, he should have given her a fuller explanation. One misstep after the other, because he'd felt some stupid need to test her.

Stupid, really, to set her up like that. As if any woman, who wasn't given any warning, would take one look around the club and be on board with whatever he wanted to do. Hell, if she had been, he wouldn't have trusted it. If he'd given her more prep or brought her here and given fuller disclosure instead of just shoving everything in her face to see how she dealt with it, maybe tonight would have gone differently.

"Don't push her," Patrick murmured in his ear, clapping his hand on his shoulder. "She likes you, but she's probably going to need some time."

"Yeah, I can see that," Rick said, but there wasn't any bite to his reply. He knew Patrick was just watching out for him. Right now Maria was looking anywhere but at him.

Dammit. He really hoped he hadn't fucked this up beyond repair. At least she hadn't run straight for the front door, he supposed he should take heart she was still comfortable enough coming over to him.

The girls split off, going straight to their boyfriends, while Olivia stayed close by Maria's side, as if offering support. Not that he really wanted Olivia acting as mother hen to Maria, but if it was going to help his little tease then he'd be grateful for it at this point.

Maria took a deep breath before looking up to meet his eyes, her own face composed but anxious. "I think I'd like to go home now."

The words 'if that's okay with you' went unspoken but he could feel them lingering in the air. And somehow he'd managed to convince himself she might not be submissive? Ha. He really was an idiot sometimes. Even though she'd been occasionally more aggressive than the submissives he was used to, she responded in a lot of ways like a submissive. She obviously wanted to please the people she cared about, the people around her. And she looked to him for approval.

As much as he really would have liked to stay and show her Stronghold wasn't as scary as it had looked, he knew he needed to listen to what she wanted. Like Patrick had said, now was not the time to push.

"Of course," he said gently, keeping his voice low. "If that's what you want."

She hesitated for just a second, and his heart leapt with hope she might change her mind and say she wanted to stay, but then she nodded her head. "Yes please."

The ride home was uncomfortable and silent. It was obvious the women had all taken to Maria. She'd gotten all of their phone numbers from Lexie before they'd left, and Lexie had insisted on including hers as well. Followed by a suspicious, dirty look at Rick, even though she couldn't possibly already know how he'd messed up. Apparently Maria's subdued countenance was enough for Lexie.

Rick was torn between wishing he'd never taken her to Stronghold, wishing he'd managed the evening better, and berating himself for being stupid enough to expose himself to one of his neighbors. Not that he thought Maria would make trouble for him, she wasn't the type, but it still would make for the occasional awkward encounter around the pool and in the stairwell. Every time, he'd feel the sting of regret for getting so close and messing it up so monumentally.

He walked her up to her door, keeping his hands in his pockets and to himself, which really sucked when all night he'd been able to reach out and touch her as much as he'd wanted. So far she hadn't really looked at him, she seemed lost in thought, at least she didn't seem afraid of him. Just distant. Untouchable. No longer his to protect or claim. It made the inside of his chest hurt.

When they got to her door, he took a deep breath and faced her. She peered up at him through thick lashes, and for a moment he could almost pretend tonight had gone well and she was waiting for a kiss. Unfortunately, that wasn't the case. "Maria, I just wanted to say I'm really sorry. I should have... well we should have talked more. A big part of... well, of the lifestyle," he said, changing his words just in case any nosy neighbors were listening at their doors, "is communication. Not that you would have been able to tell from how I behaved tonight. I fucked up. I put you in an uncomfortable situation and I just wanted to say I'm really sorry."

Dark eyes, fathoms deep, studied him. "Apology accepted. I... your friends were very nice. They explained a lot about... um... well, that stuff to me." Her eyes darted to the closed doors of her neighbors and he appreciated she was being as circumspect as he had been. Not that he expected anything less from her. "But I wish you had been the one to."

Hope surged up inside him, nearly painful in its intensity. He jammed his hands deeper into his pockets, ignoring the dominant male in him which wanted to reach out and touch her, seduce her, bend her to his will. Maria was at least a little submissive, he didn't doubt that anymore, and he was sure if he pressed now that they would end up in bed together tonight, but that wasn't how he wanted her. Free choice and logical thought, not lust and impulse... because he wanted more than just a night, he wanted a relationship.

"Would... you like to go out some other time? Not to Stronghold," he added hastily, seeing the apprehensive expression that flitted across her face. "Just for coffee or something."

Not even a real date, although he might have tried for that if her reaction hadn't been so immediate and clear. Her forehead wrinkled as she sucked in her cheeks, obviously thinking. Part of him wanted to take back his words and tell her not to worry about it, but another, more hopeful, part insisted he stay quiet and let her figure out her answer for herself.

"I'm not sure," she said finally, hesitantly. "Um... maybe? I just... I need some time to think."

Rick felt his expression harden, hiding his disappointment. He nodded. "I understand. Thank you for coming tonight. Again, I'm sorry about... well everything."

"Thanks," she said, giving him a little smile before slipping into her apartment. The door closed behind her, but he caught one last glimpse of her thoughtful expression before it shut.

Damn.

## 10

Standing on the stairwell of her apartment building, Maria watched as Rick swam his morning laps. It was a good thing her apartment didn't face the pool or she probably would have spent all morning watching him. As it was, she'd been standing in the same place, staring at the pool, for at least five minutes. Thankfully, no one had walked by to see her imitation of a statue.

This morning she'd woken up, ready to go to the pool and meet up with Rick as usual. But once she'd gotten to the stairs and been able to look across to where the pool was, and seen his powerful body plowing through the water, she'd been assailed by doubts. What would they say to each other? Would he take her presence as a declaration that she was interested in what he'd shown her last night?

And had she really stopped being upset with him?

His apology at her door last night had been completely sincere, she had no doubt of that. The hangdog look, the guilt, had been all over his face and in his body language, so she'd almost wanted to reach out and give him a hug and reassure him everything was all right. But it wasn't, entirely, was it?

Chewing on her lower lip, Maria shifted her bag to her other shoulder. Even though it only had her towel, sunscreen and pool stuff in it, it got heavy after a while of just standing there.

She liked Rick. She really did. A lot. Spending time with him at the pool was fun. Talking to him had become an integral part of her day. She liked hearing about his friends, telling him about her family, and just talking about the small stupid stuff while they flirted and tried to make each other laugh. She believed he liked her and wanted more from her than just a one-night stand. So that was something. But last night she'd put a lot of trust in him, going to a completely unknown place with a guy she'd really only known for a little less than a month, and she felt like he'd broken her trust. Not because he'd taken her to Stronghold. Heck, some parts of the night she'd really liked. Meeting his friends, seeing the private upstairs rooms... but she was still having trouble wrapping her head around the scene in the Dungeon.

More than that, she was still kind of mad he hadn't explained more about Stronghold to her once they'd gotten there. A million other questions had been raised off of that.

Could she trust him in the future?

Did she want to get kinky with him? Or even at all?

Was she actually going to date a guy who wanted to take her to a club where she might have to strip down in front of a bunch of other people? Maria made a face. No one had mentioned whether or not Rick was an exhibitionist, and Maria had forgotten to ask.

Being the eldest of four sisters, she knew very well every single woman, no matter her shape or size, had something they didn't like about their body. Every woman had crushes on guys who weren't attracted to them, dated guys who turned out to be jerks, and had to put up with snide and nasty comments from other girls. Heck, Lara, who was drop-dead gorgeous, once had a boyfriend who tried to get her to lose weight she didn't even have to lose. So Maria knew, first hand, that being slim and stunning did not mean a reprieve from body issues. She'd found her own confidence in that knowledge. There would always be things she wanted to change about herself, so she might as well just love herself the way she was.

But that didn't mean she necessarily wanted to get nekkid in a room full of people she didn't know, while they watched her get it on.

She'd never had exhibitionist tendencies. Although, Rick hadn't actually said he did either and he had pointed out the curtains at the private rooms.

For that matter, none of his friends had used the rooms or been down in the Dungeon. They'd all just hung out at the bar. Maybe Stronghold was just their hangout place? Except Olivia had talked about all of them doing scenes there before they'd met their current girlfriends.

Yeah, there was a lot of information Rick had left out. She scowled at the swimming figure in the distance, her lips tightening.

Of course, she doubted it would have been easy to bring up. Just look at the fact that she hadn't told a single one of her sisters about Rick's kink. Even Jackie who obviously would have been the most understanding. Hell, she doubted she'd be able to tell any of them about Stronghold.

Bah.

She didn't even know what she would say if she went over to the pool. Be mad? Ha, like they could talk about why with all those other people around. Act like everything was normal? Yeah... she didn't think she could do that either. They'd crossed some kind of threshold last night, some boundary line that, once crossed, couldn't be put back in place. It was like when friends had sex, except they hadn't even got to do that.

Turning on her heel, Maria started back up the stairs. Today was not the day to face Rick. She still had a lot of thinking to do, obviously. Just anticipating it had made her realize when she did face him, she needed to have more of an answer for him than 'I'm still thinking things over' and then try to act like nothing had changed between them. They could go forward or not, but they definitely couldn't go back.

Plus, she could get on her computer and do some research. Educate herself. And then eradicate her search history.

COMING UP OUT OF THE WATER, RICK LOOKED AROUND AND FELT A familiar pang of disappointment when he saw Maria still wasn't there. Not that he was really expecting her. Just hoping. Idiot that he was. Why the hell would she want to come out and see him today?

Gritting his teeth, he dove back under the surface of the pool, letting the muted noise and cool water envelope him, taking him into another world. With every stroke he thought about Maria. He'd spent the last forty-five minutes castigating himself with every mistake he'd made last night. Flaying himself with the memory of every sign she'd shown of being submissive, that he'd brushed off, every time she'd leaned into his hand for support, every stuttered breath when he'd pressed himself against her.

Then he'd tried to move past the useless merry-go-round of missed opportunities, knowing it was pointless to rehash what he'd already done wrong and thinking about what he should have done instead. Too late for that. What he needed to do now was figure out if he should try to fix it.

He wanted to. Not just because he wanted Maria, but because he hated thinking things might be uncomfortable when they ran into each other from now on. Even if she didn't want him anymore, he didn't like the idea that their future interactions would be so far removed from the flirtatious friendship they'd been forming. That he'd killed any chance of anything with her. But he didn't know what the best move to make was.

Even though part of him wanted to just show up at her door and force her to talk to him—hell she'd done it to him often enough—he knew it wasn't the best tactic to take. Not with something like this. But when was it time to stop giving her space and start pushing? He was a Dom, and right now he was a Dom out of control of the situation. It was his own fault, but he sure as hell didn't like it.

When he finally got out of the pool, his muscles felt achy, which was not the best way to start his day. At least it was a Sunday and he didn't have anything going on other than meeting up with Jared and Chris. Marissa was out of town doing something, Rick didn't really care what she was doing, he was just glad she was away from Jared. Even though he knew her constant absences were a large part of

Jared's initial issues with their relationship, Jared always seemed happier when she was away. It meant he could spend more time with his friends without her souring it, so it wasn't surprising the big man had wanted some company.

Something Rick was happy to give. Plus, maybe Jared and Chris could give him some advice. Both of them were in complicated relationships, after all, and one of them was miserable and the other completely happy. He could get pointers from both sides.

IT DIDN'T TAKE TOO LONG TO REALIZE MAYBE EVERYTHING IN Chris' life wasn't great either. For one, he barely ribbed Rick about Maria, and that was because (for two) he was definitely completely distracted. Staring off into space, eyes wandering around the room, but not actually looking at anything.

They were all sprawled out on Jared's furniture. Jared took up most of the space on his small couch while Rick and Chris were both comfortably ensconced in his leather recliners. The television was on, but no one was watching, and Jared had put out some chips and salsa, but no one was eating. Another sign there was something wrong with Chris. Jared wasn't a big snacker, but Chris sure as hell was. Rick could go either way, but despite his extended workout that morning, he didn't really feel like eating.

His stomach was too full of unaccustomed anxiety.

Looking over at Chris, it was almost like looking at Justin. Except Justin would never sit draped over both the chair and the armrests like Chris was, but at least then the serious, almost brooding expression wouldn't be an anomaly. Chris was the one who was usually smiling.

Picking up the throw pillow he'd removed from the recliner when he'd first sat down, Rick had it live up to its name and he lobbed it across the room at Chris' head.

"Hey," Chris barely batted it away in time to keep the pillow from catching him directly in the face.

"Hey," Jared repeated, frowning at Rick over the top of his beer bottle, his brow knitting together in offended dignity. "Stop throwing my cushions around."

"It's a throw pillow."

"Whatever. They're decorations, not artillery."

"You have issues," Rick said, feeling slightly lighter as the absurdity of the conversation lifted his spirits a bit. That was more like it. None of this sitting around sullenly. Chris had picked the pillow back up and looked like he was contemplating whether or not it was worth Jared's possible ire to try and return fire. "I know why I'm down, and I know why Jared's down—"

"I'm not down," Jared said, lifting his beer and smiling, as if to show how not-miserable he was. "I'm drunk."

"—but why are you so down?" Rick finished, ignoring Jared. The big man was looking a bit under the hatches, to use one of Hilary's phrases, but he figured Jared deserved it. After all, he couldn't get drunk Friday or Saturday nights since he was usually working. Being a bouncer, he tended to have off Sunday and Monday evenings. So it made sense he'd choose today to get drunk, especially since he finally had an empty apartment to do it in.

Chris sighed, dropping the pillow back onto the floor, earning a dark look from Jared that he ignored. "Liam's going to propose to Hilary soon."

"So I've heard."

"Probably within the month."

"Still not understanding what this has to do with you..."

"It's girl-pressure," Jared said solemnly, looking like a sage old wiseman. He nodded his head at both of them. "She's Jessica's best friend, and Jessica started dating Justin and Chris before Hilary and Liam got together. So now the pressure is on Justin and Chris, because once Hilary gets engaged, Jessica's going to be wondering when her ring is coming."

"How are you in such a crappy relationship when you know so much?" Chris asked, looking a bit disgruntled at the rather cavalier breakdown of his relationship problems. Jared shrugged.

"Does it really matter, if you guys aren't at the same place Hilary and Liam are?" asked Rick. "I mean... your relationship is entirely different. A lot more complicated."

Rubbing his hand over his face, in a tired kind of motion, Chris groaned and leaned back in the chair, letting his upper body hang off the edge of it before coming back upright. Kind of like a kid facing questions from his parents that he didn't want to answer. "It just brings up all sorts of questions we don't have the answer to. Like... should we have some kind of commitment ceremony? If we do, should one of us actually marry her? If so, who does? Will that change things? What about kids, parental rights and how they'll feel about having three parents? What do we do if one of us marries her and, God forbid, there's some kind of accident and the two who are married are in the hospital and the third one doesn't have any kind of visitation rights?"

Rick whistled, while Jared let out a kind of grunting 'huh.'

Truth be told, once Chris had brought up Hilary and Liam, Rick had suspected it might be something along the marriage issue lines, but honestly, he hadn't thought it out as well as Chris and Justin obviously were. To him it had seemed a simple problem of deciding to have some kind of ceremony and, if they wanted to have one of them legally married to Jessica, to play rock, paper, scissors to figure out who got to do the deed. But there were definitely considerations beyond a wedding, which he hadn't considered, but which were serious and substantial.

Actually, out of the three of them in the room, his own issues were looking a heck of a lot better. At least that was something.

"Have you talked to Jessica about it, yet?" he asked, knowing Justin and Chris had been trying to work everything out between themselves, but if there was really so much to consider then he doubted Jessica would take being left out of the conversation very well.

"Where do you think half of these questions came from?" Chris asked grumpily. "She got downright morbid when it came to accidents and deaths. I don't think she actually wants to marry either of us."

Aha. No wonder Chris was in a bad mood. He was feeling rejected. Rick could empathize with that.

"I wish I had that problem," Jared said from the couch.

Both Rick and Chris sat bolt upright.

"Marissa wants to marry you?"

"I don't know." Twirling the empty beer bottle in his hand, Jared scowled at it. "She bought a wedding magazine. It's underneath my bed. I wish she'd taken it with her. I think she's hinting."

Since he wasn't look at them, it was easy for Rick and Chris to exchange looks. Holy shit. Rick knew Jared felt responsible for Marissa, and he had loved her at one point... but he couldn't possibly be thinking about actually marrying her and living in this misery for the rest of his life... could he? Surely emotional blackmail could only go so far.

"Are you going to?" Chris asked tentatively.

It wasn't often Jared opened up about the issues in his relationship, because he knew exactly how his friends felt about Marissa and sharing tended to only make things worse. Especially since he kept getting back with her even when they did break up for short periods of time.

"Fuck no," Jared said, his scowl getting even darker. But he still hadn't taken his eyes off the beer bottle, rather than looking at either of them. "I'd rather swallow a bottle of pills myself."

From the bewildered look on Chris' face, Jared hadn't shared that particular story with him. Rick grimaced, searching for something to say which would deflect attention from what, to Chris, probably sounded like a weird declaration. Fortunately, Chris unintentionally did it for him.

"Sooo... why are you still with her?" Chris asked slowly, looking between Jared and Rick, as if searching for clues. His dark eyes were concerned, at least he wasn't looking quite so melancholy about his own issues now.

"I think it's just habit," Jared said, shrugging. He slumped back against the couch, his eyes looking slightly reddened and very tired. "Habit... and she won't let me go. But I don't fight it very hard either."

"In vino veritas," Rick murmured. Chris gave him a sharp glance, but Jared didn't appear to hear him.

The giant man looked surprisingly small, hunched in on himself in the center of the couch. He looked lost. Drunk... small and lost. It was almost humbling, because Rick had never seen Jared like this.

Shit... is this were a mismatched BDSM relationship led? Maybe he should just leave Maria the fuck alone. Lifting his own beer to his lips, Rick took a long swallow.

MONDAY MORNING HANGOVERS WERE THE WORST. JUSTIN HAD picked up Chris at some point, but Rick had stayed the night. Commiserating. Supporting. Jared had gotten drunk off of his ass, and then they'd gone out to the parking lot and burned the wedding magazine Marissa had left. He didn't know how sober-Jared would feel about that, but drunken-Jared had been downright gleeful.

It blew Rick's mind that Jared could stay in a relationship where he was so twisted around and unhappy, but that was the danger of someone like Marissa. Who was willing to use all the intimate things she'd learned about Jared to hold onto him. Sometimes Rick thought Jared was her safety net, her anchor in a world where she was constantly taking risks for her future. It was a shitty fucking situation for Jared. Marissa was a downright bitch for putting him in this position and using emotional blackmail to keep him there.

He and Jared had gone to a diner down the street and had an extremely greasy breakfast and about a gallon of coffee before Rick finally felt up to heading back home. Jared seemed surprisingly even-keeled considering his misery the night before and the fact his head must be pounding even more than Rick's. When Rick left, Jared was laid out on his couch, one arm flung over his head and his eyes closed, resting.

Rick couldn't wait to get home and do the same.

Fortunately, it was only about a ten-minute drive. His hangover was bad enough he really shouldn't be on the road for even that long, but he forced himself to stay as alert as possible until he finally managed to pull into a parking space in front of his building. Blissfully close to the stairs.

The day was just starting to heat up and he groaned as he shut the door of his car, leaning against it for support for a moment. Just a moment, before he could drag himself up to his apartment and collapse again. He hadn't gotten nearly enough sleep the night before.

"Rick?"

The soft feminine voice was tinged with shock. Great. Just what he needed right now. And yet he couldn't stop the stupid grin from spreading across his face as he looked up at his sweet little tease. The woman who'd driven him to this state.

"Good morning, beautiful."

HE LOOKED AWFUL. AND GORGEOUS. AT THE SAME TIME. THAT JUST wasn't fair.

This morning she'd come out to the pool, forcing herself not to look to see if he was there until she'd gotten onto the pool deck. Leaving it up to fate, since she'd come down later than she had been when she'd been getting up to meet him. He hadn't been there. She'd been both disappointed and relieved. She still didn't know what she wanted from him, she just hadn't been able to stay away. Right now she just wanted to talk, see where things led now that she had a better idea of what he expected from a romantic relationship. Maybe test if the knowledge changed the way she interacted with him.

Yesterday had been too soon, but today she'd felt mostly ready. And then he hadn't been there.

Now he was standing in front of her, well leaning really, all scruffy and red-eyed, and still achingly attractive. He looked like he had the hangover from hell, but even that couldn't stop the sex appeal. How did he do that?!

He stumbled forward, and Maria immediately scooted to catch him. Scruffy blond hair covered his jawline, slightly darker on the underside, and he wrapped his arm around her shoulders, pulling her into him.

"Gotcha."

The wicked twinkle in his eye made her scowl. Had he stumbled on purpose? But when he stepped forward again, she could feel he was still unbalanced.

"Are you still drunk?" she asked as she shifted her pool bag to allow her to grab his arm more securely, taking some of his weight. Good grief he was heavy, and it wasn't like she was a dainty girl.

"God, I hope not," he said, ruefully. "If this isn't my hangover, then I don't want to know what is."

Maria couldn't stop herself from giggling a bit as she helped him maneuver toward the stairs. His movements were a bit lurching, and he swayed a bit, but even if she hadn't shown up he would have been able to make it on his own. Still, he didn't relinquish his hold on her. Heck, he practically had her leaning on him a bit. She didn't know if he was just using his situation to touch her, but if he was, she didn't really feel like complaining.

It felt nice to be tucked under his arm, next to all his hard muscle. He smelled faintly of beer, coffee, and pine. Not a terrible combination really. They went up the stairs slowly, while she savored the feel of having him partially wrapped around her. Who knew if this would happen again?

When they got to his door, he fumbled with his keys, using just one hand rather than letting her go. Maria stayed quiet, although a small voice in her head was whispering she should leave now. But she wanted to know what his apartment looked like on the inside. She wanted to know how far into it he would take her. Would he let her all the way back into his bedroom or would she barely make it inside the front door like last time?

Trepidation crept through her—just like she'd wanted to know about Stronghold. Curiosity killed the cat...

Then his door was opening, and they were heading inside.

Definitely bachelor digs. His main room was almost Spartan: couch, easy chair, giant television, and a dinged-up looking coffee table. Although there was a giant bookshelf, overflowing with books along one wall. Not too surprising since he was an English teacher. She only got a glimpse of the kitchen and the small eating area as he pulled her down the hall, enough to see they were clean and mostly bare.

The hallway was narrow, and Rick stumbled into the wall a bit.

"Careful," she said, pulling him back up. He groaned.

"I just want to get in bed."

"I'll bet. Where'd you sleep last night?"

"Jared's couch." He waved his hand expressively. "Too drunk to drive last night."

It was weird to be having such a normal conversation with him, considering how the last time they'd been together had ended. Weird and a relief. Maybe it was better that their first run-in with each other was like this, completely different from the routine they'd established. Made things easier in some ways since neither of them had any expectations of how an interaction like this was supposed to go.

His room was all dark blues and light browns, with beige walls and wooden furniture.

"Nice," she said, looking around as he stumbled towards the bed, nearly taking her down with him. "Whoops! I said be careful."

Rick just gave her a lazy smile as he took the last few steps and threw himself down, stomach first onto the bed. His hand trailed down her arm, until his fingers wrapped around her wrist, keeping her in place. The dark blue of his comforter made his eyes look even bluer in the sunlight trickling in his window. He didn't have curtains, the only thing covering the window were the standard slotted blinds that came with the apartment.

"I am being careful," Rick said, his lazy smile becoming somewhat more wicked as he rolled onto his back, trying to pull her down onto the bed with him.

"Stop that," Maria said, feeling a bit flustered, not to mention more than a little turned on. Definitely not fair, right now. "Are you sure you're not still drunk?"

"If I was, would you get on top of me, little tease?" The sparkle in his eye said he was definitely feeling better now that he was lying down. Maria rolled her eyes, trying to keep an answering smile off her face. Like he needed any encouragement right now. Even if the return to playful flirting between them was making her heart flutter inside of her chest. This was more than flirting, this was playing with fire, now she knew what his kinks were. It didn't feel like he was pushing her, it just felt like his inhibitions were lowered and he was giving her the opportunity to take a step forward with him. Just a baby step.

But once she took that step, would she be able to step back?

"You want to be hungover and crushed? I'm not actually little in case you hadn't noticed," she said, one knee braced against the side of the bed to keep herself anchored, as she tried to tug her wrist free. Granted, she didn't try very hard. She wanted to find out where this was going to go.

Which accounted for her inability to actually resist when his gaze hardened, and she suddenly was yanked forward, pulled over his body so her ass was high in the air.

SMACK!

"OW! What the hell, Rick?"

Sensation and shock thrummed through her. Had he seriously just spanked her?

"You are little compared to me, my little tease," he said, his voice hard and uncompromising. He actually sounded pissed. As if she needed to hear the tone of his voice to know that—her left butt cheek still stung where he'd spanked her. "And you aren't going to crush me. Don't you dare talk about yourself like that."

SMACK!

Heat, sting, and a strange thrill of excitement spurted as his hand came down on the other side of her butt, giving it a throbbing bit of hurt to match its partner. And then she was pulled around so she was lying on top of him, looking down into his eyes. Icy blue eyes glaring fiercely up at her, waiting for her to protest.

Like she was dumb enough to do that.

His hard gaze softened, just slightly, and his hands settled on her back, one of them sliding up to her neck and pulling her down. Barely breathing, totally unable to think much less react, Maria sank against him as their lips met. Gently. So very gently... as if he was afraid she was delicate glass that might break.

No man had ever treated her like that before. Like she was something fragile, something to be cared for and cherished. Pressed against his large, hard body, she suddenly really did feel kind of little. It was a bit unnerving.

The grip on the back of her neck tightened slightly and he opened his lips, his tongue pressing forward into her mouth and Maria shuddered. Scruffy hair rasped against her chin as he kissed her, deeply but tenderly, cradling her against him. With the placement of his hand, holding her head, she couldn't have moved away if she wanted to, and she realized the way he was completely in control—even though she was on top—was making her incredibly wet.

Normally she didn't get down on herself about her body but being on top wasn't her favorite position just because she really did worry the guy beneath her was thinking about how much she weighed on top of him. With Rick, she didn't have the brain space to worry about that, it was all taken up with how hot and hard he was against her, wondering what he was going to do next, wondering if she was crazy, and being amazed at how dainty and feminine he made her feel.

This time when he pulled away, he smacked the side of her butt again, but much more playfully. His light blue eyes were darker, with lust, as he gazed up at her, examining her expression.

Sighing, he released her, and she felt a sharp slice of disappointment at the loss.

"You should go," he said, and she could hear the reluctance in his voice, which made her feel a little better. "I need to sleep, and if you stay here that's not going to happen. I don't know if you're ready for that yet."

Maria bit her lip. She wanted to say she was ready, she really did— heck the smacks he'd given her ass had been exciting, not terrifying or painful... but she couldn't possibly be thinking straight with all these hormones running through her right now.

"Okay... I'll um... I'll see you later." Her voice sounded uncertain, almost as if she was asking a question.

Giving her another lazy smile, Rick lifted his hips just enough she could feel his erection pressing into her. She gasped.

"Definitely."

Pulling herself off him, Maria couldn't help the giddy smile that bloomed when he grabbed her hand and kissed it before releasing it again, his eyes already closing. He was sprawled out across the comforter, erection pressing at the front of his jeans, and obviously horny, but he was letting her go. Telling her to go, in fact.

Strangely, it didn't make her feel rejected at all, it just made her feel like she really could trust him, as if he'd mended a bit of the breach he'd created Saturday night.

And maybe that was the scariest part of all.

## 11

A lone in her own apartment, Maria stripped out of her cover-up and bathing suit, looking at herself in the mirror. Big and curvy. But for just a short period of time this morning, she'd felt petite and dainty. Because Rick had handled her like she was.

And man, had she liked being handled. Her nipples were still hard. Giving them a little pinch, she shivered.

Yeah... after being on top of Rick, after kissing him, she was definitely taking her waterproof vibrator in the shower with her. How could she not? Hell, if she was a dude, she'd have an erection the size of Mount Everest and blue balls to match. Part of her was cursing her cowardliness when it came to what Rick wanted. But it wasn't anything like... well, like anything she'd done before. It wasn't just the concept that scared her, she realized, but she was also scared of disappointing him. Of trying it out and somehow not getting it 'right' for him. Would he lose interest in her? Even if he did, would he ditch her, or would he feel obligated to try and date her anyway? Neither idea seemed very appealing.

None of which managed to cool her libido, because right now all she could think about was what had just happened. Which had been hot, hot, hot.

Opening the door to her bathroom, neon blue vibrator in hand, she paused. It had also been their first kiss. And he'd chosen now to do it? Then again, if his plan was to seduce her into giving his kinks a try, that was not a bad tactic at all. Her defenses had definitely been lowered. She didn't kid herself; if he'd wanted to roll her on her back and fuck her senseless, maybe even do some of the kinky shit—she wouldn't have stopped him.

Regretted it later, maybe, but she wouldn't have stopped him. She had the feeling he knew it too, and that's why he'd stopped himself. Dammit, why did he have to be so perfect? Sometimes she thought it would be easier if she could just dislike him. Then she wouldn't have to deal with all these new and frightening ideas, all these new sensations and desires, but he was so freaking thoughtful and sweet. So freaking gentlemanly.

She turned the water to near scalding, because her skin always felt kind of damp and icky after being in the pool. Washing her body off first, her hands lingering over her breasts and thighs, teasing her nipples with the body wash and slick caresses, not that she really needed any extra stimulation to make herself hornier, but it felt good. Teasing. That was probably how Rick would do it, right?

His friends said he liked to have control over a woman's orgasm. That he liked to tease and withhold. Well, that's basically what she was doing to herself right now. Teasing... playing with herself. Building up the anticipation even more.

Icy blue eyes flashed through her mind as she picked up the vibrator; icy and heated at the same time, challenging and gentle. She moaned as she ran the buzzing toy over her hard nipples, the water from the shower sluicing down her back, over her shoulders, and flowing past her breasts, adding an extra kind of stimulation which wasn't exactly sexual but was definitely pleasurable.

She slid the vibrator down her stomach, teasing herself by making herself wait... not that she really had much self-control, but it helped when she imagined it was Rick. After all, he didn't just go in straight for the kill, did he? Even their flirtations had been like that. Lots of teasing. Lots of hot looks and little touches, and not much else. When he'd pressed her up against the wall, he'd never kissed her. Never given her the satisfaction even though he must have felt her pushing against him, yearning for it.

And the extra waiting had always just made her hotter.

Whimpering as she slid the vibrator around her slick folds, never letting it rest against her clit for more than a second or two, Maria turned so her back was against the wall and water was sluicing down her front. Pounding droplets onto her sensitive skin, and for the first time she wished she had a detachable shower head because she was willing to bet it would feel amazing against her pussy. Amazing, but without giving her enough stimulation to cum too quickly.

Which was how Rick would like it.

But Maria didn't have that kind of patience anymore. Her breath was already coming fast and hard as she used her left hand to splay open her pussy lips and finally drag the vibrator directly across her swollen clit, again... and again... sensation burst inside of her and she moaned, body arching as an incredibly intense orgasm shuddered through her.

"Fuck!"

The vibrations seemed to pierce her, overwhelming her, and she pulled the vibrator away as she panted for breath. Her pussy clenched emptily, hungrily, as the pulses of pleasure continued, even without direct stimulation. Closing her eyes, she clenched her jaw and let her body shudder out the last trickles of pleasure, picturing Rick's gorgeously scruffy face and piercing blue eyes in her mind as she did so.

WORK WAS STUPIDLY BUSY FOR A MONDAY, ONLY BECAUSE TWO OF her servers had called out sick and Maria had made the executive decision not to call anyone else in to cover them. After all, Mondays weren't exactly the busiest day of the week, especially for lunches, and they usually ended up sending at least one person home anyway. Of course, since she didn't have the extra coverage, this Monday had ended up being the exception to the rule. That meant she spent her time on the floor, lending the servers who were there a helping hand, jumping in as a food runner when the expo line became backed up, and clearing off tables alongside the busboys.

As did everyone else. That was one thing about working in a restaurant, everyone had to pitch in to every job when they got slammed, or it wouldn't work. Occasionally a new server to Murphy's would make the mistake of saying "that's not my job." They usually got fired on the spot or at the end of the shift. That kind of attitude wasn't acceptable—for any job, really, as far as Maria was concerned. It always astounded her when some servers thought busing tables was somehow beneath them. If the table wasn't bused, they didn't get a new one, and if they didn't get a new one, they didn't make money. So it wasn't even logical.

Fortunately, no one like that was currently working at Murphy's, so the shift went as smoothly as possible even though there were some stressful moments.

"Bye Maria. Thanks for the help." Juliet, one of their servers, waved at Maria on her way out of the door. She was grinning. Mostly because Juliet liked being super busy. Normally she hated working Monday lunches because they were so slow.

"Bye, see you tomorrow," Maria said, waving back.

By the time Maria finally left, she was relieved. She liked being busy too, rather than being slow and bored, but she didn't thrive on stressful shifts the way Juliet did. Less busy today would have been better.

Checking her phone, she saw she had a missed call and a text from Jackie. Her sister didn't like to leave voicemails.

Call me! =)

Putting the phone back in her purse, Maria got herself home and poured herself a glass of wine before settling in on the couch and took the phone back out again. It was hard to relax when she knew Rick was right downstairs; she had to fight the urge to go knock on his door.

Instead, Maria picked up her phone, pulled up Jackie's number under her contacts and swiped to call.

"Well helloooo darling, you took your time calling me back!"

Maria rolled her eyes. "I was at work, dumbass, what's up?"

"What are you doing this Saturday? Are you working in the evening?"

"Nope, I'm free." Hopefully a statement she wouldn't regret. But she knew it didn't really matter what Jackie wanted, her sister would talk her into it no matter what.

"Good! We need a sister night. It's been too long since we've all gotten together."

"Just sisters at this one?" Maria asked, trying to keep the wistfulness out of her voice. The last time it had been a 'sister' night, all of them had brought their significant others. Which was great for them, and they'd all made sure to include Maria, but it just wasn't the same with the guys there. For one, it was hard to gossip about them when they were present. There was always a difference in dynamic when men and women were in one place together and when it was just women, whether they were sisters or not.

"Just sisters at this one, I promise," Jackie said, cheerfully cajoling. "You know you're going to say yes anyway, so just say yes. You're the only one I haven't talked to. Ava and Lara are both in."

"Well then yes, of course, you nag," Maria said, laughing. She didn't doubt her other sisters were in, when Jackie decided to organize something she could be unstoppable. Maria was the only one who was ever able to reign her in to any degree, usually by pulling the older sister card, and in this case, she didn't really want to. Sure she'd been thinking recently about how nice it would be to have some female friends who weren't her sisters, but that didn't mean she wanted to replace them. She just wanted to have friends outside her family to talk to, like she had with Rick's female friends at Stronghold.

"Good. And we're expecting you to bring the juicy gossip, as the only single one..."

"Oh no," Maria said, groaning as she sank back against the couch. "Please don't tell me you told them about Rick."

Jackie laughed. "Of course I told them about Rick! But don't worry, I didn't mention he might like to do something freaky to you—you know how Ava is. By the way... now that you bring it up," she said in a sly, coaxing tone of voice. "Did you ever find out exactly what kind of freaky thing he wants to do to you?"

"Um..." Maria's mind went blank as she groped for words. To tell the truth? Not to tell the truth? Jackie was pretty open-minded—obviously since her husband apparently had a bit of a foot fetish—but how open-minded was she really? And if Maria was going to lie, what lie to tell? Of course, now that she'd hesitated, she couldn't just say she didn't know. Dammit.

"Oooo!" Jackie obviously smelled dirt from the excited squeal in her voice. She was probably bouncing up and down with excitement. Not just because she wanted Maria to find a man and join the married state of the sisters, but because girl loved gossip. "You did find out! What is it? Is it awful?"

From the enthusiasm in Jackie's voice, it almost sounded like she hoped it was something awful. Maria had to laugh at her sister's silliness.

"I guess it depends on your point of view..." she said slowly, drawing out the moment as she took a sip of wine. Might as well have some fun being dramatic about it. Better than being super serious about it, which might tip her sister off there was more going on than Maria was going to tell her. Not that Maria really knew how to explain everything Rick wanted from a relationship, so she just went for the simple, short explanation. "He's into spanking."

There was a long pause, which made Maria shift nervously. She hadn't realized how much her sister's reaction would mean to her until just this moment. If Jackie was completely against it, would she be able to talk Maria completely out of trying anything with Rick? Even if Maria was starting to think she really might want to try?

"Giving or receiving?"

Suddenly Maria wished she and Jackie were having this conversation in person, even though she was blushing up a storm, because she really couldn't tell what her sister was thinking. There was nothing in Jackie's voice to even give her a little hint.

"Definitely giving."

Another long pause. Maria swirled her wine in her glass. Stretched out her legs and stared at her toes as she flexed them against her coffee table. The pedicure she'd gotten with Jackie last week was still holding strong.

"Wow..." Jackie said finally, her voice almost a whisper. "So he's like, all Fifty Shades of Grey?"

"I have no idea what that means."

"What?! Maria! How have you not heard of Fifty Shades of Grey?"

"I've heard of it. Isn't it a Twilight spin-off?"

Jackie groaned. "You're hopeless. Never mind. Not what I'm interested in. Are you going to do it?"

"I don't know..." Maria hesitated and then decided to give her sister a little bit more of the truth. After all, she really did value Jackie's opinion and she wanted to know if it would change if Jackie knew Maria was considering more than just something casual with someone who wanted to spank her. And more, but she really didn't feel comfortable telling Jackie about the more. "He's not just looking for a good time."

This time the long pause seemed weightier. Maria took another sip of wine and waited.

"So.... you're saying the spanker wants a relationship with you?"

Maria sat up straight. "If you ever meet him, you are not allowed to call him that."

"Of course I wouldn't say it to him."

"Or if he's anywhere nearby," Maria said, going into her 'stern older sister' mode. She could only imagine how Rick and his incredibly intimidating group of dominant buddies would react to the nickname. On the other hand, she was willing to bet Olivia would be amused. So would the other women, but they probably wouldn't be able to show it. From what she'd seen on Saturday, spanking might be the least of their worries.

"Yeah, yeah okay... soooo... if I'm going to be meeting him, does that mean you're actually going to date him? A guy who wants a real relationship?"

From the hope in her sister's voice, Maria had the sudden suspicion Rick could want to do just about anything other than really hurt her and her sister would support him as long as he was looking for a real relationship and not just a casual fling. Great. Not that she thought Jackie was doing it out of pity, like some of her other relatives might, but it meant Jackie's standards for her were apparently lower than her own. Blech.

"I haven't decided yet." And wasn't that the truth.

Jackie sighed. "Alright, well I have to go, Daniel just got home... but Maria, I want you to seriously think about this. Cuz I can tell you like this guy, I could tell you liked him even when you were saying you just wanted something casual, and I don't want his um... interests to put you off. Especially if he's smart enough to want more than just a fling with you. Okay? Like... think about it. Give him a chance."

"Yeah, I'll think about it," Maria said, inwardly sighing as they said goodbye. She could hear the masculine rumble of her brother-in-law's voice in the background, filled with obvious delight at seeing his wife at the end of a long day. Must be nice.

But she hadn't told Jackie everything Rick wanted from a relationship, because she really wasn't sure her sister would understand. And she was a little scared. What if Jackie judged her for wanting to try out the things Rick wanted? Not just the spanking, but literally giving over her sexual control to a man? Letting him decide when and how she orgasmed? Her sister was open-minded, but there were limits.

Especially if Jackie realized how aroused it made Maria. Not something she really wanted to share with any of her sisters. Although she bet the ladies of Stronghold would understand.

MORNINGS JUST WEREN'T THE SAME WITHOUT MARIA. RICK HAD half-heartedly hoped she might show up on Tuesday morning, but she didn't. He wasn't sure whether his hungover performance the day before had helped or hindered him. At least she'd stopped to help him. He'd definitely needed the help, although he'd also used the opportunity to press himself up against all those soft curves... and get her into his apartment, and into his bedroom, and to kiss her. It had been a good excuse, which probably meant he was a bastard, but he didn't care.

She hadn't run screaming. She just didn't seem to have made up her mind yet.

Waiting on tenterhooks was not his style, but he was trying to be good. Trying to wait her out and give her the space and time she needed. It was making him temperamental. He wasn't sure if it was the hangover or his nerves from not knowing what Maria was going to decide that made him so snappy, but Justin and Adam avoided him pretty much all day. Which was fine, he was happy to be left alone with his pounding head and his circular thoughts.

Another man might not be so patient. Another man might decide he wanted a woman who knew she wanted him. But Rick was pretty sure she did, and she was just a bit scared. Hesitant. It was a big step. So he was trying to wait for her to figure out what she wanted. To learn from Liam, who had tried to use scare tactics on Hilary to get her to stay away, just because he'd been attracted to her but didn't think she'd be able to handle what he wanted. Especially since it hadn't worked when he'd tried it on Maria anyway.

It was frustrating as fuck.

Tuesday slid by with no word from her. So did Wednesday. Fortunately, he had distractions in the form of working for Adam, helping Andrew deliver a heavy table he'd custom-made for a client, and, finally, Wednesday evening, by helping out Angel with the women's self-defense class she was teaching at Stronghold. It was the first time any of the guys were going to get even a peek at the classes. Even though Patrick owned the place, Angel had told him that interrupting class—even just to look in—would be disruptive to the sense of security the women would have by it being an all-female class.

So when she'd asked for volunteers among Adam's friends to help with the last day and her equivalent of a final exam, Rick, Patrick, and Andrew had all jumped at the opportunity. Actually, he'd been rather surprised the other guys hadn't. Liam had to teach his own classes in the evenings, and he knew Adam was there working out tonight, but Justin and Chris had actually been asked not to participate by Jessica. She'd told them she'd be more comfortable without them there, which had both of them grumbling but they'd respected her wishes. Rick knew Andrew was looking forward to rubbing it in Chris' face that he was able to be there.

"Oh good, you're here," Angel said, grinning as he came in the door. Patrick and Andrew were already there, putting on some bulky padding with dubious expressions on their faces. He couldn't blame them; the padding was at least three inches thick and made them look like Rock 'em Sock 'em Robots. They looked ridiculous. "Come on over and get padded up."

Angel was adorable in yoga pants and a tank top show-casing her curves, her curls pulled back into a high ponytail that bounced along behind her. When he was a kid, Rick would have wanted to tug on her ponytail. Just for fun. Now he couldn't help but think of Maria's curls and how much longer and thicker they'd be in a similar hairstyle. Easy to wind around his hand.

"I feel like the Stay Puft Marshmallow Man," Patrick said, complaining. Even though the pads were a dark red color, Rick could see what he meant. Patrick was a big guy anyway, with that much padding on he looked like twice his usual size. The helmet part hung loosely from his fingers; obviously he wasn't going to put it on until he absolutely had to.

"Yeah, but just think, we could probably get hit by a car right now and not even feel it," said Andrew cheerfully. He launched himself at Patrick, chest out and arms back, and bounced off with enough force he couldn't regain his footing and ended up rolling onto the ground. Angel and Rick burst out laughing as Patrick loomed over him, trying to cross his arms and failing miserably because of all the padding. Andrew rocked himself, waving his arms and legs in the air. "Help! I'm a turtle and I can't get up!"

"Thank god Chris couldn't be here," Patrick muttered as he reached down and grabbed Andrew's wrist. "All I need is two of you acting like five-year-olds."

"Here," said Angel, still giggling as she helped Rick slide the arm pads up over his bicep. Another one covered his elbow, and then his forearm. He could move, but it wasn't exactly an easy movement. He grinned as Angel helped him with the rest of the pads while he watched Andrew continuing to try and bounce off of Patrick. The larger man just took it with a grim but painfully patient look on his face. Andrew and Chris were good friends because they had a similar sense of humor, but it wasn't often that Andrew was playful like this.

At least, not in years. Which meant Patrick was going to let him get away with it where he definitely wouldn't put up with it from anyone else.

Well, maybe Jared. But if Jared did what Andrew was doing, it would probably be Patrick hitting the ground. He wasn't ever playful like that anyway, thankfully for the sake of all their health.

"Alright children," Angel said, clapping her hands together once she was finished with Rick. She sounded like a school teacher, getting the attention of her students. A nursery school teacher. "Time to stop playing around."

The malevolent look Patrick gave her would have sent some subs—like Jessica or Hilary and probably even Lexie—straight to their knees, but Angel just smiled up at him, ignoring it. Rick wondered how Adam managed her at home. Even though Adam had never wanted a 24/7 total power exchange, he tended to try and dominate and control every aspect of his life. Whereas Angel wasn't exactly easily controlled. Rick had seen her go all soft and subbie at the club, but when they weren't in a scene, she sometimes acted like a Domme. Like right now.

She explained, in more detail, what she wanted of them. They'd already known this was going to be the 'final exam' of the class, and they were going to be playing the role of an attacker so the women could practice what they'd learned over the past weeks. But Angel wanted some very specific things. One woman at a time was going to come in, the others were going to wait out in the lobby, and Angel wanted them to stand in the center of a padded ring she'd set up. The guys were going to circle around the woman, talking in character so she could hear them, but she wasn't to open her eyes or try to get away until one of them grabbed her.

The goal was to get away. Angel had left three 'openings' in the circle she'd made of the pads for the women to 'escape' through. The guys weren't supposed to hinder their escape too much. Obviously the women couldn't actually hurt them with all the padding they had on, so they had to mime their injuries.

It sounded like fun, except for the part where they were supposed to say creepy shit to the subs. Rick wasn't sure how comfortable he was with that. Andrew grinned at the prospect, but then he was a sadist as well as a Dom. Being able to combine scaring some subbies while helping them had to be his idea of a good night. To Rick's surprise, Patrick looked a bit like he anticipated it too.

Then again, Lexie was in the class.

They could hear feminine laughter and chattering coming from the lobby area, and Angel gave them a final grin as she went to get their first victim.

Andrew grinned, stretching out his arms as much as he could even though he was hindered by the padding. "Good thing we've got all these pads on... otherwise we'd have to worry about the Dommes going for our balls."

"I thought Olivia had decided not to take the class," Rick said, looking up in surprise.

"She's not, but Lisa and Erin did," Patrick said, rumbling. He was shifting, almost uncomfortably, as if trying to find one of his usual stances and was unable to because of the bulky pads. Hard to project an aura of dominance when you felt like a marshmallow ready for roasting. Or maybe already roasted, considering the color of the pads.

"Well this might be even more fun than I expected," Andrew said, grinning. Obviously he was looking forward to tweaking the Dommes' tails. It wasn't something anyone would risk on a regular day, but hell, they had permission for it now. Chris was going to be super bummed he'd missed this.

Angel brought in the first woman, a thirty-something sweet little subbie named Laura. She was dressed in workout clothes and had pads on her knees, elbows and wrists, which meant she would still be able to move. Laura looked nervous, but as she got closer and realized who it was underneath all the padding, she giggled. Her high energy didn't dissipate at all, she was practically bouncing on her toes, but she didn't look as scared anymore.

Of course, Angel noticed too. "Now, forget who they are. Remember, you're going to stand in the center, don't move until one of them grabs you, and then do what you need to in order to get away. Okay?"

"Okay," Laura said, looking a bit nervous again after Angel said the grabbing part. Still, she gamely went into the center of the circle and closed her eyes.

There was an awkward pause for a moment as he, Patrick, and Andrew all looked at each other. Angel rolled her eyes and made an urging motion with her hands, and Andrew stepped forward, growling under his breath.

"Hey pretty girl..."

Patrick and Rick both started to circle around her, Patrick breathing heavily on purpose so she could hear him. Probably couldn't think of anything to say.

"Where you going?"

"Whatcha doing?"

Going back and forth, taking turns talking, Rick and Andrew tossed out questions and compliments, making their voices as low and rough as possible. It wasn't really about what they were saying, but about how it sounded, Rick realized. Laura's head was swiveling back and forth, her hands clenching into little fists and then stretching out again. The waiting was getting to her. Angel looked at Rick and stroked her finger gently down her own arm.

Taking the hint, Rick reached out and trailed his finger across Laura's shoulder. She flinched but didn't move from place.

Then Andrew grabbed her arm from the other side. Laura shrieked as her eyes flew open and she whipped her arm out of his grip, faster than Rick would have thought she'd be able to.

"No!" she yelled, as she followed up the spin-out with a punch right to Andrew's chest. He grunted as she took a step back away from him, obviously surprised by both her quickness and her aggressiveness. Not the sweet little subbie they'd seen in the club, not at all. Patrick and Rick both loomed closer, not wanting to overwhelm her completely, but still playing their own roles. She spun around and kicked Patrick in the shin, shouting "No!" again as she did so, and he actually staggered a bit.

Rick found out why when he got a kick to the gut. Apparently, the padding made Laura feel like she didn't need to hold back, she was giving one hundred percent to her blows. It didn't hurt, but it did knock him back, especially because the bulky padding already had him a little bit off balance. Laura sprinted for the opening in the circle of pads, jumping up and down as soon as she was outside to celebrate her escape.

"Great," Angel said, high-fiving her.

Flushed with pride, Laura reached out and grabbed Angel for a hug, who hugged her back just as fiercely. It wasn't until she looked back at the Doms she'd just hit and kicked that Laura lost a little bit of her exuberance.

"Good job," Patrick said, echoing Angel's sentiments, giving Laura an encouraging smile. Andrew and Rick immediately followed his lead and saw the sparkle come back into Laura's eyes and he realized she'd been a bit worried about how the Doms might react. As soon as she got her reassurance, from the owner of Stronghold no less, she was flying higher than ever.

Rick realized that by asking the Doms to be her test dummies, Angel had set up the final exam so the subs would be taking on men they usually craved approval from, so when they got it, their self-confidence would go even higher. Laura was practically glowing as she went out the back where Angel had set up drinks and food for a small post-class party on the patio, while Angel went to get Victim #2.

"Did you hear how loud she shrieked when I grabbed her?" Andrew said, grinning. "This is even more fun than I thought it would be."

Patrick snorted. "If you think that was loud, you've been whipping your subs incorrectly."

"Think you can do better?" Andrew asked, challengingly.

"I know I can."

"Loudest shriek wins?" Rick asked, pretending to stretch out his back nonchalantly even though he couldn't actually stretch anything. It was about the look, not the reality.

"You're on."

They all fist bumped in the center of their little circle, grinning.

"I call next turn," Rick said, just as the door opened behind them.

Turning to see who it was, Patrick just nodded his head.

Unfortunately Rick had inadvertently chosen Erin, one of the Dommes, who didn't shriek at all when he grabbed her. Although she did stomp on his foot and elbow him in what would have been his solar plexus if he hadn't been appropriately covered. He went down with a realistic groan and watched with enjoyment as she literally just pushed past Patrick, ignoring Andrew completely, as she rushed out of the closest opening.

Next up was Jessica, who did shriek and jump when Patrick grabbed her by the waist, hauling her back against him. He got an elbow to the gut for his pains, and then a jab to the head when she spun around to face him. Rick reached out and grabbed her arm, pulling her away from Patrick. It took her a second to break his hold, and by then Andrew was circling around. She broke loose and darted between them, going for the opening.

They didn't have a real problem until Ellie, who panicked and screamed with real fear when Andrew grabbed her by the hips. She burst into tears almost immediately, causing all three Doms to start panicking as well. Andrew and Angel took her off to the side, since they were the ones who knew her best. Rick knew she was a masochist and one of Andrew's favored playmates, because neither of them seemed to be looking for anything beyond a scene. She tended to work with the same Doms over and over again, as long as they didn't get attached. Rick had no idea what had set her off, but he had the sinking feeling that, for Ellie, the class wasn't just about prevention of a possible attack. Of course he knew the number of women who had been through some kind of sexual assault was infuriatingly high, he hadn't actually talked to anyone who had spoken about it from personal experience. Not that they'd told him. Knowing shy, stunning Ellie might be one of them made him want to go punch things.

Angel escorted Ellie out to the patio to calm down with the help of the other students. Rick hoped it would help. Then Angel headed to the lobby again and came back with Lexie. Neither Andrew nor Rick argued when Patrick indicated he wanted to take her first.

Lexie shrieked like a banshee when Patrick lifted her up off the ground from behind. She pounded on his arms and—going by his grunt—would have gotten him a good kick in the nuts if he hadn't been shielded by all the pads. Patrick let her go and Lexie spun around, jumping at him with her shoulder. She got him right in the chest and the big man went down, a look of surprise on his face that turned to shocked fury when she kicked him in the nuts again. That was when Rick decided to back off, stepping back with his hands in the air in a gesture of surrender, but Andrew still made a feint for her. Even though Lexie could have easily gotten out of the circle at that point, she took the time to kick Andrew in the thigh, hard, bouncing on the balls of her feet as she turned to face Rick.

"Lexie, you're supposed to be trying to escape, not take them down," Angel called out, sounding both exasperated and amused.

"You said in class to try and make sure perps couldn't follow," Lexie said as she darted out of the circle. She was grinning and bouncing just like the others had, but she also smirked at Patrick as he got to his feet, looking pretty disgruntled. Andrew and Rick exchanged looks but hid their grins before Patrick could see them.

She'd taken the big guy down hard.

"Good job," Andrew said, when it looked like Patrick wasn't going to be the first to speak.

"Yeah, I didn't even want to go after you," Rick told her, reaching out to tussle her hair, since he was close enough. Lexie made a face at him as she ducked away, trying to get her short locks back in place.

"Thanks guys," she said with another smirk, apparently unconcerned that Patrick hadn't spoken up. Sauntering out onto the patio, she looked immensely pleased with herself.

Angel raised her eyebrow at Patrick as soon as Lexie was outside. "What, no accolades for her? She did very well, even if she did forget her primary goal was to get out of the danger zone."

"She doesn't need any encouragement," Patrick said, but the very edges of his lips were curved up. Just a little.

They got through the rest of the class. Rick managed to make Hilary shriek when he tickled her as he grabbed her by the waist, high and shrill enough that he winced and let go of her immediately. That was the best he managed to do for their little contest, although she'd shrieked at least as loud as Lexie had.

And he learned a few things. Surprisingly, it was the sweetest subs who had the tendency to go for their balls, not something he would have expected. Ellie came back in at the end, grimly determined. Even though he wanted to go easier on her, Angel had warned them not to. They circled around her, whispering, brushing their fingers against her, feeling her tension. This time, Patrick grabbed her with one hand on her shoulder and the other on her waist, and Ellie screamed bloody murder again, but she didn't panic and cry this time. Nope, she managed to break away from all three of them, knocking them aside as she ran out. Fastest time out of the entire class probably. All four of them piled on the praise as she grinned up at them, absolutely buoyant and shining with happiness.

Rick saw Andrew whisper something in her ear before she headed out towards the patio. Probably a promise of a reward during the upcoming weekend.

Before joining her students, Angel helped each of them take off the pads on their hands and forearms. Then she deserted them to help each other get the rest of their gear off. During which time they debated who had won their little bet.

Granted, Ellie had screamed the loudest, but Andrew didn't feel right taking the prize for that. All he would say was she had some "issues" he knew about, although he hadn't realized it would be a problem today, her scream hadn't actually had anything to do with him. Which meant either Hilary or Lexie had been the winning shriek, and even acting as an impartial judge Andrew couldn't decide who had been louder.

Once they'd gotten their pads off, they joined the ladies outside. Grabbing a beer, they stood back along the edges of the patio and just watched the exuberant subs and the two Dommes enjoying themselves.

"I have to admit, I wasn't sure this was really a good idea when I told Angel she could have classes here, but I'm glad I did it," Patrick said, his gaze scanning over all the women. They'd clumped together in three different groups—those who wanted to sit, those who were standing by the bar, and those who were at the food table. "This is good for them."

"Her next session's already full, isn't it?" Andrew asked. Patrick nodded. Giving Rick a glance, Andrew tipped his beer towards him. "Are we going to see your girl in one of these classes anytime soon?"

"She's not my girl," Rick said, casually, even though his gut clenched. He'd like to see Maria here, getting friendly with the other subs. Glowing with confidence and delight. "Not yet anyway. Maybe not ever."

"Don't count her out yet," Patrick said, giving the group of women another casual glance. Rick noticed his friend's eyes were settling on Lexie at least twice as often as he was looking at anyone else. "She was interested Saturday. You fucked up a bit, but if she likes you—and I think she does—she'll get over that. Just give her time."

Angel sidled over to them, and Rick realized she had been just close enough to be in earshot. Granted, he'd thought she was involved in the conversation with Laura, Hilary, and Erin since she'd been standing with them at the food table, but she'd heard enough to be distracted from the female conversation.

"Are you guys talking about Maria?" she asked, popping a cube of cheese in her mouth as she smiled at Rick with interest. "I liked her."

Rick took a sip of beer, trying to shrug off his discomfort. He knew the girls had liked her. That actually made waiting for Maria to decide if she was going to take a chance on him even harder, adding to the internal pressure he already felt. If he decided he didn't like her then he wouldn't care what the group thought, but since he did like her, and he wanted her to like him, he had the uneasy feeling he'd be getting the blame if Maria didn't come around again. Probably because it was at least ninety percent his fault if she didn't.

"Don't get your hopes up that she's coming back to Stronghold," Rick said, half-talking to himself. Plus, maybe saying so would help to lower expectations. Angel pouted. "She hasn't been coming to hang out at the pool with me in the mornings like she used to."

"Have you seen her since Saturday night?" Angel asked thought-fully. "She might just need a little push."

"I saw her Monday." Rick shrugged. Patrick raised an eyebrow at him. The grapevine had probably gotten the news around that he would have been pretty hungover on Monday. Chris had probably told Justin and Jessica, and it would have just gone around from there. Their group really needed to work on personal privacy. Realistically, Rick knew it was never going to happen; it all came from a place of caring and control-freaks. Besides, sometimes the incessant grapevine was a good thing.

"Well?" Angel pushed. "Did she talk to you? Did she avoid you? What happened?"

Frowning down at her, Andrew shook his head. "Adam is way too lenient with you."

"Adam's not here." The saucy tone of her voice was almost insolent. Little brat knew she could get away with more when her Dom wasn't around.

"Are you saying you'd be behaving better if he was?"

Tilting her head, Angel thought the question over for about thirty seconds. "Yup." She grinned and pointed her finger at Rick's chest. "But he's not here to spank or plug me for being nosy, so spill."

Rick spilled. Why not? After all, getting a female's perspective on Saturday had helped him understand a bit better where he'd fucked up. Maybe Angel would have some advice. After all, she'd managed to work through a pretty major misunderstanding with Adam when they'd gotten together, and Adam wasn't exactly known for being the most forgiving person in the world.

Of course, talking about Maria meant Lexie also ended up veering into their orbit, tucking herself up next to Patrick. Not touching, but with barely an inch of space between them. Neither of them looked at each other, but they were so obvious about not looking that it caught everyone's attention.

No one was stupid enough to say anything.

"I think you're doing the right thing," Angel said, when he finished. "She likes you, that's obvious. But you kind of messed up by not talking things through with her before bringing her to Strong-hold." Angel grinned. "If anyone knows it takes a bit of time to work through that kind of miscommunication and breach of trust, it's me. But I think she'll come around."

"Just don't let her wait too long," Lexie said, still studiously not looking at Patrick. "Sometimes you need to step up and go for what you want, because otherwise she might think you don't want it enough."

Andrew coughed to cover a laugh as Rick nodded his head with a sober look on his face. Grinning even wider, Angel nodded her agreement with Lexie. His usual stoic expression on his face, Patrick just took another sip of his beer.

This was one of those times when no one needed the grapevine to know what was going on. It had become increasingly obvious to all of them Lexie had a thing for Patrick, and Patrick was doing his damndest to ignore her blatant attempts to get his attention, continuing to treat her as a little sister. Angel shot Lexie a look of sympathy.

Yeah, the girls were definitely on Lexie's side. This was going to get interesting eventually, especially if the women decided to get involved. Rick had no doubt they would if they thought Patrick was taking too long; that's just how they were.

## 12

"Maria. You've got visitors at the bar."

"Who is it?" Maria asked, looking up from the computer where she was arranging the server schedules for the next couple of weeks. Damien, one of the busboys at the bar, was hanging on the doorframe, grinning. He'd been working at Murphy's long enough to recognize her family when they came in.

"New people. And they're hot." Damien grinned at the surprised look on Maria's face and then scuttled away, heading back into the restaurant.

New people? And hot? Slightly confused, she got up from her desk. Maybe they were asking for the wrong person. If Damien had been one of the girls, or gay, she might have hoped Rick was there, but she couldn't see Damien getting excited over Rick.

As soon as she got out to the bar she looked around, but she didn't recognize anyone right away. It was crowded from Happy Hour, so that didn't necessarily mean anything. Giving a second look around, she caught Damien's eye, and he pointed to two women who were sitting at the bar, their backs mostly towards Maria.

Walking towards them, she caught a glimpse of a profile which looked familiar, but it took her a second to recognize Angel from

Stronghold. She looked different outside of the club, in the light, but Maria recognized the curls, as well as Angel's distinctive features, which were a beautiful mix of Asian and white. She was dressed in jean shorts and a t-shirt and was sitting with a slender woman whose long brown hair with blonde highlights hung down about halfway down her back. Maria couldn't fully see the other woman's face, she didn't recognize her, but going by the way her two male bartenders were drooling —and the pouting one of the cocktail waitresses was doing—the other woman was gorgeous.

Angel turned her head and saw Maria coming towards them, and her smile lit up her face. A sense of relief swept over Maria, almost surprising her; she hadn't realized how much she'd tensed when she saw Angel. A little worry in the back of her mind that Angel had come there to lecture her about Rick was quickly brushed aside in the face of Angel's obvious pleasure at seeing her. The other woman turned, surprising Maria a bit. Going by the way the guys had been salivating, she'd been expecting movie star looks; instead, the woman looked a lot like the quintessential girl next door. A very pretty girl next door, but still. Approachable. Sweet. Apparently completely unaware as to how she was affecting the male population at the bar. Hm. No wonder the guys were tripping over themselves.

"Maria, hi," Angel said, waving her hand for Maria to come join them. "I hope we didn't call you away from anything important. Maria, this is my best friend Leigh. Leigh, this is Maria—Rick's girl."

Maria coughed at Angel's bluntness, as well as the completely innocent look that went along with it. She had a feeling Angel knew very well things still were kind of up in the air with her and Rick.

"Hi Leigh, nice to meet you."

"You too. Don't mind her," Leigh said, jerking her head at Angel and smiling as she shook Maria's hand. She gave Angel a sidelong look. "Miss Nosy over here has boundary line problems. You don't have to talk to us about Rick if you don't want to." Angel made a derisive noise and smiled winningly at Maria. And Maria couldn't help but laugh.

"Actually... I wouldn't mind talking to someone about it," she said a little hesitantly. Angel's smile got even bigger. Glancing over at the bartenders who were obviously listening in to the conversation, Maria gave a little cough. "Um, maybe let's grab a table over there."

Looking over their shoulders at the bartenders, both Angel and Leigh laughed before picking up their drinks. Angel had what looked like a Manhattan, straight up, and Leigh had a Dark and Stormy, one of the house specialties. Also one of Maria's favorites. She loved ginger beer. But she still had work to do, even though she could take a break right now, so no happy hour for her yet.

Sitting down, Maria fiddled nervously with the napkin in front of her as Leigh and Angel sat down across from her. It felt weird to be about to talk about something so intimate, since she barely knew Angel and she had just met Leigh, but she also felt relieved Angel had searched her out. Especially after the other day in Rick's apartment. Since then, she'd felt more conflicted than ever. Worried, mostly, because a large part of her really wanted to date him and try to be with him, but what if they started dating and she realized she hated what he needed? Or what if she just sucked at being submissive or couldn't meet his needs in some way? The idea of disappointing him made her feel shriveled and cold inside.

"So what's on your mind?" Angel asked, smiling as she sipped her drink carefully. Most people felt the need to keep their eye on a martini glass, but Angel handled hers like someone who drank them often and felt completely comfortable with the precarious glass. "I'm hoping Rick, because I know you've been on his."

"Really?" Maria perked up for a moment, and then felt herself slump down again a bit. Okay, yeah, she wanted to be on his mind, but she was also a little bit worried about the hopes he seemed to have for her. He'd made it pretty clear he was looking for a Relationship with a capital R. That was a lot of pressure. In fact, if he wasn't so obviously confident and self-assured, she might have wondered if he was a little desperate. "I mean... yeah... I have been thinking about him."

Angel and Leigh exchanged glances. "Do you mind sharing?" Angel asked, looking a little worried. "I really don't mean to be super nosy, it's just I know he really likes you, and on Saturday it seemed like you like him."

"I do... I just... I'm a bit scared." Maria fiddled with the corner of the napkin some more, worrying it between her fingers.

"Is it the BDSM stuff?" Leigh asked. "Cuz that kind of scares me. The guys are all nice and everything, and this one," she jerked her head at Angel, "was always interested in it, but I find them all to be a little intense."

"Rick's not that intense," Angel argued, sounding like she was trying to defend him.

"Not on the surface, compared to Mr. Control Freak you're practically living with," Leigh argued back. "But from what I've heard at the club, once he gets into a scene, he makes up for being more laid back the rest of the time."

"Laid back?" Maria echoed in surprise. That was so not how she would describe him.

Seeing her expression, Angel giggled. "Well, usually. He's been wound a lot tighter ever since he met you. I've noticed all the Doms get a lot more relaxed once they feel they have a handle on a situation, and right now he definitely does not, so it's no wonder he's more tense than usual. Jared's probably the most relaxed, really."

"He's the one with the evil girlfriend, right?" Leigh asked. She smiled at Maria, to include her in the conversation. "I think he's the only one I haven't met yet."

"Which is too bad, because you two could compare notes," Angel muttered. Leigh elbowed her, making her drink slosh over the side of the martini glass. Catching it with her hand, Angel gave her friend a glare before licking it off of her palm. "Look at all the good booze you almost made me waste."

Ignoring her, Leigh turned her attention back to Maria. "So, is it the BDSM stuff? Or is it Rick?"

"I think it's mostly the BDSM stuff," Maria said softly, keeping an eye out for nosy staff coming close enough to hear their conversation. "I mean... I'd never even heard of it before this weekend. At least, not the way he does it. I've heard of bondage and stuff like that, but just... I don't know... Crap. I'm not explaining this very well."

"Well enough," Angel said with a shrug. "I read a lot of kinky books before I ever actually tried anything out and going into a club was stilly scary for me. Especially since I was doing it alone."

"Even though she told me a lot, I definitely hadn't heard about a lot of the things that go on at Stronghold," Leigh said, nodding her head. "I think a lot of it's pretty frightening. Hilary and Liam are more my speed when it comes to the kinky stuff." She sighed, looking a little bit wistful. "I love watching him watch over her."

"So you and your boyfriend don't do the BDSM thing?" Maria asked, curious. It was kind of nice to get a perspective from another outsider who still knew about the club and its members, and who thought it was both a bit scary and a bit desirable. Obviously Angel, Hilary, and Jessica were going to be encouraging about it, but it sounded like Leigh had a different viewpoint more in line with Maria's.

"No, I met him way before I knew about this stuff," Leigh said, smiling, although there was still a hint of wistfulness in her voice. "We've been together for years now and I don't think it's something he'd go for."

"But you wish he would?"

Leigh hesitated, sliding her finger around the top of her glass and knocking the straw ahead of it, like she was thinking about a way to answer which didn't involve either badmouthing her boyfriend or giving Maria a personal information overload. "I wish he was interested in some parts of it. He's really good at doing the big romantic gestures, but when I hang out with Angel and Adam and the others, I see how much the guys do a lot of little things I wish Michael would do."

"That doesn't really have anything to do with being a Dom, just a good boyfriend," Angel said darkly. Maria was getting a pretty good idea of Angel's feelings about Leigh's boyfriend, which didn't bode well for the relationship. She was definitely getting the vibe Leigh and Angel were very close, maybe as close as Maria was to her own sisters, and she couldn't imagine either herself or her sisters staying with someone whom the family didn't approve of for very long.

"He is a good boyfriend in some ways," Leigh said, defensively. "There's just some things I wish we could change, but that's true of any relationship." It had all the undertones of an old argument. One Maria knew Angel couldn't win. Even if Leigh agreed with her friend, she would feel compelled to defend her boyfriend, especially if they'd been together for years. Not that any of Maria's sisters had been with boyfriends for years when the family didn't like them, but they'd all had boyfriends who had lasted close to or a bit over a year that they had stayed with for too long.

Just like she often had with her sisters, Maria decided it was probably prudent to interrupt them. "I just wish there was a way to... I don't know, try out BDSM to see if I even like it? I mean, I'm attracted to Rick and he turns me on, and I'd be willing to see if what he likes turns me on too, but it doesn't seem like that's an option with him. He's very much into having a relationship."

"And you aren't?" Angel's attention was fixed back firmly on Maria, as was Leigh's although Leigh still seemed a bit unfocused by her own thoughts.

"If I wasn't so worried about the sex stuff I would be." Maria sighed. "I feel like we've gotten to know each other pretty well, even though we haven't exactly been dating. But we'd been hanging out on a daily basis before this past weekend. The sex stuff just threw me for a loop, but it's important if we're gonna be more than friends. I just feel like I only have two choices with him—friendship or relationship. And it seems like a lot of pressure. Not to mention, what if we try and I hate it or suck at it and then everything's just ruined?" Realizing her voice was getting a little bit loud, Maria coughed and looked back down at the stupid napkin she was now tearing into teeny tiny pieces. She was making a mess, but she didn't particularly care right now.

"You need an Introductory Scene."

"What?" Maria blinked. "What's that?"

Angel groaned. "Seriously? He didn't tell you about Introductory Scenes? We didn't mention it?"

"I'm not sure," Maria said, blushing a bit. Had he? Had the other women? "If anyone did I don't remember..."

"Oh well, you've had a lot of information thrown at you recently," Angel said sympathetically. "Introductory Scenes are for newbies to the club, submissives and dominants but it mostly seems like it's the submissives who take advantage of it. Kind of a way to find out what you like or don't like, if you're inexperienced or unsure." She grinned. "It sounds like exactly what you should do. I know Rick used to do them, so he knows how to."

Maria made a face at being reminded Rick had probably had sexual contact with quite a few of the women at Stronghold. Still definitely not something she was a fan of... although she just kept reminding herself that obviously none of those women had stuck. Rick blatantly wanted a relationship, and he'd brought her into the club to do it rather than choosing one of them. She hoped the girls had been right about the other women not being man-stealers, because if Maria caught one of them going for Rick while she was there, the end result was not going to be pretty. It might be hot when Rick got all alpha and controlling, but Maria was not a pushover and she wasn't just going to sit on the sidelines while someone made a move on her man.

Pushing past her own issues, she had to admit she liked the idea of doing what sounded like a try-out scene. Try it out, see if she liked it.

And also see if Rick liked her within it.

"I think..." she said slowly, aware Angel and Leigh were both watching her with hopeful anticipation. She smiled. "I think it sounds brilliant."

TWO JACKS AND THREE EIGHTS. A FULL HOUSE. RICK KEPT HIS FACE carefully blank as he threw down another chip, knowing Adam and Olivia would both be studying him closely. Playing poker with such highly observant people made for some brutal games.

But it was nice to sit and hang out with friends. Especially since he still hadn't heard from Maria. The distraction was very welcome. He'd been helping out in Adam's office today when Adam had asked him and Justin if they wanted to get together since Angel was going to happy hour with Leigh. Justin had preferred to go home to Chris and Jessica, but Rick had jumped at the chance. They'd ended up getting Olivia to join them as well.

Taking a sip of his beer, Rick looked up to watch as Olivia contemplated her hand.

"Fold," she said finally, putting the cards face down.

Adam studied her, as if wondering if she'd seen something he hadn't. They'd been at this for a couple of hours now and Olivia was the closest to going out. None of them had told her that whenever she had a good hand, her right eyebrow would go up. That was half the fun, discovering out each other's tells and then trying to erase their own. Rick had figured out a while ago that he had a tendency to bounce his leg when he was unsure about his hand. Now he threw in a bounce every now and then just to throw the others off.

"Call," Adam said finally, tossing in his chip.

Grinning, Rick laid out his cards and Adam cursed. The other man was only holding two pair.

"Close but not close enough," Rick said, chortling as he scooped up the chips. It was a fairly decent haul, but the real pleasure was in the win. They never bet a lot of money, but the competition was always fierce.

The doorbell rang unexpectedly, just as Rick was finishing up organizing his chips. He looked at his friends. "Did you guys know if anyone else was coming?"

Olivia shook her head at the same time Adam said, "No."

Faint hope it might be Maria, finally, sprung up in Rick's chest, but he did his best to ignore it, knowing it was a much better chance he'd be disappointed. When he looked through the peephole, it was all he could do to contain his emotions. If Adam and Olivia hadn't been there, he probably would have done some kind of stupid looking jump or motion, just to vent some of the excess energy suddenly running through his veins.

Instead, he just opened the door, putting a hopeful smile on his face. Even though he was pretty sure the nervously determined expression on Maria's face came from a tense submissive, about to admit her desires, and not from a woman who was about to turn him down, he didn't want to get his hopes up only to have them flung back in his face. There was a chance she was nervous about telling him no, but the tight feeling in his gut came from some kind of primitive male instinct that made him want to beat his chest in victory. Witnesses notwithstanding.

"Hey," he said, letting his pleasure at seeing her fill his expression.

To his delight, she smiled back, still nervously. If she was coming to reject him, she wouldn't be smiling, he was sure of that. His grin widened.

"Hey... Um..."

"Is that Maria?" Olivia called out. Rick turned to glare over his shoulder. From where Olivia was sitting she could clearly see it was Maria.

"Oh... you have company... maybe I should—"

"No," Rick cut her off, reaching out to grip her upper arm as she started to pull back. Fuck no. She was finally here, and he wasn't going to chance her going away and changing her mind. Or even just making him wait longer to know for sure what she was going to say. "It's just Adam and Olivia. Want to come in? We're playing poker."

Maria fidgeted, still obviously a bit nervous, although she waved at Olivia. Adam had turned around in his chair, Rick saw, but from the other side of the doorway Maria couldn't see him. "No, I've got some stuff I have to do. I just came by to um... well..."

"Say yes to going on a date with me?" Rick asked, keeping his tone playfully hopeful. Trying to help her out and hoping the answer was yes.

"Well, sort of." She gave herself a little shake, as if gathering her courage. "I wanted to ask you if we could do an Introductory Scene. Um... at Stronghold."

Whatever he had been expecting from her, it definitely hadn't been that. His first instinct was to say no, but he clamped his jaw down against the word, because he couldn't think of an immediate reason as to why not. Also, because she looked so hopeful, while simultaneously anxious for even asking.

"Why?" he asked, realizing his tone had changed substantially. Tighter. Definitely not happy. Immediately she reacted, her shoulders coming forward as she clasped her elbows. A protective gesture that made him inwardly curse. He hadn't meant to sound upset, but for some reason he kind of was. It felt almost like a delaying tactic, another way to make him wait while she tried to figure out what she wanted. Even though he recognized insecurity on his part as being kind of illogical, because she didn't really know what she wanted, he couldn't stop the emotion.

"I'm just... I've never done anything like this before. And I don't know if I'll like it. Or be good at it." The real worry he saw her in eyes was that of a submissive afraid of disappointing her Dom and it definitely made the hard tension in his lungs soften. "So when Angel suggested—"

"Angel suggested?"

"When did you see Angel?"

Rick's and Adam's questions overlapped in exactly the same slightly suspicious and demanding tones. Meddling female. After all her questions at Stronghold about Maria he should have realized she wouldn't leave the situation alone. He ignored Olivia's giggle.

Wide eyed, Maria glanced over Rick's shoulder, where he was sure Adam was now in her line of view.

"She came in to happy hour tonight with her friend Leigh," Maria replied hesitantly, obviously unsure of whether or not she was getting Angel into trouble.

Behind him, Rick could hear Adam mutter something while Olivia laughed. Probably something about how he ought to beat his sub's ass for interfering. A sentiment which Rick would echo.

The idea of doing an Introductory Scene with Maria was just... scary. He'd done them before, with other subs, but never with one who meant anything to him. It felt like a test. Which made him feel both prickly and a tiny bit fearful. Prickly because he didn't like the idea she was just playing with him, trying him out, and simultaneously afraid that at the end of it, she would realize she didn't want him or what he had to offer. Even worse, he knew her interest in BDSM had already been piqued, so what if she rejected him but went looking for someone else at Stronghold? Then he'd not only have to live in the same building as her, but he'd be running into her at the club.

Did he really have a choice? It was a reasonable request, especially for a complete newbie.

It wasn't until Adam spoke up behind him that Rick realized how long he'd been making Maria wait for an answer.

"If Rick doesn't want to do it, I'm sure Patrick could suggest someone who would be more than willing."

Rick snarled in response. Fuck. He was already so in over his head. He already considered Maria his girl, even if she wasn't his sub yet.

"That won't be necessary," he said tightly, ignoring Olivia's answering giggle and Adam's chuckle. Maria looked up at him, worriedly, and he softened his expression. "I'll talk to Patrick and set it up. Will next Thursday work for you?"

Hope, fear, and desire all flashed across Maria's face and she nodded. Stepping out into the hall, Rick pulled the door behind him so it was only open a crack.

Letting go of the doorknob, Rick took Maria's face in his hands, tilting her head back so he could look directly into her dark eyes. Her pupils dilated as her lips parted automatically for him, and he felt his cock begin to harden in response.

"I want you to do some research online. I'll have Patrick send you the questionnaire all the newbie subs who are doing the Introductory Scene get. I want you to really think about what you want and need." Something inside his stomach twisted at the thought that her desires might not align closely enough with his. Compromise was possible on a lot of things, but not everything. At least he'd be able to look over the survey and see if there was anywhere they were glaringly incompatible. "Okay?"

"Okay," she whispered, her tongue flicking out along her bottom lip. He could tell she wanted him to kiss her, but he held himself back.

Just in case.

He was already in too deep, emotionally, but he didn't have to go deeper until he knew he wasn't the only one.

"Good girl," he said, watching the arousal and desire flare in her eyes at the words. Then he released her. Without the kiss they were both aching for. "Have a good night."

Confused and off-balance—which made him feel more satisfied and centered—Maria nodded her head. "You too."

He watched her head up the stairs before he turned and went back into his apartment. Both of his friends were sitting there, waiting for him, not even looking at the cards and chips on the table.

"Soooo...." Olivia prompted. "Why didn't you want to do an Introductory Scene with Maria?"

"It's not that I don't want to," Rick hedged, sitting down across from them and trying not to feel like he'd just set himself up for an interrogation as Adam and Olivia exchanged glances. Unfortunately his poker face didn't feel like it was working. "I love the idea of getting her into Stronghold again. I just don't like feeling like I'm being tested."

"Ah," said Adam, thoughtfully. "I think I can understand that. The Introductory Scenes are supposed to be for introducing newbies to the scene, but with Maria it's also going to be specifically giving her a scene catered to your tastes and her reactions are going to be more than just indicative about whether or not she'll be into BDSM, but whether or not you two might work as a couple."

Trust Adam to be able to immediately put Rick's conflicted emotions and subconscious thoughts and worries into coherent statements. Then again, Adam probably kind of understood the feeling a bit too, since he'd been interested in Angel when he'd ended up doing her Introductory Scene. It wasn't quite the same but close enough Adam could definitely feel some empathy.

Olivia looked surprisingly thoughtful, as if that was an angle she hadn't considered before, one which held merit. Which meant she probably wasn't going to give him too hard a time anymore, which Rick could be grateful for.

"That's exactly it," he said with relief. "I feel like I'm putting myself out there. All the things I want and need, and she's either going to reject me or accept me... and that really sucks." Especially because, as a Dom, he was a bit of a control freak. Even more so when it came to sex than some of his other friends. He loved it when a woman gave up control to him; but even if Maria submitted to him at Stronghold, it would be like being on probation. Not a happy feeling for anyone, much less someone with his inclinations.

"She's doing the same thing though," Olivia said. "Maybe not as blatantly, because you know what you want and need from the scene and she doesn't yet, but just by showing up here and telling you that she wants to try, she's putting herself out there. For her, it's all one big unknown."

"Plus, she's definitely worried about disappointing you," Adam said, backing Olivia up. "Don't discount that. Angel will get bratty with me if I'm ticked at her about something, but if she thinks she's disappointing me she'll run in circles trying to find a way to either fix it or make it up to me."

"Right before bursting into tears if she thinks she's failed," Olivia murmured so softly Rick barely heard her. Adam shot her an exasperated look. He must have been getting relationship advice from the outspoken Domme. Coughing, Rick hid his grin. It was nice to know he wasn't the only one dealing with issues out of his depth. He could only imagine how panicked Adam would be over Angel crying. Talk about feeling out of control. Part of him wanted to ask what had happened, but going by the closed expression on Adam's face, he doubted the man would answer. He knew the two were having some issues because Adam wanted her to move in and Angel wasn't ready to take that step yet. Another situation where Adam felt out of control, but he was working through it and doing whatever he needed to keep Angel happy.

The little trickles of doubt and insecurity were still inside of Rick, but he definitely felt much better already. After all, Maria was being brave just by wanting to try something she had little knowledge and no experience with, especially when he'd mishandled her first introduction to the scene so badly. No wonder she wanted to try it before she committed to it, and he needed to remember this was completely new to her and she wasn't auditioning him. At least, he hoped she wasn't.

She was showing a great deal of trust in him, trust that he'd worried he'd completely broken. So he was going to man up and trust she wasn't going to reject him outright, and she wanted to try an Introductory Scene because she really wanted him and not just the kink she now knew existed.

## 13

Rick was coming up on the pool's wall when he saw two legs dangling down in front of him. Reaching out to grasp the ankle, he really hoped it was Maria's leg, as he used his other hand to tickle the sole. Rising up from the water, even with it filling his ears, he could hear her shriek and giggling.

Grinning, he raised his eyebrow at her. "Don't you know to keep your feet out of the lap lanes?

An expression which looked a lot like relief was on her face as she smiled back at him. Going by her body language, he could see she felt a little awkward, her muscles were tensed as if she was ready to flee in case he wasn't happy to see her. But he'd responded playfully, and she was taking her lead from him.

"What are you going to do, spank me?" She was half-defiant, half-anxious, and Rick couldn't help but laugh, seeing right through her brave front. Maria was probably going to be a bit of a bratty sub. Right now she was acting out a bit because she didn't know exactly how to handle herself. On the other hand, she was completely honest with her emotions, and she wasn't going to avoid talking about the elephant in the room. Nope, it was going to come spilling out of her mouth and make her blush a bright red that matched her bathing suit. Rick eyed her bathing suit and the snug fit it had on her curves, wondering if one day he might be able to fulfill his reoccurring fantasy of sliding his fingers under the fabric and making her so wet she'd have to get in the pool or give away her state.

Gripping her ankle tighter, he tickled her foot again as she shrieked, water splashing him in the face when she kicked out with her other foot.

"It seems to me maybe you want the spanking," Rick said, teasingly. Keeping it light. Non-threatening. He had the feeling she was probably going to try and top from the bottom at first—she was too assertive and too untrained not to—and he was going to very gently show her it wasn't going to happen. Sassiness was all well and good, he liked that, but he wasn't going to allow her to take control of any scene between them. Just by basically daring him to spank her, she'd initiated a kind of scene and he was going to respond appropriately. "Tickling is probably a better punishment."

Maria gasped, trying to yank her ankle out of his hand. Even with the water making her soft skin slick, he had too tight a grip for that to work. Instead she just went slightly off balance, her breasts wobbling in an incredibly enticing way. "Tickling isn't a punishment."

The screech of the lifeguard's whistle from across the pool got both of their attention. The teen in the chair pointed at Rick and then jerked her thumb at the main part of the pool. He got the message—if you're not swimming laps, get out of the lap lane. Grinning, happy Maria was there, he decided he didn't need to finish his workout. Giving her foot one last tickle, he laughed at her outraged shriek as he finally released her ankle and ducked under the rope to head to the main pool.

When he resurfaced, he saw Maria already sliding into the water, giving him a moment to reorganize his thoughts.

They'd been pretty flirtatious before he'd taken her to Stronghold, afterwards he hadn't been sure whether or not she'd show up again here. Now that she was here, he still didn't know whether or not she'd want to be with him after her Introductory Scene. He needed to revise how he was going to deal with her until after the scene. Not that he was going to stop flirting with her, but definitely nothing more than that.

Last night it had been instinct not to kiss her, to hold back, to take control of the situation. Denying her had, in some ways, been almost petty, but it had also been self-protective and had given him back the steering wheel in the situation. Something which, at that point, he'd needed. Right now he needed to stay in control and not let things go beyond where they already had, not until after next Thursday.

It soothed him to see she was back to being nervous as she approached him. Rick smiled and started chatting with her, not reaching out to touch her, but keeping things friendly and just a bit flirty. Slowly, Maria relaxed as she told him about her week at work, including Leigh and Angel's visit. When he told her about assisting Angel for her class' final exam, she laughed so hard she actually went underwater for a few seconds. Especially when he told her about Lexie's turn and the way she'd managed to get Patrick in the nuts, twice.

By the time Rick had to leave to get ready to head over to Andrew's, whom he was helping today, he was feeling a million times better. He and Maria weren't quite back to where they had been before, but that was okay. The biggest change was that the sexual tension between them was even higher than before. As well as their anxiety about the Introductory Scene. When he told her that he'd scheduled the scene and gotten the okay from Patrick, she'd brightened and then immediately looked anxious again.

He didn't try to soothe her too much. A bit of anxiety, and even fear, was good for a scene.

"Don't forget to do your research," he said, tapping her on the nose with his finger before he left. The temptation to kiss her was incredible, especially because the bikini she wore made him want to put his hands all over her and he could tell she wanted him to when she tilted her head up at him, but he held onto his self-control.

Maria narrowed her eyes at him. "Yes, Professor."

Rick raised his eyebrow, letting his voice deepen to a more powerful and threatening tone. "I'll tell Patrick to make sure he reserves the school room for us."

Chuckling at Maria's dropped jaw, Rick considered that a fitting exit line.

PUSHING AWAY FROM HER COMPUTER DESK, MARIA DECIDED SHE needed a break.

Friday night... less than a week until her Introductory Scene. Excitement and tension fluttered in her belly in equal measure, the same way they always did every time she thought about Rick and Stronghold. It was still hard for her to reconcile the man she flirted with and chatted with in the mornings with the stuff she was reading online.

Granted, she knew he wasn't going to be interested in everything she was finding online, but still, she didn't know everything about him. And she didn't think his female friends possibly could either. Even if Jessica had slept with him at that school.

*I really need to stop dwelling on that.*

Going through her fridge, Maria pulled out the bottle of sparkling red she had put in there to chill the night before. She wasn't really a white wine drinker, so over the summer she tended to drink a lot of rosè and sparkling reds instead of the heavier cabernets she preferred in the winter.

It felt like her head was swimming with information. Spankings. Whips. Golden showers. Pony girls. Chastity belts. Cuffs and chains. The differences between a submissive, a slave, a baby girl, etc.

She had to admit, the baby girl thing sounded kind of fun... Maybe just because she was the oldest of a large group of girls and had often felt a bit like a mother-figure in some ways, but the idea of being a brat and getting to just relax and play for a bit sounded great. But it definitely wasn't something she'd want to do a lot, or even for very long. Some of the other parts of it didn't sound so great though... she wouldn't want to pretend to be anything younger than an eight-year-old. And again, not for very long. Maybe it was just a repressed desire for a coloring book that she didn't have to share.

The chastity belt... was that something Rick would be interested in? One of the girls had said he was into orgasm control and that kind of seemed like the same thing. Taking a sip of wine, letting the bubbles pop and fizz on her tongue, she rolled the liquid around her mouth as she thought. The fantasy of it actually made her a little hot, the idea he'd want her goodies locked up and he'd have the only key, so she couldn't even play with herself without his say-so... It made her feel like a bit of a freak that it turned her on, but it really did.

Of course, then she started thinking about the actual logistics of such a thing. Things like, how would she go to the bathroom? And how comfortable were they actually? The ones she saw online did not look comfortable. Yes, she had looked them up. They didn't look anything like what she'd expected—she'd been picturing something along the lines of Maid Marion's belt in Robin Hood: Men in Tights. The ones online had looked more practical, but still not comfortable.

"Oh my God... what am I even thinking?!"

Her voice echoed in the room.

Was she considering compromising what she wanted just because she really liked Rick? That didn't seem like her. But then again, she really liked Rick. And she was wondering why she'd never explored these kinds of things before, worrying the only reason they were turning her on was because she was picturing Rick doing them to her. That it had more to do with him and her wanting him than it did with her wanting the kinks.

She was so worried about disappointing him, about not being what he wanted and needed... was she somehow forcing herself to be aroused by these things?

Or was it just that she'd never known anyone who was into this stuff and so she'd never had the opportunity to even think about it? After all, none of her sisters were. Jackie had been married for years and Maria had just found out Daniel had a bit of a thing for her sister's feet. The whole not having a lot of close friends outside of her sisters, at any point in her life, was probably working against her. She'd drifted away from all of her female friends eventually, so maybe she'd just never been close enough to any of them to even know if they'd tried out bondage or role play or spanking.

So, was it that she was actually really kinky and just hadn't known it, or did it have everything to do with Rick?

"Sleeping Beauty!"

"No, Little Mermaid!"

"We can watch both," Maria shouted over both of her sisters while Ava cackled maniacally in the background. Good grief, it was just like when they were all kids. Jackie and Lara, the youngest, going at it while Maria had to play the arbitrator and Ava gleefully spectated. Although, Maria had to admit, she'd thought they'd long since moved past arguments about what Disney movie to put on. Talk about regression.

At least they were arguing over stupid stuff now, instead of grilling Maria about Rick. She'd told them as much as she could, about meeting him at the pool and hanging out with him in the mornings. Jackie had been winking at her throughout, since Lara and Ava were totally pro-Rick, but didn't know what Jackie knew. And Jackie didn't even know the whole of it. Finally, she got them off her back by telling them she had a date with him on Thursday. Which was kind of what the Introductory Scene was, right?

Initially she'd been relieved when they'd started trying to decide what movie to watch.

"Fine," said Lara, glaring at Jackie. "But—"

"Little Mermaid first!" Jackie yelled over top of Lara.

Lara beaned a pillow right at Jackie's face and Maria reached out and expertly snagged it out of its trajectory.

"Rock, paper, scissors."

"What?!" Jackie looked outraged. "It's my house. I should get to choose which movie we watch first."

"Rock, paper, scissors," Maria repeated firmly, trying to hide her smile.

Man, she loved her sisters. Even if they were being idiots. She could tell they were enjoying dragging out this particular scene from their childhood.

"Oh whatever, just give the little brat what she wants," Jackie said, slumping dramatically back onto the couch. Maria was impressed she managed a slump that could actually be considered dramatic. Unfortunately for Jackie, Lara wasn't as impressed; squealing with delight at her win, Lara popped up to grab the DVD off the shelf and put it in the DVD player.

"You two are going to be a terrible example when you finally have kids," Ava said, grinning as she shook her head.

If Maria hadn't been looking right at Jackie, she wouldn't have noticed her sister's sudden stillness and blank expression.

"Oh my God!" Maria snatched up the glass Jackie had been drinking and sniffed it. Not a single fume of alcohol wafted from what Jackie had claimed was a cranberry vodka. Jackie turned beet red. "You're pregnant!"

Lara squealed even louder than she had before, throwing the DVD up in the air just as all the sisters launched themselves at the couch Jackie was on. It was a squirming, writhing pile of sister hugging and shrieking with excitement while Jackie laughed and tried to push them off of her.

"You're smothering me."

Still giggling, they all pulled back enough to let Jackie breathe, Ava and Maria on either side of her, with Lara kneeling and resting her arms on Jackie's knees, as they peppered her with questions.

"When did you know?"

"How far along are you?"

"Was it an accident?"

"How do you feel?"

"Who else knows?"

"One at a time," Jackie laughed, waving her hands at them, but her eyes sparkled with happiness. "I'm only a month along, which is why I hadn't told any of you yet, thanks Maria." Maria just grinned and shrugged. "No, we weren't trying, but we aren't upset, we're ecstatic."

Her hand resting on her belly, Jackie was absolutely glowing. All of them were. After all, this was going to be the first kid in the family. God... their mom was going to explode with excitement. No wonder

Jackie hadn't told any of them yet, she and David had probably wanted to just enjoy the news for themselves.

"Now... I'll tell Mom and Dad tomorrow, but no telling anyone else," Jackie said, pointing her finger at each sister in turn and reiterating Maria's own thoughts. "Except your husbands," she said, adding the modification for Ava and Lara. "We're not announcing til the third month. Although, I guess I can tell Daniel he should tell his sister and parents now, too."

Baby talk eventually devolved into wedding talk for Lara, all of which Maria was both a part of and completely separate from. The strangest mix of delight, awe, and a little bit of melancholy filled her. Spending time with her sisters was wonderful. Finding out she was going to be an aunt was even more so. So why the melancholy?

Maybe it was just that her sisters all seemed so much farther ahead in their lives than she was, especially now with Jackie pregnant. They'd spent a lot of time talking about Lara's wedding and even more time talking about Jackie's pregnancy. In the back of her head, as content as Maria was with her life, she'd always kind of figured she'd at least be engaged, if not married, by the time any of her sisters started having babies. It wasn't a competition, but it just bought up the question, why wasn't she further ahead in her life?

Not to mention, it also made her worry even more about her reactions to Rick and her upcoming introduction to kink. Would she be able to separate her multitude of desires? Her desire for him, her desire for what her sisters had, and her already confused sexual desires? It just suddenly felt like there was a lot hinging on Thursday evening.

Fortunately, none of her sisters noticed anything strange about her behavior. They finally settled down enough to watch The Little Mermaid—although they spent half the time talking over the movie. When they weren't singing along.

In between movies, Maria went into Jackie's kitchen to reload the snacks and get another drink. After a minute, Jackie followed her in, leaving Ava and Lara chattering away about wedding stuff again in the other room.

"Hey. So... I want an update," Jackie said, poking Maria's side and nearly making her drop the bag of chips she was holding.

"An update?" Maria asked, momentarily confused.

"Yeah." Jackie hopped up onto the counter, watching Maria refill the tray of goodies. "An update on this date. So, you're gonna give the spanking thing a try?"

"I don't know," Maria said, averting her eyes as she felt a hot blush spreading up into her cheeks. She felt like a bad older sister, like she was setting a bad example, even though she knew it was kind of stupid. It was just habit to try and do everything correctly, to not let her sisters know when she was doing something that... well, wasn't on the straight and narrow. Which was why she still wasn't going to tell Jackie she was going to a kinky sex club as her 'date.' "It's just a date to... you know, see if we're compatible."

Except she had a feeling she probably was going to be getting spanked. It seemed very likely. But she didn't know for sure, so she wasn't lying exactly.

"Well, I'm glad you're not just giving up on him," Jackie said, snagging a grape from the tray and popping into her mouth. "Every relationship has things you have to compromise on, and a little spanking shouldn't be a deal breaker. Who knows, it might even be exciting." Now it was Maria's turn to give Jackie a suspicious look. Her younger sister grinned. "I'm not saying I've tried it. It's just I would have never thought I'd find it sexy to do anything with my feet... but Daniel's reactions make it sexy for me."

"I just wonder if I'm going to have to compromise too much," Maria said, hedging her answer a little bit. "You know? Like, what if I'm just doing it because I like Rick?"

"What's wrong with that?" Jackie asked. "As long as he's not asking you to do something you actively dislike. Maybe you'll try it and you'll hate it, and he'll have to decide if he likes you enough to go without. Or maybe you'll try it and not hate it, but not love it, and just tolerate it for his sake. Like I tolerate Daniel's yearly depression over the Redskins." She rolled her eyes. "I wish he would just cheer for the Ravens, he'd be a much happier man."

Maria laughed. "I'm not sure if we can compare being a Redskins fan to getting a spanking."

"But you see my point."

"Yeah..." Maria picked up the tray, fully loaded with food again. "I'll think about it."

And she would. Her sister had made some good points, which applied to everything Rick wanted, not just spanking. Not that she really thought she was going to hate anything he did to her, at least she hoped not, but she had worried about things she didn't love. On the other hand, she could put up with one or two kinks that maybe she didn't love but didn't hate either. There were some she definitely wouldn't do. Those were called "hard limits," as she'd discovered during her research.

Ugh. She wished it was just Thursday already so she could stop worrying over it in her head.

## 𝔰𝔩 14 𝔰𝔢

It felt like nervous energy was fizzing through Rick's veins in place of blood as he knocked on Maria's door.

They'd fallen back into their habit of spending time together at the pool in the morning, to the point where Adam never expected to see him before ten on the days when Rick came in to help out, but things had changed a bit. Both of them were flirtatious, but more cautious about pushing the line, knowing they were waiting for the evening at Stronghold. Now that the day was finally here, Rick felt a jumpy tension in the pit of his stomach that had made getting through the day almost unbearable. Especially after Patrick had sent him her survey. For the most part it looked like she was willing to try a lot of things, although he wasn't sure how much was because she wanted to make sure she didn't automatically dismiss something he might want to do, and her hard limits were definitely along the same line as his. Just thinking about all the things she was apparently willing to let him try with her had left him distracted and horny.

He took a lengthy and goal-oriented shower, and even though he didn't have a hard-on anymore, his leathers felt tighter than usual, and not just because his cock was looking forward to finally getting a chance at Maria.

Really, he didn't know yet how far she was going to be willing to go today, but he was allowed his fantasies. Even if, logically, he knew it was a better idea to hold off on any real intimacies until she was sure of what she wanted. Hope welled and stuck inside his chest. After all, the fact that she was willing to return to Stronghold for an Introduction Scene at all, everyone seemed to think it meant something significant.

When Maria opened the door, Rick's cock made the front of his leathers even tighter. She looked stunning in a dark red tank top which looked like it was barely holding in her breasts, clinging to every inch of her curves, and a short black skirt that made her legs look miles long. It was a loose skirt, rather than a tight one, but he wasn't going to complain, although eventually he'd like to see her in some tight-fitting PVC or latex. Her curls had been put back into a loose pony tail keeping it off her shoulders and back but gave him fantasies about winding the heavy mass around his hand and using it to guide her movements.

The way her head was slightly ducked, her shoulders slightly hunched, and the little glances she was giving him through her eyelashes made her the very picture of an uncertain, anxiously nervous little subbie.

"Hi," she said in a breathy voice.

Rather than responding immediately, Rick took the time to make a lengthy and obvious perusal of her body, very similar to what he'd done the first time they'd gone to Stronghold. But this time, he was looking at her with much more intent. Tonight he was finally going to get his hands on her, maybe even put them all over her. She squirmed uncomfortably at his close scrutiny, but underneath her tank top her nipples were already hardening. The air between them seemed tight with tension. He could see her throat muscles work as she swallowed, obviously wanting to say something, but finding herself waiting for him instead. When he met her eyes again, they were wide and she was no longer just peeking at him, but actively waiting for what was going to happen next with bated breath.

"Hello gorgeous," he finally said in a low voice. Leaning forward, he brushed his lips over hers, teasing her with the lightest of kisses. She tried to follow him back up as he straightened, but he reached out with one hand, placing it on her hip and keeping her in place. "Ready to go?"

For a moment he thought she was going to change her mind as something like fear flitted through her eyes, but then her expression firmed, and she nodded her head. Pulling on her hip, Rick turned, sliding his hand along her back and tucking her under his arm as they headed down the stairs.

"So uh... how was your day?" Maria asked after a minute. Rick laughed. She was so nervous and cute, trying to sound normal, like nothing out of the ordinary was happening.

"Not too bad. I spent most of it helping out Justin," he said, feeling her slowly relaxing under his arm as he told her about Justin's current social media issues. Currently Justin was working with Adam's employees and his temps on how to keep their social media private. It was mind-boggling how many people didn't even bother to look up things like privacy settings, allowing the entire world to see what party they went to the weekend before. Not exactly something most people wanted a future employer to come across.

They chatted the entire way to Stronghold, which relaxed Maria at first, although he could sense her becoming more and more anxious again as they got closer to the club. By the time they arrived, she was practically vibrating in her seat. While Rick thought a bit of nervous energy was a good thing for a submissive, and perfectly normal in a new one, he didn't want her to be too scared.

As she reached for the handle to open her door, Rick grabbed her other hand. "Maria." With a blink of surprise, she let go of the door handle and turned her head to face him. "We aren't going to do anything tonight you don't want. You understand that right?"

"Um... I think so?"

Rick smiled, squeezing her hand. "Really. All you have to do is say 'red' and everything stops. I want us to talk more once we get inside, before we do anything. Patrick sent me your survey this morning and I've looked it over, but I think we'll both feel better if we talk things through before your scene."

"And if I say yellow?"

He smiled again. Someone had been doing her research.

"Then we slow things down and talk about them before I continue. I might occasionally make you uncomfortable and I might mix a little pain with pleasure, but I will never hurt you and I will always honor your safe word. Do you trust me?"

There was only the slightest hesitation before Maria nodded her head. All things considered, Rick decided it was only understandable she would be a bit hesitant. What was important was that she was still willing to try.

"Okay sweetheart. Let's go in."

Tension wrapped around her body again, but this time it had more excitement in it than fear, which was what Rick wanted to see. A little bit of fear was good, but excitement warring with fear was better.

Surprisingly, no one was standing at the entrance to the main room, but Lexie was at the front desk, looking kind of pissed about something, but when she saw Rick and Maria her entire demeanor perked up. She grinned at them, straightening in her chair. Tonight she was wearing a bright pink bra underneath an electric blue mesh shirt. Compared to some of the things she'd been wearing for a while, Rick was always grateful to see she was wearing underwear underneath her tops. At first that had freaked him and the other guys out, now it was a relief that she was mostly decently covered.

As if she could read his thoughts, Lexie narrowed her eyes at him a bit, but the smile she gave Maria was genuinely welcome.

"Hello again. I'm so glad you came back," Lexie said as they came to the front desk to sign in.

"Hi um... glad to be here."

Lexie laughed. "That sounded very convincing. I won't hold you up here, although I may hunt you down later. Have a good evening."

Just as they reached the door, it opened and Mistress Lisa stepped through. The Dommes only occasionally acted as the door guard, usually they preferred Dungeon Monitor duty when they were helping Patrick out. She looked startled for a moment, obviously not expecting anyone to have been standing outside, and then grinned.

"Hello Rick." Holding the door open, she made an elaborate sweeping gesture for them to pass her by as she winked at Maria. "Have a good evening."

Inwardly groaning, Rick wished the club wasn't such a hotbed of gossip sometimes. Did everyone know he was bringing Maria here tonight? Probably.

"Thank you," Maria said, sweetly, still obviously nervous. Taking her by the hand, Rick pulled her past Lisa, giving the grinning Domme a short nod. Getting a clear view of the bar, he groaned out loud this time. He could sense Maria peeking around him to see what he was looking at. "What? Oh..."

Angel and Adam were there, along with Olivia, Liam and Hilary, and Andrew. Of course, Andrew was working bar, but he was still obviously watching for Rick and Maria's entrance. As if on cue, they all waved. Rick growled under his breath.

He glanced down at Maria, who was now standing at his side rather than behind him, her fingers wrapped rather tightly around his. "Do you want to go say hi?"

"Yeah," she said, relief flitting across her face. He tried not to feel hurt by her desire to delay their scene even further. Maybe talking to the others would help calm her. After all, it was partially Angel's doing that Maria was even here tonight.

His friends didn't even bother to pretend like they were there to do anything but gawk. All of them were looking at him and Maria, and grinning, as they approached. Hilary and Liam were sitting beside each other, Liam's hand under the table, probably on Hilary's thigh. She waved at Maria. The bright pink PVC corset she was wearing was definitely one of Angel's creations; she, Jessica, and Lexie had all started buying a lot of their club clothing from Angel. Angel herself was wearing a more daring outfit that looked a little bit like a leather bikini on top and a school girl uniform on the bottom. Surprisingly, she was seated beside Adam, rather than being wedged between his legs or on his lap. Andrew was leaning against the bar, on the wrong side of it for working, but since no one was sitting at the bar it didn't really matter.

Angel greeted Maria with a hug, Hilary automatically following her example, and Rick knew he'd made the right decision as Maria's smile became a little brighter and a little more natural. He did raise his eyebrow at Adam though.

The big blond shrugged. "What? You should be grateful it's just us." His smile took on a more wicked turn. "Justin, Chris, and Jessica were planning on coming too, but they ah... got held up."

"Where's Patrick?" That was the only surprise, that the owner wasn't out here to personally watch over and ensure Rick didn't fuck up the way he had last time.

Andrew leaned in and lowered his voice to a stage whisper that was clearly audible. "We think Lexie did something to him, but no one knows what."

Beside him, Olivia snickered while Angel got a smug expression on her face and Hilary giggled. The Doms all raised their eyebrows, which of course Olivia could ignore. Avoiding Liam's gaze, Hilary looked at Angel, whose expression was so innocent it screamed treachery. Adam sighed.

"What did you do?"

"Me?" The outrage in Angel's reaction as she placed a delicate hand on ample cleavage, deliberately drawing attention to her in-drawn breath, was so overdone it was obvious she knew she was caught and didn't care. Because normally, she was a much better actress. "Why would you think that?"

Crossing his arms over his chest, Adam glared down at his sub. "You know I don't like being lied to."

"Lying? Who's lying?" Angel turned to Hilary, practically bouncing with supposed indignation. "Am I lying? Have you heard one single lie drop from my mouth? All I did was ask a question. You can't lie by asking a question, right Rick?" Angel spun around to point at him. "You're the English teacher. Lying by asking a question is impossible, isn't it?"

"Does she have a snooze button?" Rick asked Adam, feeling the side of his mouth quirk up into a reluctant smile. Even though it was obvious Angel had either done or knew something, and he shouldn't encourage her, he couldn't help but find her entertaining.

"Nope, he's looked," Angel said brightly, cutting Adam off before he could even respond. The blond frowned down even more fiercely at her, which she ignored. Man, she was just asking for it, wasn't she? "Besides, you don't need a snooze button, you just need to tell Mr. Grouchy here that he's wrong and—EEP!"

Her short shriek was cut off as her stomach bounced against Adam's shoulder.

"Put me down you Neanderthal!"

"I thought I was a Viking," Adam said, looking decidedly more cheerful as he swung around and started to maneuver between the tables. "And you, you little brat, are asking to get this fine ass beat." Angel shrieked again as Adam smacked her upturned ass hard with his free hand.

Beside him, Rick could feel Maria shift, and he pulled her closer, putting his arm around her so he could whisper in her ear. "Don't interfere... remember, all she has to do is say her safe word and Adam would stop immediately. Besides, Angel likes getting spanked."

Just as he said that, Angel used one hand to push herself away from Adam's back and her other hand to give his ass a hefty smack. Adam froze mid-step. His back was to them, so Rick couldn't see his expression, but he bet it was priceless. Angel laughed smugly.

"Ha! So you can dish it out but you can't take it, huh?"

"Little terror. Are you feeling neglected sweetheart?" Adam asked, his voice syrupy with false sympathy as he strode away, heading towards the Dungeon. His tone deepened, becoming more darkly threatening. "All you needed to do was tell me you needed a good spanking, I would have been more than happy to oblige."

Rick saw Angel look up at Maria and send her a wink and he suddenly wondered if Adam and Angel had engineered the entire little scene to help set Maria at ease. In some ways, Adam had gone remarkably easy on his disrespectful little sub. He bet she wasn't supposed to spank him though; she was going to pay for that.

Seeing Angel wink had definitely made Maria relax even more, underscoring Rick's reassurance that Angel wasn't in any kind of real trouble. Although, Angel might not entirely agree with the assessment by the time Adam was done with her. He didn't know what the troublesome sub had been thinking. She'd definitely pushed Adam more than he'd ever seen Adam put up with from any other woman. Then again, Rick had never seen Adam in love before either.

Hilary was beside herself with giggles, even as Liam shook his head. "You'd better not be getting any ideas, love."

"If you want to spank his ass, I'll protect you," Andrew told her. Liam just laughed.

"Like you could take me."

"I think that's our cue," Rick whispered in Maria's ear, taking advantage of his friends' macho posturing to pull her away. She went somewhat reluctantly, obviously just as amused as Hilary was, watching as Andrew insisted he could totally take Liam because he'd fight dirty and Liam had too much pride to stoop to his level.

HANGING OUT WITH RICK'S FRIENDS WAS SO EASY AND FUN, BUT SHE didn't protest when Rick led her away. Dragging out the inevitable was just making her more and more nervous, even though at first it had been nice to stop by and say hello to them. Watching the interaction between Angel and Adam had been both revealing and amusing. Like the beginning of a little play, at the end of which was hot sexy time. It just so happened that hot sexy time was going to include a spanking. So maybe more like a porno than a play, except she'd never really been interested in watching porn.

She gave Rick a little glance through her eyelashes as he led her up the stairs. The leather pants and tight black shirt he was wearing made him look mouthwateringly good, his skin and hair appearing even more brightly golden against the dark clothes.

Part of her was relieved they weren't heading for the Dungeon, another part of her was a little disappointed because she would have liked to see what happened between Angel and Adam. The next part in the play (or porno) so to speak. Did that make her perverted? Or just curious?

Moving with firm, sure steps, Rick led her straight down the hall to the last door on the left. As soon as they stepped in, Maria's cheeks flamed brightly as she remembered Rick had teasingly said he thought she'd like the school room. Apparently he hadn't been teasing. Heat and hard muscle pressed into her from behind and Maria realized she'd come a halt. Blushing even hotter, she jumped forward and away from him as if scalded, increasingly unnerved by the situation.

Unnerved and excited. As she spun around to face him, Rick closed the door behind him, and her pussy actually clenched at the sound. They were all alone. And he was going to... what? Spank her? Fuck her? She didn't know if she was ready for any of that, but this was what she wanted.

Those icy colored eyes studied her, making her even more nervous as she shifted her weight back and forth. She wanted to keep still, but with all the adrenaline and nervous energy running through her body it was impossible. She had a suspicion that, not only was he drawing this moment out on purpose, but that he liked how anxious she was.

As if to corroborate her suspicions, Rick smiled slightly. "Why don't you go ahead and have a seat, Maria, and we'll talk."

"Yeah, okay."

Turning back around, Maria realized there were only two places for her to sit. Either at one of the student desks or at the teacher's. And she was pretty sure which one Rick meant for her. For just a moment she considered trying to sit at the teacher's, but she had a feeling it would probably be justifiable cause for spanking. Maybe she shouldn't start this off by antagonizing him.

So she went and sat dutifully at one of the student desks. Thankfully it was more comfortable than it looked, built for an adult and not a teenager, so she didn't feel oversized in it the way she often had in high school. No need to feel like she was wedged into a small space. One of the other desks looked like it was more the standard size, but that's why she hadn't sat in it. It would work well for someone who was petite and slim, and she appreciated Stronghold had multiple sizes for different body types.

Rather than sitting at the teacher's desk, Rick leaned against the front of it, which meant there was a lot less space between them than there would have been otherwise. If it wasn't for the leather pants, he would have looked like the epitome of a relaxed, sexy teacher. Man... if his students could see him now... She didn't doubt Rick was probably the fantasy of many a teenage girl; if they saw him like this their heads would probably explode.

"So let's talk about your survey."

Damn. She'd thought she couldn't blush any more than she already had been. Seriously, it felt like the heat had spread from her face down to her neck and chest. Was it possible to have a full body blush?

"I thought the point of the survey was to answer all your questions before I even got here," Maria said a little lamely. For some reason, now that they were sitting here and about to actually talk, having an actual conversation about her answers just seemed incredibly embarrassing. She'd kind of liked the idea of Rick just knowing everything about her and her burgeoning fantasies without her actually having to say them out loud.

The twinkle in his blue eyes said he was enjoying her discomfiture. "Communication is one of the most important aspects of BDSM, and one which I've been particularly bad with when it comes to you. I told you we'd talk things through before we start. Besides, I think you'll be more comfortable if we go over some guidelines for the scene."

Guidelines. Talking things through. Communication. Okay, she could handle that. Maria nodded, relaxing a bit.

"We definitely have a lot of the same hard limits," Rick said, casually crossing his arms over his chest. Which just made his biceps stand out more. Yum. He was way more relaxed than she was. "But you left a lot of options open to explore, and I have to admit, not all of them are my cup of tea but if there's anything you're particularly interested in trying, then it's my job to make sure you get to." He raised his eyebrow at her.

"I just didn't want to say no to everything," Maria muttered, twining her fingers together as she glanced away from him.

"Do you even know what caning is?"

"I looked it up." Now she really couldn't look at him. She'd had to look up an awful lot of stuff and at a certain point she'd figured, what did it really matter what implement he hit her butt with? And what if there was a certain implement he really liked? "I just didn't want to say no to something you liked and I haven't tried before."

Now Rick moved away from the desk, stepping forward and putting his hand under her chin to force her to look at him. Maria bit her lip as his blue eyes seemed to bore into her, like icicles. After a long moment they softened slightly.

"I have no interest in caning you, sweetheart, and I don't think you'd care for it if I did. But I appreciate your bravery in wanting to please me."

The compliment warmed her even as she opened her mouth to protest she wasn't trying to please him. She shut it before she could get the words out. Because, after all, that's what she had been doing, and even though some part of her brain insisted she was giving him all the power by admitting to it, he hadn't said it like it was a bad thing. Or like it was something he expected of her. No, he'd said it like it was something to be cherished, like it was an honor she'd given him.

"Good girl," Rick said, rubbing his thumb over her lower lip. It parted immediately from the upper as she drew in a quick breath, wondering if he was going to kiss her. Instead he pulled away, resuming his position leaning against the desk in front of her, and she scowled. The amused look he gave her only made her scowl deepen. "You also indicated on the survey you're willing to engage in sexual intercourse during a scene."

"Isn't that what this is about?" she asked, a bit hesitantly.

"Not necessarily. There are plenty of scenes which don't involve any sexual contact at all. Usually Introductory Scenes don't have a lot of actual physical intimate contact."

"Oh." She couldn't decide what she was feeling. Disappointment? Relief? Both? There was only a brief flash of rejection and worry that he'd decided he was no longer interested in her before she banished the thought as both stupid and illogical. Emotions were allowed to be illogical, but that didn't mean she had to give into them when they didn't make any sense at all.

So, did that mean he wasn't going to touch her at all?

After a long moment of silence, she realized Rick was watching her reactions very closely. Staring at her face in fact. And she wondered how much of her thoughts he'd been able to see. She scowled up at him again, getting a flash of white teeth in response.

"No, we're not going to have sex tonight," Rick said. "But definitely not because I don't want to. I do. But this isn't the right time or place, and definitely not the right circumstances." Right, because it's not like they were an actual couple or anything. Maria blew out a breath. Maybe she should be glad he was being so controlled and authoritarian about this. After all, how much would it suck to have sex with him and then discover she wasn't able to give him what he needed? Much better to stick with fooling around and then deciding where to go from there.

Still, the fact that he was so controlled while she was feeling so very vulnerable and out of control was starting to irk her. After all, she'd been ready to jump into bed with him tonight. Hell, she'd been trying to get him to jump into bed with her for weeks now, and here he was, finally giving in, but not really.

And he called her a tease. He was a bigger tease than she'd ever been.

Maria tilted her chin up. "So what are we going to do?"

She could hear how bratty and demanding she sounded, but she only regretted it for a second. It kind of felt like Rick was still withholding information from her. After all, he'd said they were going to talk, but so far it seemed like all they were talking about were the things he wasn't going to do to her.

He raised his eyebrow at her again for her tone. "That's what I wanted to ask you. Are you comfortable with me using my hands and or mouth on you, or would you prefer to stick to just toys?"

Yikes, talk about a loaded question. Maria desperately wanted his hands and mouth on her, she could use toys on herself any old time. On the other hand, would she actually sound desperate if she said so? Would he be insulted if she said hands but not mouth? If she was trying to protect her heart, not knowing whether or not he'd even want her at the end of tonight, what was the smartest decision?

"Didn't the survey cover this?" she complained, feeling kind sullen. Crossing her arms over her own chest, she glared at him. After all, she'd said in the survey she was willing to have sex... it had been easier to just click an option on the computer than it was to actually give him the go-ahead in person. It didn't seem fair that she was the only one who had to open up and make herself vulnerable like this. He hadn't said a word about whether or not he wanted to put his hands and mouth on her. Just that they weren't going to have sex tonight.

She wondered what the right time, place, and circumstances would be to him.

The whole situation was making her more and more uncomfortable. She'd thought by now he would have touched her, that they'd at least be making out or doing something kinky. That was the point of her filling out a survey and then coming here tonight. Instead he was probing her wants without giving away any of his own. When they'd first gotten here, and he'd said they'd talk things through before the scene, she'd found that reassuring. Now she wished he would shut up and get started. If he'd just started kissing her, overwhelming her, the way he had the few times they had kissed, it would have been so easy to become putty in his hands and just let him do what he wanted, try what he wanted.

This wasn't easy at all and it was aggravating her. And apparently amusing him. Which only aggravated her more.

"I told you I wanted to go over guidelines for tonight, because the survey didn't cover what your preferences for tonight would be," Rick said. His tone was just a bit patronizing and he was still standing so casually, so under control, that it made Maria want to do something to shake him up.

Time to change tactics. Getting annoyed and snappy wasn't getting her what she wanted, which was for him to jump her. And she knew he wanted her. He wanted her to talk? Fine, she'd talk. On her terms. Screw the stammering, blushing, vulnerable thing.

Maria leaned back against the desk's chair, letting her lower body slide forward and her knees fall apart. The look of surprise on Rick's face was incredibly vindicating, and it helped motivate the sultry smile that she gave him and to dissipate some of her frustration with him.

"I don't mind toys," she said, letting her voice become a bit husky as she spread her legs even further apart. Chances were, he couldn't see anything of her lap under the desk, but that wasn't the point. He'd be able to imagine it; and he'd know that if he had the correct angle, he'd be able to see whether or not she was wearing panties.

Which she wasn't.

Rick's jaw clenched, and his eyes flashed, his gaze becoming harder, hotter as he stared down at her. The amusement she'd seen earlier had been wiped clean away by his surprise and now it was being replaced with lust.

Bringing her finger up to her cleavage, she traced the line of skin. "I don't mind if you use your hands and mouth here..." She ran her finger down over her breast, circling her nipple which was already hardening. The way he was looking at her was making her feel hot and horny all over. The air in the room seemed to thicken, the entire dynamic had changed between them.

All because she'd stopped pussy-footing around. Good. Being unsure wasn't like her and she hadn't enjoyed it, or the way he'd been drawing things out. Now, going by the growing bulge at the front of his pants, both of them were on a more equal playing field.

"Or down here..."

Letting her finger trail down below the desk, below his eye level, Maria didn't even manage to touch herself before Rick growled, "Stop."

She froze, waiting. There had been something extra in his order, something that demanded she listen. With any other man, she would have just laughed and done what she wanted, but the little bit of extra strength in his command had made her want to obey him. Which her brain told her was silly, but there was no denying her body found it hot. Her pussy had clenched immediately, getting even wetter.

"Stand up."

Maria obeyed, feeling even more vulnerable now that she didn't have the desk between her and Rick. Although he was still leaning against the teacher's desk, there was a vibrating tension in his body that made her think of a predator about to pounce. That casual pose was no longer so convincing, not when his jaw was locked and his muscles were hard with tension. She pressed her thighs together, feeling how soaked her pussy was between them.

Standing was scary, but this was definitely more of what she wanted.

Uncoiling from his leaning posture, Rick stepped sideways and gestured at the desk.

"Bend over this, little tease." His voice was hard and uncompromising, laced through with desire. Maria was moving before she stopped to think, blindly obeying. Which, when she reached the desk and started to bend over, was more than a little startling.

She shot an uncertain glance at Rick.

The look she got back was unyielding. "Bend over, Maria. I want your forearms down on the desk and your sweet ass in the air..." His voice softened just a touch. "And don't forget, you can say 'red' at any time and this stops."

Right. Or yellow to slow things down and talk about them. But she really didn't want to slow down, because if she did, she might never get the courage to start again.

Taking a deep breath, she turned her head away and leaned over the desk, very aware of the way the back of her skirt was lifting to expose her pussy. Spreading her legs to help her maintain her balance only made the entire area feel more exposed. She wasn't sure how much of her bare ass and pussy Rick could see, but she knew he was getting at least a little bit of a show.

"Good girl," he murmured, and a wash of warmth went through her.

Braced on her forearms, she peeked over her shoulder to see his eyes were locked onto the lower part of her body, and she couldn't help but wiggle her ass at him a bit. For a brief moment she enjoyed his quick intake of breath, and then she squealed as he smacked her ass. Her skirt fluttered as her head snapped back around.

It stung where his hand had landed, but not too badly. Then he placed his hand directly over the spot he'd just smacked her, rubbing the sting away and replacing it with a strange warmth that made her pussy throb even harder. Maria moaned a little with approval.

Of course, that didn't last too long.

"Little tease."

He smacked the other side of her ass and then rubbed the sting away again, making her wag her bottom up and down a bit. The rubbing felt incredibly good, and while she wasn't sure she liked the stinging part, she could definitely put up with it for the aftermath. Maria's head hung down as she waited for whatever was going to happen next, practically panting with the arousal coursing through her.

This was way hotter than she'd even imagined.

# 15

Flipping up the short little skirt Maria was wearing, Rick had to bite back his own groan as the gorgeous curve of her ass was finally fully revealed to him. The tiny garment had been driving him crazy—in a good way—as it fluttered teasingly over her buttocks when he'd spanked her the first two times. His little tease wasn't wearing any underwear. He didn't know why he was surprised, her self-confidence was definitely part of what appealed to him, but he hadn't really expected for her to be so comfortable at Stronghold that she'd come without panties. Most of the submissives had to be told not to wear underwear. Hell, he'd heard Hilary get into an argument with Liam about it before.

But here was Maria, completely bare beneath, without a stitch of clothes on her gorgeous ass, and so ready and wet for him to touch. His cock was practically straining the seams of his pants, he was so hard.

The glistening lips of her pussy were swollen, and he could already see her clit peeking out from its hood. He knew she was anxious, as well as sexually excited, and the combination would only heighten the sensations she was experiencing.

"Do you know what topping from the bottom is, Maria?"

"No," she said in a breathy voice. He needed to talk to Patrick about getting some kind of mirror or something set up in here. As much as he was enjoying the view from this angle, he also wished he could see her face.

"It's what you were just trying to do," Rick said silkily. "You were trying to manipulate me into giving you what you wanted, instead of following where I lead."

"No, I..." Her protest trailed off and he felt a surge of both pride and arousal as she came to her own conclusion. "Oh, I think I see."

Even though she didn't apologize, she sounded contrite. Although, to be honest, this time he didn't need an apology, because he was sure she hadn't realized what she was doing. Still, he did need to lay down the law and this was as good a time as ever to introduce her to funishment.

"Which is why I'm going to spank you now."

"Oh! But..." Her voice trailed off again as she looked over him with those wide brown eyes. Rick could practically see the thoughts going through her head. After all, she'd agreed to this. He had already started spanking her—and going by her reaction there was no doubt in his mind that she'd liked it more than she'd thought she would. Granted, he was going pretty easy on her, but the way her bottom had wiggled had looked an awful lot like her body begging for more.

He gave her a little, reassuring smile, running his hand over the smooth curve of her ass at the same time. It teased both of them, as well as giving her physical reassurance that she hadn't actually done anything really wrong.

"I'm going to spank this sweet ass until it's nice and pink, so you'll know for next time what happens when you try to force my hand." He said it firmly, giving her ass cheek a squeeze where he'd already slapped her before, and watched as her pupils dilated even more. Yeah, his little tease liked being bossed around, she liked being told exactly what he was going to do to her, and she liked being spanked.

All of which was enough to make Rick wish he was the kind of guy to lose control, so he could just say the hell with it and bury his cock inside of her wet heat.

Instead, he raised his hand. "Face front, Maria."

As much as he wanted to see her expression, her neck would be more comfortable with her facing away from him. Besides, the anticipation of not knowing where or when the next blow was going to land would make her even more amped up.

Admiring the creamy expanse he had to work with, as the previous slaps had barely pinked her cheeks, Rick brought his hand down right in the center of her right buttock. Her breathy gasp was music to his ears and food for his desire. All that ample flesh jiggled in the most enticing way possible as the pink handprint on her skin bloomed and immediately began to fade.

SMACK!

This time he caught the center of her left cheek, watching the same reaction with pleasure.

SMACK! SMACK! SMACK!

Working his way up to the top of her buttocks and then right back down again, Rick measured out his strokes carefully and methodically. First came the gentler but firm slaps heating her skin and allowed her to get used to the sensation, eventually growing in strength as her bottom was 'warmed' and she was able to take more and more. In fact, crave more and more. Maria's head was hanging down, her breathy moans and squeals coming in rhythm with his smacks, every line of her body screaming her submission to the spanking.

The heady sensation of being completely in control over her, of knowing she'd given herself over to his care, to his discipline, made Rick's head whirl, even as he continued to pinken her ass. The cheeks of her butt were much lighter in color than the rest of her, having been covered by her bikini bottoms all summer, and they were easily turning a bright pink. Between her legs, the dark brownish-pink of her pussy lips were shiny with her honey; her pussy was practically dripping with need.

When he rubbed his hands over her warm ass, Maria moaned and arched almost like a cat, lifting her bottom into the air. He knew that after the spanking it would feel good, but he still reveled in her uninhibited reactions.

"Good girl," he said, squeezing the soft flesh of her ass slightly and enjoying the shudder that rippled through her body in response. Taking her by the waist, he pulled her up to face him.

Her dark eyes were hazed with passion, her pupils fully dilated, and her cheeks were nearly as pink as he'd turned her ass. Pressing his hands against her back, he held her flush against him, watching as her tongue flicked nervously against her parted lips as she tilted her head slightly back to look up at him. He didn't think he'd ever get tired of feeling all those soft curves against his body, pressing against his cock. Reaching down, he cupped her ass, grinding himself against her and enjoying the sensual expressions that crossed her face as her fingers clutched at his shirt and she moaned for him again.

When she opened her mouth, he leaned down and captured her moan with his lips, thrusting his tongue between them, the way he wanted to thrust his cock into her pussy. Massaging her tenderized ass cheeks with his hands, he kissed her deeply, bending her back so she had no choice but to hold onto his shoulders or risk losing her balance. He swallowed her little mewling cries of pained pleasure, as she rubbed herself against him and he squeezed her spanked ass, knowing she'd probably never felt anything quite like that heady mix before.

The way she pressed herself against him with abandon, not even paying attention to her balance, just trusting him to catch her, said a lot about her state of mind. It was heaven to Rick, holding her propped against him, knowing that without his support she would fall, and knowing she knew he'd never let that happen. Devouring her mouth, he could feel all the blood in his body pumping through his cock, pounding in his ears... it was the ultimate rush for a man like him.

When he finally pulled himself away, Maria whimpered, her lips swollen from passion, and tried to follow. Smoothing a hand down her back, Rick pushed her back down onto the balls of her feet and off of her tiptoes.

"Feeling hot for teacher yet, little tease?" he asked, his lips spreading out in a smile. To be truthful, he'd never really had the teacher fantasy. Maybe because it was his job and the idea of going there with an actual student made him feel a little sick, but with

Maria, here in the fantasy classroom setting, he was definitely starting to see the appeal.

Maria's hands fisted in his shirt as she glared up at him, trembling in his arms with how much he'd roused her body to passion. "You are such a giant hypocrite."

"And you have obviously not learned your lesson," Rick said, although his grin widened even further. It wasn't a happy grin, it was more like the gleeful grin of a predator whose prey just walked within reach. The hitch in Maria's breath and the sudden worry that flashed across her face indicated she saw the difference.

Stepping back enough that she would be able to balance on her own once he released her, Rick slid his hands up her back and to the straps of her tank top. Maria stilled as he pulled the straps off of her shoulders and down her arms. Looking directly into her eyes, he captured her gaze, watching as the pace of her breathing picked up as he tugged her tank top down.

The top had a built-in bra, which barely contained the bounty of her breasts. He stopped pulling when he reached that part, although he tugged the straps off of her arms, leaving her midsection clothed but her breasts completely bared. As much as he wanted to strip her down completely naked for him, he could sense her unease. Which was kind of funny, considering this was the woman who had worn nothing but a trench coat to his door and then flashed him. Then again, they were out in what she knew was a public space now, where the Dungeon Monitors would occasionally check in on a scene. And she was new to this.

So he left her clothed up top, except for her breasts—it wasn't going to make a difference anyway, as long as he had access to all the parts of her that he wanted.

"Beautiful," he murmured, cupping her breasts in his hands, although he continued to watch her face carefully, to make sure he wasn't pushing her too far, too fast.

Maria just shivered and closed her eyes, wetting her lips with her tongue again, as her back arched lightly, pushing her breasts further into his hands. That was all the invitation Rick needed. Shifting so she could lean against the teacher's desk behind her, resting her hands on the edge and thrusting her breasts upwards toward him, Rick squeezed and kneaded the heavy globes as he lowered his mouth to one perfect, budded brown nipple. She moaned as he sucked the little bud into his mouth, biting it gently with his teeth.

Pinching the other nipple and rolling it between his fingers, his cock seemed to pulse as Maria squirmed and moaned. Her bottom probably wasn't entirely comfortable, pressed against the hardwood of the desk after the spanking he'd given her, even if the spanking hadn't been particularly hard. Biting down, he tugged the sensitive nubbin and she shuddered as she moaned even louder.

Yeah, even if she hadn't known it, his little minx definitely liked a bit of pain with her pleasure. Her hips were moving, searching for some kind of pressure, but she couldn't bring her legs together and she couldn't reach him, because of her position against the desk. Trapped between nothing and a hard place... delightful.

This time when he released her, he didn't step back far enough for her to stand straight. Instead, he bent just enough to get his arm under her legs and use it to swing her up onto the desk completely. Maria fell back onto her elbows, her breasts jiggling, her skirt sliding up to expose her thighs and pussy. Both of her nipples were fully erect, one shiny from the ministrations of his mouth, the other dark and full from his pinching fingers.

"Lie down," he said, almost gently as he walked around to the other side of the desk where the drawers were.

Every piece of furniture in Stronghold was set up to easily restrain a submissive, and the teacher's desk was no exception; each of the four legs on the desk was equipped with restraints. Even though Rick hadn't used the desk before, it took no time at all for him to get Maria situated exactly how he wanted her.

Arms above her head, spread apart, and cuffed to the corners of the desk, her legs spread even wider, knees pointed to the ceiling. He cuffed her ankles to the desk and her thighs to her calves, forcing her to keep her legs in position and spread wide. The only real movement she had was her head and she could bring her knees together if she wanted to, but it would put a strain on her hips.

With her tank top rolled down and her skirt flipped up, she was only covered around her middle and the rest of her was completely open and vulnerable to him, the puffy lips of her pussy spread to reveal the soft heart. Her wide eyes were filled with arousal and anxiety when she tugged on the restraints and realized how tightly bound she was, her breathing stuttered, and he could practically see her arousal climbing even higher.

It took his breath away.

Other submissives had responded like this to him, other submissives had been eager to be tied up and played with, but none of them had affected him like Maria. Maybe it was because she was new to kink, maybe it was just because his emotions had already become entangled in her, but whatever the reason, this moment felt more potently powerful than any he'd ever experienced.

I CAN'T MOVE.

The thought should have been terrifying. Horrifying. She should have been rebelling, screaming "Red" and demanding to be released.

This should not be the most sexually potent, highly erotic, panty-dropping (if she were wearing any) moment of her life.

And the smoldering look Rick gave her shouldn't make her feel like a sex goddess. Seriously, shouldn't she be feeling oppressed right now?

Oh yeah... I've got a couple of spots on my body I'd really like you to oppress.

Whatever. She'd always been of the school of feminism that said women should be able to choose what they wanted. And she wanted this. Really, really badly.

The straps holding her body down, holding her open, were both restrictive and exciting. It hadn't escaped her notice how careful Rick had been about restraining her, checking to make sure none of them were too tight, warning her to let him know if any of her limbs started to tingle or feel uncomfortable. While he might not want her to be able to move, he was just as concerned and attentive to her safety and comfort as he was to securing her in place.

Rick was standing down at the end of the desk, which meant he had a perfect view right up between her legs. Even though she'd been pretty brazen with him, she wasn't sure she'd ever had a man examine her girly bits so closely without touching them. It made her feel squirmy. But with her legs strapped together the way they were, it wasn't very comfortable to try and close off the view—which she had a feeling was the point. The straps around her thighs and calves were perfectly comfortable until she tried to close her legs.

One warm hand wrapped around her ankle. It was insane how such small contact, so far away from any of the parts that were aching to be touched, could feel so good. So reassuring. And, as his finger caressed the soft spot between her ankle and heel, so erotic.

"Fingers and mouth, right?" Rick asked, a glint in his eye said she was definitely going to pay for teasing him.

Maria was so ready to pay. She wriggled, watching his eyes immediately lock onto her breasts as the mounds jiggled with her body. Rick might be a very dominant alpha male, but he was still a male and boobs were boobs.

"Yes, please," she said, a little shocked at how breathless she sounded. Who cared though? Rick definitely looked pleased.

His hand slid up the inside of her calf, making her skin tingle in anticipation as his fingers moved up to her thighs. They were on a direct line of sensation to her pussy, and her breath came faster as his fingers slowed on their path, watching her reactions. Shuddering, Maria lifted her hips as much as she was able, encouraging Rick to move his fingers faster.

Instead, halfway up her thigh, his touched disappeared.

She actually whimpered.

"What's wrong?" she asked. "Why'd you stop?"

"Because I wanted to," Rick said easily. So casually that if her legs had been free she might have kicked him out of frustration as he moved around the side of the desk and opened some of the drawers there. Maria glared at him as he opened a baggie he found in there. "Something to learn little tease, when it comes to sex, things move at my pace. Not yours. You are still trying to top from the bottom."

Damn if her heart didn't race even faster at his words. At his deliberate control. Yeah, she'd wiggled her ass, trying to get him to move faster, trying to get his hands on her pussy. Now she blushed red hot at being called out on it.

But who could blame her? She was wetter than she'd ever been in her life, without direct stimulation, and she really wanted the direct touch. Unfortunately, Rick moved up to the end of the desk where her head was and Maria felt like whimpering again. Something metallic clinked against the wooden surface, right next to her head, although she didn't see what he'd put down, and then his hands were on her breasts.

Cupping them. Squeezing them. Maria moaned, her eyelashes fluttering as she looked up at him towering above her. He didn't go straight for her nipples, which were beginning to ache to be touched, but wrapped his fingers around her flesh and kneaded.

"Beautiful," he murmured, and Maria truly felt it.

How could she not when his gaze was so admiring as he looked down her body, plumping her breasts and torturing her wonderfully.

When his fingers finally did close around her nipples, her entire body felt like it might levitate as her back arched, thrusting her breasts upwards. It was pain and pleasure as he rolled the tight buds between his fingers, the culmination of anxious anticipation that made her pussy throb. She badly wanted to be able to rub her thighs together, to put some pressure on her clit, but there was no way she could get her legs closed with the way he'd trussed her up.

All she could do was writhe and arch, her body moving with need rather than intent. Now she wasn't teasing or trying to get him to touch her where she wanted. She just couldn't stop moving with all the adrenaline and erotic energy flowing through her.

"Oh God..." She gasped as Rick tugged on her nipples, pulling them upwards, and twisting slightly, before covering her entire breasts with his hands again and squeezing.

"Hands..." he murmured. "And mouth."

Maria let out a strangled cry as he bent over and took one of her nipples into his mouth. It was then that she also realized he was still fully clothed. If he hadn't been, he would have been close enough to lick. Instead, as he scraped his teeth along the sensitive bud of her nipple, she pushed her head up and laid a kiss on his stomach through his shirt.

Unfortunately, her neck muscles weren't strong enough for her to maintain the position long enough to do anything, but she at least got a chuckle of amusement from him. Right before he suckled her nipple hard, taking it deep into his mouth and making her moan and pant as her hips bucked uselessly.

"Rick... Please... stop teasing!"

She moaned again as he switched breasts, taking her other nipple into his mouth, completely ignoring her plea. The one that had just been freed felt cool in the open air, as wet heat engulfed the other. He sucked on her nipple with long, deep pulls, his tongue swiping across the surface. Maria hadn't realized how very sensitive her nipples could be. Every suck was followed by twisting pull deep inside her stomach, giving her the sensory illusion that he was sucking on her clit as well even though he was nowhere near it.

It felt like her body was burning up with heat, with the need to orgasm, and yet she couldn't quite get there... because Rick wasn't where he needed to be for her to cum. Remembering what the girls had said about Rick's kinks when it came to orgasm control and denial, Maria wished she hadn't brushed off that part so easily. She'd been more worried about her mental state, she'd had no idea the physical distraction to which he could drive her.

While he lavished attention on her breasts, her core was feeling more and more empty, pulsing and clenching around nothing while her pussy wept cream in its neediness. The demand for relief was becoming uncomfortable in its intensity, something she'd never experienced before. If her upper body was on fire, her lower body was the molten core of a volcano about to burst, swirling and building with pressure.

By the time he pulled away again she felt nearly mindless. It took her a moment to come back to herself enough to realize he was asking her a question; his voice had sounded so very far away.

"What?"

Fingers traced little pathways across her breasts, circling around her nipples, distracting her even more.

"Do you know what nipple clamps are, sweetheart?"

Maria nodded. She'd seen them online when she'd been looking around and she wasn't sure how she felt about them. Some of them had been weighted, dragging the women's breasts and nipples down with them and she hadn't really liked the way that looked. But some of the pictures had been kind of sexy, plump nipples surrounded by silver and black, the women's faces an erotic mix of pleasure and pain.

"I'd like to decorate these pretty little nipples," Rick said, giving the little nubs a tug. "I want you to feel the bite while I move down to your sweet pussy. Do you need to say either of your safe words?"

"No," Maria said immediately. Hell, she'd agree to anything now that he said he was going to move down to her pussy. Her body was humming with need, demanding she give in to whatever he wanted. And having the sensation of her nipples being pinched while he played with her pussy sounded wonderful.

The scraping sound at the side of her head was her first clue that Rick had been planning this from the start; the clamps had been what he'd gotten out of the desk. Maria shivered as she felt the brush of cold steel against the mound of her breast while he got the clamp in place.

"I've kept these from being too tight for your first time, but you're going to feel a sharp pinch and then it's going to fade. Just breathe through it."

She cried out as the clamp closed down around the tingling bud. Sharp pinch! HA! Her back arched, pussy spasming as the biting pain rushed through her, followed almost immediately by a surge of pleasure. It was like he was pinching her nipple very, very tightly, except the pressure was steadier than any human fingers could provide.

Seeing she was alright, Rick immediately followed with the next one, balancing out the pain on her chest. Maria sucked in air, breathing in deeply like he'd told her to, as the initial sting around the tender bud faded to the painfully pleasurable pinch. It felt like her nipples were now throbbing in time to her pulse. When Rick brushed his fingers over the tips, it felt like tiny needles were sticking into the tenderized nubbins, tiny needles that made her gasp and writhe in confused ecstasy.

"Good girl. How does that feel?"

"Tight... Hurts... but a good hurt," she admitted, shivering as he cupped her breasts again, gently stroking the undersides. Their sensitivity of her entire chest felt magnified with the clamps tightly confining her nipples. "Are you going to touch my pussy now?"

An unfamiliar note of pleading had entered her voice again. Maria couldn't remember the last time she'd ever begged during sex, or even if she ever had, but Rick's slow pace made her feel wanton, even as his tender care made her feel safe enough to do so. She didn't worry he would mock her.

Nope. Fucker just looked smugly satisfied as he moved back down between her legs, trailing his hand along her stomach.

"Yes Maria," he said, his voice dark and rich with sensual promise. "I'm going to touch your pussy now. I'm going to do what I've been fantasizing about for weeks and taste this sweet pussy."

This time when she writhed as his hand curved over her mound, her breasts jiggled and her nipples stung with renewed pain as the clamps moved. Oh fuck... this was going to kill her. Keeping still made her want to scream with frustration but moving at all just made her even more needy and aroused as the stabbing pain and pleasure of the clamps washed through her.

Settling himself between her legs, Rick wrapped one arm under and around her thigh, pressing his hand flat down on her belly just above the landing strip she had on her mound, holding her hips in place as he used his other hand to spread over the lips of her pussy and gently blow on the swollen, wet flesh. Maria groaned, jerking at the wrist restraints, which made her nipples flare to life again as her breasts jiggled. She should have known he wouldn't just get down to it and get her off.

Keeping his hand firmly placed on her lower belly, holding her exactly where he wanted her, Rick took one long lap with his tongue right up her creamy center. But just when he got to her clit, he pulled away.

Maria practically sobbed, feeling the tiny little bundle of nerves swell even further in dismayed protest at the teasing lack of stimulation. "Rick pleaaaaaase..."

"Shhh..." His hand made little circles on her belly. "You'll get to cum, Maria, I promise, but right now I'm going to enjoy this. And you are too."

Enjoy was both an under and an overstatement.

It was blissful agony as Rick went about his business of tasting her. He savored her. She'd never had a man explore her so minutely, so thoroughly, with his mouth. In her experience, when a man went down on her, it was with the goal of getting her off. Whatever Rick's goal was, it wasn't that.

He could have had her going like a rocket at any second, but instead he seemed to deliberately avoid doing anything which would send her over the edge. Maria lost track of the different ways she begged, as it all fell on deaf ears, while his tongue made long, slow strokes up and down every crevice of her pussy, hot breath brushing against her clit but never his mouth, and fingers pressing down on her stomach as she tried to arch, to writhe, to move her body against his lips.

When his tongue speared her, actually shoving into her, Maria tried to rub her pussy against his face, desperate for the climax circling her insides. She was so wound up it had become painful, dancing on the edge of ecstasy without being able to go over. Mindless, needy, her world had been swamped by sensation, overwhelmed by the chaos of pleasure and pain that sizzled along her nerve endings. The hand pressing down on her stomach, keeping her from moving her hips, was unyielding and she wanted to rip it away from her, knowing if she could just move...

Fingers slid inside of her, replacing his tongue, going deeper, opening her wider. Not that she was truly conscious of what the change was, but she felt it deep inside of her and her body responded to it.

His voice came through the haze, through the roaring in her ears, self-assured and commanding. "Come for me, Maria."

And the fingers inside her curved as her clit was swallowed by heat that sucked at the swollen nub. Maria screamed as her body bowed, jerking against the restraints, shuddering as wave after wave of inexplicable rapture buried her.

STUNNING... SO FUCKING GORGEOUS HE WAS ALMOST ABLE TO FORGET the way his cock was throbbing in his pants and the painful knowledge that he was going to have blue balls for the rest of the night.

Maria had given herself over to him completely. He didn't even think she'd been aware she'd been chanting nothing but "please, please, please" for the past five minutes while he'd licked, nibbled, and thoroughly enjoyed her pussy. Hell, she'd been begging long before that, but it had all degraded down into the one simple plea as the need to orgasm had overwhelmed her.

There had been a lot more he'd wanted to do to her, but he'd reminded himself that she was new, and he didn't want to scare her off. Now he was thinking he shouldn't have been so worried. She'd taken to the bondage, the clamps, the edging, and loved every second of it.

Her pussy was clamping so hard around his fingers that he nearly shot off in his pants thinking about what it would feel like around his cock. The screaming, passionate cries that heralded the initial impact of a long-denied orgasm were winding down into the softer, whimpering moans of a well-pleasured woman. Damn but he'd love to keep her chained to this desk, making her come for him again and again.

But they were nearly out of time. Too much longer in here and Patrick or one of the other guys would probably be by to check on them. Rick had never really considered himself possessive, but he suddenly realized he didn't want anyone else to see Maria like this. All soft, vulnerable, and submissive.

Ignoring the ache in his balls, Rick gave her pussy one last swipe, savoring the sweet, musky taste of honeyed woman, and got to his feet. One look at the dreamy, unfocused expression on Maria's face told him she was pretty far gone in her head. She wasn't used to playing like this, so it was probably a good thing he wasn't going to get the chance to really test her boundaries tonight.

There were so many things he wanted to do with her. Tie her up and really take his time with her body. Spank her until her ass was cherry red, use toys and his hands and mouth to edge her before fucking her hard while she climaxed over and over again on his cock, put her in vibrating underwear and torment her while they were out in public, and feel the glory of having her give over control of her orgasms to him. Let him decide when and where she got her pleasure.

Hell, his imagination was running wild, wanting to go further with her than he ever had with any other woman. Wanting to see how far he could push her, make her wait for days for an orgasm, until he could spend hours making her cum again and again. Tying her legs apart, with a strap across her hips to hold her in place instead of just his hand, so he could do whatever he wanted to her, force her to take the pleasure until she passed out. He'd never done that to a woman, but he'd seen it done before... to him, there was a level of intimacy and trust necessary for that kind of play that he hadn't wanted between him and another woman before.

But with Maria...

Forcing himself to stop spinning the possibilities and focus on the matter at hand, Rick gently removed the clamps on her nipples. Her unhappy, feminine whimpers quickly faded as he sucked gently on the tender little buds. They were a dark, reddish-brown from their time in confinement, and she'd probably be feeling rather sensitive tomorrow. He liked the idea that lingering aches would remind her of the scene.

Getting her covered up again and uncuffed, Rick did a quick clean-up around her before gathering her up in his arms. There was some movement in the window and then the door opened before he could get there.

Olivia stood on the other side, giving the possessive caveman that had taken over part of his brain a feeling of relief.

"How'd it go?" she asked, peering at Maria, who had snuggled her head against Rick's shoulder, one arm around his neck. Olivia grinned as she looked them both over. "She looks pretty happy."

"She's perfect," Rick said, grinning as he snugged Maria's soft curves against him, enjoying the weight of her in his arms. "Come on, let's go sit down, she's still pretty out of it."

Fortunately the couch at the end of the hall was empty. Settling himself in the corner, Maria against him, Rick accepted the blanket Olivia got from the bin beside the couch. Maria made happy, contented murmuring noises as he tucked the blanket around her.

"Must have been intense," Olivia commented. Rick snapped her a sharp look. For a second, he thought he heard a hint of envy in her voice, but if he had there was nothing of it on her face. Just a kind of professional interest and a bit of smugness.

"Very," Rick said, feeling a kind of contented calm he'd never experienced after a scene before. He didn't mind Olivia's satisfied smile. He knew there was a good chance that without her and the other women, he and Maria might not be where they were now. "Where's Patrick?"

Even though he preferred Olivia right now, he was surprised the big man hadn't shown up yet, especially since he missed seeing Maria before the scene. Olivia smirked again.

"Still in his office. Lexie and Angel managed to rig a little surprise for him when he opened his door."

"Bucket of water?" Rick asked, feeling slightly confused. That was the only prank he could think of, but it didn't really make sense.

"Bucket of glitter. The herpes of the art world. He's probably still trying to scrub it all off, but you just can't get rid of that shit."

Rick choked on a laugh. Holy shit… Patrick must be livid. There was also no way the man was showing himself in the club if he suspected there was one single speck of glitter left on his body. Good thing he had a private bathroom in the office of his or he'd really be SOL.

"Is she trying to get herself fired?"

"I don't think that's exactly the punishment she's looking for," Olivia said, her gray eyes glittering with amusement. Rick snorted. Poor Patrick. Poor Lexie. Even though he didn't like the idea of her getting kinky, he couldn't help but feel bad for her when she so obviously wanted in. Especially when the person she wanted in with was Patrick. Although, he was starting to think she and Patrick would actually make a pretty good couple.

He doubted her brother Jake would agree.

Wriggling movement brought his attention back to the woman in his arms, who was finally coming out of her sex-induced stupor.

"Rick?" her voice floated up as she pushed away from him, her face still flushed and eyes a bit unfocused.

"Hey sweetheart, welcome back to the world."

"I—oh." Catching sight of Olivia, Maria blushed, and her mouth snapped shut.

"Don't mind me, I'm on my way out. I'll see you around," Olivia said, tipping Maria a wink as she pushed herself up from the couch. The Domme sauntered off down the hallway, leaving Rick and Maria curled up on the couch.

"So? How do you feel?" Rick tried to keep the smugness out of his voice, but he didn't entirely succeed. But he was also entitled to some smugness. Not only had Maria proven to be both submissive and responsive to his needs, but that scene had been the most thrillingly intense one of his life. There was no way it hadn't been the same for her.

"Good... um... very good." Maria sighed and snuggled back down into his chest, letting him hold her.

Deciding to just enjoy the moment, Rick let her settle in, figuring she'd need a few minutes to gather herself. And in the meantime, he could just savor the feel of her against him, while telling his cock it was just going to have to wait.

HOLY SHIT SNACKS ON A POPSICLE STICK.

She felt drunk. High. Okay, she'd never been high before, but this was what she imagined it felt like. Some of her friends in college had done ecstasy once and right now she kind of felt like that; all lovey and glowy and wanting to rub herself all over Rick. The clothes on her body felt restrictive and she wanted to just strip them all off and roll around on top of him like a cat. She felt so connected to him, like there was a special bond between them now.

And at the same time, there was a frightened little voice deep inside of her screaming what she was feeling wasn't real.

Endorphins, adrenaline, all chemical reactions in her brain... but her body was still screaming at her that Rick was the perfect man and to never let him go. But how could she trust that feeling? How could she even begin process what had just happened between them when she was on a physical and emotional overload?

Which made it the worst possible time for his next question.

"So sweetheart..." Something nuzzled the top of her head and she got the impression he was gently kissing her hair. Which just made tears spring into her eyes. Which was so unlike her. More proof that she was not entirely herself right now. "Want to do dinner tomorrow night and then maybe make our way back here? There's a lot I'd like to show you."

Her body thrilled, urging her to immediately say yes. But that small, logical part of her brain which wasn't sure what to make of all these new experiences. That part thought she should wait until she wasn't drunk on crazy, kinky, ridiculously satisfying sex to consider what should happen next between them. Even though her body was totally on board with the idea, deep down she knew she wanted more between them than a sexual relationship. And she wanted more than sex at the club... was it possible he only wanted her if he could have her here?

More thoughts and doubts began to fill her, dampening her high.

"Um... Can we talk about it tomorrow?" she asked, pressing her cheek against his shoulder as she clung to him. She could tell not all of her thoughts were making sense; she just didn't feel lucid. Everything seemed kind of hazy and dream-like and she knew she shouldn't make any firm decisions right now. "I just... I need to think."

"Yeah... sure."

So wrapped up in her own thoughts, trying to sort through her emotions and the lingering responses in her body, Maria didn't even notice how he'd tensed.

## ❧ 16 ❧

Why did he do this to himself?

After a sleepless night, Rick was not feeling up for his usual morning workout. He forced himself to go down to the pool anyway. Asking himself the same question over and over while he was swimming at least felt more productive than doing it while sitting on his couch staring at the wall. He'd been beating himself up ever since he realized Maria hadn't been as into the scene as he'd thought, as into it as he had been.

While he'd been congratulating himself about finding the perfect woman and thinking about a future with her, he'd really just been setting himself up for rejection. Maybe he'd pushed too fast. Too hard. Maybe she hadn't been as ready for everything as he'd thought, not as into the scene as he'd thought.

Or maybe she was just running scared. Some people did that when they encountered something overwhelming.

Either way, he realized he'd done exactly what his friends had warned him about. He'd built something up in his head that wasn't there, romanticizing the encounter and garnering expectations from it based on nothing more than his own desires. Rick had never considered himself to be a romantic. Obviously he was wrong.

Obviously he was an idiot.

Small consolation that it also meant Olivia was finally wrong in her advice. He really wished she'd been wrong when it came to someone other than him.

Breaking through the water, Rick pulled himself out. Today was just about working out and hopefully exhausting himself so tonight he'd be able to get some sleep. That he'd be able to close his eyes without Maria's face, her body, her responsiveness popping into his mind, because the second that happened he started questioning all of his observations. Because once the scene was over, she'd changed. She'd been silent on the way home and when he'd walked her up to her door, he'd given her a kiss on the forehead. His way of saying goodbye.

Rubbing his towel hurriedly over his face, he didn't even admit to himself that he was trying to get out of there before she got to the pool. While he wasn't going to change up his routine over this, he wasn't going to linger to chat with her either. He didn't want to hear any careful explanations about why she wasn't interested in dating him, why it was too much for her.

Hell, he just wished he could forget it had ever happened. This was what he got for not following his own rules and trying something with one of his neighbors. He'd known from the beginning what he was risking, and he'd decided to do it anyway. Lesson learned.

"Rick?"

Fuck. Taking a deep breath, Rick dragged the towel down and turned to face the one woman he really didn't want to see right now. She was earlier than usual, but if he'd just been a couple of minutes faster he could have avoided this.

"Hey, I was just heading in," he said, sliding his feet into his flip flops as he swung the towel over his shoulder. Trying not to notice how fucking gorgeous she looked or the fact that she was wearing his favorite red bikini. Trying not to remember what the paler skin under her bikini looked like.

Instead, he focused on how nervous she obviously was, her fingers clutching at each other in front of her as she shifted her weight back and forth on her feet. Her wrists showed the faintest signs of being a bit red where she'd been restrained last night and had tugged on them while she writhed—no, stop it. Not going there.

"Oh... Um.... I thought maybe we should talk..."

"It's fine. Nothing to say and I've got things to do." He hated the brief hurt that flashed across her eyes, but he couldn't deal with the 'let's just be friends' talk right now. Maybe in a couple days when looking at her didn't hurt so much. It wasn't her fault he'd gotten things built up in his head but letting go of all those stupid little dreams was more painful than he'd realized it would be, especially when he was face to face with her. In a few days he could face her, be civil and even friendly with her, but not today. Not when seeing her made him feel like his nerve endings were scraped raw. "I'll see you later."

There. That way she knew that eventually they'd hang out. Just not right now. Rick gave her as much of a smile as he could, knowing it was fake as hell looking, and walked away as quickly as he could while she blinked and looked confused. Probably she'd been expecting some kind of confrontation, he thought as he went through the men's room and out towards the apartment building. Maybe some kind of deep heart to heart. Okay, maybe not that at the pool, but at least some kind of conversation or whatever.

Not today. Maybe tomorrow.

Maybe never.

IT FELT LIKE THERE WAS A FIST IN HER CHEST, AND IT WAS squeezing the shit out of her heart.

Maria slowly set down her pool stuff, blinking back tears. There were enough people around the pool that she didn't want to go running back out, making Rick's rejection plain to anyone who happened to be watching. Thank God she was wearing sunglasses.

He hadn't been. And his eyes had been as icy and cold as his last name.

What had she done wrong? What had changed between last night and this morning? He'd been so caring, so attentive last night... he'd asked if she wanted to go to dinner, and then he'd dropped her off at her door with a sweet, gentle kiss to her forehead...

She'd only gotten a few hours of sleep last night after her body had wound down from the intensity of their scene at Stronghold and she'd spent hours thinking through everything that had happened. It hadn't taken her too long to realize that yes, she'd been a bit high on pleasure and declaring undying devotion to Rick was definitely not where she was actually at emotionally, but she definitely felt a lot for him that went beyond mere affection. Their attraction to each other had led to explosively hot intimacy and she could only imagine actual sex would be even better.

But maybe after the scene he'd had time to sit and think too... maybe he'd been high on the chemistry but had ultimately decided he didn't want her for whatever reason. After all, he'd asked her to dinner right after the scene. Maybe after they'd both come down from the high, he'd realized she didn't actually have what he wanted. Needed.

The Introductory Scene hadn't been much like she'd imagined. Sure, she'd been spanked—and it had been pretty hot—and he'd teased the hell out of her before letting her orgasm, but that definitely didn't encompass everything that was possible. Had he tried to do anything she didn't like? Sitting on the pool chair, she cast her mind back, trying to think.

Some parts of the night were a big blur. She couldn't remember everything. But she trusted Rick had taken care of her through that. If she just knew what he wanted from her now, she was more than willing to try. Heck, she'd been half out of her mind last night... if she hadn't been able to do something for him...

There was no way she was chasing after him to find out what though. She didn't think she could do it without crying and she sure as hell didn't want him to try again with her out of pity or guilt or something.

Feeling small and cold, as if the sun was just glancing off of her skin without warming it, Maria looked around the pool. One of the moms waved to her and she waved back. Fuck it. She didn't care what any of these people thought if she spent less than ten minutes poolside. They all recognized her, but they didn't know her.

She couldn't just sit here acting like everything was normal. She needed to find out what she'd done wrong. Fortunately, she knew just who to call.

Grabbing her bag, Maria swept back up to her apartment, only hesitating in front of Rick's door for a moment. Nope. She wasn't going to knock. Not right now. Maybe later if no one picked up their phones. And only if she could get her roiling emotions under control.

The second she was alone in her apartment, with the door securely closed behind her, Maria dug her phone out of her pool bag.

"Please pick up, please pick up," she murmured as the phone rang. Relief flooded her as the call connected.

"Maria! Hey, what's up?" Angel's warm, excited voice seemed to wrap around Maria, promising support and friendship and all the things Maria desperately wanted from the women of Stronghold.

Emotion welled in her throat and chest. She'd been on such a roller coaster ride for the past twenty-four hours. All the fear and anxiety last night, combined with excitement and arousal, followed by passion and pleasure, then confusion and caution and now this morning... rejection and doubts.

"I—" Maria choked and burst into tears. She didn't even know how to say what had just happened or what to say. Everything was just hitting her all at once and she sank down, leaning on the arm of her couch as she cried.

"Maria?! Maria, are you okay? Are you having sub-drop? Shit, do you know what sub-drop is? Maria? Should I call Rick?"

"No!" Well that word got out okay and it was the catalyst which allowed Maria to start to get control over herself again. Her cheeks were wet with her tears and her chest still ached, the fist inside of it clenching even harder, but at least she could get words out. "Don't call him. Please. He doesn't... he doesn't..." want me. The tears threatened again as she swallowed the words.

"Are you sure?" Frantic concern laced Angel's voice, helping to buoy Maria's spirits. "What's wrong? What happened?"

"I don't think Rick wants me." God, she sounded so broken, and the sobs welled up again, tears spilling back down her cheeks. Stupid emotions. When had she gotten so wrapped up in him? Sure, she'd wanted him, and she'd thought, hey let's try the sex thing to see if it'll work out, see if a relationship is possible, but she hadn't expected to feel like this if it didn't. As if her heart was already breaking.

Through tears and sniffles, Maria dragged herself up and onto the couch, rather than kneeling beside it, curled in a little ball and hugging one of her cushions for comfort, she choked out the whole story to a sympathetically furious Angel. All the while, her head pounded, and her chest ached as if her rib cage was compressing inward.

By the time she was done, she was leaning her head on the back of the couch, feeling more than a little lost and forlorn, although at least the tears had finally stopped.

"I just don't know what I did... or didn't do. I was hoping maybe... maybe you'd heard something from Adam or... or knew something..."

"No, sweetie, I'm sorry," Angel said, her voice low and soothing. Comforting. "Rick didn't talk to anyone after you guys left last night, but I'll bet—I'm sure—this is just some kind of misunderstanding. You didn't do anything wrong. He told Olivia last night after your scene that you were perfect."

"Then why doesn't he want me now?" Maria practically wailed, although now that she wasn't crying, she was starting to feel kind of pissed. What the hell was wrong with the man? Last night he was all communication, communication, communication and then this morning he wouldn't even talk to her! How could they fix whatever had gone wrong if he wouldn't talk?!

"I don't know what happened, but you can bet I'm going to find out." Despite the fact that Angel sounded grim and rather threatening, Maria just found that even more comforting. She had someone in her corner. Someone who wasn't one of her sisters, which was a nice feeling. "Can I call you later?"

Sniffling a little, Maria glanced at the clock and groaned. "I have to leave for work in an hour, I'll be there until around seven or eight tonight probably. But you can leave me a message. Or just come by and see me."

"Awesome. I will get back to you today. You can count on it."

Angel sounded an awful lot like Maria when she went into Mama

Bear mode over one of her sisters. Was this how her sisters felt when that happened? All comforted and taken care of?

"Thanks," Maria said with a little laugh. She wasn't happy, but she was feeling much better. At the very least, she was hoping maybe if Rick wasn't going to talk to her that he'd at least talk to someone, and she could at least find out what happened.

Maria could handle rejection, it had happened before, even if it hadn't hurt this much. What she couldn't handle was not knowing why. Especially when, from her end, everything had seemed so good. And Rick had told Olivia she was perfect, so seriously... what the fuck?

"WHAT THE FUCK, RICK?"

Great. Angry, fire-breathing Adam. Definitely not what Rick felt like dealing with right now. Even worse, he had no idea what Adam was mad about. Could be just about anything. Rick had been at Adam's office all morning, doing stuff for Justin, but he couldn't actually remember what he'd done because his head was so fogged over and distracted.

Going by the expression on Adam's face, he'd probably fucked up something major.

"Sorry man... I'm kind of out of it. What'd I do?"

Adam stalked into Rick's makeshift office, slamming the door behind him as he glared at Rick, crossing his arms over his chest and making the suit jacket he was wearing go very tight around his shoulders.

"Would you like to explain what happened between you and Maria?" Adam asked, practically looming over Rick from across the desk.

Anger flickered. "How is that your business?"

"Well it becomes my business when my girlfriend calls me and rants to me for thirty straight minutes about my asshole friends who made their new sister-friend—whatever the fuck that means—cry this morning."

Ouch. It felt like someone had just punched Rick in the gut. "She was crying?" He couldn't even fake indifference or keep the concern out of his voice.

Raising one blond eyebrow, Adam's glare turned even more contemptuous. "Sobbing, according to Angel, because you don't want her anymore and she has no idea why. Which, after an intense scene like I hear you two had last night, she's probably feeling like you've seriously fucked with her head. So now my girlfriend would like to know why I'm friends with such a fucktard and, additionally, wants to kick your ass. When I tried to defend you, she told me she hopes I step on a thousand Legos and then she hung up on me." Adam glared. "The yelling and nagging I can take. It hurts my ears but at least she's just talking at me. Hanging up on me means she's probably scattering Lego booby traps around my house. So yeah, this is my fucking business because somehow, I got dragged into this shit and now I'm going to have to watch my every step in my own goddamn house. Now. Would you like to explain what happened between you and Maria?"

Rick tried to feel angry again, but the strongest emotion he could summon was maudlin. He should probably be mad Angel was getting into his business, and dragging Adam into it as well, but if Maria was really that upset about the end of their friendship then he was glad she had someone there for her. Even if it was one of his best friend's girlfriends, who happened to be a good friend herself. Although he didn't think he'd be giving Angel a call to chat anytime soon.

"The scene was intense and afterwards she didn't want anything to do with me. I realized I'd gotten everything built up in my head, exactly the way Olivia warned me about, and I'd spun this perfect little fantasy of the future. This morning I didn't really want to hear the 'let's just be friends' talk from her and so I kind of brushed her off. And I'm sorry if that hurt her, I'll apologize to her later, but I just couldn't deal with it."

For a long moment, Adam and Rick just stared at each other, and then Adam seemed to soften. Well, as much as he ever did. Sighing, the other man uncrossed his arms and tugged on the bottom of his suit jacket to straighten it back to its usual, impeccable state.

"Just so you know, I got the impression from Angel that Maria is not upset over the loss of your friendship. I don't know where you got the idea she just wants to be friends, but you should probably have some kind of talk with her or you're going to have trouble getting any of the girls to talk to you."

"Better than nagging me," Rick muttered under his breath as Adam reached the door. Adam shook his head, a smile breaking out on his face.

"You have a lot to learn, Rick. Nagging is a sign she cares and hasn't given up on you. Silence means she's plotting your death." Adam sighed, but the stupid little smile stayed on his face. "Or planting Lego booby-traps."

Looking surprisingly content for a man who was contemplating serious foot pain, Adam left. Rick groaned and let his head fall down onto the desk, banging it several times. What the fuck was going on? Had he misinterpreted Maria last night? No... she'd definitely wanted to be left alone. Hell, he'd asked her if she wanted to have dinner and go back to the club and she'd put him off. Then she'd been silent the entire car ride home. And hadn't said anything beyond "Good night" when he'd walked her to the door. How else was he supposed to have taken that?

Maybe Angel had misinterpreted when she'd talked to Maria. He could see that happening. Or maybe Maria had changed her mind again? Did he really want to try to start something with someone who constantly changed their mind about what they wanted?

Then again, he was already miserable. Maybe being miserable in a relationship with an uncertain Maria would be less miserable than not having her in his life at all. Rick gave a short laugh. Yeah, all he needed to do was look at Jared and Marissa to know that was a seriously fucked up way to go.

No, he wanted what Angel and Adam had. A real relationship, where even though she called him up, yelled at him, and threatened him with stupid pranks, the man was walking around with a smile on his face. Probably because he was already contemplating her punishment. Rick wished he was contemplating punishments for Maria and not just wallowing in his own little personal hell.

"Hey Rick?"

Glaring, Rick lifted his head up again. "Are you here to yell at me too?"

Justin's lips quirked as he eased more of himself into the doorway, leaning against it rather than just poking his head in. "I don't know, should I be?"

"No, no definitely not."

The dark-haired man studied him for a moment before nodding his head. Rick didn't doubt his friend would be stopping by Adam's office immediately after this to find out what was going on. A bunch of gossip girls, that's what his friends were.

"I just wanted to see if you had the resumes ready for Dana yet."

Right, that's what he'd been doing. Going through the resumes they'd gotten over the website and doing the initial sorting of the good ones from the bad ones. Adam called it using Rick's English teacher profession to his advantage. All Rick had to do was weed out all the ones with spelling or grammatical mistakes and then send the good batch on to HR to go through.

He glanced at the computer screen. "Almost done."

Hesitating, Justin tapped his fingers against the door frame. "Maybe you should take a break after. Wanna go out to lunch today?"

Not really, but he knew what his answer better be unless he wanted a male pow-wow in this stupid office during the afternoon.

"Yeah, sure."

Giving him an encouraging nod, Justin vacated the doorway. Rick let his head slam against the desk a couple more times for good measure before taking a deep breath and getting back to work.

MARIA WAS ALREADY AT THE BAR, HELPING OUT THE BARTENDERS who had gotten a bit overwhelmed, when Angel, Jessica, and Lexie showed up. Apparently everyone wanted to get out and celebrate the end of the week, and she couldn't blame them. Today had been hectically busy, which she'd been grateful for because it kept her from moping and checking her phone every five minutes to see if either Rick or Angel had tried to get in contact with her.

Still, her spirits lifted for the first time all day when she saw those three smiling faces. People who, she realized, she already considered her friends. Fastest friends she'd ever made, and yet she trusted them. Maybe it was because of what they had in common. They pretty much had to trust each other on a certain level because of what they knew about each other.

Despite how crowded the bar was, they didn't have any trouble getting to the counter. A group of college guys willingly moved aside when Lexie tapped one of them on the shoulder and gave him a brilliant smile. Wearing a lacy black tank top, dark gray shorts, and some pretty heels that gave her several extra inches of height, she still looked delicate and pixie-like. And those bright blue eyes of hers stood out because of the lack of other colors she was wearing. One look at her, and the curvier brunettes behind her, and the guys were practically falling over themselves to show their courtesy by letting the girls through to the bar.

Jessica's hazel eyes were sparkling with amusement as she gave Lexie a sidelong look, obviously thinking it was only the younger woman the guys were interested in. Maria wondered if Jessica realized three of the guys behind her were currently checking out her ass.

"Hey ladies, what can I get you?" The forced smile on Maria's face had started to feel almost natural, but she could tell they weren't fooled.

Angel glanced at her watch which was set into a delicate looking bracelet made up of gold and tiny sparkling gems. It went surprisingly well with the casual peach sundress she was wearing, probably because of the gold chain wrapped twice around her neck. "Depends... do you know what time you're off?"

"Ummm...." Maria glanced around the bar. It was after seven, but she always stayed until she was no longer needed. Still, most of the rush already had their drinks which meant things behind the bar would slow down to a more even keel soon. "I can probably get out of here in half an hour."

"Soooo... one drink. Pre-gaming!" Lexie said gleefully.

"Pre-gaming?"

Jessica grinned. "For Stronghold girls' night. As soon as you're done here, we're taking you to Olivia's."

"That..." Relief and a kind of awed happiness filled her. "That sounds amazing."

Girl time, with these ladies, where she could vent and ask questions, and not have to worry about being judged... yeah, that sounded fucking awesome. Otherwise she'd be tempted to call up Jackie and would probably end up spilling a lot more than she meant to.

"Great. In the meantime, I'll have a glass of white wine," Jessica said.

Angel looked at the board where Murphy's listed their specials. "Dark and Stormy."

"Tequila sunrise." Lexie just grinned at Jessica's look. "What, I already called out of work tonight."

"That's going to get you in trouble," Angel murmured as Maria poured Jessica's glass of wine. Maria looked at her with raised eyebrows, wondering why Patrick would object to Lexie calling out of work. "Lexie and I might have arranged for a bucket of glitter to fall on Patrick's head yesterday... completely covering him and quite a bit of his carpet."

"Pink glitter," Lexie chimed in, her blue eyes sparkling. "So for my punishment he's got me working every shift possible for the next month... supposedly it's supposed to keep my idle hands busy."

"Personally, I think he's just doing it to keep you off the club floor," Jessica pointed out, taking a sip of her wine. Keeping quiet, Maria mixed the drinks and just listened to the club gossip, a small smile on her face. She'd wondered what Lexie had done yesterday.

"Whatever, he can't keep me from getting someone to cover my shift, and since I'm not going to be on the club floor tonight anyway he can't even yell at me about it," Lexie said smugly.

Laughing, Angel accepted her drink from Maria. "At least, not tonight. You are just asking for a spanking."

Fluttering her ridiculously long lashes, Lexie gave Angel a sweet smile. "Why yes... yes I am."

"From Patrick?" All three of them looked at Maria, who blushed a bit as she realized the surprise in her voice could be considered kind of insulting. "Sorry... just... he's kind of intimidating." Both Angel and Jessica nodded agreement, but Lexie just shrugged. Unfortunately Maria didn't get to finish the conversation because she had finished making their drinks and there were already other people behind them trying to catch her eye so they could order. Moving away from the bar, the three stood together, talking and laughing, and also keeping an eye out for Maria.

Even though they were no longer talking to her, she still felt included. She knew they were waiting for her. Doing a girls night with them sounded perfect. Heck, even if things didn't work out between her and Rick, there was no way she was giving up these girls now. Especially since it seemed like they liked her just as much as she liked them.

MARIA WAS IN HEAVEN. GIRL HEAVEN, THAT WAS.

Hanging out with the girls of Stronghold was just as much fun as hanging out with her sisters. Maybe more so because she felt a little freer, and she didn't already know everything about them already. So far the night had held several shocking revelations, all coming out after multiple drinks.

Olivia was sitting pretty as Queen Bee in a plush, red velvet armchair just barely a dark enough shade to keep from clashing with her red hair. Even the fuzzy little sheep on her pajama pants couldn't take away from her regal posture. On the love seat, Hilary and Jessica were cuddling, both of them in pajama pants and tank tops. Hilary's were a shocking shade of pink while Jessica was wearing what looked suspiciously like men's boxers and a ragged blue t-shirt.

On the couch with Maria were Lexie and Angel. Lexie was sprawled out and taking up at least half the couch, her legs resting over both Angel and Maria's laps. Unlike the others, Maria, Lexie, and Angel were all still in their regular clothes. Jessica had brought some to change into and Hilary had been at Olivia's and already in her pjs when they'd arrived.

Jessica was finishing up explaining her solution to the marriage question, which Maria was completely fascinated by. The whole three-some relationship kind of boggled her mind, especially once they'd gotten on the topic of marriage. Apparently, Chris and Justin wanted a wedding, but the big question was which one of them would actually, legally marry her. And apparently, so far, the two were trying to work it out on their own without including Jessica in their conversation. Jessica's solution was brilliant simplicity—and Maria was pretty sure it wasn't just the alcohol talking.

She didn't want to legally marry either of them. Have a ceremony and say vows, making a commitment? Sure. But she figured they could set up trusts and legal avenues for all the financial stuff in case something happened to one of them, and same thing for any kids they might have. Jessica was perfectly happy to just be with both of them, and she was worried being legally married to only one of them would upset the balance their relationship had achieved.

"So what do the guys think?" Lexie asked, tapping the rim of her glass. Maria had no idea what Lexie was drinking, they'd all been making their own concoctions out of the ample options Olivia had supplied.

"Ha." Jessica snorted. "I'll tell them as soon as they get around to asking me what I think we should do."

Olivia laughed while Angel shook her head, amused.

"Alpha men. Go figure. Idiots."

Now Maria laughed. "And Rick kept going on about 'communication' in BDSM relationships, what the hell."

"By communication, they mean they tell you what to do and then you do it," Lexie said succinctly, wagging her finger at Maria. "It works out so well for them too." The saccharine sweetness in her voice was more effective than sarcasm, and everyone burst out laughing.

Lexie was so right though, it did seem like Rick had some issues with listening to what Maria had to say. Hell, this morning he hadn't even given her a chance to talk. Stupid men.

"Men suck." She scowled at her drink. Which was her... what? Third one? Fourth one? Shit, she was starting to lose track.

"Ha, try living with one of them." Belying her statement, Angel grinned. "Actually, right now, I technically live with three of them, but even combined they're easier to deal with than Adam."

"That's because you don't live with men, you live with minions," Olivia said, grinning. "Anytime you want to send them over here, feel free. I could use some minions around this place."

"Oh Lord..." Hilary rolled her eyes. "You would eat Sam alive, Olivia."

"Yeah, but Q could probably go toe to toe with me." Her tone was surprisingly wistful.

Maria looked at the redhead curiously. "You want a guy who can go toe to toe with you?"

"Yep. Right up until I put him on his knees." The redhead grinned wickedly.

Drunken giggles broke out around the room. Yeah, Maria could see that. Olivia was a Domme who liked a challenge, kind of like how Angel challenged Adam and Lexie challenged Patrick. Hilary and Jessica seemed more sedate. What did Rick want? Maria had a sinking feeling she was kind of a challenge; did Rick want someone who was more like Jessica? Or was she only thinking that because she knew they had once had sex?

"I need more booze," Hilary announced, pushing Jessica off of her and distracting Maria from her thoughts. The brunette protested, flopping down behind Hilary's back as the blonde leaned forward to refill her drink. Picking up a bottle of salted caramel vodka, she gave it a loving little rub on the side before unscrewing the cap. "Hello vodka... goodbye dignity..."

"Dignity is overrated," Jessica said, pumping her fist in the air so it was just visible over Hilary's shoulder, her voice slightly muffled from being smushed between Hilary and the love seat. Maria had to laugh, and her insecurities about Jessica faded again. She was just being stupid about that and she needed to get over it.

Not surprisingly, two and a half hours later, Maria was drunker than she'd been in a really, really long time. Somehow she'd ended up on the floor with Lexie and Angel behind her. Lexie's head was in Angel's lap while Angel played with her hair and Lexie played with Maria's, utterly, drunkenly fascinated by the little curls at the back of

Maria's neck. Olivia was still on her throne, except now she was kind of sprawled on it and was drinking straight from an almost empty bottle of Jack. The last time she'd gone for a refill she'd realized it was almost gone and had decided to just take the bottle.

"Hey... hey... anyone got a camera?" Olivia held up the bottle, grinning like a loon. "I need a drink of me finishing this!"

Blinking owlishly, Hilary peered at her. "A drink?"

"I mean a picture!"

"Maybe you shouldn't finish that."

Giving Hilary a one-fingered salute, Olivia brought the bottle to her lips and swallowed the last couple of gulps. Maria was in awe. "Hot damn."

"Did anyone take a picture?" Olivia looked around at all of them. None of them had moved and she scowled. "You subbies are useless. Useless I say! Spankings for everyone!" Even she couldn't keep a straight face through the threat though, and they all ended up laughing hysterically.

Lexie was laughing so hard she nearly fell off the couch.

"Whoa!" Maria rolled the other woman back. Even though she was "drunk as a skunk," as Hilary had said earlier, Lexie managed to keep her glass held straight up so she didn't spill a single drop.

Sniffing at the cup, Maria smelled cinnamon. "You're not drinking straight Goldschlagger are you?

"Oh God no," Lexie said, pushing herself up to a mostly sitting position. Even though Maria's vision was kind of swirly and fuzzy, she could see Lexie was just as bad off. "It's Goldschlagger, Malibu, and triple sec."

She said it so reasonably Maria didn't even catch the issue until Angel smacked Lexie on the arm. "That's like, three times the alcohol."

"There's ice in it..." Smiling, Lexie took another sip of her drink.

"You puke, you clean it up," Olivia said regally. Lexie just gave her a thumbs up.

"You're so tiny," Maria said, watching in wonderment. "How can you drink so much?"

"Lots of practice..." Lexie said, but instead of sounding snarky she almost sounded a little sad. "My guy friends all still see me as a kid, I can't get into the fun parts of Stronghold and Patrick won't fuck me... what else do I have to do?"

Maria patted Lexie's knee comfortingly, because everyone else was too busy choking. "I'm sorry honey. I'm not getting laid either."

"You didn't get laid last night?" Jessica sounded shocked.

"Nope. Was totally okay with it too, but Rick said he didn't want to do it there... not that he wants to do it anywhere now. Fucker wouldn't even talk to me this morning. I wanna do it. But not if he doesn't want me."

"Oh honey, he wants you," Angel said, reaching down to pat her head. "I've been waiting for the right time to tell you. I had a little chat with Adam and he had a little chat with Rick... and apparently Rick said something to the effect that you don't want him."

"What?!" Outraged, Maria sat straight up, nearly spilling her drink. Which, might not be a bad thing at this point, because she was immediately dizzy from the fast movement, a clear indication she'd gone well past her usual alcohol limit.

Angel snickered. "Yeah, apparently he thought you were going to give the 'let's just be friends' talk."

Olivia burst out laughing. "Oh gawd... Maria you should see the look on your face."

Laughing ruefully along with the others, Maria tried to clamp down on an emotion. Any one emotion. They were all kind of distant and fuzzy feeling. Hope, confusion, relief, anger... all mingled together and yet somehow separate from her. Probably an effect of the booze.

"Why the hell would he think I just wanna be friends," Maria complained, putting down her drink on the coffee table so she could throw her hands up in the air. "I let him spank me, tie me up, and then put his hands and fingers all over me! And in me! My nipples have been sore all day!"

About to say something, Jessica paused, thinking over Maria's words. "Your nipples?"

"Yeah, he put little pinchy thingies on them." Maria pouted, rubbing her hands over her breasts.

"Oooooh, clamps. I like clamps." Angel made a happy little sighing noise. Dammit. Maria wanted to sound like that when she talked about Rick. What the fuck was wrong with him?

"Oh honey, he's a man," Lexie said, sympathetically. Oops. Maria had spoken out loud. "Did you guys talk after the scene last night?"

"Yeah..." Maria tried to focus and remember. "He was super nice and cuddly. Asked if I wanted to go out for dinner and back to Stronghold tonight and I asked if we could talk about it today. Except when I went to the pool to talk to him about it, I got the cold shoulder."

"Awww Rick... nooooo..." Jessica groaned, running her hands over her face while Hilary giggled at the dramatics.

"What? What am I missing?"

"Boy logic," Angel said sagely, nodding her head. "Trust me, I'm like the guru of boy logic. I will bet you... I will bet you anything, that when you didn't immediately say yes to dinner and sexy time, he took it as a 'no.'"

"But that's not what I said."

"Yeah, but I bet that's what he heard," Olivia chimed in. "You'd be amazed at how sensitive some of these alpha guys can be. Especially when they're worried about being rejected. Rick was already second guessing himself constantly when it came to you."

"So when you said you wanted to talk today, he thought everything was a big fat no go," Angel finished up triumphantly.

"But I meant what I said. I wanted to talk," Maria griped, clenching down her jaw. An emotion was definitely coming through more clearly now. Anger. She was pissed off. "I just needed some time... last night was just a bit overwhelming, you know?"

"We know. He even probably knows. But..." Olivia sighed. "Try to remember that he was probably overwhelmed too. And Rick's a full-steam ahead kind of guy. Once he gets going, it's hard for him to remember that 'slow-down' doesn't mean full stop."

"A trait most of our men share," Hilary said, shaking her head with amusement. "I swear, I think that's why they like the stoplight safe word system. Very clear directions for them."

Maria shook her head, disbelieving. "Great. Okay. So obviously he and I need to talk but... ARGH. Why couldn't he just speak up last night? Or this morning? Dumbass."

"You know what we should do," Lexie said slowly, as if thinking out loud. "We should go make him talk."

Brilliant. Lexie was fucking brilliant. That's exactly what they should do. After all, Rick had said BDSM was key to communication. No wait, communication was key to BDSM. Yeah, that's what he'd said. So she was gonna make him communicate.

Dammit.

## ❧ 17 ❧

**M**audlin. That's how he felt. Fucking maudlin.

It hadn't been the best evening. When he'd gotten home from Adam's office he'd hung around his apartment, passing the time by going on a cleaning spree which had left his kitchen and bathroom sparkling. He'd even dusted all the surfaces and then vacuumed. Just trying to get time to pass faster until Maria should be home from work.

He'd knocked on her door at seven o'clock.

Again at eight.

And one last time at nine.

No answer. No movement on the inside. Yes, he'd pressed his ear to the door to listen. Yes, he'd realized how creepy that would make him look if any of her neighbors had happened to open their doors while he was doing it. Hadn't stopped him. Unfortunately, he'd had to come to the conclusion she wasn't home.

So he sat out on his balcony until about ten o'clock. Somehow sitting on his balcony wasn't really something he did much of, even though part of the reason he'd chosen the apartment was because it had a nice balcony. Private. Not adjacent to any of his neighbors.

Bonus: it looked out over the parking lot. When Maria finally got off work and came home, he'd be able to see her coming in.

Of course she'd be able to see him too, but he was okay with that.

He was feeling more balanced now. Less raw. Like he could handle it if she gave him the friends talk. Although, he was hoping maybe he'd misread the situation.

Hope for the best, prepare for the worst. That was his motto for tonight. He hoped he'd misread the situation and once they talked today she'd have a good reason for putting off talking to him last night. But he wasn't going to get all amped up just in case he hadn't been the one to misunderstand.

After way too long with his thoughts, staring up at a sky whose stars he could barely see because of all the lights from the apartment complex, Rick had gone back inside and sat down in front of the television. Obviously Maria was coming home late tonight. Maybe the night manager had called out. Or maybe she'd accepted a date with some other guy. Yeah, he knew he was being kind of illogical.

That's why he'd turned the TV on. Distraction, pure and simple. Although it was just soundless noise and meaningless shapes because he wasn't really paying attention to it at all. Still it helped him fuzz out his brain. Sink into the couch. Let his thoughts go and clear his head.

So when someone pounded on his door, it came as a bit of a shock to his system. Even more shocking were the giggles that followed immediately afterwards.

"Rick! Rick, I know you're in there, open up!"

It was Maria's voice, but different. The words slightly slurred. A slower cadence. Rick practically vaulted over the back of his sofa and was at his door in two steps, a frown already forming on his face. Was she drunk? And who was giggling?

Whatever he'd expected to see when he opened the door, it definitely wasn't Maria leaning against the door jamb with Lexie and Angel standing just a foot behind her, leaning against each other for support.

"What—"

"You!" Maria poked her finger into the center of his chest, pushing herself up to stand straight, as she cut him off. "We are talking! Communicating."

"Um...." Rick rubbed his chest, his other hand still on his door, as he took in the scene. Shit, he needed to get all three of them inside. Angel and Lexie's giggles were getting louder and while Maria hadn't exactly shouted her demand, she wasn't quiet about it either. "Right. All three of you, in here, now."

Sticking her chin up in the air, Maria swanned past him, only stumbling slightly, her gait definitely unsteady. Rick pinched the bridge of his nose where he could already feel a headache forming as Angel and Lexie passed him, both weaving as they walked. The three of them were completely wasted. Digging into his pocket, he watched the very drunk trio stumble their way to his couch, falling onto it like a pile of unruly puppies, while he sent identical text messages to two recipients.

She's at my place and she's wasted.

What he really wanted to say was 'get your ass over here now so I don't have to deal with this,' but he knew what he'd actually sent would get faster results.

The giggling, feminine pile of limbs and bodies just made him sigh. This was not how he'd expected to talk to Maria tonight. He'd expected her sober and without back-up. Although at least he should feel grateful Angel had been giggling and not plotting mayhem.

He was going to have to keep an eye out for Legos.

Looking at a giggling Lexie, who had somehow ended up on the bottom of the pile and was currently fighting her way to the top, he amended that thought: and glitter.

Something occurred to him that made him frown again.

"How did you all get here?"

"Cabbed it. From Olivia's," Angel said, grinning gleefully. Kind of vindictively actually. He glanced down at the floor as he made his way to the ottoman in front of the couch, so he could face it. No Legos. Yet. "Hilary and Jessica didn't come. They didn't want to get in trouble." She drawled the last word, which made the others burst into more giggles.

Rick couldn't help the smile breaking through, even though he was trying to look stern. They were all cute, piled up, and drunkenly happy. Maria's eyes met his and she scowled again. Which was also kind of cute, not that he was dumb enough to mention it.

"You!" She pointed her finger at him again. The other two immediately quieted, expectant expressions on their faces, like they were waiting for Maria to make some grand pronouncement. "You are a dumbass." Angel and Lexie nodded their agreement.

He raised his eyebrows at all three of them. "Alright."

This was definitely not the time to argue. Not when it looked like Maria was having trouble just stringing together sentences. Best thing to do in this situation was just sit tight and wait for his own back-up to arrive.

"I like you. And you could've had aaaaaaall this." Maria's words were accompanied by the most hilariously awkward sexy gyration he'd ever seen, even if it hadn't been hampered by Angel leaning on her side and Lexie half on her lap. Granted, "all that" was looking pretty hot in her work attire, which consisted of a dark blue cotton blouse and creamy linen pants that looked business casual but would also allow her to keep cool in the summer's heat. Somehow Rick managed to keep a straight face though, even though he was definitely beginning to see the amusement in the situation. "You and your talking. And non-talking."

Okay. So he'd gotten it wrong. Maria liked him. At the very least. And somehow he doubted she'd show up this drunk at his door to tell him so unless she meant as more than friends. On one hand, he was relieved. On the other hand, he wished she'd been a little bit more forthcoming last night rather than shutting him down right after the scene. It would have saved both of them a lot of angst today.

Rick nodded his head amiably. "Yeah, we should talk. Probably tomorrow."

"No, I wanted to talk tomorrow. I mean today. I mean, yesterday I wanted to talk tomorrow!" Maria glared at him.

"Yes, you did," he said in a placating tone. "We should have talked this morning. I'm sorry we didn't." Well, now he was sorry. If he had to do it over again, maybe he would have made a different decision, but maybe not. After all, she really hadn't given him much to go on last night, despite their talk about communication. Which was something he'd explain to her when she was sober.

"Oh…" Seemingly struck by his apology, Maria deflated, leeched of the anger that had puffed her up. Lexie gave him a thumbs up from behind Maria's back.

Although Rick would have liked to see what Maria said next, he was also incredibly relieved when his doorbell rang. All three women twisted around, trying to look toward the noise with a look of surprise on their faces.

"Who's that?"

"Back-up," Rick replied dryly, already halfway to the door.

Both parties, as it turned out.

"Uh oh…" Angel said it in a sing-song way, but she was definitely looking a bit like a trapped kitten when Adam caught her eye from across the room. She smiled hopefully and then tried to hide under Maria's hair when Adam didn't smile back.

"Well shit." Lexie glared at Patrick, who glared right back. Truthfully, Rick hadn't been entirely sure who to contact for her, but he figured Patrick was better than her parents.

Patrick crossed his arms over his chest at almost the exact same time as Adam. For a moment, Rick almost felt sorry for the little troublemakers. Almost.

"What are you doing here?"

"I thought we talked about not interfering in our friends' relationships," Adam said, right on top of Patrick's question.

All three men winced as the room erupted with sound, Lexie, Angel, and Maria all trying to explain at once. At the top of their lungs. Rick slammed the door shut behind him. He'd done it to keep the noise out of the hall, but it had the added benefit of making the women jump in surprise and shut up.

"Come on, Angel," Adam said, sighing as he let his arms drop, his hard expression already softening. Sometimes Rick couldn't believe how much Angel had changed his friend. Mostly in good ways, although Adam was turning into a big softie when it came to her. "Let's go home and we'll talk about this tomorrow."

Making a face, Angel pushed herself up and stumbled, nearly falling on the floor before Adam darted forward to catch her. "Okay pest—"

"Don't call me that!"

"Time to go." He swung her up into his arms and turned, heading for the door. Which Rick obligingly opened for him.

Patrick and Lexie were still caught up in a glaring match. Next to Lexie, Maria had shrunken in on herself as if trying to avoid Patrick's gaze. She really didn't need to worry about that. Rick was pretty sure Patrick was solely focused on Lexie, to the exclusion of everything else going on around him.

"Why weren't you at work tonight?" Patrick barked out finally.

"Umm... girls' night. Duh. Don't worry, Olivia was there to keep an eye on me." Lexie rolled her eyes expressively.

"Obviously not a very good one."

"Obviously she recognizes I've grown up and treats me like an adult."

"I'll treat you like an adult when you act like one."

Lexie flipped him off, sticking her tongue out at him at the same time. Patrick snorted.

"Yeah, that's exactly what I mean," he said, shaking his head as he moved forward, obviously intending to pick her up from the couch.

"I can stand on my own," she said furiously, pushing herself up and away from Maria, who was watching the whole scene with big eyes, trying not to do anything to draw attention to herself. Rick couldn't blame her, he was finding it pretty fascinating too.

"Barely." But Patrick stopped just a couple feet short of her. "You're so drunk it's amazing you can stand at all."

"I'm twenty-four, I can handle my liquor."

"You're twenty-three."

"I—oh. Yeah, but I'm almost twenty-four, my birthday's—"

"Not for another two months," Patrick said grimly, reaching out his hand for her to take. His other hand was balled up by his side, as if he was using pure force of will to keep from picking her up instead of just offering his assistance. Lexie kind of wilted, as if just realizing how drunk she really was. His voice softened, turning coaxing and gentle, almost tender. "Come on, little pixie."

"Okay." Lexie finally gave in, practically melting against Patrick as he slung his arm around her, supporting her. Wrapping both of her slim arms around his waist, she nuzzled her face into his chest.

Seeing Patrick's clenched jaw expression, Rick knew for sure, for the first time, that Patrick definitely no longer saw Lexie as his little sister. But Rick didn't comment. Just held the door open for them. That was going to be complicated as fuck when Jake finally came home.

Rick also didn't mention the specks of pink glitter clinging to the back of Patrick's neck.

Shutting the door behind him, Rick turned to face his own troublemaker. She was sitting on the couch, hands in her lap, fingers wrapped tightly together, and looking up at him with a worried expression as she nibbled on her lower lip.

"Are you mad?"

"Nope. Just tired. Come on," he said, walking over to her and taking her hands to pull her up. Like Lexie had with Patrick, Maria practically fell against him. "We're going to bed."

"Okay..." Maria instinctively started toward the front door, but Rick tugged her around to head down the hallway. "Oh... We're..."

"Going to sleep," he said firmly. There was no way he was going to do anything with her but sleep tonight, but he also didn't like the idea of her going home alone when she was this drunk. Better to have her here where he could keep an eye on her. "Tomorrow morning, we're going to have the talk we should have had either last night or today."

"Mmmmm kay."

Getting her undressed and into one of his t-shirts was a process. Not just because he would have been turned on anyway, but because she kept giggling and trying to snuggle up against him. Which was definitely testing his self-control. He ached to press her breasts into his hands, to run his hands all over her smooth skin... but he fought the impulses down. Not going to happen. Not like this.

Finally he got her situated in his bed, wearing a t-shirt and a pair of his boxers over her underwear. Sleepily, she tried to wrap her arms around his neck and kiss him, but he managed to veer off enough to give her a kiss on the forehead instead, ignoring her mumbling complaints. Hopefully tomorrow she'd remember and be appropriately grateful for his restraint. Because he should seriously get some kind of award for being such a fucking boy scout.

Stripping down to his boxers, Rick felt the most incredible surge of rightness seeing her in his bed. Another emotion he needed to tamp down until they'd talked.

Sliding in beside her, he wrapped his body around hers, snugging her curves up against him. He groaned softly as she wiggled her bottom into his crotch, his dick snuggling into the warm cleft of her ass. Tightening his arm around her, he tried to breathe through the fairly painful ache in his lower body and relax himself. Which was pretty much a useless endeavor. He knew he would probably relax better if he moved farther away from her... but he didn't want to.

Closing his eyes, he breathed in the warm, womanly scent of her and focused on relaxing his muscles one by one. Surprisingly, even though he was horny as hell, with Maria safe in his arms, he found himself drifting easily to sleep

IT WAS A COMBINATION OF THINGS THAT WOKE HER. THE AWFUL taste in her mouth. The throbbing in her head. The nauseous gurgling of her stomach. And the nagging instinct she wasn't in her own bed.

Oh God... what did I do?

Warily, Maria opened her eyes, whimpering a little bit at how bright and piercing the light seemed to be, even though there wasn't very much of it. It took a couple of moments for her eyes to focus and a few more to recognize she was in Rick's room.

Okay, seriously... what the fuck did I do last night?

Immediately she put her hand under the covers. Shirt... shorts... panties... yeah, they hadn't had sex. Relief and disappointment swamped her, although there was definitely more relief than disappointment in the mix. For one, if they'd had sex, she'd really want to remember that. For two, they really needed to talk before they had sex.

Rolling onto her back, she looked at the other side of the bed which was rumpled and empty. So they'd slept in the same bed at any rate. She put her hand over her eyes, blocking out the light while she tried to remember exactly what had happened last night.

Going to Olivia's for girls' night and having a blast, she remembered. Lots of girl talk. Lots of insight into what the other girls were into. Angel telling her that Rick thought she didn't want him—as if! Then Lexie suggested... aw shit. Well that explained how she'd ended up here. Although she couldn't really remember what had happened once they got here. Everything was kind of fuzzy and disjointed by then.

Very faint sounds were coming from the other side of the door, which meant Rick was both awake and moving around. Sneaking out probably wasn't an option. Maria moaned as she pushed herself up to a sitting position. It wasn't just her head that hurt; her whole body ached.

"I'm getting too old for this shit," she muttered. She could remember a time, heck five years ago, when she could have gotten shit-faced, stayed up all night and then been at work with just a headache the next morning. One of the hazards of getting older. Or maybe it was just that she didn't do it as often anymore. No tolerance. Either way, it sucked.

Her clothes from the day before were folded on top of Rick's dresser. Maria reluctantly took off what were obviously his t-shirt and boxers. She'd have to wait till she got home to change her panties, so she left those on and put on her bra, pants, and blouse. Wearing her dirty clothes made her feel kind of grimy, but she just couldn't face Rick while she was still wearing his. Yanking the rubberband out of her curls, she grabbed the heavy mass and put it up into a messy bun. There was no point in trying to do anything more with it right now.

Opening the bedroom door, the faint sounds resolved into the familiar clinks and sizzles of someone cooking. It smelled delicious. Even though she was still kind of nauseous, her stomach perked up.

Taking a deep breath, she made herself shuffle down the hallway to look into the kitchen. Seeing the movement, Rick looked up from the pan he was pushing eggs around. If her body didn't hurt so much, she would have appreciated the view a lot more. Sexy bare chest, pajama pants hugging his hips, ruffled morning hair, and cooking breakfast; he was like a woman's wet dream. Maria didn't even want to think about what she looked like.

"Good morning," Rick said, his lips curving into a grin. "How are you feeling, sunshine?" Maria just whimpered, and he chuckled sympathetically. "Come on and sit down." Setting down his spatula, he reached out and she automatically took his hand, allowing him to lead her over to the table. When she winced at the sunlight, even though he had the shades down, he sat her down at a seat where her back would be facing the outdoors.

"Coffee?" she asked, a hint of begging in her voice.

"Water first, you need to be hydrated before you have something that will dehydrate you further. Eat the banana."

Blinking at the table in front of her, she realized there was indeed both a glass of water and a banana sitting in front of her. The water was cool, not cold, and it felt wonderful. She had only meant to take a sip, but she found herself gulping it down and by the time she lowered the glass it was half gone.

"Good girl."

Maria looked up to find Rick watching her from his position at the stove, an approving look on his face. She wrinkled her nose at him, even though just hearing him say that made a strange little tingle of happiness go through her. This definitely wasn't a sexual situation, so she shouldn't like that, should she? Having him take care of her felt really nice, even though he wasn't supposed to be bossy outside of the bedroom.

Deciding to ignore him for now, because she could really only concentrate on one thing at a time at the moment anyway, she peeled the banana and took a bite. Ugh. Bananas weren't her favorite anyway, and right now her stomach was even less of a fan. But she chewed and swallowed the one bite while she watched Rick. Definitely a view worth watching. Even though he was shirtless, he didn't seem to get a single spatter of food or grease on him. She was envious; she always wore an apron when she was cooking bacon.

He was very purposeful, no motion wasted, as he finished up the eggs and put the bacon on a paper towel to soak up some of the grease. There was a pretty large pile of it already.

"Why don't you just microwave the bacon?" she asked. Even though it was kind of fun to watch him take each piece from the sizzling pan and add it to the pile, she realized he must have done at least three separate shifts of bacon to get the pile that large.

"I can control how crispy it gets more easily if it's in the pan," Rick replied, setting the last slice down just as the toast popped up out of the toaster. "I'm picky about my bacon." He winked at her as she fell silent again, just enjoying watching him plate the eggs, bacon, and toast.

The plate he set in front of her had way too much food on it, but she didn't say anything for now. She'd just eat what she could. Rick pulled butter and jelly out of the fridge for the toast and set it down between them, sliding into his own chair.

"So," he said, picking up his fork and scooping up some eggs. "How was your night last night?"

The twinkle in his blue eyes made her want to stab him with her fork. Instead she just set the utensil down and picked up a piece of bacon. Much less dangerous.

"What I remember was fun." She eyed him. "Hopefully not too embarrassing. What happened to Lexie and Angel?"

"Patrick and Adam picked them up. You don't remember?"

"Bits and pieces." Although now that he'd told her, she felt like she remembered a little more, as if he'd added some puzzle pieces to her memory and the picture was becoming clearer.

This time Rick's smile was slow, amused, spreading across his face until the corners of his eye crinkled. "Well, you may or may not remember, but I promised we would talk this morning. You seemed pretty mad we didn't talk yesterday. Which, I know was my fault. On Thursday, after the scene, I felt like you shut me out and were pushing me off. I thought the scene had gone really well and when you didn't even want to talk to me afterwards... well I thought that pretty much said it all."

"Oh I'm sorry..." Maria dropped the piece of bacon as guilt sparked. She'd been pretty mad yesterday that he'd made assumptions, but when he put it like that, she could see where he was coming from. If she'd been the one who'd immediately said 'let's get together again' and he'd told her they should wait until the next day to talk about it, she probably would have felt pretty rejected and thought a lot of the same things. "I didn't even think. I wasn't even capable of thinking at that point... I was just so overwhelmed by everything and I knew I wasn't thinking clearly and I just didn't want to make any decisions or anything while I was all spacy in my head. I wish you'd said something. I wish I'd said something."

"It was both our faults," Rick said, reaching over to hold her hand. His fingers curled around hers, strong and comforting. Even more comforting was how easily he took his portion of the blame. There were a lot of people out there, of both genders, who were quick to assign blame without acknowledging their own part in a misunderstanding. Maria had been quick to see where she'd gone wrong, but she did feel better knowing Rick felt like there were things he could have done to prevent the misunderstanding too. His smile turned rueful. "I shouldn't have jumped to conclusions and you should have been just a bit more forthcoming about where you were at post-scene. After all that talk about communication, we both kind of fell apart on that one. I wish I'd just let you talk yesterday morning, I had a really shit day thinking you just wanted to be friends. Which I was down with, it just hurt, and I needed some space to recover."

"I definitely don't want to just be friends," she said shyly, squeezing his hand. "I had a shitty day yesterday too, but the night before was... I don't even have words."

Rick's eyes sparkled at her as he gave her hand another squeeze before pushing it back towards her. "I know what you mean. Now eat your breakfast. You need something in your stomach."

"Bossy," she murmured, but there was no heat in her voice. Truthfully, she kind of liked how bossy he was, because right now it was making her feel cared about. Taken care of.

In the past when she'd gotten drunk, she'd pretty much always had to take care of herself. Unless she was going through a break-up or some kind of personal trauma, and then of course her sisters were there for her, but in the mornings she had always been the one fighting through her hangover to make sure everyone else was fed, hydrated and recovering. That had always been her job as eldest. Having someone else taking care of her felt weird but also really nice.

She told Rick some of what she and the other girls had talked about, nothing private of course, and then he told her more about all of his friends, in between making sure that she was eating and finally supplying her with coffee. Afterwards, he let her go upstairs to change while he did the dishes, although he made her promise to come right back downstairs once she was done so they could talk some more.

They'd gotten the whole misunderstanding and apologies out of the way quickly enough, but apparently Rick wanted to talk about the scene and what she'd liked, didn't like. He'd tried to start the conversation with her right then, but she'd asked for time to take a shower and change so she could feel more like herself before having to face that kind of conversation, and he'd relented.

"Oh noooo..." She groaned when she went to her bathroom and got a good look at herself. Going to bed in her make-up, even though she didn't wear that much to work, had given her raccoon eyes. And her hair looked freaking awful, even if the bun was supposed to look messy. It was like a bush on top of her head, one that was in desperate need of a bird to nest in it.

First things first. Her bladder was uncomfortably full, and she needed to brush her teeth so she could return to some sense of normalcy. Then came the hot shower, which helped to wake her up even more, even soothing some of the aches in her body.

By the time she was back at Rick's door, in fresh clothing (although still work clothes since she only had about an hour before she had to head over to the restaurant), with her curls tamed and her face scrubbed, she felt like a new person. Still an achy, slightly nauseous person, but a new person.

"Hey beautiful," Rick said, drawing her in through the door and brushing a swift kiss over her lips. "Welcome back." Even though she wanted to just press herself against him and get to the fun stuff, Maria made herself move past him into the apartment.

Standing awkwardly, not sure of where to go, she smiled as Rick took her by the arm and led her over to the couch. When he sat down, he pulled her down with him, practically on his lap. Maria tried to squirm away. "I thought we were going to talk."

"No reason why we can't cuddle while we talk."

Sure there was; because she couldn't think straight when she was pressed up against him and thinking about all the amazing things he'd done to her body and how hot and sexy he was. And she did need to think straight, because this was a relationship unlike any she'd ever been in—or ever known anyone else to be in—and she wanted to be able to use her head. Because right now, she wasn't entirely sure whether her heart or her head was in charge. She had a feeling her libido was running the show with her heart sitting in as V.P. It would be so easy to be overwhelmed by hot sex and Rick's caring, dominant nature. Maria was a little worried it would be too easy, and she didn't want to lose herself.

Still, she could compromise. She slid her legs over his lap while she turned to face him, pulling her upper body away. At first he looked surprised, but then he grinned and rested his hands on her legs, rubbing her thigh through the thin material of her summer pants.

"So... how do we talk about this?" Her voice came across almost business-like, which made Rick grin even wider.

"Well, first you tell me how you think the scene went, what you liked, what you didn't like."

Maria made a face. "Why does it seem like I'm always the one who has to tell you what's going on in my head first before you tell me anything?"

"Because I'm in charge," Rick said, giving her a meaningful look. "At least when it comes to the bedroom stuff. But I don't mind at all telling you that I loved every second of the scene, it was the hottest scene I've ever had in my life. I think that's because of the connection we have, and I want more." The calm tone he used was completely at odds with the hot, hungry look in his eyes. Maria felt her stomach flip over as he squeezed her thigh, just above her knee.

With other guys, she'd occasionally worried about casual touching on her more fleshy parts, even though she would have dumped any of their asses if they'd said anything derogatory about her body. With Rick she didn't even feel a flash of worry, because of the way he was looking at her. It was crystal clear Rick liked touching all her parts, and not just during sexy time.

"Okay..." Maria took a deep breath, a little bit shocked by how much he'd just revealed. "Then um... yeah. I really liked the scene. Everything about it." Even using words like "the scene" to distance herself a bit from it, she could feel a blush coming on.

Rick raised his eyebrows at her. "Everything?"

"Well, there were a couple of times when I kind of wanted to smack you and tell you to get on with it," Maria said, poking him in the arm and making him laugh. He squeezed her thigh again, his thumb stroking slightly, and she could feel her body hum with pleasure.

"That's what I like," he said, his smile fading just a bit as he became more serious, his gaze becoming more intent. "I like to draw everything out. In fact, I went easy on you the other night because you're so new to all of this and I was pretty sure you aren't used to being denied orgasm, but that's exactly what I want. I want to control your orgasms, so you only have them when I say you can, and that will mostly be when I give them to you. I might tie you up and tease you for hours before letting you come... or I might tie you up and make you come over and over again until you're begging me to stop. That's the kind of control which turns me on."

It was so, so wrong, but her pussy was clenching at both of those images. Had she already forgotten her railing frustration when he'd been taking his sweet time? And yet... the idea of being at his mercy again was... wow. Plus, come on, like she'd ever begged a guy to let her stop coming. That was something she'd like to experience.

"Okay... that's a lot. But um... I'm getting hot and bothered just hearing you talk about it and I don't know if it's just that it's you or if I'll actually like it, but I like you and I want to try..."

"Even though you wanted to smack me the other night?"

"Yeah, but even so it was still the most... well it was the best orgasm I've ever had." Maria rubbed her cheek, which felt like it was on fire from blushing. Even though she was looking at Rick, she couldn't quite look him in the eye while she said this, but he didn't call her on it, obviously realizing it was hard for her. "The best sexual experience I've had all around, really. Sometimes I think the only reason I'm not immediately down with all this is because there's a little voice in the back of my head that says I'm an independent woman and I shouldn't want to give up control over my body."

"Which is why it's such a gift when you do," Rick said softly. Reaching out, he pulled her a little bit closer, so she was practically on his lap again. This time Maria didn't resist, warming to the tenderness in his voice. "It's not something I, or any good Dom, takes for granted. I absolutely see you as an independent woman, who can take care of herself and doesn't need me—especially not to give you an orgasm. So when you give up your control, when you trust me to tie you up and have my wicked way with you," he winked, "when you submit to my desires and my control and wait for my say so to find pleasure... it means a great deal more to me than if you were completely dependent on me for everything or didn't know how to give yourself an orgasm." Maria giggled.

"Yeah, okay, I can see that," she said, feeling reassured. He'd said similar things to her already, but now that she'd gone through a scene with him, she had a much better understanding of exactly how much trust, how much submission it would require of her. "So, what about outside of that? Like, dating-wise. How does that work?"

"Just the way it's been working, except we start spending time together outside of just the mornings," Rick said, grinning. Reaching up, he brushed some strands of hair out of her face, cupping her cheek with his hand. Maria leaned into the caress, feeling even more of her nervousness trickle away. "I can't promise I won't be at least a little bit pushy outside of the bedroom, but I have no doubt you can hold your own. Just look at Adam and Angel for an example. In day to day life, he's a much bigger control freak than I am, he'd run someone like Hilary or Jessica right over, but Angel stands up to him no problem."

"And gets spanked for it."

"Only when she does it in the club. And you liked your spanking, sweetheart." He drawled the last part, making her body heat at the salacious way he said it and the memory of how much she'd liked being spanked. "So does she. That's not a real punishment for her."

Maria giggled. "Yeah, I did kinda get that impression."

"So what do you think?" Rick stroked his finger down her cheek. "Wanna have dinner with me tonight?"

That didn't even take a moment of thought.

"Yes, please."

$\mathscr{H}$   18   $\mathscr{H}$

**R**ick was on cloud nine, if cloud nine also happened to include blue ball hell.

Having decided it was best if he and Maria took a step back after the Introductory Scene, he'd ensured they didn't do more than kiss while they were together. Saturday morning he'd taken her to pick up her car so she could go to work. That afternoon he'd finally gone to her restaurant to visit her and then they'd ended up having dinner there. Which meant he didn't pay, but that was alright. He wasn't that much of a control freak. Afterwards he'd brought her back to his place and sat her down to watch A New Hope, because he still considered it a crime she hadn't seen any of the Star Wars movies.

She giggled through the light saber battle between Obi-Wan and Darth Vader at the end. Even Rick had to admit it didn't hold up compared to some of the later battles, much less modern technology, but otherwise she enjoyed the movie. Afterwards they'd cuddled on the couch talking some more, until they'd started kissing.

It took all of his self-control to walk her back up to her apartment that night, rather than dragging her down the hall to his bedroom like the horny animal he was. After that came the very long shower and right arm workout while he remembered her softness, her wet heat, and the way she writhed and begged while he tasted her. Unfortunately, jerking off one night didn't do anything to cool his libido the next day at the pool.

They had to keep it PG for the kids there, but they still flirted and splashed and kissed.

But most of all, they learned about each other. Rick told her about the camps his parents would send him to as a kid and how he'd come to his love of nature from that. Maria had never been camping, except for when she was in the Girl Scouts, which was definitely something he wanted to remedy. He told her about his brother Kenneth, whom he rarely talked about because they weren't exactly close anymore. Kenneth lived in Philly; three years Rick's senior, he'd been shocked and appalled when he'd walked in on Rick with a gagged woman tied to his bed. They'd explained things to Kenneth, after everyone was decently dressed, and his brother said he understood, but he'd never been comfortable with Rick after that. Which was why Rick only visited Kenneth and his wife Clara about once a year, usually on a holiday when he couldn't get down to his parents. And they never came to his place.

Maria had already told him a lot about herself, especially her family and her place in it. Always the older sister, always the caretaker. Always the good example. When she admitted to him that Jackie's pregnancy made her both excited and jealous, he hugged her close and told her it was only natural. After all, he'd felt the same way about his friends settling down into real relationships. It wasn't quite the same, but he knew the guilt that cluttered around feeling envious over someone else's happiness.

On Tuesday she texted him several times from work, which wasn't unusual. What was unusual was the depressing tone of her texts. She was having a rough day. Their food shipment had been late, which meant the kitchen had started off the day behind on their prep-work and weren't quite ready when the restaurant opened, which messed things up for the servers. Then, during the shift, they'd had several problem customers. On top of that, one of her long-term servers had been caught basically stealing, under-reporting his cash tips so he didn't have to give as much in tip-out to the busboys and food runners, and he was late without calling in for the third shift in a row, so she'd had to fire him.

By the time he got the text about the server she'd had to fire, he was already elbow deep in making dinner for her, hoping to give her an end-of-the-day pick-up. He'd even had Justin give him some ideas.

Filets wrapped in bacon with oven roasted asparagus and tomatoes and homemade macaroni and cheese with crumbled bacon on top. Rick had noticed how much she liked bacon when he'd made her breakfast Saturday morning; she'd eaten nearly as much as he had. The mac'n'cheese recipe was one of Justin's specialties, definitely not Kraft. Made out of gruyere and cheddar cheeses, cream, a bit of mustard for extra flavoring, put it all in a little individual baking dish and sprinkle panko bread crumbs and bacon on top. Healthy it was not, but it was mouthwateringly good, with the added benefit of being comfort food.

Come to my place when you get off work... I've got a surprise for you.

After a few minutes, his phone buzzed.

I should be out of here in twenty... I hope the surprise is a hug. =(

Aw. Cute. He'd hug her. Then he'd feed her and take care of her. And then he'd crawl on top of her and see if he couldn't find another way to ease her tension.

Sure, he'd wanted to take a step back after their scene and the misunderstandings, especially because she still seemed like she was finding her footing with the whole submission thing. He hadn't wanted her to think everything was about sex, but he could tell she was getting just as sexually frustrated as he was. So tonight was about TLC and then, if the mood was right, taking a small step forward.

The mac'n'cheese and tomatoes were in the oven and the steaks and asparagus were sitting on the counter, waiting for their turn, when Maria knocked on his door. Rick bounded over, swung the door open, and pulled her into his arms for a hug before she could even say hello.

Ooohhh... I needed this.

It was the perfect way to be greeted at the end of a long, hard day of work. Maria melted into Rick's body, clutching at him like he was a life raft, and he secured her in the circle of his arms and filled her back up with warmth. Today had sucked beyond all measure, but all of that seemed to float away while he was holding her.

"Hey sweetheart," he said, kissing the top of her head. He did that a lot, she noticed, kissing her forehead or cheek or the top of her head. At first she'd thought it was a little weird, like something a father or brother would do, but it also made her feel cared about. She was quickly learning to like those tender little kisses. "I made you dinner."

As if in response, Maria's stomach growled. She smiled a real smile for the first time in what felt like hours as she lifted her head and sniffed the air. "Oh my God, it smells amazing."

"Good, come on in and I can finish up."

Rick swept her into his apartment, dropping her purse on the table by the door and getting her seated in the breakfast nook with a glass of wine, while he finished up making her dinner. The filets with bacon sizzled while he talked, telling her about his own day and slowly lightening her mood as he described the custom-furniture pieces he'd helped Andrew with that morning and how he'd been fascinated by watching Andrew actually burn patterns into the pieces.

Even though it wasn't exactly fascinating conversational material, it helped her to relax as his easy tone soothed her. She sipped at the wine, because she didn't want more than one glass for the evening and she definitely wanted some of it with dinner. The conglomeration of amazing smells had her mouth watering.

"Oh... heaven..." Maria said after she'd swallowed her first mouthful of macaroni and cheese. It was creamy, tangy, and just a bit smoky, plus the little crunchy bits, all contributed to making it the best mac'n'cheese she'd ever had.

"Unfortunately not something I can take the real credit for," Rick said, smiling as he watched her eat. The pale blue t-shirt he was wearing matched his glowing eyes exactly, giving him kind of a surfer-boy look. Scruffy surfer boy, since he hadn't shaved today. Being blond, he didn't really need to, but sitting across the table from him she could see the scruff on his chin and cheeks. It was pretty hot. "I got the recipe from Justin."

"Mmmm... I should get the recipe from Justin and take it to Murphy's. We'd make a killing." Maria licked her spoon without thinking about it. Then she caught Rick's eye, saw the heat suddenly kindled there, and felt her insides clench.

He'd been making her crazy for the past few days, kissing and caressing her but never going beyond that. At first it had been reassuring that he wasn't just going to jump on her, that he obviously wanted to build a real relationship and not just one based on their compatibility in bed, but she was also starting to go a little stir crazy. Since they hadn't really talked about it, and even though she knew he wanted to control her orgasms, she'd gone ahead and taken care of her own needs when the itch became too much. But she would really, really like for it to be him.

Because he was way better than any vibrator.

"Glad you like it," he said, giving her a slow sexy smile.

"Love it," Maria replied, flicking her tongue along the underside of the spoon. The entire atmosphere around the table changed, tensed, and then Rick deliberately leaned back, breaking it.

His eyes sparkled. "More eating, less flirting."

"I can multi-task."

"Good to know," he said cheerfully, but the heat had already dwindled from his eyes and she knew he wasn't going to flirt back until he was satisfied she'd had enough to eat. Sometimes she thought he didn't realize exactly how dominant he was outside of the bedroom, but since he never actually ordered her around and he was usually just doing something to take care of her, it wasn't like she could complain.

It wasn't overwhelming, which was the important thing to her. Their interactions really hadn't changed much, except that now they touched and kissed a lot more than before. And she felt more and more comfortable around him as he became a more integral part of her life.

Sitting like this, eating the dinner he'd so thoughtfully made for her, made all sorts of warm fuzzies go off in her chest.

They talked and teased and then she insisted on helping with the dishes. It felt domestic and natural, even more comforting emotionally than the mac'n'cheese had been.

"Alright, beautiful," Rick said, turning her around and pressing her against the counter, trapping her between the hard surface and his hard body. His hands came down on either side of her, as if he didn't already have her immobilized just by the way he was leaning on her. "Now what do you want to do?"

It felt like every nerve in Maria's body came to life as he nuzzled along the side of her cheek and down to her neck. She clutched at the front of his shirt as her head fell back, giving him better access.

"Um... gee... I don't know... what do you want to do?" she asked. Her voice had gone all high and girlishly breathy as heat pooled in her stomach.

Rick's lips pressed against where her neck met her shoulder and she moaned, grateful she'd worn an open collar shirt today. Teeth grazed the same spot, not enough to hurt but just enough to sting a bit and she clutched at his shirt even harder, her fingers digging through the fabric.

She felt the front of her shirt give as he began unbuttoning it. "I was thinking I'd like to strip you down... and use my hands and mouth again..."

"Oh... yeah that sounds good," Maria said, nodding happily. She pulled him up by his shirt to give him a kiss, feeling him chuckle at her audacity, before he plundered her mouth. Their tongues danced together, as he got his hands on her hips, rocking his hips against her soft stomach so she could feel his cock digging into her.

And then he pulled away and flipped her around so she was facing the counter, bending forward slightly. "What did I tell you about topping from the bottom?" Rick asked, sounding amused as he pulled her shirt down over her arms and dropped it on the floor. "I'm in charge now."

"But we're not in the bedroom," she said, wiggling her bottom against him.

SMACK!

Maria shrieked as his hand came down hard on her ass, his body moving away just enough to allow him to whack her, before pressing back up against her. She gasped, throwing her hands out to catch herself on the counter, keeping her balance.

"Brat," he said, but he didn't actually sound upset. "If you're going to backtalk, I can think of better things for you to do with that mouth of yours."

That made her moan again. Maria was usually indifferent about giving head, to her it was a foreplay thing, but the idea of getting on her knees for Rick was a lot hotter than she'd have thought. Something about being in such a submissive posture before him and taking him into her mouth, pleasuring him, made her incredibly horny. With him it felt like it was going to be more than foreplay, like it could be pleasurable for her in and of itself. She rocked back against his cock as he undid her bra and pulled it from her body, before pushing her upper body down so she was bent over the counter again.

"Stay right there, just like that," he murmured, running his hand over her back, caressing her where her bra had just been.

Her nipples brushed the cool surface, making them even harder than they already were, and she shivered. Maria blinked as she stared down at the dark tan surface, her hands splayed out across it to help keep her balance as Rick's fingers quickly took care of the button and zipper on her pants. She felt him kneel down as he tugged her panties off along with her pants, leaving her completely naked and bent over his counter.

Warm hands pressed against her inner thighs, making her wiggle as she spread her legs further for him, knowing he was staring right at her pussy. It was slightly less awkward for her since this time she couldn't actually see him doing so. In fact, not being able to see him was rather exciting, she had no idea what he was going to do next.

The warmth of his hands moved up and down the backs of her thighs, coming closer and closer to her spread pussy with every sweep. Maria moaned, leaning forward even more to thrust her bottom out at him, her nipples pressing and flattening against the cool counter.

A kiss pressed against the under curve of her buttock, near her pussy but not nearly close enough. Maria's legs trembled, but she tried to hold still, remembering how the last time he'd teased her even more when she'd tried to make him move faster. Another kiss pressed against the other side, his hands cupping her buttocks and squeezing them. With a moan, Maria found herself arching involuntarily before she pushed her hips back down to press against the counter.

"Good girl, you're learning." The words were like a whisper across her skin and then she felt his hot breath on her pussy lips, his fingers sliding down the folds and gathering wetness as they went. She whimpered, closing her eyes as the sensations sparked little blazes in her pussy. "But... this isn't where I wanted to do this."

"What?!" Maria's eyes popped open and then she shrieked as Rick grabbed her and swung her up into his arms. Holy hell! This was the first time she'd ever been picked up in her adult life. She'd always assumed that, as a bigger girl, it wasn't something she was ever going to experience. To be honest, she'd always thought it was a bit silly in romance novels, but right now it felt kind of awesome. It made her feel tiny and delicate in a way that she hadn't experienced before.

Even if she did have to tuck in her legs as Rick moved through the apartment, heading for his bedroom, to avoid having her feet bang into the walls. That wasn't a weight thing, it was a height thing. Clinging to his neck, definitely a little bit worried he might drop her, she wasn't able to relax until he was tossing her onto his bed.

Bastard wasn't even breathing hard, she'd been worried for nothing.

"And here I thought those muscles were merely decorative," she murmured as he pulled off his shirt and started on his pants. Propping herself up on her elbows, she just enjoyed the quickly improving scenery as he stripped, barely pausing to give her a wink at her words.

Yeah, lots to admire here. Not just the muscles, but also the fact that they were nicely sized without being overdone. The scattering of blond curls on his chest, the slightly darker patch that led down from his belly to curls around his cock, which was jutting upwards perfectly.

"Does this mean I'm going to get to use my mouth too?" she asked, surprised at how wistful her voice sounded.

Rick's head swung up to look at her and he froze, one leg still in his pants, his gaze suddenly focused like a predator's. "If you're ready for that, sweetheart, I would like nothing better."

Mouth dry, unable to speak, Maria just nodded her head. The heat in his eyes went supernova as he stepped out of his pants and stalked towards the bed. To her surprise, he didn't immediately join her, he went to the nightstand first and pulled out a pair of leather cuffs, tethered together by a short metal chain. Maria's eyes widened as her heart rate picked up in excitement.

"Wrist." Rick held out his open palm and Maria immediately put her hand into it. He wrapped the leather around her wrist, tightening it and buckling it. "How does that feel? Too tight?"

The soft lining of the cuff was snug, but not at all tight. Like a strong embrace around her arm. "No it's good."

And it felt good too. Her heart beat faster, knowing she wasn't going to be able to move her arms, that she was going to have to trust Rick. She'd never considered being without her hands while giving head. It was both frightening and exciting. Realizing exactly how much she trusted him just aroused her even more.

He turned her, cuffing her wrists behind her back. Immediately it made her feel vulnerable and sexy as her breasts were thrust out by the position and she knew she could no longer use her hands or arms. The things he could do to her... but she trusted him not to, and that level of confidence in him made her feel almost transcendent. His hands slid up her arms to her shoulders and then down to her breasts, cupping them as he pulled her upper body back against him.

"Does being cuffed excite you, little tease? Do you like being at my mercy?" He nipped at her ear and little tingles went up and down her body as he squeezed her breasts, pinching her nipples between his fingers.

"Yes. Oh..." Maria moaned, long and low, as the pressure on her nipples increased and he rolled them back and forth. Her pussy pulsed. With her hands cuffed the way they were, she could feel his hard cock against her palm, and she just couldn't help herself... her fingers closed around it, making her feel wicked because she knew he was going to love the way it felt while simultaneously disapproving of what she was doing.

Rick huffed with laughter. "Are you trying to get a spanking? I think you might like that too much."

He pushed her forward then, and she cried out, before he caught her wrists and helped her slowly lower her upper body down onto the bed. The push and the catch turned her on just as much as everything else had, as strange as that sounded. Maybe because even when he'd pushed her, she hadn't really believed he'd forgotten she couldn't catch herself, she hadn't believed he'd let her fall.

Now she was rump up on the bed on her knees, her hands cuffed behind her, one side of her face pressed against the mattress, and absolutely desperate for Rick to touch her.

Two swift slaps to either side of her ass weren't exactly what she had in mind. They were hard, stinging, and then gone and she found herself disappointed he wasn't continuing. Instead, she heard plastic crinkling.

"Something else I did today that I forgot to mention until now," Rick said, his voice calm but eager, with a hint of anticipation. "I went to the store and picked up some new toys. Just for my little tease."

Something pressed against her pussy, cool and hard, and she moaned. It wasn't very long although it was bulbous shaped; she could feel it pressing into her, followed by his fingers. When his fingers retreated, she could feel something hanging down from her pussy and she clenched around the intruder, trying to figure out what it was.

Sensation hummed to life inside of her and she shuddered. It was some kind of vibrator, attached to a remote by a long wire, which Rick must be holding. Maria moaned as it buzzed away inside of her, making her pussy spasm with pleasure. This was hot.

This is hell, she thought, ten minutes later, her body clenching with need as the vibrator turned off again. Her moaning protest was muffled by the thick length of Rick's cock as she sucked him even harder.

It killed her that her response to being tormented was to suck for all she was worth, but it was the only kind of satisfaction he was giving her. He'd gotten himself situated on his back, the remote in one hand, while she crouched between his thighs and licked her way up and down his cock. At first they'd teased each other, as he switched the remote on and off at random intervals, alternating between throbbing, humming, and pulsing vibrations inside of her while she explored the veined length of his dick with her tongue.

Then he'd wrapped his fingers in her hair, pulling her mouth more firmly onto his cock, groaning as he slowly thrust between her lips and she sucked him deep. The writhing need in her body made her crave being filled in a way she'd never experienced before. Even though the vibrating egg inside of her was pleasuring her, it didn't fill her. If it wasn't moving, she would have barely noticed it was there.

The only place she was being filled was her mouth, and she found herself craving more, wanting to draw him deeper, because it was the only way she could have him inside of her right now. Feeling his pleasure, knowing it was pleasing him to torment her, was as sexy as it was frustrating.

Her neck and back were starting to have trouble, because she'd been bobbing up and down without the use of her hands, and he took up the slack to help her. For the first time in her life, she felt a man push against the back of her throat and actually go past her gag reflex. Panic flared for a moment, but then he was already pulling out, giving her room to breathe, before thrusting back in again.

Somehow he'd taken over complete control, holding her head in place and pushing his cock in and out of her mouth on his own. Maria cried out as the vibrator came to life inside of her again, making her body clench as he speared her throat. From his groans and quickening pace, she was sure he was going to cum soon.

And she wanted it. Needed to taste him. Then it would be her turn. But also because she truly wanted to experience his pleasure, to see him at the mercy of the passion between them, and to know she was satisfying his needs the way he was hers.

When he pressed her down, she couldn't help but fight it somewhat as hot liquid spurted inside of her mouth. She pulled her head back, needing the space to help her swallow as the salty-sweet, bitter flavor coated her tongue and warmth slid down her throat. Maria sucked, swallowed hard as he relaxed his hold on her, allowing her the space to breathe and swallow at the same time.

She hummed her pleasure, a warm feeling of glowing satisfaction spreading through her even though she hadn't reached her own climax. The gentle stroking of his fingers and his low sigh of completion were their own reward.

Although, she really did want to cum too.

"Good girl," Rick said, his voice filled with male satisfaction. His eyes glittered as she sat up, her lips feeling swollen, her belly full of his cum, and her pussy so wet and needy between her legs that she was desperate to rub up against something, anything, to get herself off.

Not that she had the chance.

Rick flipped her onto her back, being careful not to crush her arms or wrists beneath her, holding her legs and hips up so he could gently settle them down on top of her bound hands. Except he didn't settle them down all the way; his arms went underneath her thighs, wrapping around her legs and pressing his shoulders against them, bending her nearly in half and filling his hands with her breasts.

Right before he did that, he flipped the vibrator onto a shockingly high intensity pulse that made it almost feel as though it was thrusting inside of her. Maria's toes actually curled, digging into the sides of his back as she shrieked at the sudden sensation increase; his warm mouth finding her clit as his fingers pinched her nipples.

"Oh fuck!"

The sensations were almost too much after all the teasing, nearly painful in their pleasurable intensity, and Maria tried to writhe— except she couldn't. Rick was holding her too tightly and the cuffs on her wrists didn't have any give, and that just made her hotter and wetter. She was at the mercy of his mouth and hands and the vibrator pulsing inside of her, pinned in place and completely vulnerable.

He didn't make her wait for it; the steady suction of his mouth on her clit, the way he was pinching her nipples in time with the suction, and the matching pulsations of the vibrator sent her right over the edge.

"Rick! Oh fuck... oh fuck... oh fuck Rick!"

Hot, liquid ecstasy ran through her, making her want to pull away, to get some kind of a breather, but her position didn't allow it and she rode out the intense pleasure with tears beginning to roll down her cheeks. It was the first time she'd ever cried during an orgasm, but it was just too much for her body to bear and it felt like the excess was leaking out of her through her eyes.

"Rick... please... stop... fuck... please stop..."

It was becoming too much, her amped up body already revving right back up again; unable to descend from the high it had already reached, she found herself ascending to heights she hadn't thought were possible. She jerked and shuddered against him, succeeding only in adding to the sensations wrecking her brain as he gripped her nipples even more tightly to avoid releasing them.

"I want you to cum for me again," he said, releasing the suction on her clit just long enough to tongue it, to tease the folds with his mouth. His hands tightened on her breasts, making her moan in a kind of sexual anguish as the erotic tingles became almost stinging. Every inch of her skin felt doubly sensitive, doubly responsive to what he was doing to her.

His mouth closed over her clit again and sucked. She was going to explode.

Red! Say Red!!!

Her mouth opened, but just when she thought she couldn't take it anymore, something inside of her felt like it burst open. A release valve that flooded her system with blinding rapture, an orgasm so intense that all thought was vanquished from her mind. Not just tears, she was now sobbing, another way of releasing the built-up tension from her body. The humming vibrator inside of her felt like it was stabbing against the sensitized walls of her pussy, the pleasure becoming painful because her brain couldn't process what was happening to her.

Maria's heels drummed against Rick's back, not purposefully, but because she couldn't control her body's reactions. It was all too much. She felt like she was sinking, melting, and she suddenly understood why an orgasm was called a little death.

DIALING BACK THE VIBRATOR TO A STEADY, LOW HUM, RICK couldn't believe he was already hard and ready to go again. Maybe it wasn't that surprising. Feeling Maria struggle to move beneath him, tasting her on his tongue, feeling her softness in his hands, hearing her cry out his name... not to mention knowing she was riding a sexual high, was all extremely arousing to him. Even if he had just cum ten minutes ago.

He could hear the ragged, near-panic in her voice as she'd hit her second orgasm, known he was pushing her close to the edge... but he wanted to show her the other side of his desire for control over her orgasms. Although withholding pleasure could be rewarding, he also wanted to overload her with it, to drown her in it.

Right now, that meant pulling back slightly. Her sobs had quieted to whimpers as he laved his tongue over her pussy, soothing the hot, swollen flesh as it quivered under his touch. Gentling his hold on her breasts, he caressed and squeezed them, barely running his fingers over her nipples.

Just like a man needed time between orgasms before he could come again, so did a woman. Multiple orgasms were different, but right now Maria needed a bit of a break before her body would be able to peak again. After all, mountains couldn't exist without valleys.

"Rick?" Her voice was breathless, questioning, and slightly confused.

"Yes, sweetheart?" he asked, looking up the curvy length of her body to meet her eyes, enjoying the sight of all her swells and dips along the way. Lots of nice valleys there to appreciate.

Her eyes were slightly reddened, tear tracks down the sides of her face, and her cheeks were pink, her hair slightly mussed from both his manipulations while she'd been giving him head and the way she'd been tossing her head back and forth while she was on her back. Rick's cock jerked, pressing hard against the bed beneath him. Fuck she was gorgeous. He licked up her creamy center, enjoying the shudder that went through her. A few more minutes and she'd be ready for him to ramp things up again.

"What are... are you... um... I thought we were done?" It came out as a question, making him chuckle a bit. She squirmed a little, obviously slightly uncomfortable about having a conversation with him while he was still licking her pussy.

"Mmmm... no," he replied, sliding his tongue into her hole, spearing her pussy with it and then pulling back out. The humming vibrations echoing up and down her channel actually made his tongue tickle a little bit when he did that, but it was worth it to see her reaction and feel the lift of her hips in response. "I'm not done eating this gorgeous pussy... I'd like to have you come on my face at least one more time."

Consternation, arousal, anxiety, excitement... he kept a careful watch on her expressions as they flitted across her face. Her legs tensed, trying to push him down and away from her. Ha, not gonna happen. Even better, when she wasn't able to dislodge him, he could see the way that aroused her even further, her eyes getting big as her nipples plumped again.

"Okay... yellow, I'm not sure I can handle that." Her voice quavered, but he could see the curiosity in her eyes, feeling the way her pussy was fluttering around the vibe.

But he pulled back enough to rest his cheek on her thigh, still close to her pussy but no longer licking it. More confusion in her expression, as if she'd just realized some part of her hadn't really wanted him to stop. Rick plucked at her nipples and she shuddered, looking at him suspiciously.

"I thought yellow meant we slow down and talk about things."

"It does." Rick grinned. "But slow down doesn't mean stop." He nuzzled his face against her thigh, pinching her nipples and rolling them through his fingers, keeping her body primed. If he stopped playing with her completely, she might lose some of the needy edge he was working so hard on building back up.

She squirmed. "Can you at least turn off the vibrator?"

"No."

Yeah, that turned her on. Apparently Maria liked being denied. It was turning Rick on too, although before today he wouldn't have said it was a particular kink of his. Seeing Maria's arousal was what made his cock twitch; although he did have to admit he liked this kind of control over her too. The subs at the club would never ask for something like that, they knew to leave it up to the Dom. Rick had already decided he didn't want to change that about Maria, he liked that she was constantly talking, asking... he didn't want to train any of that out of her. It was refreshing, even if it wasn't what he'd once imagined when he'd been fantasizing about the sub he'd settle down with.

Maria's breathing was becoming heavier, her slick pussy calling to him… but she'd said yellow and he wasn't going to break her trust.

"So what's wrong, sweetheart? What can't you handle?"

She bit her lip, looking adorably uncomfortable. "Another orgasm… it's just… it's so much, I feel… um… I can't even think of the word."

"Overwhelmed?"

"Yeah, that." She nodded, looking relieved he understood.

Of course he understood, but that wasn't going to save her. "Good. I want you to feel overwhelmed. I told you before… I want you at my mercy…" His words were becoming more ragged. He licked a line up her pussy. "I want you screaming with pleasure, until you're begging me to stop."

"I already did that." Her voice was husky, aroused.

"Yeah, and you're going to do it again… I want to watch you come on my tongue one more time. And sweetheart, this time, unless you say 'red,' I'm not going to stop."

Rick let go of one of her breasts to flick the switch on the vibrator, amping the intensity back up and changing it from a steady hum to a throbbing pulse. As she moaned, her hips lifting up, he renewed his feast on her pussy.

A deep shudder went through her body as she tried to tighten her legs around his head, an instinctive reaction to try and gain control over the amount of sensation running through her. Rick didn't give her the chance. Releasing her breasts, he wrapped his hands around her thighs, prying them apart and tilting her hips even further up. She cried out, her back arching as her pussy was opened completely to him, unable to protect herself from the onslaught of his tongue.

He suckled her clit into his mouth, sliding his tongue around the tiny nubbin, ignoring her renewed pleas for him to stop. She called out his name and begged him to go slower, to stop, but she didn't say 'red.' Like a good submissive, she wanted to please him. More than that, she trusted him. Even though she thought she couldn't handle it, she gave over the control to him and allowed him to push her past the point where she would have stopped. His cock was practically throbbing, and he wondered if he was going to cum without even touching himself.

Then, she came. Gloriously. Beautifully. Screaming his name with a ragged passion that had him groaning against her soft flesh. She was crying again, and if he hadn't had such a firm hold on her legs, he was pretty sure she would have kicked the shit out of him in the throes of her climax. Which just turned him on even more.

Slowing the steady sucking on her clit, he lowered her hips back down, reaching out for the remote and muting it back down to a low buzz. Maria moaned, whimpering as he released her clit, her body still spasming with the after effects of so many orgasms.

With her legs spread to show her swollen pussy, her arms still bound behind her, and her eyes glazed with satisfied passion, she was like a wet dream come true. Planting one hand on the bed next to her shoulder, Rick wrapped his other hand around his cock. The shaft was hot and hard in his hand and he groaned with pleasure as he squeezed, fisting the iron rod and pumping, fast and hard.

It took him less than a minute for his amped up sexual frustration to peak and spill out all over Maria's body, thick streams of cum landing on her stomach and breasts. He looked down to see her watching in fascination, and he groaned as the sight caused another spurt of ecstasy.

The complete loss of his self-control was almost frightening, except he loved it too. Being with Maria made more than just his emotions spill out all over the place. With other women maintaining control had been easier, because he hadn't felt the same way about them as he did with her.

Breathing heavily, he worked the last few drops of cum from his cock, a feeling of complete satisfaction rolling over him as he looked down at his handiwork. A spatter pattern of his seed over her belly and breasts, marking her as his. It satisfied something dark and primitive inside of him.

Studying fluid patterns on her belly and breasts, Maria had a slightly different reaction.

"You know... I always thought this would be gross, but that was actually kind of hot," she murmured, and Rick had to laugh.

He loved the things that came out of her mouth. It might not have been the sexiest thing to say, or the most complimentary, but it was honest, and she brought a sense of humor to the situation most women didn't. At least, most women he'd encountered.

Helping her to sit up, he undid the cuffs from her wrists. She winced as she rotated her shoulders, shrugging the soreness from them, and he immediately felt bad. If he was going to play for so long with her, he shouldn't have kept her in that position; it wasn't an easy one on the body.

Bundling her up into his arms, Rick took her to the shower. She was a bit wobbly on her feet, still kind of out of it, and he enjoyed the way she clung to him in the shower, her body all slick and wet. One day, he promised himself, he'd have her like this, all wrung out and wobbly in the shower, and then he'd press her up against the wall and fuck another orgasm out of her while she begged for a respite. But not today.

Today he let her lean against him, enjoying her soft breasts on his chest, her happy humming in his ear as he wrapped his arms around her and soaped down her back. He kissed her forehead, her closed eyelids, her cheeks, her lips, as he cleaned her off.

Afterwards, he wrapped her in a towel. The heat had obviously gotten to her—and to him a bit as well—and she was practically dead on her feet. Sitting her down on the toilet, he brushed through her hair and pressed as much water out of it as he could, not wanting her to go to bed with completely wet hair.

He took far too much satisfaction in getting her settled naked into his bed, her head on his shoulder, half-dried hair spread out across his arm, breasts tucked against his side and one leg over his thighs. Maria mumbled something incoherent as he arranged her. Rick would have liked to talk a bit, but sleep had already taken her.

Well, at least he was pretty sure he'd made her day better.

### ❦  19  ❦

**M**aria woke up alone in Rick's bed. At least this time she wasn't hungover. Unless there was such a thing as a sex hangover. Her pussy felt like there was. It was sore in the most delicious way, even brushing her fingers over it made her wince, and yet her body tingled as she remembered the fucking phenomenal night they'd had. Without having actual intercourse once.

At this point, she wasn't sure she'd survive sex with Rick. Was there such a thing as being too good in bed?

Or maybe, with prolonged exposure, she'd become more acclimated to it. Like alcohol tolerance.

Grabbing one of his t-shirts so she didn't have to walk naked out into his main rooms, she went looking for her clothes. She was a little let down he hadn't had them all ready for her the way he had the other day, but it turned out they weren't just lying in the little piles in the kitchen where they'd be left. Nope. He'd folded them up and stacked them and put them on his couch.

A little smile flitted on her lips. Maybe he'd wanted her to be naked while walking around his apartment.

There was also a sticky note sticking to her bra, which was on the top of the pile.

Out for my swim. Come join me?

Maria was pulling on her pants, so she could go upstairs to get her bathing suit, when his front door opened.

"Aww, I'm too late?" she asked, trying not to wince as her pants settled into place, brushing against her sensitive pussy lips.

Wearing a blue striped bathing suit, a towel around his neck, and nothing else, Rick looked incredibly surfer-boy sexy. "Hey sleepyhead."

"How did you wake up so early?" she grumbled, going over to him and stretching up for a kiss. Mindful of her morning breath, she kept her lips closed, but she wanted to kiss him anyway. His skin was slightly clammy under her hands.

"Habit. Although I was a little later for my swim than usual." He glanced at the clock. "I've got just enough time to shower and get out of here... what are you doing tonight?"

"Dinner with my family," she said. A little voice in the back of her head said she should invite him, but that seemed like it was moving really fast. As far as they knew, her first date with him had been last Thursday. Maria never introduced guys to her family right away, at least not since high school.

Fortunately, Rick just smiled at her, taking away her anxiety and the pushy voice in the back of her head. "That sounds like fun. If you feel like stopping by afterwards, I'll be around."

"You're not doing anything tonight?" As soon as the words were out of her mouth, she kind of felt like an idiot. Duh, of course he wasn't, otherwise he wouldn't have asked her what she was doing.

"Well, since you're not around I'll probably go to Liam's dojo," he said, wrapping his arm around her waist. "But I'll be home by eight."

"Okay."

One more kiss to her lips and then she was out the door and on her way up to her own apartment. Not quite a walk of shame since she was at least wearing his t-shirt and not her shirt from yesterday. It was a nice soft t-shirt too, long enough it covered her butt, and in a dark slate gray color that was somehow flattering to both of their skin tones. Maria grinned as she went into her apartment, picking it up by the collar to sniff at it.

Yeah, it smelled like him.

"I hope he doesn't think he's getting this back," she mumbled to herself.

DAMMIT, SHE SHOULD HAVE JUST INVITED RICK. DINNER WITH HER family had somehow turned into a barbecue at her parents with her family plus about ten other people. Some of her parents' neighbors had ended up being invited over, because they were 'like' family. Ava had brought her friends Wendy and Cara because... well Maria still wasn't entirely sure she understood the full convoluted story, just something about men sucking and Wendy needing support. Then, worst of all, when Lara had arrived and seen that there were extra people, she'd texted Victor and told him to go ahead and bring his buddies he'd been having happy hour with. Maria definitely didn't have a problem with Victor's friend Sameer, who was friendly, articulate, and intelligent, but she would never understand why either of them were friends with Jeremy.

At least there were enough people that it was relatively easy for her to stay out of whatever group Jeremy was currently having a conversation with. She had absolutely no desire to say another word to him after the way their conversation had ended at Lara and Victor's engagement party. Although, technically she supposed she'd taken his advice about getting laid, but it definitely didn't make her want to be a nicer person to him.

"...I swear, it's like a chainsaw ripping through my eardrums, but the second I touch his shoulder he's awake and telling me he couldn't possibly have been snoring because he hadn't even fallen asleep yet." Barbara, who lived next door to Maria's parents, waved her hands in the air in frustration. Her husband Gerry just smiled indulgently and shook his head.

"She's making this all up," he told Lara, grinning at the look of outrage his wife gave him in response. They were giving Lara 'marital' advice, with the exact same stories—and arguments—that they'd given all of Maria's sisters before their weddings. No one ever tried to stop their recitations, they obviously enjoyed it so much. The two of them had been married for over thirty years and were thoroughly enjoying their retirement together.

"I am not."

"That's okay," Lara interrupted, laughing at the older couples' bickering. "We don't have that problem, Victor doesn't snore."

"Just wait till he gets older," Barbara said, shaking her head sadly. "You think this one snored like that when we first got married? Ha! I would've left in the first year. Now I've got too much time invested with him. I finally got him trained to put the toilet seat down and he starts in on this."

Maria giggled along with Lara, as much at the couples' antics as at their words. For all their constant bickering and sniping, Barbara and Gerry always did it with a note of loving amusement in their voices. Kind of like her and Rick in a way maybe. Except he would also spank her ass if she took it too far.

Looking to her left she caught Jackie's eye and immediately blushed, since Jackie was the only one of her sisters who knew anything about that side of Rick. So far none of her sisters had been able to grill her about her "date" with Rick last Thursday. Too many people around. But the speculation on Jackie's face said that might not last for too long.

Sure enough, five minutes later, Jackie was calling her over, asking for help in the kitchen. Uh huh. Maria sighed inwardly. Interrogation time.

"Soooo... how are you?" Jackie asked as soon as they got to the kitchen, her dark eyes sparkling with eagerness as she started to load up slices of bread onto a tray. They'd run out of bruschetta outside.

"Doing okay, how are you?" Maria asked, mimicking her sister's syrupy tones. More than okay, really. She was still sore down between her legs, but in a mostly good way, although she managed not to think about it too much while she was outside and surrounded by people. Mostly because it was really super awkward thinking about that when half of the people around her were family. She grabbed the bowl of bruschetta topping her mom had in the fridge and put it on the counter next to Jackie.

"Oh, I'm great. Just wondering how my sister's hot date went," Jackie winked at her. "Since you didn't call or anything afterwards."

"You didn't call me either," Maria pointed out, although she did feel a bit guilty. She'd always been close to her sisters, even though they'd drifted a bit after they'd all gotten married and she hadn't. Any other guy and she probably would have been on the phone with each of them within the first forty-eight hours post-date. Then again, things with Rick had gotten pretty complicated quickly, and she'd known none of her sisters would be able to understand. Not that she was going to explain it to Jackie right now. It felt weird, but there were just some things she wasn't going to be able to share with her sisters about her and Rick's relationship. "I thought maybe you weren't interested."

Jackie rolled her eyes, spooning the tomatoes onto the bread. "I just thought you might be still thinking things over because of... you know." Her voice went sly and she gave Maria a significant look. Complete with eyebrow waggling.

"Well it went great. Even um... that part." Maria blushed as Jackie's jaw dropped open.

"You—you didn't... you already—?"

"Shhh," Maria hushed her, automatically looking over her shoulder to make sure no one had snuck up on them. Her face felt like it was burning up. Even speaking so ambiguously felt dangerous. She lowered her voice, leaning in towards her sister. "I haven't slept with him yet but yes, we tried out the you know, and it went fine. Better than fine."

"Told you so," Jackie said, gleeful.

"Yeah, just... don't mention it to Lara and Ava. I'll tell them the date went well. We spent some more time together over the weekend. Last night he made me dinner," Maria said, feeling warmth swelling in her chest. This was the good stuff, the stuff she could share with her sisters. The stuff she wanted them to know. She was dating a man and he was freaking awesome. They'd just skip over talking about the freaky in the sack part. "Surprised me with it because I'd been having a bad day."

Jackie's eyes practically glowed, reflecting Maria's own feelings back at her. She could tell how happy she must look, because of how happy Jackie looked right now.

"Now that's the kind of thing I like to hear," she said, leaning against the counter. The bruschetta lay next to her on the tray, basically forgotten, Maria was amused to see. "When are you seeing him next?"

"Well, he told me to stop by tonight. I might have brought him here if I'd realized how crazy this 'family dinner' was going to be," she said, glancing out the window into the backyard full of people. Maybe she wouldn't have. It was kind of early in their relationship to be introducing him to her family, but she was surprised by how much she wanted to.

"Trying to scare him away already?" Jackie asked, amused, as she looked over her shoulder at the fracas. "That's not nice."

"Oh shut up and go back outside," Maria said, pushing her sister back toward the door so she could finish up the bruschetta. Laughing, Jackie did as she was told, satisfied now that she'd gotten the dirt. Maria had no doubt by the time she got outside again, Ava and Lara would know her date had gone well, and she'd be seeing him again.

At least no one would tell their parents. That was sister-code. They would gossip as much as they wanted about boys among themselves, but everyone got to tell mom and dad in their own time. Maria grinned, wondering how Rick would handle her parents and sisters. She had a feeling he and her dad would get along pretty well, and he'd fit right in with her brother-in-laws. Come to think of it, they were all kind of alpha-males in their own way. And none of them quite knew how to deal with her mother.

Theresa Arias was like a small whirlwind, able to herd large groups of alpha males into doing what she wanted. Unless her husband put his foot down, of course. Then she was just sneakier about it. Maria grinned, wondering if she would ever be able to be quite like that. Somehow she doubted it. Besides, in Rick's group of friends that seemed to be Olivia's job.

"Guess I shouldn't be surprised to find you in here." The sneering, deep voice could only belong to one person.

Maria made a face, putting the bruschetta in the oven before turning to face Jeremy. He was leaning against the doorway, looking both bored and contemptuous, with his arms crossed over his chest.

"And what do you mean by that?" She supposed she could have played nice, but that was just so not her style. Especially not in her parents' home. Maybe if they'd been in public, but here? This wasn't her sister's engagement party and Maria didn't care if she made a scene. Not like there was anyone else inside the house right now anyway, they were all out back, so if Jeremy wasn't going to play nice then she sure as hell wasn't either.

"You know... the kitchen..." He untucked one of his hands and waved his finger in a small circle to indicate the room. "Where all the food is."

"Actually, most of the food is in the backyard right now, jackass," she said, not at all surprised he was back to the fat jokes. Seriously, would he ever grow up? She'd heard enough of them in high school, and even college, but at this point in her life, most people were more aware of themselves and most people weren't so shallow.

"So you're not hiding out in here, trying to drown your sorrows in food?"

Maria snorted. "Seriously? What sorrows exactly?"

"Oh, I don't know... the fact that you're the oldest sister and the only one who doesn't have a ring on her finger," Jeremy said, tossing his head back. It made his dark hair kind of do a little flip, and she wondered if he thought that was somehow attractive. Well, maybe it would be if he didn't have such an ugly personality. "Making up some imaginary boyfriend who just couldn't come tonight."

Wow... apparently word got around fast. Jackie must have said something to either Ava or Lara where Jeremy could hear. Not Jackie's fault really, but it made Maria's insides burn that she had to deal with this jackass and his insinuations. She was fine with how she looked. Seriously. His words didn't hurt, but they sure as hell pissed her off.

Clenching her fists by her sides, she looked at him coldly. "I think you should get your ass back outside and find some people who actually like you before I kick you out of here."

To her further frustration, Jeremy just smirked and shook his head at her like she was a naughty child as he straightened up. "And then go outside and tell everyone what... that you kicked out your sister's best man in her wedding because he called you out on your imaginary boyfriend? Come on, Maria, don't be like that."

Dammit he was probably right. Which just made her more furious. Not the imaginary boyfriend part, of course, but if she actually kicked him out then she'd have to be the one to explain it. Kicking him out would be descending to his level.

Why was she letting him get to her anyway? This entire conversation was pointless and stupid and the best thing to do was to show complete indifference to him.

She flipped her hand at him. "Whatever. I'll go. Keep an eye on the bruschetta and take it out in about ten minutes."

Turning to go out the other entryway, even though it would mean she'd have to go out the front and walk around the entire house on the outside, Maria wasn't too surprised to hear movement behind her. She looked back, expecting to see him retreating so he wouldn't have to watch over the bruschetta, but instead he was halfway across the kitchen and moving closer.

"Aw, come on Maria, don't be like that," he said, giving her a smarmy kind of grin. "I just wanted to tell you you don't have to make-up boyfriends, I'll take you out."

She froze, completely and utterly poleaxed as she re-ran his words through her head. "Are you asking me out on a date?"

Even more surprising, Jeremy stopped walking toward her, suddenly looked incredibly awkward, even though he was trying to pull off nonchalance. He shoved his hands into his shorts' pockets and shrugged. "I guess. So you wanna?"

"No." She started to turn again.

"Why not?"

And right back around again. "Seriously? What are you, the five-year old on the playground who thinks being a jerk is the way to win over the girl?"

"I was just teasing." He grinned, as if inviting her to share in the joke. Maria was not impressed. "I mean, you're a big girl, but you're still pretty hot. You were kind of a bitch at Victor and Lara's engagement party, but that was kinda hot too."

Maria stared at him for a long moment. "You have issues Jeremy.

And no. Sorry, but my boyfriend is neither imaginary nor into shar-ing." Turning on her heel, she quick-stepped out of the room before he could respond, only taking a moment to call back: "Don't forget about the bruschetta!"

Stepping back outside, she started to make her way around the house, shaking her head. Would wonders never cease. The sad thing was, before she'd met Rick, she might have thought Jeremy's little performance back there in the kitchen kind of cute. Now it was just sad, sad, sad. And a little entertaining. She actually almost felt a little sorry for Jeremy. No wonder he didn't have a girlfriend, he had no game.

She put a smile on her face as she joined the crowd in the backyard again. Ava and Lara immediately came over, making a little sister huddle no one else was going to interrupt with all the giggling and whispering. A few minutes later, Jeremy came outside with the tray of bruschetta. He shot Maria a nasty look, which she ignored, and strolled over to join a conversation on the opposite side of the yard.

Definitely should have brought Rick. Then they could have avoided the whole scene altogether. Maria wondered if she and Rick would still be together closer to Lara's wedding, when she'd have to be seeing more of the wedding party anyway. She imagined bringing Rick to her sister's wedding and seeing the look on Jeremy's face when he saw her imaginary boyfriend.

It gave her a little shiver of both apprehension and hope when she realized how far into the future she was picturing Rick and herself.

BODIES WERE SPRAWLED OUT, IN VARIOUS LIMP POSITIONS, ACROSS the mats. They were supposed to be stretching, but that had pretty much devolved into basically resting. Even Liam seemed tired, he was the only one still stretching, but he was doing it slowly and almost disinterestedly.

Rick groaned as a sore muscle in his back twinged when he tried to roll over. Andrew had gotten him good there during their sparring match. Maybe he could convince Maria to give him a massage tonight.

Extra bonus of having a girlfriend—someone to help relieve his aches and pains.

Next to him, Jared stretched out his leg and nudged Rick with his foot. "So what are you doing here tonight? I thought you'd be hanging out with Maria."

"She had a family dinner... I'm just wasting time with you guys till she's back."

"Family dinner and she didn't invite you?" That was Andrew, pushing himself up to a sitting position. Sweat had visibly soaked through his white tank; he'd been working out some kind of emotional angst tonight for sure, sparring with both Rick and Liam. He'd definitely be feeling it tomorrow too.

"We haven't exactly been going out long," Rick reminded him, trying not to feel defensive. Although he knew very well that if she had invited him, he would have been delighted. But he wasn't going to get upset she hadn't. "I'll meet them eventually. We're still figuring things out."

Andrew's eyebrows went up. "What does that mean?"

"It means she's a newbie to the scene," Rick said, shrugging as he moved his head back and forth, trying to work out some of the kinks in his neck. "She's just a little apprehensive, so we're taking things slow."

"Good idea," Liam said, interjecting while Andrew scowled. "You don't want to overwhelm her."

"I liked her when I met her, but don't let her twist you around or lead you on if she's not sure she's actually into this lifestyle. All you'll end up with is a bunch of regrets and doubts," Andrew said, his voice dark. He pushed himself up to a standing position. "No woman is worth that. I'm gonna hit the showers."

Now Rick was definitely feeling defensive, but he kept his mouth shut while Andrew stalked from the room. All of them knew it was his past speaking for him. Rick didn't know all the details about Andrew's last relationship, but he knew it had been right when Andrew had first started exploring BDSM and his girlfriend had been doing so with him. Then everything had gone to shit, and Andrew hadn't had anything more than scenes at the club ever since. So he knew Andrew wasn't really talking about Maria leading Rick on, he was talking about his ex leading him on. Which made Rick even more curious about exactly what had gone down between them. He wasn't sure he'd ever know.

"Don't mind him," Liam said quietly. "He's just a wee bit biased."

"Besides, newbies work out for some of us," Jared said, giving Liam a significant look. The big man was looking pretty relaxed these days, with Marissa out of town. Sure, he wasn't playing at the club, but at least he didn't look constantly miserable either.

"Pretty darn well too," Liam said. He grinned, boyishly, and suddenly looked almost sheepish. "I'm ah... well, I meant to tell you guys when Andrew was still in here, but um... This weekend I'm going to ask Hilary to marry me."

Rick let out a whoop of joy, doing a kind of sitting leap to land on Liam, hugging the fucker for all he was worth. A heavy weight crashed into both of them, taking them down to the mat as a laughing Jared piled on.

"Fuck yeah! Congratulations man."

"You're the man."

"Get off of me. You're both sweaty and gross." Liam pushed upwards, using momentum to stand and shove both Jared and Rick off of him. Laughing, they rolled away on the floor. All of Rick's lethargy from the workout had vanished. He was too happy for his friend to be anything but super energized.

"So you think she's gonna say yes?"

"Fuck you."

THE TELEVISION WAS ON, BUT NO ONE WAS PAYING ANY ATTENTION to it. They'd all wanted to do a small celebration with Liam, because no one really thought Hilary's answer would be anything but 'yes,' and Rick had convinced them to come back to his place so he could keep his promise to Maria about being there. He supposed he could have just texted her he was going out and why, but he wanted to see his girl.

For some reason, knowing the first of his friends was getting engaged, was making Rick feel even more anxious to see her. Almost needy. He didn't like that word. Needy. But he couldn't deny that was how he felt. Maybe especially because of Andrew's words. He still didn't know what had happened to end Andrew and Kate's relationship, but he definitely didn't want to go that way with Maria. It made him want to get his hands on her and ensure she wasn't going anywhere.

Plus, it was cheaper than going out to a bar. They'd bought a couple six packs on the way back to his place to share. Liam had already told Olivia, Justin, and Chris, he called Adam and Patrick from Rick's to tell them. Adam declined the invitation to come over, saying he was all tied up with Angel that evening—Rick had a feeling Angel was probably all tied up while Adam took the call. Patrick didn't answer his phone, but since it was Swingers Night at the club that wasn't too surprising; he was likely walking the floor and keeping an eye on things.

They weren't looking to get drunk, just have a good time and enjoy each other. Liam admitted he was nervous.

"I was gonna do it last week, but I chickened out."

"You guys have talked about it though, right?" Jared asked. "I mean, it's not just going to come out of the blue."

"Well I'm hoping to surprise her, but yeah we've talked about getting married." Liam grinned. "Talked through the important things like how many kids we'd like, whether or not to go to church, how we'd want to do our finances. All that kind of stuff."

Geez. Just hearing Liam say it made everything seem more real. He and Hilary were really going to do this and make babies and be a family. It hit Rick that he and his friends were really, fully adults now. Being responsible for yourself was one thing, but taking on the responsibility of having a family? That almost seemed like a fantasy to him, something for the far away future, but now Liam was bringing it home.

He found himself wondering if Maria would want kids, hoping she would. Where she might want to live... did she see herself in this apartment building forever? And what about her job? She worked late evenings sometimes and—okay, get yourself together jackass.

This is exactly what your friends mean about getting ahead of yourself.

Fortunately no one had noticed his distraction. Jared and Liam were still talking about the topics people who were getting married should work out before the wedding and swapping stories about people they'd known who hadn't. Andrew was just as lost in his own little world as Rick was. While he was putting a smile on his face, and nodding his head, Rick could see Andrew's dark eyes weren't entirely focused. He also wasn't contributing much to the conversation, he was mostly drinking.

Rick suddenly wondered if it was hard for Andrew, seeing his friends suddenly shacking up in serious relationships when for so long all of them had been single or just casually dating. They were falling like flies, one after the other. Hell, Justin and Chris had started it by going down together. Well technically he supposed Jared and Marissa had been the first to be in a serious relationship, but no one in their group of friends counted them as a serious couple. Mostly because they didn't want to. But out of all of them, Andrew was the least interested in having a relationship. Was he worried he might lose his friends as he lost things in common with them?

Rick didn't have time to try and bring Andrew back into the conversation, because his doorbell rang. The sound made his heart leap in his chest with excitement as a single thought rolled through his mind: Maria.

Sure enough, his gorgeous girl was outside his door, looking tired, but her brilliant smile as she saw him lit up her entire face. A guy could get used to putting that expression on his girl's face. He grinned back at her, feeling warm and happy all the way down to his toes.

"Maria."

"Hey Maria."

The guys all called out their greetings, and Maria blinked in surprise as she turned to look at them. Rick realized he'd forgotten to text her to give her a heads up that some of the guys were over.

"Come on in, we're just having an impromptu celebration for Liam," he said, explaining. "He made a very important announcement this evening."

Liam puffed up in his chair, beaming at Maria. He was definitely a little drunk. "I'm gonna ask Hilary to marry me this weekend."

Immediately Maria's face lit up and she clapped her hands in excitement, bouncing slightly. "Oh my God, Liam, that's amazing!" she squealed, dropping her purse as she darted across the room to hug him. Rick had to squash down the instant surge of jealousy as Maria practically sat on Liam's lap in order to wrap her arms around him. "I'm so happy for you."

Hugs were good, but enough was enough. Rick had moved close enough to see Liam was getting a fantastic view of Maria's cleavage. Those were his boobs to ogle. Wrapping his arm around her waist, he pulled her up and dragged her the few steps back so he could sit back in his previous seat, taking her with him.

She went with him easily enough, relinquishing her hold on Liam. Practically bouncing on Rick's lap, her eyes sparkled with glee, but she gave Rick an almost apologetic look. "Are you sure you want me here? You guys can have boy time, it's not like I have far to go to get home."

"No need," Rick said, tightening his arm around her. "We've had boy time all night."

"Ooookay," she said, drawing out the word as she laughed at him, settling back into his arms. "Just didn't want to interrupt the sausage fest." She snuggled close. Out of the corner of his eye, Rick could see Andrew watching her behavior, almost warily but also approvingly. Probably both because of her offer, and the way she'd immediately given into Rick's wishes once they were known.

"Olivia was busy tonight," Jared said, grinning at her. "Angel's all tied up, and Justin and Chris haven't told Jessica yet because they aren't sure she'd be able to keep her excitement from Hilary."

Maria snickered when Jared said Angel was all tied up, not even the hint of a blush rising in her cheeks. No surprise or worry either. His little tease had already come a long way from not knowing anything about BDSM to accepting the aspects of his friends' lives that were part of the scene. Rick stroked her back, sliding his fingers under the hem of her shirt and enjoying the way she stiffened and squirmed a bit against him. Just small movements, obviously not wanting to draw attention as the conversation shifted to when Justin and Chris might be making Jessica a similar proposal, but enough for him to know she was getting turned on.

So was Rick for that matter. But he controlled himself, enjoying the small touches, the teasing touches, until later when he could get her alone.

SUNLIGHT WOKE MARIA AND SHE WAS SURPRISED TO SEE RICK WAS still in bed. Then again, he'd ended up having a fair amount to drink the night before. Andrew hadn't been sober enough to drive when Jared and Liam left, so the three of them had stayed up talking for a long time before Andrew had eventually passed out on the couch. Had Rick been drunk when they fell asleep? Maybe. He hadn't had much after she'd gotten there but she knew he'd had a few before that.

Deciding that, hungover or not, he would at least appreciate having someone else make him breakfast, she started to slip from his bed.

Instead, a firm hand grabbed her wrist and pulled her back down. Maria stifled a surprised shriek as she fell into his hard body, looking up into amused blue eyes.

"And where do you think you're going?" he asked, maneuvering her so she was pressed up against him again. She'd realized there were certain positions he liked her to be in, and most of them involved her being somehow draped across him.

"I was gonna go make coffee and get some breakfast together," she said, planting a kiss on his lips. "I wanted to take care of you the way you took care of me on Saturday." She wriggled, trying to pull away, but his arms tightened around her, unyielding and unwilling to let her go.

"Mmm, I have a way you can take care of me." His blue eyes sparkled wickedly as he took her hand and laid it on his very hard cock.

Maria gasped and tried to yank her hand away, but his grip was too strong. Last night he'd insisted she sleep over, and they'd made out before going to sleep, but it hadn't gone any further than that. She'd assumed because Andrew was in the next room and Rick hadn't wanted his friend overhearing. Although, maybe she'd assumed that because she hadn't wanted Andrew overhearing.

"Andrew might still be here," she hissed at him, tugging on his hand. Rick chuffed a laugh.

"So what? I can guarantee you, he's heard and seen worse at the club."

The reminder that Rick had been sexually active with other women at Stronghold was definitely not helping his case. Maria stiffened, pushing away the sudden hurt she felt. Immediately, Rick let go of her hand, sensing her change in mood, and cupped her cheek with his hand, forcing her to look at him. "That's not a good look. What just went through your head?"

"Reminding me that Andrew's probably seen you with other women at the club is not the way to convince me to ignore the fact that he's in the next room right now," she said tartly but matter-of-factly, doing her best to keep any jealousy out of her voice.

Rick's eyes narrowed.

Suddenly she found herself on her back, breathless, with a large, angry, aroused male looming over her body. His hands were planted on either side of her, trapping her beneath him. Maria stared up at him with both shock and arousal. Even if she was still feeling a little pissy, that had been a seriously hot throw-down. She'd have to be dead for her body not to react to something like that.

"I wasn't talking about me specifically," he said, just as matter-of-fact as she'd been. "I was talking about at the club in general. I scened with a fair amount of women yes, but I didn't have sex with all of them. Hell, I didn't have sex with most of them. And the only woman I'm interested in right now, the only woman I've wanted a relationship with in years, is you." His eyes scanned down her body, looking over her curves, which were laid out beneath him, and she could see his expression change slightly, his anger leaking away as sexual interest reasserted itself.

She was just as interested even if she was still feeling a little bit of jealousy. Or maybe because of it. Knowing he hadn't been talking about Andrew watching him at the club did help a bit, but she also knew she couldn't get too wrapped up in Rick's sexual past. It wasn't like he'd hidden the whole club—or even the sex school—stuff from her. She would just have to concentrate on being smug that he wanted to be with her, rather than jealous over brief affairs of the past.

"Alright."

Something flickered in his eyes. "That's it? Just 'alright?'"

Maria smiled sweetly up at him. "Yep. Except you still need to get off of me because we are not having sex for the first time while Andrew's in the next room."

The heat in his gaze flared and solidified, narrowing in on her. Maria found herself holding her breath, waiting to see what he would do. Yeah... probably shouldn't have tried ordering him around while lying in his bed. With him on top of her.

"Alright."

Then he kissed her, not giving her even a moment to worry about morning breath. His body was hot and hard on top of hers, and as she reached up to push him away, he grabbed her wrists and forced them above her head, holding them down. Suddenly Maria understood the scene she'd seen in Stronghold's dungeon a little better, understood the whole forced reluctant sex thing. Not that she felt like fighting with or begging Rick to stop, but just having him take the choice away from her was so freaking hot. She knew she could say one word at any time and everything would stop, but otherwise, he was just going to keep pushing to get what he wanted.

Her nipples were hard, aching little buds that rubbed against the crinkled hair on his chest. Her legs were spread slightly, but his were outside of hers, so his cock rubbed against her mound rather than her slit. Maria whimpered and bumped her hips upwards, trying to get more friction as his free hand swept down her side, following the line of her curves, caressing the side of her breast, stomach, and hip as it traveled.

Then, when his hand reached her hips, his own lifted and he slid his hand between their bodies, his fingers seeking out her wetness. Because of the way his legs had hers imprisoned, she couldn't spread her thighs very much, but his finger dipped in anyway, coating itself in her growing wetness. Maria moaned against his lips, arching her back underneath him, giving herself over to the sensations beginning to course through her. Submitting herself to him.

Rick's finger probed, slid, teased, and she tried to press her legs open further, wriggling when he wouldn't budge and let her. After making out with him last night and the way he was touching her this morning, she was starting to feel a bit frantic with the need to cum. Her pussy pulsed eagerly as his finger circled her clit.

When he pulled away, lifting himself off her, she blinked up in dazed confusion. Rick just grinned at her, settling onto his side and resting his hand on her stomach. She was free. He'd released her hands, taken his weight off of her... and her body throbbed with disappointment. What the hell had just happened?!

"Okay, sweetheart," he said, as she stared up at him speechless. "You can go make coffee now."

"What?!" Maria fought the urge to punch him in his smug-looking face.

"You wanted to go make coffee and get some breakfast together. Go ahead."

"But you... we..." Her body was tingling with need from his caresses and he was just going to stop and send her to the kitchen?

Rick's face became more serious. "This is part of what I want, Maria. Control over your body, over your orgasms, including for punishment. I don't like that you seemed to think I would push you into sex before you're ready or that you thought I was throwing other women in your face." His hand started to caress her stomach, moving lower, and she froze, hoping he would put his fingers back between her legs, worried about what her punishment might be. "So today, you're going to go to work, all hot and wet and ready to come, but you're not going to. You're not going to touch yourself at all. You're going to wait until tonight when you'll come back here to me and then I'll make you come. When I'm ready to."

His voice had gone low, intimate, as his fingers caressed the very top of her slit, teasingly close to her clitoris, but not quite touching it, even when she bucked her hips. Maria whimpered. This was so wrong. She shouldn't be so turned on by his demand, but she was. The idea of going through her day, feeling like this, was kind of horrifying because of how uncomfortable she was going to be, but knowing she was doing it for him also aroused her.

Rick slapped the top of her pussy, his fingers just curving over to cup and punish the sensitive folds, and Maria gasped as her body shuddered. It stung, but it felt good too, the contact almost enough to make her cum. Being denied was painfully uncomfortable and she looked up at him pleadingly.

Leaning down, he kissed her forehead. "Go make coffee, sweetheart, I'll be there in a minute."

## 20

Glancing at the clock again, Rick wondered when Maria would show up at his door. He wondered if she'd be horny or pissed when she did so. Or maybe some delightful combination of both.

This morning had definitely caught her off-guard, but he had seen in her eyes that the idea of waiting all day for her orgasm had also appealed to her on some level. Which appealed to him. Pleased him. Honestly, if they never did more than what they'd done together so far when it came to BDSM, he'd be just fine with that. Sure there were other things he'd like to explore, but just doing some spanking, some bondage, and having Maria let him control when and how she orgasmed was enough to satisfy the kinky needs which lay in his psyche.

He didn't doubt she would make it through the day, thinking of him the entire time, until she came home to him.

The little angsty looks she'd given him over breakfast had definitely kept her on his mind all day. She'd been downright squirmy. He was pretty sure Andrew had noticed, and been amused, but neither of them had said anything to draw attention to her agitation. Rick might have if Andrew wasn't there, but he'd already come to the conclusion she was definitely not an exhibitionist. She liked her private things to be private. So, instead, he contented himself with small little touches to help keep her on edge.

Now he was just waiting for her to get home. To his home, he meant. She was upstairs getting ready, which he knew because they'd been texting all day and he'd told her he wanted to take her out to dinner. But she'd wanted to shower and change first, so he was being patient... although he was also wondering if she was making him wait on purpose. That was okay, as long as she didn't masturbate.

Great, now he was thinking about her naked body, all wet and slick in the shower, with her hand between her legs. Maybe he'd have her play with herself for him tonight. Rick grinned wickedly. Yeah, she was so going to regret giving him so much time to think.

He almost jumped when his phone went off to let him know she was ready.

They didn't go to Murphy's this time. Although Rick had really liked the food there, and also the people, he wanted to take Maria out on a real date where he paid. Somewhere she could completely relax; because he'd noticed that at Murphy's she'd been watching how service was going. Tonight, he was determined all of her focus was going to be on him.

It wasn't that hard.

They'd held hands in the car and when they'd gotten to the restaurant he'd asked for one of the corner booths. So he could sit next to her, keep his hands on her.

Maria's hair was gloriously curly, pulled back away from her face, but still tumbling down her back. She was dressed in a little black dress that dipped low into a loose front which hinted at showing more than it actually was, as if he waited long enough he might be lucky enough to be looking at exactly the right moment to see it completely expose her. It cinched in at her waist and hugged her hips, flaring out into a flippy little skirt just underneath her ass. The kind of dress designed to torture a man.

Which meant it was his job to torture her right back. He kept his arm around her shoulders while they looked at the menu, drawing little circles on her bare skin, watching her nipples harden under the thin fabric of her dress. Sitting next to her also meant he got to keep peeking down the front of her dress, trying to see more skin. Instead he just got a hint of the lacy black bra she was wearing, which was enough to give him a hard-on at the dinner table while he wondered if her panties matched. He shifted his hand down to her lower back, caressing just above the curve of her ass.

After the server took their order, she gave Rick a dirty look.

"Would you stop that?" she whispered, but her voice was breathy, excited, not just annoyed. She was squirming a bit in her seat. Rick grinned, leaning in to whisper in her ear.

"No. You like it." He was starting to get more of a feel for Maria's personal kinks. No exhibitionism, but the danger of being caught did appeal to her. Being teased out in public got her going too, because she knew she wasn't going to get her satisfaction there. While Rick kind of liked the idea of making her orgasm at the table, he knew she wouldn't be down for that. He was happy to tease and torment her, rousing her without giving her satisfaction. He splayed his hand on her lower back, his other coming down to rest on her thigh, fingers resting only a few inches below her pussy. Her quick, indrawn breath was all the validation he needed. "You like it when I touch you and get you wet. You like the idea someone might notice—as long as no one actually does."

Maria shivered as his hand tightened on her thigh. Rick fought the urge to slide his hand under her skirt and up her leg.

Something clattered on their table and Maria jerked away and Rick slightly straightened, amused. Their server looked amused too, giving Rick a wink, before walking away.

"Oh my God, that's so embarrassing," Maria muttered, reaching quickly for the bread and butter the server had just dropped off.

Rick chuckled, but backed off, just keeping his hand on her back. He liked touching her, even though it was just as much a sexual torment to him as it was to her. As she buttered her bread, Maria shot him a little look from underneath her eyelashes, both shy and seductive. Definitely aroused, not upset with him.

Still, she'd said she'd wanted him to stop, so now he'd give her a little taste of that. And it might help him keep his own rampant libido under control.

By the time dinner was over, Maria felt ready to jump out of her skin. The day had been torture. She didn't think she'd ever been so aware of her body. Every time she'd walked, she'd felt her pants brushing against her inner thighs and pussy, every time she'd sat down, she'd felt them tighten over those same areas. Her nipples had been incredibly sensitive all day. And then Rick had spent all of dinner making her even more wet and squirmy, to the point where she almost didn't care they were in public—she just wanted to come.

Even worse, it just turned her on even more that she knew she wasn't going to get off until he got her off.

Man, she was one sick puppy. The physical stuff was hot, but it was the mental stuff that made her feel the most confused and the most turned on. She felt like she wasn't supposed to like this—but maybe that was part of what she liked. It wasn't forbidden to be following a man's orders or allowing him control over her body, but it did have a feeling of taboo around it, like she was being somehow naughty.

Although, when she compared her and Rick to some of the other couples at Stronghold—like Paul and Christina—she felt almost tame by comparison, so that was kind of reassuring.

Walking back to the car, Rick had his arm wrapped around her waist, and she leaned into him, rubbing her curves against him. He looked down at her, grinning. "Little tease."

She snorted. "Like you're one to talk."

Conversation at dinner had been easier while they were eating, because he'd had to stop touching her. Nothing they'd talked about had been consequential, but it had all been enjoyable. Of course, as soon as he was done eating, he'd gone right back to teasing her, caressing her with small little touches that made her feel sensitive all over her body.

"Careful brat," he warned, patting the side of her bottom in mimicry of a spanking. Maria shivered and raised her eyebrow at him.

"We're not in the bedroom."

"Doesn't mean you won't pay when we get there."

She jumped him the moment they walked through his front door, using her foot to kick it shut behind her. The suddenness of her sexual assault caught him off-guard and he fell back against the wall, with her on top of him. For one long moment, Maria had the upper hand, her arms around his neck and her lips pressed against hers. Having the upper hand didn't turn her on though; what flat out made her pussy gush was when he took it away.

Even though he was the one pressed up against the wall, he took control. His thigh thrust between hers as his hands pulled her forward, making her skirt ride up and her pussy rub against his leg. Gripping her ass, he squeezed the soft flesh tightly in his hands, holding her still against his thigh so she couldn't do more than squirm. It felt like hot flashes of pleasure were sparking in her clit. She was so turned on—had been so turned on all day—that she could feel her body shuddering as her climax began to build.

Then he pushed her away, forcing her to slide away from his leg, and Maria cried out in protest. Her arms still clinging around his neck, she looked up at him, needy pleading in every line of her body. There was no doubt he was turned on too; his cock had created a substantial bulge at the front of his pants. Maria wondered where the hell he got his self-control from... and then she wondered if the reason she felt free to become so out of control was because she knew Rick wasn't going to lose his.

Theoretical questions like that weren't really her priority though. Getting off was.

"Rick please... I've been dying all day and I was good, I haven't touched myself once... please, I need to come," she begged. It felt strange to beg, and also strangely exciting, especially when she saw his eyes flash with hungry heat in response. Maria had never been into lots of talking during sex, but the words just seemed to flow from her, without conscious thought. "Please Rick, I need you to touch me... I need you to make me come..."

"How am I supposed to say no to that?" He lowered his lips to hers, almost gently, his hands reaching down to her ass, and somehow she knew he wanted her to jump up on him.

Definitely something she'd never done, considering she'd never trusted a man to be able to catch and hold her weight like that. Not since her prom date had tried to dip her and ended up dropping her on the dance floor. But for Rick, she jumped, wrapping her legs around him, knowing he would catch her and he wouldn't let her fall.

His hands were strong and sure, holding her right where her ass and thighs met, her legs wrapped around his waist pressing her pussy against his body. They kissed, deeply, passionately, as he started walking her back down the hall toward the bedroom. Maria's body buzzed with excitement, loving the way he'd completely taken control, feeling warm and languid with her trust in him, and absolutely aching for more.

RICK MENTALLY APPLAUDED HIMSELF ON HAVING ENOUGH SELF-restraint to get Maria back to his bedroom instead of fucking her up against his front door. Although he liked the front door idea for some-time in the future, that was definitely not how their first time together was going to go. He had no doubt tonight was going to be their first time together.

It was all he could do not to bump her into the walls on the way back to his room, because walking straight while he was kissing her like her kisses were air and he was suffocating, wasn't exactly easy.

He bumped his arm against his light switch so he didn't have to maneuver to the bed in the dark. About a foot away from the bed, he slowly let Maria slide down his body until she was standing in front of him, enjoying the way it felt to have her rubbing against his cock on the way down. Gentling his kiss, he slid his hand up and into her hair, wrapping it around his fingers and using it to tug her head back, exposing her neck to him.

A feminine whimper made his cock swell even further as he moved his lips down the line of her neck and to her collarbone. With his free hand, he tugged the straps of her dress off of her shoulders. Because the front was loose, it fell down, exposing the black lacy bra, the top hung around her waist as she pulled her arms all the way through.

"Fuck that's hot, sweetheart," he said, bending to rub his face over those lace-clad mounds, biting at her nipple through the fabric. Maria moaned, her hands coming up to clutch at his head. "Do they match?"

"Does what match?" she asked, after a moment, her voice thick with passion.

"The panties," Rick said, kneeling down so he could begin to tug her dress down over the curve of her stomach. He looked up at her, enjoying the view of her breasts and then her face with her big eyes watching him. "Do they match?"

"Yes."

"That's even hotter." He pulled the dress down, revealing her midsection and then her panties, and then the dress fell to the floor, leaving her in nothing but lace and heels. Rick was practically panting for breath. Leaning forward he pressed a kiss to her pussy through the panties, right over her clit, and Maria made a low sound in her throat that was like an aural aphrodisiac. As if he needed anything to help turn him on right now.

Her hands rested on the top of his head as she swayed lightly, trying to keep her balance. One hand cupping her butt to help her, he slid the fingers of his other hand beneath her panties, feeling the wetness coating her pussy lips, barely contained by the fabric of her underwear. Maria moaned again, moving her hips.

"Maria, I want you to do something for me." He swirled his fingers around her creamy folds, just barely pushing inside of her body and then pulling away again.

"What?"

"I don't want you to come until I'm inside you. Can you do that for me sweetheart?"

The unhappy groan he got in response made him grin.

"I'm not sure I can help it. Fuck!" Her hips jerked as he ran his fingers over her clit. "Especially if you keep touching me like that."

"I know but I want you to try. You're new to this, so I won't punish you if you come... but I want you to try not to. Because it will please me."

It was like he'd said the magic words. His little subbie tease seemed to melt just a bit, her body relaxing as she nodded her head. She wanted to try. Rick's pulse pounded inside of his head. Yeah, he wasn't going to make her wait too long, because he sure as hell wasn't going to be able to.

MARIA'S LEGS WOBBLED, FEELING LIKE THEY MIGHT MELT AS RICK'S finger slid inside of her. She clenched around him, whimpering at how fucking good it felt, trying not to focus on how fucking good it felt. The idea that she was supposed to stave off an orgasm, instead of trying to reach for it was completely foreign to her... but then again, she'd never been with a man who made her orgasm so easily. Normally, if she wanted one then she had to work for it.

She felt like she could go off like a rocket at any second, and Rick's finger moving inside her wasn't helping at all. What did guys think about at a time like this? Baseball? Great, now she was picturing Rick's fabulous ass in a baseball uniform. Not helping. His finger moved again, and her mind felt like it splintered under the wave of sexual need.

How was she supposed to keep from coming when he was touching her like that? She tried to move her hips away, but he just gripped her tighter, pumping his finger inside of her. Swaying in her heels, with him on his knees before her, she should have felt powerful. Instead she felt soft and submissive and wholly feminine. And also, really, really close to coming.

"Rick pleeaaase," she begged, and then moaned with disappointment as his finger slid out of her. The loss of contact made it easier for her not to come, but since right now what she really needed was for all the tension in her body to have somewhere to go. It was swirling around inside of her, making her skin feel tight, like her body was too small to contain it.

"Up on the bed and spread your legs, sweetheart."

Dammit that shouldn't sound so sexy, but in his deep, gravelly voice that one sentence seemed to reach deep inside her and pluck at her needy, feminine core. Maria crawled onto the bed, purposefully giving him a fantastic view of her ass and the way her cheeky panties barely contained her curves. If she had to suffer then so did he.

When she turned around, his eyes slowly moved up her body from where she'd been putting her butt on display, until his eyes clashed with hers. Watching as he stripped off his shirt, Maria kicked off her heels over the side of the bed and lay on her back with her hands at her side. She felt both awkward and excited as she spread her legs, never losing eye contact with him as she did so.

Rick shucked off his pants and his giant erection was pointing straight at her, intimidatingly large and angry-looking. Wrapping his hand around it, he pumped his fist down and up one time before releasing it again. Maria felt like she should be running as he stalked toward the bed and crawled onto it, over her. Instead, she was just laying there like a tasty treat for him to devour.

"You're so beautiful," he murmured as he positioned himself between her legs. That's when Maria realized she still had her panties on and she groaned. Dammit, she wanted—needed—him inside of her or she was never going to be able to do as he asked.

As if he could read her thoughts, Rick gave her a wicked look as he leaned over and sucked one of her nipples into his mouth. The lace itched against the tender bud, increasing the sensation. Maria reached up to grab him, but he took her wrists and pinioned them on either side of her head.

"Please let me touch you," she begged.

Chuckling, Rick released her nipple from his mouth with a pop. "So you can try to hurry me along? I don't think so, sweetheart."

She groaned again, knowing the truth to his words. Yeah, she wanted to touch him just because she wanted to run her hands all over his body, but she also wanted it because she was sure she could make him lose some of his self-control. Push him along.

And then very likely get punished for trying to top from the bottom, so it was probably better he wasn't even giving her the chance to. If he made her wait even longer while he spanked her, she was likely to explode.

When he reached behind her back with one hand to undo her bra, she arched upwards to help give his hand space to work. And, not so incidentally, press her breasts against his chest in a way he couldn't rebuke her for.

Pushing the bra up her arms, he stopped about halfway between her elbows and wrists and started wrapping the straps around her limbs. Maria stared. He was restraining her with her own lingerie.

"That's better," Rick murmured, before sliding back down her body so his face was at her breasts. Maria groaned as he cupped them, wriggling beneath him, gasping when he sucked a rigid nipple into his mouth. She loved being restrained and controlled like this, now that she knew what it felt like. Rick sucked deep and then released her nipple again, pinching both buds between his fingers and tugging gently. Her pussy pulsed in response. "You said on your Stronghold survey that you're on birth control, do you want me to wear a condom?"

"What?" Maria felt dazed, like his words didn't entirely make sense. He tugged on her nipples again, the corners of his mouth turning up. She tried to focus. "No... no, don't. I want to feel you."

This time she hadn't been trying to get a reaction from him, she really hadn't, it was just the honest truth, but she could definitely feel his response to it.

FUCK, HE WAS GOING TO COME LIKE A RANDY TEENAGER IF HE didn't get a hold of himself. Deciding they had both waited long enough, Rick moved up to kiss Maria on that luscious, smart mouth of hers. He was brutally glad she didn't want a condom. While he would have worn one if she'd wanted, he wanted to feel every inch of her when he buried himself in her lush body. He wanted her cream to coat his cock, and he wanted to mark her with himself inside and out.

As he kissed her, rocking his hips against her, he could feel the frantic movements of her body beneath his. Pushing her legs together, he moved his body enough that she could bend so he could yank her panties down her thighs, over her knees, and off her body completely, tossing them away into his room without looking. Leaving her completely open to him.

He pressed one hand between her legs, the other one holding down her arms above her head, as his fingers stroked her slit. Maria cried out in frustration, her panting breaths signaling how close she was to cumming, as he toyed with her.

"Not yet, sweetheart, don't come yet."

If looks could kill... except the glare she sent him was also filled with passion, hot need, and submission, because she was still trying to please him. Still fighting the sensations riding her hard, fighting his fingers as they threatened to push her over the edge.

Rick groaned.

Enough.

The head of his cock pressed against her soft wetness and they both moaned. If he wasn't holding her down, Maria might have levitated off the bed. Hot, tight, wet silk coated his sensitive head, and he gritted his teeth, forcing himself to slowly thrust forward rather than just burying himself in her body the way he wanted to. It wasn't fast enough for her, and her hips jerked upwards. If he ever wanted to take things as slowly as possible with his little tease, he was going to have to tie her down completely.

Her legs wrapped around his back, urging him forward, and he let himself slide slowly into her silken heat. Fuck she felt amazing. He savored every inch of her body as it took him in, clenching around him as she gasped and writhed, the heels of her feet digging into his back.

"Rick! Oh fuck... Rick!" Maria was practically vibrating beneath him.

Leaning forward, he shoved the rest of his dick into her, slamming against her body and placing his lips next to her ear. "You can cum now, sweetheart."

She was off like a shot, her body tensing and clenching around him, moving beneath him as he ground his groin against her splayed pussy lips and clit. Despite the fact that he was stronger, heavier, he could barely hold her arms down as she orgasmed, creaming herself all over his cock. The ripples of her body, the heated clasping of her pussy milking his cock, nearly made him lose it right then and there.

Breathing deeply, he looked up at the wall, rather than continuing to look down at her face as she came for him. Tears had already started to leak from her eyes, her mouth open as she gasped for air through the tumultuous sensations.

When he felt her slowly start to still beneath him, he pulled his hips back, dragging his cock back out of her, and then slowly began to thrust in again. He had to go slow right now, it was that or be a less-than-a-minute-man. Maria's pussy spasmed around him as he moved, her pleasure still ongoing as his cock rubbed against her sensitive insides. Deliberately tilting his groin to rub against her clit, he was rewarded with a gasping shudder from the woman beneath him every time his body sank completely into hers.

MARIA'S LEGS TIGHTENED, HER HEAD THRASHING BACK AND FORTH at the dragging sensation of Rick's cock pushing in and out of her body. The inner walls of her pussy were incredibly sensitized, she could feel every inch of his cock as it moved inside of her, and the pleasure was overwhelming. All that unbearable tension had exploded when he'd told her she could come, and now it was like a spool unraveling without end, flowing out of her and making her shake and gasp as it went.

Impossibly, Rick's cock seemed to get harder, thicker, stretching her body as he began to move faster. The long, hard strokes came quicker, and she cried out as the vortex of painful pleasure increased the pace of her unraveling. Heat burst inside of her and Rick groaned, his hands tightening on her as he sank deep and held himself there. Their bodies rubbed together, and he whispered her name in a ragged voice that sent shivers up her spine as she felt him pulse inside of her. She could actually feel every spurt of his cum in her sensitized channel, and her pussy automatically clenched around him, trying to pull every last drop into her body.

She'd never felt so close to anyone as she did to him at this moment, their bodies wrapped around each other, his hand holding her wrists immobile above her head, and their climaxes intimately mingling. Lips descended as she felt him relax on top of her, his own tension fleeing quickly. He kissed her, gently, tenderly, as he unwrapped the bra from around her arms.

They held each other, and Maria took the opportunity to really explore him with her hands, tracing his muscles as they continued to kiss, enjoying the feel of him all around her and inside of her. A lot of the time after sex, she wanted to get up and clean up as soon as possible, but right now she was just enjoying the moment too much. She didn't want to give up the intimate joining of their bodies, she didn't want to stop Rick's tender caresses or spoil how cherished she felt as he held her.

When he did move away, it was reluctantly, and he rolled onto his back, pulling her with him to cuddle. Maria snuggled her head into his shoulder.

"I should go clean up," she murmured, although she didn't even twitch much less actually try to move away.

"In a minute," Rick murmured back, his hand trailing up and down her spine. He planted a kiss on the top of her head.

Relaxing into his cuddling, Maria took stock of her body. The intense sexual tension that had gripped her throughout the day was completely gone. She'd thought she'd need several orgasms to get rid of that kind of need; apparently one really big one which lasted the entire time they'd been having sex would do the trick. Good to know.

Every muscle in her body felt limp and satisfied, especially her rather sore internal muscles. It had been a long time since she'd had sex, and she didn't think she'd ever had sex quite like that.

"Do you want to go to Stronghold sometime this weekend?"

Maria hesitated. She hadn't realized how ambivalent she felt about going to the club. It didn't exactly pierce the happy morning-after glow she was enjoying, but it did make her stop and think. "Um... I don't know." She could see Rick was surprised and she tried to pinpoint the source of her anxiety about going back. "It kinda seems like every time we go there, something bad happens."

"It was bad last time?" Rick's eyebrows came together in consternation and alarm, and Maria had to roll her eyes at his surprising insecurity.

"No, the scene wasn't bad... but the next morning pretty much sucked for me, and I know that after the scene wasn't so great for you."

"Oh..." He seemed to think it over. Maria was glad he wasn't just brushing off her concern, considering it wasn't exactly a logical one. But she couldn't help feeling that things did go better for them outside of Stronghold. Both times they'd gone there some sort of problem had cropped up. Everything they'd done outside of there, had been great. Last night, for example. They had incredible sex, showered, and then fallen asleep in each other's arms. Maria hadn't even missed her own bed, she liked being in Rick's too much. He grinned at her. "Well you know what they say, third time's the charm. And we don't have to do anything there, sometimes I go just to hang out with my friends—although that isn't the only place we go to hang out."

She giggled. "I hope so... just, do you think we could wait a little bit longer?"

She wasn't sure what he would make of the request. This definitely wasn't a time she was trying to top from the bottom, she really just wanted to get more comfortable with the two of them and all this new sex stuff between them before going back to Stronghold. It wasn't like she had bad memories there really, it was just that the thought of going back made her feel anxious and not in the sexy way.

To her relief, Rick just smiled and reached across the table to hold her hand, his thumb caressing her skin. "Of course, sweetheart."

## ❧ 21 ❧

Two weeks later, Rick found himself facing an interrogation of the like he'd never experienced before. He'd met dads, brothers, mothers, but nothing compared to having to meet three sisters all at once. Three younger sisters who had benefited from their older sister's mothering their entire lives and were absolutely determined to do just as good a job now that it was their turn to watch out for her.

Off to the side, Maria was watching as she chatted with her mom and one of their neighbors, her eyes twinkling at Rick over her sister Ava's head. Seeing her amusement almost made the interrogation worth it.

He wasn't quite sure when he would say they'd started dating, since they'd started to really get to know each other at the pool before he'd taken her to Stronghold, but he often found himself adding up all their time together in his head as being their relationship. So far they hadn't been back to Stronghold yet, but that was okay. They'd hung out with his friends and would be hanging out with them again tonight in fact. Adam was throwing a little party at his place to celebrate Hilary and Liam's engagement. Adam had always enjoyed having people over, and now that he was with Angel, the parties tended to be even more well organized than they had been before. Today Maria had taken the full day off of work so she could bring him to her parents' for an afternoon barbecue before the party.

"So what have you been doing over the summer since you don't start at your new school until the fall?" Ava asked. Out of all of Maria's sisters, she was definitely the least resistant to being charmed by him. Jackie had obviously liked him right away, Lara had warmed up to him throughout the interrogation when he'd been willing to answer all of their questions with both patience and charm, all of which seemed to make Ava even more determined to ensure someone was still giving him the third degree.

Not that he minded. He could tell Maria's sisters all loved her and were just looking out for her, so he had no problem taking the time to set them all at ease. Although he did find it kind of amusing that their Dad hadn't seemed to feel the need to join in. They'd talked for a bit when Maria had first introduced them, and then the sisters had descended. Mr. Arias listened to Rick's answers for the first couple questions and then had given Rick a sympathetic look and strolled away. Rick had decided to take that as a good sign.

"I've been making extra money where I can, since I'm used to teaching summer school. A couple of my friends have needed help over the summer with their businesses, not enough to hire someone full time, but perfect for someone like me."

"What do your friends do?" Jackie asked, obviously curious. She'd said a couple of things that made Rick think Maria had spoken with at least one of her sisters fairly frankly about some of the things they did in the bedroom. Girls talked, he didn't mind that. Especially since she'd mostly hinted around the spanking thing, which had turned Maria a nice beet red, and that had been kind of fun to watch.

"My friend Adam owns a company which does head-hunting and temporary employment; he's the one I spend most of my time helping out around the office. I also help with paperwork at a friend's dojo and another friend's club. Sometimes I do manual labor for my friend Andrew, who has his own carpentry business." When he said manual labor, he grinned as all three sisters immediately looked at his biceps. Jackie and Lara were frankly admiring, Ava a little more grudgingly so.

Out of the corner of his eye he saw Maria drifting over to them and he immediately felt himself straightening in anticipation. The three sisters all turned their heads to see what he was looking at.

"Isn't that Jeremy over there?" Ava asked as she turned back. Rick glanced over and saw a dark-haired guy, probably about his age, had joined the conversation with Maria's mom and neighbor. Fairly attractive, but with kind of a sleazy look to him. Or maybe it was just the name was ringing a bell.

Lara giggled. "No wonder she's coming over here then, she can't stand him."

"You don't think it's just to save me?" Rick stage-whispered to her, making her giggle again.

"Well she might just feel uncomfortable with Jeremy," Ava said smugly. "He's got a thing for her." Her eyes glinted as she watched Rick's reaction, probably to see if she was finally getting a rise out of him.

Nope. While he might feel a bit more possessive than he had a second ago, Maria had mentioned Jeremy's name before, but only as the obnoxious best man in her sister's wedding party. Definitely not someone he was going to feel threatened by. After all, even if Ava was right and Jeremy did have a thing for Maria, Maria had a thing for Rick.

"Hey sweetheart," he said loudly, reaching out his arm to Maria and ignoring Ava. Maria grinned at him as she slid underneath his arm, wrapping her own around his waist. "Are you here to save me from your sisters?"

"Are you admitting you need saving?" she asked, teasing.

"Only from Ava," he whispered into her ear, loudly enough that all three of her sisters would be able to hear. "I think I have the other two fooled."

Giggling, Maria elbowed him in the ribs and he grunted. Giving her a look, he slid his hand down to her waist and patted her bottom warningly. Unperturbed, she just smiled up at him.

Turning his attention back to her sisters, he noticed Jackie was staring at his hand where it was on Maria's hip, fascinated. Neither Lara nor Ava seemed to have noticed though.

"He'll do," Ava said, giving him an amused look. Now that Maria was here she seemed to have dropped the animosity and was actually looking at them with approval. Guess he'd passed her test, although he had no idea exactly what had done it.

Maria's arrival seemed to indicate it was time to break up the interrogation and the sisters drifted away one by one, allowing him and Maria to wander and find their way into another conversation group. This one close to the food, which was good because Rick was starving.

OKAY, SO SHE WAS SHOWING OFF RICK A LITTLE BIT. MARIA couldn't help it. She felt incredibly smug about proving to Jeremy that her boyfriend wasn't in the least bit imaginary. Plus, Meg, an obnoxious and superficial brat who used to live across the street from Maria and was now home visiting her parents (and therefore unfortunately invited to the barbecue) was practically drooling over Rick. But he had eyes for no one but Maria. The slender redhead looked like she was drowning in jealousy and Maria felt incredibly vindicated after having endured years of Meg's taunts about how she was fat.

Rick liked her curves. And he hadn't given Meg a second glance.

Take that, bitch.

Maybe Meg and Jeremy should get together. They'd make a perfect couple. Although Jeremy hadn't given Meg a second glance either. He'd also steered away from Maria all afternoon, which suited her fine. Hopefully he was embarrassed. Or intimidated by Rick. Either worked for her.

It felt good to be here with Rick and her family. A couple of her aunts and uncles were here too, and they were all suitably impressed by him. Not once, not once, in the past few hours had she been subjected to pitying looks or well-meaning comments that made her hackles rise. She was able to just relax and enjoy the company. Well, most of the company.

Barbara, her parents' neighbor and good friend, sat down next to her, on the opposite side from Rick. The older woman's eyes were gleaming with interest. She truly did love giving Maria and her sisters relationship advice. Maria often got the impression Barbara had been waiting for her to bring someone home she was serious about.

"You've got yourself a live one there," she said, nodding to Rick, who was holding Maria's hand but involved in a conversation with Daniel and Victor on the other side of him. "Where'd you pick him up?"

"The pool," Maria said, grinning at the brash older woman. "He couldn't resist my red bikini."

Nodding approvingly, Barbara stabbed her fork into her potato salad. "Smart man. How long have you two been together now?"

Maria hesitated. "Well, we've been spending time together for over a month... I guess our first real date was a few weeks ago though."

"Spending time together is important," Barbara said sagely, with an approving nod. "Don't knock it. Nowadays all you kids are just jumping right into bed together, it's better to get to know each other first. Makes the sex better too."

Choking on a laugh, Maria tried to stifle her hilarity, not wanting to draw too much attention. Sometimes Barbara said the most outrageous things. Maria wanted to be her when she grew up.

"Excuse me? What's going on over here?" Rick was suddenly leaning across Maria, looking highly amused. "Sounds like there must be an interesting conversation happening."

Barbara wagged her finger at him. "You just heard the word 'sex,' didn't you?"

"Yes, ma'am." Completely unapologetic. Maria choked on a giggle, kind of shocked he'd immediately read Barbara's personality so correctly.

"This one's a keeper," Barbara said to Maria and tipped Rick a wink. "You always want to hold onto the honest ones."

"Thanks, I plan to hold onto him," she said, squeezing Rick's hand. Turning her head slightly so Barbara couldn't see the hot, sensuous look she gave Rick. "Very tightly."

"Tease," he mouthed at her, before turning back to Barbara and formally introducing himself. It wasn't too long before the three of them were laughing again, drawing more people to their conversation, including Barbara's husband Gerry. The two of them together were like a comedy team. Barbara was in her element, enjoying being the center of attention as Rick drew story after story from her, Gerry always providing humorous counterpoint to whatever she said. Even though Maria had heard all the stories before, they seemed to have new life as she was able to watch Rick's reactions to them.

Rick got along with everyone he talked to. Maria's mother had been very impressed, not to mention charmed to the point where Daniel complained he was obviously no longer the favorite significant other of her daughters. Which, of course, Galio and Vincent had pretended fury at, insisting Daniel had never been the favorite. She loved watching Rick interact with her family; he really fit in seamlessly, in a way none of her previous boyfriends ever had.

They lingered to help clean up, Rick assisting her dad with the grill —a job all of her brothers-in-law were more than happy to give up to him, while she picked up trash around the yard with Jackie. Who whispered gleefully to Maria that she just adored Rick, a declaration which was followed by multiple whispered "I told you so"s and "aren't you glad you listened to me?"s.

Yeah. Yeah, she really was. Ever since she and Rick had first slept together, they'd spent every night together. Sometimes at his place, sometimes at hers. They didn't have sex every single night, but definitely most nights. Maria loved that when she initiated, he would usually give her control for a little bit before swiftly and unexpectedly taking it away. Her body had never been so well-satisfied.

Most mornings he teased her when they first woke up, with caresses and kisses that made her want to jump him, and then he'd leave her aching and needy all day so she was practically a sex-starved maniac by the time she got home. Then, most of the time, he'd tie her up and play with her until she was nearly senseless with need before fucking her into sensual oblivion. He never made her wait more than the length of the day for her orgasms, which she was grateful for. The withholding thing was hot, but she didn't think she could go for longer than twenty-four hours without orgasming, not the way he liked to tease.

It was always different with him and always satisfying. Sometimes he tied her up so she couldn't move an inch, sometimes he tied just her arms or just her legs, and sometimes he didn't tie her up or hold her down at all. She couldn't decide what she liked best. Usually whatever he was doing to her at that time. This morning he'd bent her over her kitchen table, held her down by her wrists and taken her from behind.

Maria still shivered just thinking about it.

The sex was just the cherry on top of the sundae though. They spent just as much time cuddling, talking, and just spending time together. She'd even started getting up a little earlier so she could swim laps with him. Not for his full work out, but she would wake up around the same time as him, move a heck of a lot slower, and join him for the last twenty minutes or so of his swim. It was surprisingly soothing. Not to mention fun when he would come up behind her and try to grab at her ankles to pull her under.

She'd love to do the same to him, but she knew she wasn't ever going to be able to catch him, much less get a hand around one of his ankles.

They'd been on several dates, but a lot of the time they just stayed in and spent time together watching TV or movies and playing the occasional board game. He'd offered to teach her how to play chess, and then had ended up buck ass naked when she told him she played a little and asked if he wanted to play strip-chess. She had more fun with him than she'd ever had with any of her past boyfriends. At first she'd worried about how much time they were spending together, worried they might get sick of each other, but if anything, their time together was homey and domestic.

Well, homey and domestic plus hot sex. It was a pretty great way to live. Everything about her life seemed easier and happier. Even stressful days at work weren't so bad because she knew she was going home to Rick. Things would probably change a bit once school started and he went back to work at regular hours, but Maria wasn't worried about it.

By the time they headed over to Adam's for Liam and Hilary's engagement party, Maria was feeling incredibly cheerful. The day had gone so well. Her family liked Rick and he liked her family, she hadn't had to deal with Jeremy or Meg at all, and now she was going to go hang out with her new friends. It was a little daunting to know they'd all be there at once, but she'd seen a fair bit of them separately over the past couple of weeks. The girls had come in more than once to visit her during happy hour at work. She enjoyed having real friends, especially ones she could talk about the sexy stuff with.

"Hey guys!" Angel greeted them exuberantly at the door, pulling Maria into an immediate hug. "Come on in. Everyone else is already here."

"Oops," said Maria, apologetically. "My family's barbecue ran a little longer than I expected."

"No worries," Angel reassured her breezily. "Trust me, this is a casual kind of thing. None of Adam's parties have a real start time. Olivia and Andrew have been here for hours. Come on, let me give you the tour."

Rick's hand on the small of Maria's back propelled her forward down the hall after Angel. Adam's house was gorgeous, all the rooms impeccably neat, except for one room that looked like a study converted into a sewing room for Angel's projects. Adam, Patrick, and Jessica were in the kitchen, snacking on the food laid out on the counter. It looked delicious, but Maria was so not hungry yet, although she and Rick each picked up a drink while they were there.

After that, Angel led the way downstairs to Adam's basement, and the obvious social center of the house. There was more food, as well as a huge television and a ton of video games.

"Hey guys. We're having a tournament, want in?" Chris asked, grinning as he glanced up from looking at the screen. He, Lexie, Liam, and Hilary were all sitting on the floor with controllers in their hands and were focused on whatever they were playing. Olivia, Jared, and Andrew were sitting on the huge sectional couch with them, along with three guys Maria didn't know.

Looking at the television, Maria blinked in surprise. "Is that Mario Kart?"

"Yeah, the version for the Wii," Andrew said, trying to distract

Chris by putting his foot up near the other man's face and slowly bringing it closer. "It's the only game Jessica and Hilary will play."

"It's the only game I'm not entirely terrible at," said Hilary cheerfully. "Oh no, no, no!" Her words belied her first statement as she wailed. "I hate Rainbow Road."

"Everybody hates Rainbow Road, honey-girl," her fiancé said, his voice filled with false sympathy. Hilary leaned over and knocked into him with her shoulder, sending the Yoshi on the screen careening off the edge of the road. "Hey!"

"Oops," she said, smirking at him. Everyone laughed, except for Chris and Lexie, they were too focused on their own characters.

"So you guys want in?" Chris asked again, focused on the screen. Going by the quadrant he seemed to be looking at, Maria guessed he was Donkey Kong, which meant Lexie was playing as Mario. Hilary was Princess Peach of course.

"Not me, thanks."

"I'm in," said Rick behind her. "Unless Sam's playing."

"I've been disallowed," said the skinniest of the three guys on the couch. He was dressed kind of nerdy fashionable, with skinny jeans, a striped green and orange shirt that was only a little loose on him, and thick glasses. "I'm just here to offer impartial judgments, when needed, and occasional advice."

"Maria, these are my housemates, Sam, Q, and Mark," Angel said cheerfully, pointing to each of them in turn. Ah, that explained it. Maria had heard about the three of them, from both Rick and Angel, and she knew Adam was still frustrated about the fact that, technically, Angel didn't actually live with him. Going by what Maria had seen around the house, Angel had basically moved in, but the fact that she still had a room with her old housemates was a bit of a bone of contention between the couple.

"Are Leigh and Mike coming?" she asked. She'd only seen Leigh one more time since meeting her, and last week Angel had come in with a tall, dark and handsome friend named Mike. If she wasn't already involved with Rick, Maria might have been drooling over him. Then again, that was true of all of Rick's friends, but he was the only one who she really had a spark with. Still, they were all fantastic eye candy individually, and en masse the whole picture was pulse-pounding.

"Nah, Leigh's got date night with her boyfriend and Mike's in a show right now. I'm gonna head back upstairs to check on my man. Anyone need anything?"

There was a chorus of no's, so Angel just waved her hand and headed back upstairs. Maria and Rick made their way over to the couch to squeeze in between Olivia and Jared. The Domme was talking with Angel's housemates, making Maria bite her lip in amusement when she remembered Olivia referring to them as Angel's harem. And talking about making them her own. As if she could read Maria's thoughts, Olivia gave her an amused look before turning back to the conversation.

"So how was meeting the family?" Andrew asked, leaning forward so he could see Rick and Maria, despite Jared's hulking form between them.

"I thought it went pretty well," Maria said with a laugh. "He made it out alive." Andrew and Jared both chuckled. Andrew slapped Rick a high five.

It didn't take too long until everyone was gathered down in the basement. As soon as Hilary was done playing, Maria did the girl thing and demanded to see the ring. The center diamond was gorgeous, a one carat princess cut with two smaller emerald cut diamonds on each side, set in an intricate, delicate gold band.

"Wow," Maria said, impressed. The ring looked exactly like the kind of thing Hilary should be wearing. "He did a good job."

"I cheated," Liam said, his eyes dancing as he kissed Hilary's temple. "Jessica helped me pick it out."

"Don't listen to him." Hilary patted his chest with her free hand. Her soft brown eyes glowed with happiness as she looked up at her fiancé. The tenderness in his eyes as he gazed back at her was heartwarming. "He picked it out, Jessica just approved it."

The two of them were so obviously happy together, it made Maria's heart ache. She wondered if Rick would ever look at her like that. Sometimes she felt like she got a little hint of it from him. Yeah, they'd only known each other for about a month and a half, but at her age she wasn't going to be dating someone unless she could see a future with them and she knew he felt the same way. Even if they hadn't really talked explicitly about it, since they hadn't been together long, they'd both expressed that much.

Angel put on some dance music and all the girls except Olivia ended up on that side of the basement, dancing in between their turns playing Mario Kart. The final battle came down to Mark, Q, Angel, and Patrick. The girls stopped dancing to watch, Jessica insisted, and Maria soon found out why.

Her sides ached from laughing so hard. Angel was the meanest, loudest video game player she'd ever seen. The smack talk was epic. Adam sat behind her on the couch, occasionally putting his hand over her mouth whenever he thought she was becoming too offensive. Which, once or twice when Angel was particularly frustrated, led to him getting bitten.

"You're gonna pay for that," he growled, but he didn't interrupt her game to punish her. It was kind of sweet in a threatening, scary way.

"Dammit, I thought Asians were supposed to be terrible drivers," Patrick cursed as Angel shoved his Luigi right into some hot lava, overtaking him. "Princess Daisy is supposed to fucking suck."

"Suck it up, buttercup. I'm only half-Asian and the white half's driving," Angel said, laughing as she zoomed around another corner, using a mushroom to get her closer to Q, who was driving Mario. "Take that you mangy bastard."

"She refuses to play anything but the girl characters, so she's had a lot of practice," Sam said, rolling his eyes at Angel's idiosyncrasies. Maria had the feeling Sam used whatever character he thought was the best, regardless of gender.

"You fucker, come back here," Angel roared as Q managed to side-swipe her, knocking her slightly off course and keeping his lead. The small smug smile on Q's face said it all.

"Your friends are crazy," Maria whispered in Rick's ear. It was so crowded on the couch that he'd gotten her to sit on his lap. He squeezed his arms a bit tighter around her.

"They're your friends now too," he whispered back, amused. Maria giggled.

Q ended up winning the tournament, much to the disappointment of all the females in the room, who—of course—had been cheering for Angel. Afterwards, everyone trooped upstairs to gather round the kitchen counter while Adam and Angel poured glasses of champagne.

Adam held his up and turned to face Liam and Hilary who were standing at the end of the island, their arms around each other, faces glowing. "To Hilary and Liam. Who, despite Liam's original intentions," everyone laughed, "managed to find the person they want to spend the rest of their life with. Congratulations."

Everyone cheered and raised their glasses as Hilary and Liam kissed. Looking around, Maria saw Adam giving Angel a kiss, his arm wrapped securely around her waist, Jessica wedged between Justin and Chris with a giant smile on her face, and then she felt Rick's arm slide around her. It was a moment for celebrating love and hope for the future. Smiling at him, she pressed back when he leaned down to kiss her, tasting like champagne and chocolate. A little hope kindled in her heart that one day, all the people gathered here might be toasting them like this.

Somehow, as the evening wound down, it was the people in relationships who were left at Adam's. Since there were less of them, they'd ended up in Adam's entertainment room on the main floor, which had a slightly smaller television than the one downstairs, a large couch and several armchairs all situated for talking. Well, people in relationships plus Lexie and Patrick. Rick grinned to himself. He wondered if they'd noticed that. Maybe. Lexie was sitting between Patrick's legs, both of them with their attention apparently completely focused on the conversation they were having with Jessica, Justin, and Chris.

He'd pulled Maria onto the armchair he was sitting in, which had a large enough seat that she was only half on his lap; her butt was on the chair, but he had her legs across his and she was all snugged up under his arm. Just where he liked her.

Liam and Hilary were sitting in another armchair, lost in their own little world, murmuring things no one else could hear and exchanging kisses. It was fucking adorable is what it was, but for once Rick wasn't overcome with envy. Because he had his own gorgeous woman on his lap and he felt like their relationship was actually going somewhere. He felt a kind of hopefulness that he was looking at his and Maria's future.

Adam and Angel came back into the room, Angel looking both a bit aroused and uncomfortable. Rick coughed, hiding his laugh. They'd disappeared for about twenty minutes and he had no doubt Adam had come through with some kind of retribution for when she'd bitten his hand during the Mario Kart tournament. Her cheeks were flushed and her eyes a little glassy, and she didn't have the sexy rolling gait to her walk that she normally did.

When she sat down gingerly on the couch, Maria stiffened, and Rick looked at his girlfriend only to realize she was watching Angel with a worried expression on her face.

"Are you okay?" Maria asked, looking Angel over with concern.

"She's fine," Adam answered immediately, settling himself down next to Angel. His face was bland, but his voice was filled with smug satisfaction. "Probably a little uncomfortable, but fine." He leered at Angel who scowled back at him, shifting slightly. Maria relaxed, seeing the interplay between them.

She'd taken so easily to Rick's brand of kink that he sometimes forgot she wasn't used to the scene and the many different ways it could be implemented between couples.

Shifting her slightly on his lap so her ear was near his lips, he whispered directly into her ear. "Remember when he told her she'd pay for biting him earlier? Angel probably just got spanked. Or she's got a plug up her ass. Which is why she's sitting so carefully... but look closely at her. Whatever just happened, she enjoyed it. Adam doesn't really care that she bites, it gives him an excuse to punish her, except it's more like funishment."

Maria turned her head to whisper back in his ear. "A plug?!"

She sounded slightly shocked... and also interested? Rick's cock twitched.

"Would you like that sweetheart?" His fingers caressed her inner thigh, making her squirm slightly and his cock came to attention, thickening against the softness of her body in his lap. "Maybe next time you're a mouthy little brat, I'll put a plug up your ass."

"I didn't check off anal as one of my interests on the survey."

"You didn't put it as a hard limit either." Going by the way she was getting even squirmier, her breathing coming faster, she was more interested in it than she thought. At least in the play part. Rick was open to whatever she wanted. He wasn't a complete ass-man like Adam, although he did like the idea of breaching what he was pretty sure was Maria's virgin hole.

Someone saying his name caught his attention, which was probably a good thing, because he needed a distraction from the sweet armful of woman in his lap before he ended up with a painful erection that would have to wait. He looked up at Lexie, who was grinning at him from between Patrick's knees.

"I said you haven't been to the club in a while, are you guys coming back soon?"

To his surprise, Maria didn't stiffen on his lap this time. Instead, when he looked at her, she seemed rather thoughtful and he felt a small spurt of excitement. As much as he loved having Maria to himself at home, he did miss the club. They had equipment he didn't, plus the theme rooms provided a more exotic atmosphere than he could ever have at home. Plus, he kind of wanted to show off his gorgeous girlfriend, since everyone there knew he'd been looking. Quite a few of them had been there the last two times Maria had; it'd be nice for them all to see things had worked out.

"We've been giving it some time," he said casually, just in case Maria still wasn't comfortable going back.

"I think I'd like to go sometime when everyone else is going to be there," Maria said, only a little bit hesitant. Rick suddenly felt like jumping into the air, pumping his fist with excitement. Which, if he'd been alone, he might have actually done. Instead he just sat there quietly, with a stupid grin on his face he couldn't get rid of.

She's ready!

It wasn't just about being in the club, it was a testament of her trust in him. Even if they didn't play there, she trusted nothing was going to go wrong this time and that meant a lot to him.

"Most of us are usually there on Saturdays," Angel said. She gave Adam a fond look. "If it wasn't for the party tonight, that's where we all would have been."

"Come next Saturday," Lexie suggested, a big smile spreading across her face. "I'm sure Patrick won't mind someone covering my shift, if it will make you more comfortable to have people you know around."

"Oh it does, I would appreciate that," Maria said, completely sincerely, obviously not realizing the way Lexie had just manipulated the situation. Patrick's face looked like a thundercloud. Lexie hadn't been on the main floor since the glitter incident and Rick was pretty sure the big Dom had been planning on milking her punishment for that for as long as possible. He was glaring at the back of Lexie's head, his eyes narrowed and his jaw tense, but he didn't say anything. Like any Dom, his larger concern was going to be a new submissive's comfort level. Rick knew Patrick would probably be breathing down Lexie's neck the entire evening.

"Great," said Lexie, ignoring the rise of tension in the room. Rick was pretty sure Maria noticed it, but she also chose to ignore it, possibly not realizing what the issue was. Even if she did know, all of the women sided with Lexie when it came to her desire for entrance into Stronghold, so it didn't surprise him Maria would too.

"We're free next Saturday, so we'll be there," Hilary said, Jessica chiming in right after her with her own promise to be there as well.

With Lexie on the floor next week, Rick didn't doubt all of the others would come out too. Olivia to support Lexie. Andrew and Jared to help Patrick watch over her. He realized his own level of caring what Lexie did had definitely diminished since he'd become involved with Maria. Maybe it was because he was realizing she was finally grown up, or maybe it was just because he had something better to focus on. Either way, he trusted his friends to look after her. Especially because he was pretty sure Lexie didn't have an interest in scening with anyone other than Patrick. Which definitely wouldn't be happening any time soon.

He wasn't the only one who seemed unconcerned with Lexie's determination to get back on the floor of Stronghold. Chris was more amused than anything else, Liam hadn't done anything but roll his eyes, and Justin just looked resigned.

Only Patrick was truly bothered.

## 22

Wednesday night, while Rick was at Liam's dojo, Maria found herself in a place unlike anywhere she'd ever been before.

"Oh my God," she whispered, staring at the huge toy, too horrified to even touch the plastic packaging. Just in case touching it made the thing come to life, escape the protective cover and come after her. It was that scary. Her voice went up to a squeak. "That goes in your ass?!"

Coming into the aisle, Angel took one look at the big, round plug and snorted. "Not my ass, that's for sure. Adam might be an ass-man, but he's not a sadist. Maybe Andrew would."

"Nah, he prefers impact play for causing pain." That came from Lexie who was browsing one aisle over in what looked like toys exclusively for nipples. Maria had had no idea there were so many different kinds of things to torture people's nipples with. Some of them even vibrated. They looked a lot less frightening than a lot of things in her aisle though.

"Ladies, you've gotten distracted again," Olivia called from the clothes section, where she was standing with Hilary. Jessica had wandered too, although Maria couldn't see what toys were displayed in her aisle. Kinky ones, she was sure.

They were all there to help Maria find an outfit for Saturday. She didn't want to go back to Stronghold wearing something anyone on the street might wear. Rick hadn't understood what the problem was, so she'd texted Angel who had organized a little girls' night out shopping for an outfit. Of course, that had devolved almost as soon as they'd gotten to the store. It was filled to the brim with all sorts of interesting things, from clothes, to shoes with the highest heels Maria had ever seen, to vibrators, to restraints, etc. etc. Maria had never seen so many things related to sex in one place.

A whole new world had opened for her when she'd met Rick, but she was still learning new things about it.

At first she'd started wandering the aisles until Olivia had pulled her over to the clothing. Then she'd been looking at the clothing, but had gotten distracted by a purple knobby vibrator on the shelf, and then from there she'd moved around the corner of the aisle to look at the realistic dildos, and then she'd just kept moving until she'd ended up where she currently was; surrounded by giant butt plugs called crazy names like "The Dominator" and "The Destroyer." Okay, it wasn't really called the Destroyer, but it might as well have been.

While she was willing to maybe try some anal stuff with Rick, this was so not inside her comfort zone. But it was kind of like a train wreck, she just couldn't look away.

Angel grabbed her arm and tugged her out of the aisle. "Don't worry, Rick's not going to want to put anything like that in you, I promise."

"He'd better not," Maria muttered as she let Angel drag her over to Olivia and Hilary.

An hour later, Maria walked out of the store with several bags, all filled with clothing. She had a dress, two tops, and two skirts that were interchangeable, a corset (which she still wasn't too sure she liked, mostly because she'd always liked breathing), and a pair of four inch heels—which were the shortest the store offered. It was, hands down, the sexiest stuff she'd ever bought. She couldn't wait to show it to Rick.

For the first time in a while, Rick felt a little nervous as he bounded up the stairs to Maria's apartment. They'd gotten pretty comfortable in each other's spaces, easily interchanging whose place they stayed at. Even though they lived so close to each other, a lot of their things had started to travel. They both had a toothbrush at each apartment, Maria had a small case of extra makeup and hair things in his bathroom, and both of them had clothes in both closets.

Rick had found he rather liked seeing her things around his place. He liked he had his things in her place as well. He'd fallen for her. Hard. Probably since day one and his feelings were only getting stronger.

The intermingling of their lives gave him a sense of profound satisfaction and also of possessiveness. Now that they were going back to Stronghold, he felt it even more so. His nervousness about tonight came from the items he was carrying in a small bag.

He wasn't really sure what Maria's reaction was going to be, but he was hoping for a positive one.

When she opened the door he nearly said fuck Stronghold. Maria looked like a kinky wet dream come true. She was wearing a dark purple PVC dress wrapped lovingly around her curves that showed off every inch of her gorgeous cleavage. In fact, it looked like her breasts could easily pop out the top, which was really just two large triangles over each breast, connected to the dress on the bottom. All he'd have to do to access those beauties was pull down the straps.

Her hair was piled haphazardly onto the back of her head, a riot of curls, which made his fingers itch to tug it all down. The incredibly high heels she had strapped onto her feet made her legs look miles long, an effect enhanced by how very short the skirt of the dress was.

Rick looked her up and down, his cock already hardening in his pants. "You aren't allowed to move more than two feet away from me," he said, his voice sounding almost harsh. "All night."

Maria giggled, her face lighting up as she curved her body slightly against the door, managing to look both shy and sexy with that one little movement. "Yes Sir."

Groaning, Rick stepped into her apartment and pulled her to him, letting the door swing shut behind him so he could kiss the hell out of his gorgeous, sexy girlfriend. She kissed him back hungrily. He could feel the nervous tension in her body as he ran his hand down to her ass and cupped it. The skirt was so short his fingers easily curled underneath to touch bare skin and Maria shuddered against him.

"Enough of that," he said, pulling away. "Or we're not going to make it to the club."

"Oh, we're definitely going to the club," Maria said mischievously, stepping back and running her hands up the sides of her dress, a look of supremely feminine satisfaction on her face. "I need to show off my new clothes."

To his own surprise, he growled a bit under his breath at the idea of her wanting to show herself off. Maria just giggled.

"What's that?" she asked, pointing at his hand. "I mean, I kind of know what it is because I recognize the bag, but what exactly is in it?" The look on her face was one of eager anticipation. He should have realized she'd recognize the black bag with its distinctive gold bars since she'd been there earlier in the week to get clothes.

Still, that only added to the anticipation. Rick grinned. "Let's sit down and I'll show you."

Except when they got to the couch, Rick sat and then grabbed her hand, easily pulling her over his lap while she was off balance and teetering slightly in those devilish heels. They looked like they could do serious damage to a man's back and Rick wondered if he'd let her leave them on later and risk it. Although if he tied her legs down then he could still enjoy the visual effect...

He shook himself slightly, bringing himself back to the matter at hand as Maria twisted slightly to glare up at him. "What are you doing?"

"Showing you what's in the bag," he replied cheerfully, pushing the skirt further up to expose her bottom. She was wearing a cute little black thong, the thin fabric bisecting her ass cheeks perfectly. Too bad it was going to have to go. He pulled it down and off of her legs, leaving her bottom half completely exposed. Even though she was muttering under her breath, he could see how turned on she was already. Letting his fingers drift up her inner thighs and to her pussy, he used his other hand to pull a small bottle out of the bag. Massaging

330

her pussy, just above her clit, he flipped open the cap and expertly let a few drops of fluid slide out onto his finger.

Dropping the bottle onto the couch, he brought his wet finger down to rest on the crinkled little star of her anus. Maria jumped slightly, one of her hands wrapping around his ankle to grip it tightly.

"What are you doing?" She looked up at him again, this time her face slightly more worried.

"I want you to wear a couple of things for me tonight when we go to Stronghold," Rick said, massaging both her clit and her anus at the same time, watching her pupils dilate as her body registered the pleasure. "I've got a small plug, a very small plug, for your ass... do you think you can handle that?" He pushed his finger in, just slightly, and smiled as she moaned.

Her body hung over his lap, her head going back down towards the ground as he manipulated those two small bundles of nerves. If she'd never done any kind of anal play before then she was probably struggling a bit with the new sensation of pleasure in an area she'd never experienced before. Deciding he'd spread enough lube around it, he pushed his finger in again slightly, feeling the tight grip of her muscle clench down around it.

"Relax sweetheart, open up for me... I promise it's going to feel good."

A little feminine whimper came from down near the floor, and then he felt her body relax slightly. Using tiny increments, Rick pushed his finger in and out, continuing to stroke her pussy with his other hand so she was becoming more and more aroused as he played with her tight little virgin asshole. Even though she wasn't saying anything, he could tell she liked it, because her pussy was becoming soaking wet. His dick was hard as a rock, pressed against her side, but he knew he wasn't going to be getting any real satisfaction for at least a couple of hours.

However, he was going to have the satisfaction of tormenting her and he could be happy with that.

Eventually he worked his entire finger into the hot, tight vise of her ass. She squirmed on his lap, her breathing heavy, as he fucked her with his finger. Damn, she'd liked this way more than he'd expected...

one day Maria was definitely going to give up her ass to him. Not tonight, maybe not any time soon, but eventually it was going to happen.

THIS WAS SO STRANGE AND SO WRONG AND SO HOT. MARIA HADN'T really thought she'd like anything anal. Sure, she'd been kind of curious, especially after the frank talk she'd had with the other girls in the locker room during her first visit to Stronghold, but she really hadn't expected to actually like it. Rick's finger felt invasive, like it wasn't supposed to be there, but also good. It stretched her in a way she hadn't experienced before, drawing a surprising response from her pussy. While she could probably blame some of that on the way he was stroking her wet folds and clit, she knew at least part of it was from the way he was fingering her ass.

The nice thing about being over his lap was that it took away some of her embarrassment. She didn't have to face him or see him while he gently probed a hole she'd always thought of as a big N-O. All she had to do was let him take control of her body while she drowned in the sensations.

When his finger slid out, she actually whimpered a little and he chuckled.

"I knew you'd like that."

The things he knew about her body always surprised her, cuz she definitely hadn't known she'd like it. Then again, he just knew a lot more things than her period. There was a sound like plastic splitting apart and then a couple of seconds later something cool and wet nudged against her anus. Maria groaned as it pushed it, much faster than Rick had done with his finger, stretching open the tight hole and making her shiver as the cool toy entered her.

"That's it sweetheart, just relax."

It felt huge, even though she knew it probably wasn't. Maria clenched a bit and then felt her muscles relax. They burned slightly as Rick pushed it all of the way inside her, until it felt like there was a slight pop and her sphincter closed around the base. She could feel the flat part that was outside of her, in between her cheeks, and she clenched again, this time experimentally. It felt... surprisingly good.

"Good girl. There's one more thing I want you to wear for me tonight."

Panties. He was slipping panties up her legs. Maria scowled. She'd put on a hot little thong, just for him, and he was having her wear real panties? Sighing a little bit, she didn't protest as he settled them into place. There must be a reason.

One which she found out as soon as he pushed her back up to a standing position and she felt something firm and nubby settle against her clit. "Oh!"

Eyes glinting with appreciation, Rick stood. With her dress still up around her waist it was easy for him to cup the mound of her pussy, pressing whatever was in the panties more firmly against the sensitive little nub.

"Feel that sweetheart?"

Maria clung to dark blue shirt he was wearing, nodding her head. "What is it?"

"Something for later."

Frustratingly, he wouldn't say anything else. He just led her down to his car—which was an experience in and of itself. The plug felt like it was jostling around inside of her and she automatically clenched to keep it from falling out, making walking even more difficult in her high heels. Now she knew why Angel had been walking weird last weekend. It felt so full and strange, but also exciting in a darkly sensual kind of way. The hard bump at the front of her panties rubbed against her clit with every movement she made; sexual distraction at its worst.

Then Rick started the car.

Maria felt every bump, every turn, every divot in a way she'd never experienced before. She tried to keep up her conversation with Rick, but she was all too aware she wasn't tracking all of the time. The sensations were just too distracting. Sitting on the plug wasn't exactly comfortable, but at the same time the discomfort just turned her on even more. She had to sit with her legs slightly apart, despite the super short skirt, or put too much pressure on the panties over her clit.

Added on to all of that, was Rick's hand on her bare thigh, his fingers gently caressing her skin. She'd put her hand on top of his, but that didn't stop the tiny sweeping movements of his fingers.

It was utter sensual torture. The upside was that by the time they got to Stronghold, she'd definitely forgotten to be nervous. She was too distracted by all the new stimuli Rick had hooked her up to.

A young man with sandy blonde hair was sitting behind the front desk, smiling at them warmly before sending them in. Jared was standing guard at the door. He gave Maria a smile as they approached.

"Good evening, Master Rick." His eyes flicked up to Rick's for just a moment and then submissively back down. "Welcome back."

"Thanks," Rick said, handing over the small duffel bag he'd brought in with them. Maria wondered what it was for, but the young man behind the desk didn't seem to think there was anything unusual about it. She didn't want to ask.

"Have a good night."

"Thank you," she said, smiling up at him as naturally as she could when her ass was clenching around a plug and with every step her panties rubbed her. Then she gasped as the plug suddenly fizzed and hummed inside of her, her eyes unfocusing and her steps stuttering.

Rick immediately wrapped a strong arm around her, keeping her from falling. Despite the sudden distractions going on inside of her, Maria didn't miss the glint of amusement in Jared's dark coffee-colored eyes.

"You asshole," she hissed at Rick as he helped her in through the door.

At home that would have gotten her an amused look. Here it got her a short, sharp slap on the ass. One which stung. The look Rick gave her was far from amused too. "Be respectful in the club, sweetheart, or I'll have to give you some punishment tonight instead of funishment."

Dammit, that was something they'd already talked about, that she knew. She'd just forgotten in her distraction. To her relief, he put his hand in his pocket and the buzzing in her ass stopped. Not that it had felt bad, just shocking... and maybe a little too good.

THE SHELL-SHOCKED EXPRESSION ON MARIA'S FACE WHEN HE'D SET off the vibrator in her ass had been worth it. Even if she had called him an asshole. Not that he really minded, except at Stronghold she needed to be more respectful than when it was just the two of them. Although he'd rather have her slip up with him than accidentally insult another Dom. He wondered what her reaction would be when he turned on the vibrator in the panties.

The little toys were already giving her some trouble, he could tell. She was taking much smaller steps than usual, although that might be because of her heels, but he didn't think so.

Hand on the small of her back, he steered her over toward his friends. They were all already gathered—no surprise there. On the way, he enjoyed the envious looks of the other dominants who were at the club as they gave Maria a once over. He felt incredibly smug, showing her off as his submissive, and not just a visitor to the club.

Mine, mine, mine.

Smug and a little territorial.

His group of friends had taken over the far corner of the bar and the table closest to it. Andrew was behind the bar, working that end, with Will working the other end of the bar. Sitting on one of the stools was Liam, with Hilary standing between his thighs, leaning against him, and next to them were Olivia and Patrick. Patrick was sitting on the bar stool closest to Lexie's seat at the table with Adam and Angel, glaring at any Dom who even looked at the occupants of the table.

He and Maria were welcomed with excitement. Not in any rush, Rick put her down on a stool next to his, enjoying the way she squirmed as she tried to find a comfortable way to sit on the hard wood with a plug in her ass. Adam tipped him a wink, obviously realizing what Maria's problem with getting comfortably seated was.

Although Rick was fairly sure Adam didn't use vibrating plugs. As Maria started to answer Angel's question about how her weekend had been so far, Rick hit the little button on the remote that made the plug pulse. Immediately, Maria stiffened, her voice quavering before she got control over it again. She shot him a dirty look before turning back to Angel, answering her friend with determination in her voice.

"What'd you do?" Patrick asked, low in his ear. Turning his body slightly, so only Patrick would be able to see, Rick pulled the two remotes from his pocket to show the club owner. Patrick chuckled. "Nice."

"I'm not sure she'd agree with you," Rick said back, just as quietly. He was going to enjoy playing with Maria and the toys, but he didn't want her to be embarrassed by knowing their friends knew what was going on. Pushing the button on the plug remote, he stopped the vibrations and watched his girl relax minutely.

Patrick grinned. "That's half the fun." As Lexie started to stand, Patrick reached out and grabbed the belly chain hanging around her bare midriff, stopping her mid-step. "Where do you think you're going?"

Glaring, Lexie turned around and scowled at him. "The bathroom."

"There and back. I'm watching you."

For a second, Rick thought Lexie was going to snap back at the big Dom. Instead, she just clenched her hands into fists for a moment and then nodded her head, letting her gaze fall to the floor before turning around once Patrick had released his grip on her chain. Patrick's expression was so hard, it might as well have been carved of granite.

Rick felt a moment of pity for the big guy. Whenever Lexie capitulated to one of Patrick's demands, or submitted instead of mouthing off or fighting back, it would actually make it harder on the Dom to resist her. Whether or not Lexie had figured that out or if she was just showing she could behave so Patrick didn't make her leave the main floor, he knew her little show of submission had probably called to something within Patrick the other man didn't want called out when it came to Lexie.

"So are you letting her do any big party nights here any time soon?" he asked, dragging Patrick's gaze away from watching Lexie cross the room to the bathroom. He doubted Patrick would want anyone noticing his all-too-revealing attention to Lexie's every movement.

Turning his head to face Rick, Patrick kept himself positioned so he could still keep an eye on the door to the ladies' room, but he wasn't staring at it anymore. "She wanted to do an end-of-summer thing, but I convinced her to hold off till Halloween." He sighed. "I'm sure she'll want to do Christmas and New Years'."

Not that Patrick had to let her, but Rick knew he would.

"Is she trying to get off this floor?" He was kind of curious as to why Patrick was watching over her like a hawk tonight. Not that it was unusual, but he'd never made Lexie account for where she was going or used an article of her clothing like a leash before.

Patrick scowled, the expression tugging at the scar that ran down the left side of his face. "No, but some of those fuckers keep looking over here," he said, jerking his head to indicate the other Doms walking around the main floor. Since most of them were probably looking for who they wanted to play with for the night, that would definitely set Patrick on edge if any of them were actually eyeing Lexie. "They're getting too used to seeing her in here and they're getting ideas."

"You're not going to be able to keep her out forever you know."

"I know." He looked a bit haunted. Or maybe that was hunted. "But I can at least hold her off till Jake's home and then maybe he can talk some sense into her."

"Oh yeah, both of them will just love having that talk."

"Well, she sure as hell hasn't listened to any of us."

None of them were going to tell Jake while he was overseas. The man was in a war zone, they weren't going to distract him with things they could take care of until he got home. That was something all of them were in agreement about, even Olivia. Although Olivia's idea of taking care of the situation was probably more along the lines of getting Lexie entrenched in the scene before Jake got home so there was nothing he could do about it when he finally arrived.

Both men sighed at the same time and shared a look of sympathy. Although at least Rick didn't have feelings for Lexie that were anything other than brotherly. He had his own little minx to take care of.

Which reminded him...

Reaching into his pocket, he found the more triangularly shaped remote, the one for her panties, and hit the button. Maria actually jumped in her seat, her legs pressing together underneath the table. Putting his hand so it curved over her shoulder and neck, he could feel the rapid beat of her pulse against his palm. He'd timed it so he touched her right as he'd turned on the vibrator in the panties, giving her a secondary reason to have jumped, one the people around them could see.

Maria looked up at him, dark eyes filled with growing need, and he was so close he could hear the small whimpering sound she made in the back of her throat. Smiling genially at her, he could practically feel the frustration coming off of her in waves as he turned he gave her shoulder a squeeze and released it, turning his attention back to Patrick.

He glanced at the clock on the wall. Since he'd wanted a private room with a bed, he'd booked the Arabian Nights themed room. It'd be ready for them in about half an hour. Until then, he was going to truly enjoy using his new toys.

GRIPPING THE UNDERSIDE OF THE TABLE, MARIA TRIED TO KEEP from moaning or screaming as the panties and plug went off simultaneously inside of her for the first time. She was recklessly on edge, almost past the point of caring that people were watching if she could just freaking cum. Rubbing her thighs together, she could feel the slickness at the top of them; she'd soaked through her panties already, and yet found no relief.

The clit vibrator turned off again, leaving just the anal one humming away inside of her. Rick was too damned good at keeping the clit vibrator from becoming stimulating enough to get her off. She'd have to rock herself against the stool she was sitting on in order to get enough stimulation to come, and it would be pretty obvious to everyone what she was doing. Maria wasn't quite at that point.

Yet.

At first she'd glared at Rick every time he tormented her with the little toys. Now the looks she was giving him were a lot more pleading. The smug bastard sat there, with a smug little smile on his face, talking with Patrick and acting like there was absolutely nothing going on. Except for the stupid, smug little gleam in his eye.

If she wasn't so turned on, she might have smacked him.

If she thought he'd put up with it, she'd definitely jump him. But she was pretty sure it would just lead to some kind of punishment for trying to top from the bottom. Especially since they were in Stronghold, and if the punishment was more teasing than he'd already planned, she didn't think she could take it.

So her only option was to just sit here and try to follow his example, keep acting normal, until he was ready to stop the teasing.

Concentrating on the conversations going on around her was freaking impossible. Fortunately no one seemed to mind if she just smiled and nodded a lot.

Suddenly Rick was at her side, his hand gripping her arm. She looked up at him in surprise; the world had kind of fuzzed out for a minute. "What?"

"I said it's time for us to head up to our room," he said, his stupid grin becoming even smugger.

"Oh thank God," she said, without thinking. And then blushed as the chuckles and giggles erupting around her.

Angel patted her hand sympathetically, although she didn't hide her smile. Whatever. Maria didn't care. Right now she was a horny slut and they could laugh all they wanted as long as she got her orgasm.

Tottering in her heels, she had to cling to Rick going up the stairs. Partly because she wasn't used to wearing heels that high and partly because her leg muscles felt weak from all the stimulation between them. Fortunately nothing was vibrating right now or she might have just collapsed on the floor.

"In here, beautiful," Rick said, opening the door and ushering her in. It was like walking into a desert fantasy, something straight out of a cheesy romance novel, with the entire room draped in fabric and just a hint of incense in the air. Rick's hand on her back pressed her forward, pushing her toward the large circular bed on the left side of the room.

Maria was feeling incredibly submissive, maybe as a result of her desperate need to come, and so she just stood there and let Rick undress her before ordering her into the center of the bed. The bed was equipped with restraints on long chains, allowing Rick to arrange in her the shape of a large X.

There was very little give in the bonds after he was done, her body was stretched out and completely open to him. She watched as he went over to what looked kind of like a closet and pulled his bag out, setting it down beside the bed where it would be within easy reach.

Then he crawled up onto the bed, still fully clothed, laying himself down on top of her and kissed her.

And kissed her.

And kissed her.

Whimpering into his mouth, Maria undulated beneath him, trying to rub her body against his as he did nothing more than take his time with long, drugging kisses. It was torture of the worst kind when she desperately wanted, needed, more from him. Heat sizzled up her spine as she tried to rock against him, but Rick's hands just went down to her hips and held them in place as he continued kissing her.

The muffled sounds she was making were becoming increasingly desperate, but she couldn't seem to stop.

"Please, oh God please, Rick, touch me," she begged as soon as he pulled away from the kiss. She was on fire, every inch of her screaming with need, and his lips burned as they traveled leisurely down her neck. Maria shuddered, arching, pressing, wanting.

"I am touching you, sweetheart," he murmured against her skin, licking and then nibbling at her collarbone as his hands slid up her sides to caress the sides of her breasts and then back down. "I'm just taking my time about it."

Maria groaned. She wanted to tell him to stop, but she knew it would be useless. In fact, it might make him take longer. Perverse man that he was.

His body shifted, and he planted a leg on either side of her torso, leaning over to kiss her some more as he filled his hands with her breasts. At least it was some kind of contact, something new. Her insides ached emptily, her ass clenching around the plug in a rhythmic fashion so it almost felt like the plug was fucking her.

Roughly squeezing her soft mounds, Rick's fingers searched out her nipples and pinched, tugging the tender buds. A wave of euphoria swept through Maria's body at the firm contact, the intense pleasure that went straight down to her pussy. She arched, her hips lifting and searching for something to rub against, but Rick's entire focus was on her upper body. Rolling, tugging, rolling, tugging, and all the while his hands squeezed her breasts and he devoured her cries of needy pleasure.

She felt almost light-headed, as if she was losing her grip on reality, as she gave up the fight and just went with the sensations. Knowing there was nothing she could do to spur Rick on. The restraints on her wrists and ankles gave her the freedom to give up and let him take her where he willed.

The exquisite aching of her breasts in his hands was building, tension coiling, as if they were swelling to their limit and about to burst. The tugging, rolling, pinching of her nipples which left her gasping, also sent her flying. She cried out against Rick's kiss as the strangest sensation rippled through her; like an orgasm, but not quite like one, as some of the build-up of pressure inside her body released in a rush of ecstasy.

Just as it happened, the plug in her bottom buzzed to life again and her body writhed... it was just like an orgasm, her pussy clenching around nothing, the tugging on her nipples triggering wave after wave of rapture that flowed through her. It was intensely gratifying... and yet still not enough.

PURE SATISFACTION FILLED RICK AS HE FELT MARIA ORGASM UNDER his hands, from nothing but nipple play. It wasn't something that happened often, and it hadn't actually been his intention—he'd just wanted to take his time with her—but he was more than a little pleased about it. He could hear the confusion in her cries, laced through with the pleasure, as if she wasn't sure what was happening even as she lived it.

His cock was throbbing against the front of his pants, aching to be buried inside of her... but he knew once he did that it was going to be all over for both of them. There was no way he'd have the will power to draw back out and take his time then. Besides, right now they could have a little bit of funishment.

"Bad girl," he murmured as he pulled away from their kiss, although there was no actual censure in his voice. He grinned down at her, squeezing the soft flesh of her breasts in his hands and stroking his thumbs over her nipples to keep the little buds hard. "I didn't say you could come yet."

"But I..." Her words sputtered out as her dazed eyes took in what he'd just said. She moaned, shuddering and pressing her breasts upwards even as she realized she definitely had just orgasmed, even though he hadn't touched her pussy.

Reluctantly pulling himself off of her, Rick quickly reached into his bag. It only took him a few moments to find what he was looking for; rubber tipped little clamps that made Maria's eyes go big when she saw them. Pinching her nipple to full hardness, he looked right into her eyes as he let the clamp close around the swollen bud, enjoying the hissing of her breath as she reacted to the pain. At the same time, the arousal in her eyes flared. Swiftly, Rick attached the second clamp to her other nipple.

"You look so gorgeous with these pretty little nipples decorated," he said, leaning over to lave his tongue over each one. Maria cried out a little, squirming at his touch on her sensitive buds. "I should do this more often."

She moaned but didn't protest, and Rick grinned. Then he picked up the other item he'd pulled from his bag. "Do you know what this is, sweetheart?"

Maria looked up, her eyes focusing on the toy in his hand. "A really wimpy looking whip?"

He laughed. For a while there she'd been so softly submissive he'd almost forgotten she could be a mouthy little thing when she wanted. Apparently her orgasm had taken the edge off of her need. That actually suited his needs, because it meant he could take his time without having to worry he was driving her beyond her capacity.

The whip was made up of tiny little rubber strands, very thin and only about a foot long. Not at all threatening. However, there was a reason for that.

"It's not wimpy, it's just designed for very specific areas of the body," he said, his eyes glinting. Flicking his wrist in three quick movements, he watched as Maria gasped and writhed as he lashed the strands against each of her breasts and then her open pussy. "Maria." He waited till she looked at him, those big brown eyes filled with pain and pleasure and need. "You're not allowed to come without permission this time."

Her mouth slightly open as she stared up with something like awe at the whip, she nodded her head only slightly. Just like that, she had stepped down from being a brat and rediscovered her submissive softness. Rick flicked the whip against the outsides of each of her breasts, hard enough to make the contact sting slightly. Especially for the strands that snapped against her confined nipples. Her breasts jiggled, and Maria gasped, arching her back and thrusting them up as if asking for more.

Rick obliged. The whip snapped against the soft undersides, and then two direct hits from above that splayed over the full mounds and her nipples. She cried out, writhing. Putting his hand in his pocket, Rick pressed the remote for the plug in her ass, amping up the intensity, before flicking the whip against her breasts again, catching the soft mounds from every angle, aiming for the pale skin usually covered by her bikini.

"Rick! Oh fuck... Rick... fuck... please!" Her skin was turning a pleasing pink color, her nipples darkening to a deep reddish brown as she started to beg while he whipped her tits. Kneeling between her thighs, he could glance down and actually see the base of the plug moving as her asshole clenched around it, pulling it even deeper into her body before releasing again.

He changed his angle and hit three rapid slaps of the whip against her pussy. Maria shrieked, her body bowing as it reacted to the shocking mix of pain and pleasure emanating from between her legs. "Rick!"

"You're not allowed to come yet," he said, his voice surprisingly steady, not at all a true barometer of the overwhelming lust he was feeling. Laying the whip into her inner thighs, he drew the line of blows up each thigh, only to avoid her pussy and return to her breasts.

Maria whimpered, her hips moving and thrusting her glossy pussy lips upwards, as if inviting the whip to return there again, and he knew he'd pushed her to the point where her body was having trouble differentiating between pleasure and pain.

Laying the whip into her breasts a little bit harder, he started alternating between her breasts and her pussy. Except he kept it unpredictable, only occasionally snapping the whip between her legs, making those swollen lips puff up even more, her juices dripping down to create a wet spot on the bed beneath her. Her dark eyes were slowly glazing over, her body jerking whenever he landed a blow to her cunt, but otherwise just quietly submitting to the erotic lash.

"Please," she would whisper every few seconds. "Oh please." Soft. Breathy. Like a caress along his cock, which was straining against the front of his pants.

She was beautiful. Sensual. Perfect.

Mine.

Time to claim her.

Rick tossed the whip to the side, stripping off his clothes with alacrity while at the same time he pulled the clamps from her nipples. Did the first one, sucked the swollen bud into his mouth while Maria shook and moaned, pulled away and tore off his shirt. Did the second one with one hand while his other hand undid the front of his pants and sucked and soothed that tortured bit of flesh with his mouth while pushing his pants down.

The entrance of her pussy was soaking wet and the second he pressed his cock against her flesh he could feel the slight hum of the vibrator in her ass. He knew the plug was going to make her feel even tighter and he didn't know how long he was going to last.

Bracing himself on his forearms, he moved his mouth over hers. "You can come now, Maria."

He pushed in as he spoke, filling her as he gave permission. They both moaned as his tongue and cock invaded her, pushing in fast and deep, taking her in one rough stroke that had her body clenching around him. The humming vibrations of the plug in her ass traveled along his cock as he buried himself inside of her, pleasuring both of them simultaneously.

Fuck.

He drew his hips back and thrust, not bothering to take his time now, feeling the heat of her pussy engulf him over and over again. Beneath him Maria writhed and screamed, already clenching around in him orgasm, cumming hard as he fucked her, unable to stop the waves of pleasure that overtook her body. Her abused nipples rubbed against his chest, swollen little sensitive buds, and he slid one arm underneath her, crushing her to him.

She sobbed with ecstasy, her pussy spasming around him, making sloppy wet sounds with every thrust of his cock. Rick could feel his own pleasure tightening his balls, tingling in the base of his spine, but he didn't stop thrusting. Didn't stop riding her through her own relentless climax.

"Fuck! Maria... fuck!"

Heat and bliss boiled up through his body, the vibrations in her ass tingling along his shaft as he started to cum, searing her insides with jets of cream. The vibrations were almost too intense for him to bear, but he did because he knew it was even more powerful for her. Grinding his body against her pussy, he trapped her clit between them and rubbed the swollen little bundle of nerves mercilessly.

Maria screamed, an almost triumphant sound, and he felt her tighten and release beneath him, her pussy squeezing and milking him of every last ounce of fluid. The vibrations were too much on his cock and he pulled out almost immediately, leaving her still whimpering and shivering.

"Dumbass," he muttered under his breath, grabbing for his pants and pulling the remote from it so he could turn off the vibrator. Immediately Maria's body relaxed, going so limp for a moment he thought she'd passed out.

Then her eyes slowly opened, lashes wet with tears. "Rick?"

"I'm right here sweetheart, just hold still. I'm gonna take care of you."

"Mmm." She closed her eyes again, a sweet smile on her face, utterly trusting.

Undoing the restraints from her wrists and ankles, Rick rubbed her slightly reddened skin. She'd done a fair amount of pulling on the restraints, which were fortunately lined to keep them soft and easy on a sub's body. The only time she moved was when he pulled the plug from her bottom, and she sighed with a kind of satisfied relief when it was out. Using a wet cloth, he gently cleaned her swollen folds, while she sighed with pleasure.

Grinning to himself, Rick took the plug and the cloth over to the closet and the hidden sink and tossed them in. He'd use the provided toy cleaner in a bit; aftercare came first. And he was aching to cuddle and praise Maria.

Pulling her away from the wet spot they'd left on the bed, he cuddled her into his arms, tucking her against him in the way he liked so he could feel her pressed to his side all along their bodies. Maria snuggled in right away, rubbing her cheek against his skin. Running his fingers through the mess he'd made of her hair, Rick pictured holding her just like this for the rest of his life, and desire that had nothing to do with sex made him breathless.

WARMTH. COMFORT. LOVE.

Maria opened her eyes, aware she'd lost some time somewhere in there. The last thing she remembered was Rick telling her he'd take care of everything; she'd still been tied up and stretched out. Now she was cuddled up beside him with his arms around her, making her feel like she was enclosed in a safe haven where she would always be protected and cherished.

It was a nice feeling.

She ran her fingers through his chest hair and felt him shift to look down at her.

"Hey there."

Twisting her neck slightly to look up at him, she smiled. "Hi."

"How're you feeling?"

"Good." She shifted and winced as one of her nipples brushed against the wiry hair on his body and a muscle in her pussy twinged. "Um, a little sore."

His hand slid down her back, fingers massaging slightly. "I'm not surprised. Was I too rough?"

"No," she said immediately, shaking her head. "No, it was um... good. Really, really good." Actually, good seemed like such a lackluster word, but she wasn't about to go into rapturous detail about how spectacular it was to have a sex god for a boyfriend. Rick didn't need any encouragement. "Even the mean parts."

She felt his chuckle vibrate through her ear and then she was tipping onto her back and he was on his side, leaning over her slightly. The expression of tenderness on his face nearly made her tear up again. Had a man ever looked at her quite like that before?

Fingers stroked down the side of her face, making her feel warm and cherished all over again as he leaned down and kissed her gently. She kissed him back, both of them taking their time, kissing with such sweetness that she thought she might actually melt.

"Maria," he said, the second his lips left hers again.

"Mmmhmm?" She opened her eyes to look up into those stunningly gorgeous blue ones. Which weren't in the least bit wintry.

"I know it might be kind of soon for this..." He cleared his throat, his voice kind of rough. Something welled inside of her stomach, something hopeful, something yearning. "But I think I'm falling in love with you."

"Oh." She took a moment, just to torment him, and then smiled. "Good." She closed her eyes.

Rick growled, and Maria shrieked as he rolled her toward him, pulling her on top of him so he could have unfettered access to her ass —which he spanked hard and fast. Fast enough she didn't even have time to get her hands back there to protect her tender glutes. Her cheeks burned with the aftereffects of his hard slaps, tingling delightfully.

Giggling, she pushed herself up off of him slightly so that she could look down at him. "I think I'm falling in love with you too."

"Tease."

"Always."

Cupping his hand around the back of her head, he pulled her down for a kiss. Maria sank into it, letting him take her. She might tease, but so did he, and that's how they liked it.

# EPILOGUE

"I did it. I gave up," Angel announced as she walked into Olivia's apartment, a wine bottle in one hand and two bags of chips in the other.

Maria and Hilary looked up with interest as Jessica poked her head out of the kitchen. It was Maria's first sleepover with the Stronghold girls. They'd decided to have a girls' night in at Olivia's. A planned one where all of them could sleep over. Hilary had confided to Maria that Girls' Night Out was all too often invaded by the men as soon as they figured out where the night out was being held. Well, not quite invaded—watched over would be more correct.

So if they wanted real privacy, they had to stay in and Olivia's was the safest. None of the guys were going to try and storm her castle.

"Did what? Gave up what?" Olivia asked, looking amused as Angel pranced past her.

"Gave up the fight with Adam. I'm moving in with him."

"Finally," Jessica called from the kitchen, laughing as she went back to whatever she was doing.

Grinning, Angel swept in and sat down on the couch next to Maria. Her purple pajama pants matched the purple tank top she was wearing, and the purple polish she had on her nails and toes. The coordination made Maria feel like she should have tried harder. She was wearing her Sugar Baby pajama pants with one of Rick's shirts that she'd stolen. At least no one else was quite as coordinated, although Hilary was, as usual, wearing shades of pink.

"So what made you finally give?" Hilary asked, looking curious. She was fiddling with the ring on her finger, something Maria had noticed the pretty blonde doing on a regular basis ever since she'd gotten it. Like she was afraid it would disappear if she didn't touch it often enough. Pretty cute, really.

"No one thing... I mean, it just makes sense to since I'm there all the time anyway and he's made the space for me. Plus, Adam's been pretty patient, even if he's been growly about the whole thing. And it just feels like it's time." Angel shrugged, but she had a huge smile on her lips and her eyes were sparkling with happiness. "Adam's thrilled."

"So when are you making the big move?"

"After the Labor Day party," Angel said firmly, which gave the impression Adam had probably wanted her moved in before. "I am not dealing with having a party while we're still dealing with organizing and unpacking post-move."

"Seems reasonable," Maria said.

"One would think." Angel's voice was very dry, making Olivia laugh as she came over to join them. Obviously Adam must not think so. Jessica came in from the kitchen, carrying the tray of dips and hummus she'd been putting together.

Looking around at the group of women, Maria couldn't believe how much her life had changed since meeting Rick. She'd not only gone from wanting just a casual fling to falling in love, she now had something else she'd always wanted; a group of women outside of her sisters to be real friends with. They were like a second group of sisters, almost, except it was okay to talk about sex. There was a closeness between all of them that she'd never had with other women aside from her sisters, and they'd definitely welcomed her in with open arms and made her one of their own.

The door slammed open, making all of them jump and crane their heads around to see what was going on. Lexie stormed in the door, looking absolutely furious. She stopped in place, just standing there glaring at the wall, as the door slammed shut behind her.

"Lex?" Hilary asked tentatively. "Um... everything okay?"

For a long moment, Lexie tipped her head back and stared up at the ceiling, her fists clenching and unclenching by her sides. Then she took a deep breath and swung around to look at them.

It wasn't just anger in her face, Maria realized, there was also hurt and a sense of hopelessness. The latter was something she'd never seen in Lexie's expression.

"No. No, everything is not okay."

The support system sprang into action. It took them less than five minutes to get Lexie situated in the center of the couch, Angel and Olivia on either side of her, Maria, Jessica, and Hilary seated on the chairs across from her, with a drink in her hand. The anger seemed to have leeched from her while they were taking care of her, leaving her looking very lost and very young. It made Maria's heart ache to see the usually bouncy, confident Lexie looking like that.

"What happened, honey?" Olivia asked, brushing Lexie's hair back from her face.

Lexie's bright blue eyes looked suspiciously watery as she took a deep breath. "Okay... I've never actually come right out and said, but I think everyone knows I have a thing for Patrick. To put it mildly." They all nodded. "So, today, I decided to go for it. I showed up at Stronghold and told him I had something I wanted to show him..."

Her voice trickled off, her eyes unfocused.

"Lex? What did you want to show Patrick?" Angel asked, patting her on the leg to get her attention.

"Oh, right." To everyone's surprise, Lexie actually blushed. "I don't know if you guys have noticed, but I stopped doing the tape over the nipples look... and I did it for a reason."

"Oh shit," Olivia whispered, obviously realizing what Lexie was implying, even before Lexie pulled down the front of her tank top and the padded bra she was wearing. Two bright silver hoops decorated her nipples, gleaming against her pale skin. "You go girl."

"Yeah," Lexie smiled half-heartedly. "I was pretty excited about them."

"That's hot... did it hurt?" Jessica asked, looking both interested and a little scared.

"Like a bitch. Especially for the first few days afterwards. That's why I've been wearing the padded bras, it helped to keep them from rubbing against things and then it helped keep them hidden so no one knew."

Suddenly Hilary let out a chortle. "Oh my God... and all the guys were so relieved you were covering up more that none of them even thought about it."

Everyone laughed, including Lexie, lightening the moment. When they all looked back at her again she seemed slightly calmer after the brief moment of levity.

"So yeah. I was wearing a thong and a waist cincher and heels, and nothing else under my jacket. So I opened it up and for a minute I thought it was really going to happen. He looked at me like I was a real woman, you know, and not just... me." Her expression was so openly wistful for just a brief moment. "He told me to bend over his desk, and I did..." The wistfulness began to slide quickly into anger and hurt again. "I did everything perfectly dammit. I did exactly what he told me to, but all he did was spank me and then kick me out of his goddamn office. He told me I wasn't allowed to dress like that in the club, ever, as long as I was working for him... so I told him... I told him I quit."

The defiant look Lexie gave all of them made it clear she expected some kind of censure from them.

Instead, Angel pulled the younger woman into her arms and hugged her tight. Olivia came in from the other side, and then they were all piling on, wrapping Lexie in a sisterhood of warmth and support. A muffled sob came from the center of the pile, while they all murmured words of encouragement for her and threats against the idiot Dom.

Finally they all pulled back, only Angel keeping her arm around Lexie as she sniffled a bit, her eyes rimmed with red but she was under control.

"I just thought... I don't know what I was thinking. I've had a crush on him for so long and then I grew up and I think I might be in love with him, but how can I be in love with someone I've never done anything romantic with?" She sniffled again. Maria sat silently, not sure what to say, because it wasn't like she'd been around for very long or really understood the situation. Of course, none of the others seemed to know what to say either. "He was just always my white knight, you know? Rushing in to save me from whatever... but then instead of getting kissed I always got a pat on the head instead."

Angel squeezed her. "I'm sorry honey, but sometimes your knight in shining armor is just another idiot in tinfoil."

Staring up at her, Lexie choked on a giggle. Then giggled again, and then suddenly everyone was laughing hysterically... it was somehow all too easy to picture Patrick wrapped in tinfoil, stomping alongside a frustrated Lexie. Scaring off all her other potential suitors along the way.

Eventually though, the mirth died down and they returned back to the seriousness of the situation. It was serious, because even Maria could tell Patrick had a thing for Lexie too.

"I think he definitely has more than friendly or brotherly feelings for you," Olivia said, looking around the room for support, and getting a bunch of nodding heads in return. "He just doesn't know what to do about them. He's the biggest control freak out of the bunch, and he has no control over how you've grown up. My guess is he has no idea what to do now that he sees you as a woman and not a little sister."

Lexie rolled her eyes. "It's not that hard. Naked girl in front you, insert penis here." She pointed between her legs, at which point Angel lost it completely and burst out laughing again, setting off another round of hilarity. Maria actually had tears in her eyes from laughing so hard.

"So... if you quit, are you able to go back to the club?" Maria asked, once she got her giggles under control. She couldn't imagine Stronghold without Lexie, either welcoming people at the front desk or earnestly enjoying herself at the bar. The guys would miss her too, for all their grumblings about her presence.

"I can bring her, any time she wants to go," Olivia said. Her smile was almost evil. "In fact, it would be my pleasure."

"Yeah, but that's not really going to help the issue," Lexie said sadly. "All the guys still see me as a little girl. What I need is to actually do a scene at the club. I need to prove to him—all of them—I'm old enough to know what I want, this is what I want, and I can handle it. I've tried everything I can think of to goad Patrick into spanking me, but the second he was done, it's like he shut down again. There's no way he'll approve me for an Introductory Scene much less a membership."

"I could do a scene with you," Olivia offered, although she didn't look very enthusiastic about it.

Lexie immediately shook her head. "No, although thank you. But it's the same problem. They'll see you as safe because we're friends and no matter what you do, they'll feel like you're going easy on me. Plus, it's not like there'll be any sexual tension. They'll think it's like play time or something, or like you're placating me... Patrick will find any excuse to see something other than what I'm trying to show him. I've learned that lesson by now. I need to shove it in their faces, in a way they can't ignore, but there isn't a single Dom there who will help me do that. Whenever I've been on the main floor, no one even approaches me. They're all too intimidated to do something that might cause trouble with Patrick or the rest of the Sentinels."

Silence fell over the room.

"I know someone who likes to cause trouble," Angel said suddenly. They all looked at her, but she was looking thoughtfully out into the distance, straightening her posture as she began to look more and more excited. "I know someone who likes to cause trouble, has a membership, all of them would take seriously, and would probably be happy to help..."

The gleeful look in her eyes made Olivia look at her worriedly, but then her eyes lit up too and she nodded, a slow smile spreading across her face. Angel jumped up and ran over to her purse, all eyes following her. Lexie looked confused, and also like she wanted to be hopeful but didn't quite dare to be. Maria was caught up in the suspense of the moment, because it felt like something big was about to happen... something important, something game-changing.

Holding the phone to her ear, Angel's eyes lit up. The room was so quiet everyone could hear the deep murmur of a man's voice answering the phone, but going by the looks they were giving each other, no one had any idea who Angel had just called. She grinned at them, eyes dancing with mischief.

"Hey pretty boy," she purred.

*I hope you enjoyed Master Rick and Maria's story! Master Patrick and Lexie get their happily-ever-after next!*

*If you'd like to know more about Liam's proposal to Hilary, Make sure to sign up for my newsletter! On His Knees is available exclusively to my subscribers.*

# ABOUT THE AUTHOR

Golden Angel is a USA Today best-selling author of heart and bottom warming romance.

She is happily married, old enough to know better but still too young to care, and a big fan of happily-ever-afters, strong heroes and heroines, and sizzling chemistry.

When she's not writing, she can often be found on the couch reading, in front of her sewing machine making a new cosplay, hanging out with her friends, or wandering the Maryland Renaissance Fair.

www.goldenangelromance.com

BB bookbub.com/authors/golden-angel

g goodreads.com/goldeniangel

f facebook.com/GoldenAngelAuthor

instagram.com/goldeniangel

# OTHER BOOKS BY GOLDEN ANGEL

## CONTEMPORARY BDSM ROMANCE

### Venus Rising Series (MFM Romance)

The Venus School

Venus Aspiring

Venus Desiring

Venus Transcendent

Venus Wedding

Venus Rising Box Set

### Stronghold Doms Series

The Sassy Submissive

Taming the Tease

Mastering Lexie

Pieces of Stronghold

Breaking the Chain

Bound to the Past

Stripping the Sub

Tempting the Domme

Hardcore Vanilla

Steamy Stocking Stuffers

A Sassy Christmas

Entering Stronghold Box Set

Nights at Stronghold Box Set

Stronghold: Closing Time Box Set

**Masters of Marquis Series**

Bondage Buddies

Master Chef

Law & Disorder

Switch Play

Legally Bound

Shallow Submission

Hidden Away

Giant Tamer

Third Wheel

**Dungeons & Doms Series**

Dungeon Master

Dungeon Daddy

Dungeon Showdown

**Daddies Everywhere**

Chef Daddy

Foosball Daddies

Taco Daddy

Little Villain

HISTORICAL SPANKING ROMANCE

**Domestic Discipline Quartet**

Birching His Bride

Dealing With Discipline

Punishing His Ward

Claiming His Wife

The Domestic Discipline Quartet Box Set

## Bridal Discipline Series

Philip's Rules

Gabrielle's Discipline

Lydia's Penance

Benedict's Commands

Arabella's Taming

Pride and Punishment Box Set

Commands and Consequences Box Set

## Deception and Discipline

A Season for Treason

A Season for Scandal

A Season for Smugglers

A Season for Spies

## Desire and Discipline

A Season for Bliss

A Season for Desire

A Season for Christmas

## Bridgewater Brides

Their Harlot Bride

## Standalone

Marriage Training

The Duke's Pursuit

Rogue Booty

## SCI-FI ROMANCE

## Tsenturion Masters Series with Lee Savino

Alien Captive

Alien Tribute

Alien Abduction

**Standalone**

Mated on Hades


SHIFTER ROMANCE

**Big Bad Bunnies Series**

Chasing His Bunny

Chasing His Squirrel

Chasing His Puma

Chasing His Polar Bear

Chasing His Honey Badger

Chasing Her Lion

Night of the Wild Stags


Chasing Tail Box Set

Chasing Tail... Again Box Set

Printed in Dunstable, United Kingdom

63634269R10211